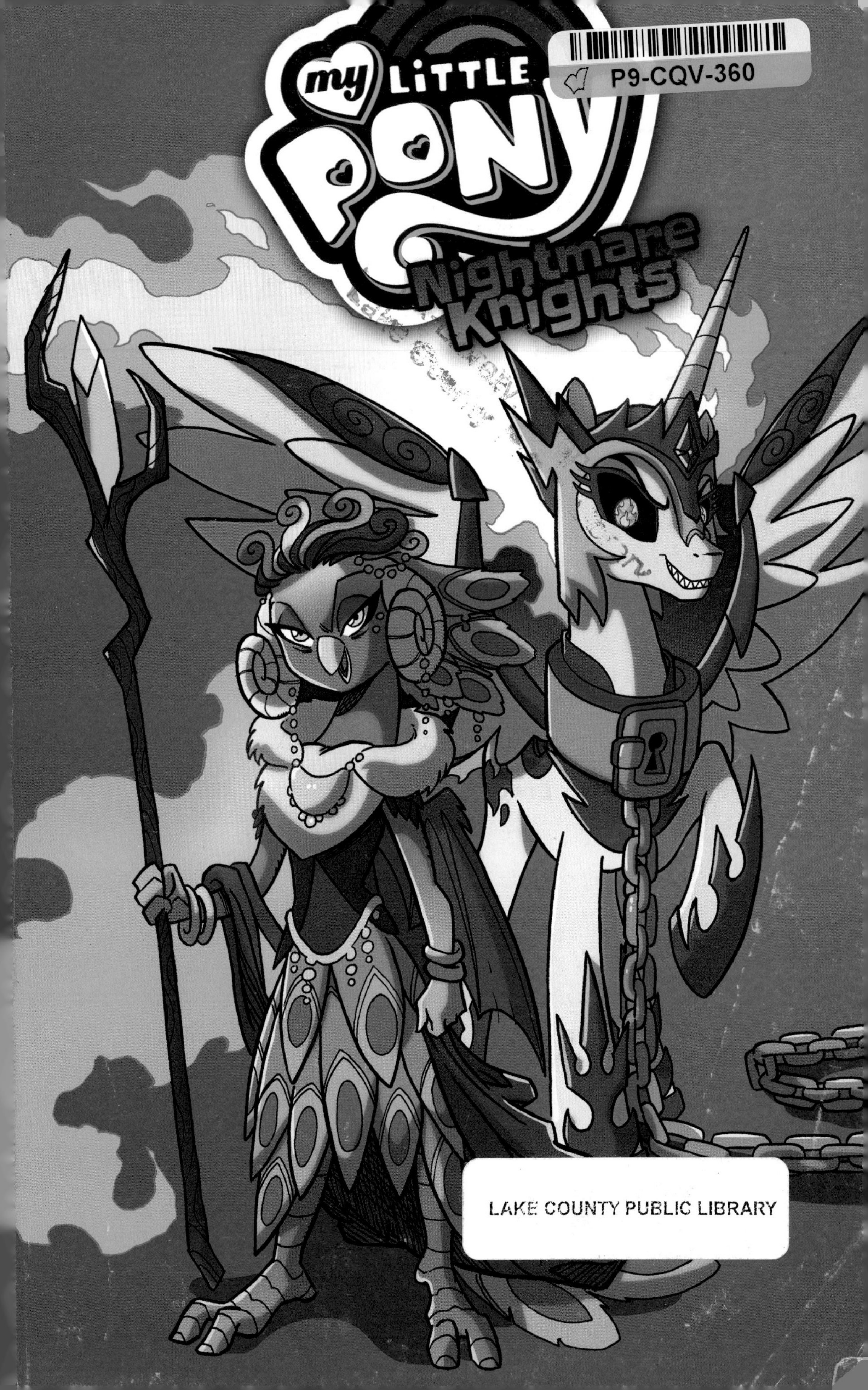
my LITTLE PONY
Nightmare Knights

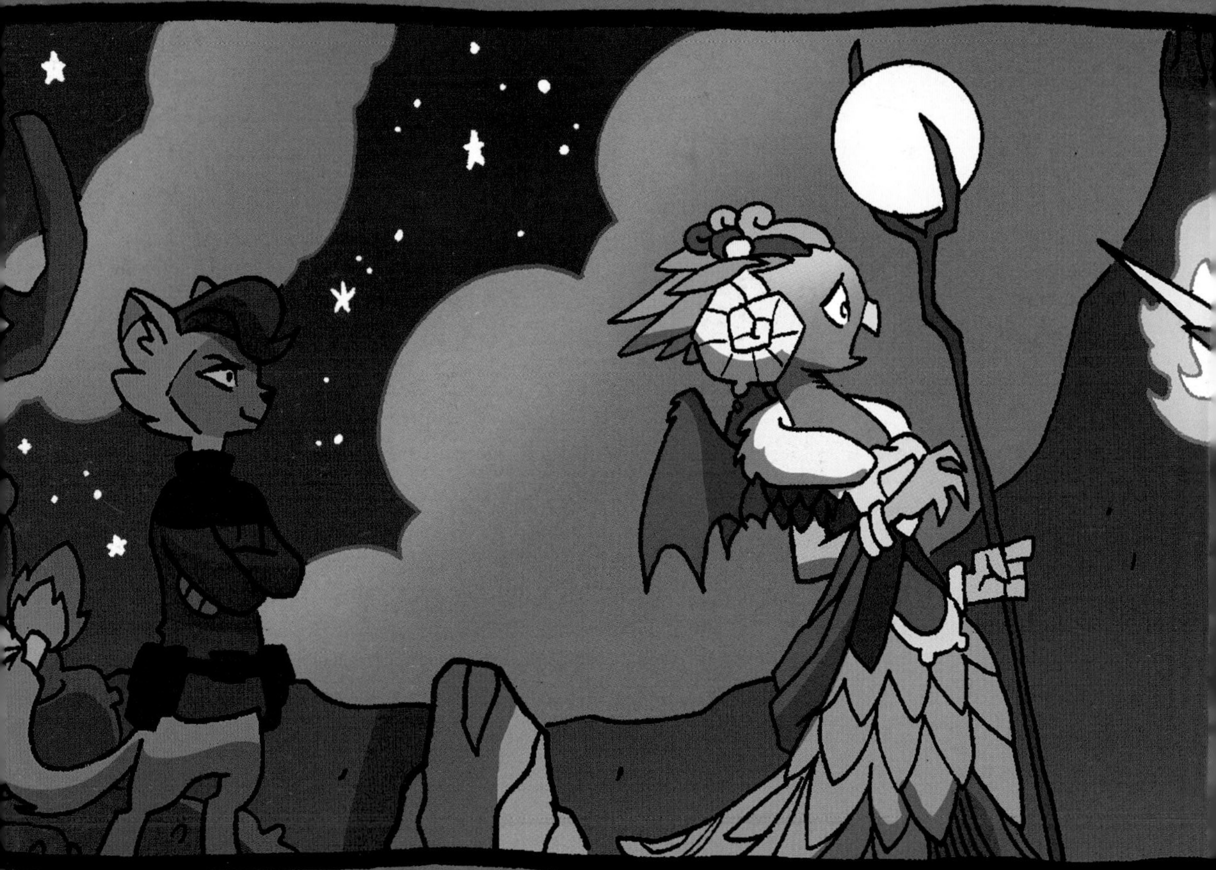

cover art by
Tony Fleecs

collection edits by
Justin Eisinger & Alonzo Simon

collection design by
Neil Uyetake

Special thanks to Meghan McCarthy, Eliza Hart, Ed Lane, Beth Artale, and Michael Kelly.

For international rights, contact licensing@idwpublishing.com

ISBN: 978-1-68405-477-0

22 21 20 19 1 2 3 4

IDW® www.IDWPUBLISHING.com

Chris Ryall, President & Publisher/CCO • **John Barber**, Editor-in-Chief • **Robbie Robbins**, EVP/Sr. Art Director • **Cara Morrison**, Chief Financial Officer • **Matthew Ruzicka**, Chief Accounting Officer • **Anita Frazier**, SVP of Sales and Marketing • **David Hedgecock**, Associate Publisher • **Jerry Bennington**, VP of New Product Development • **Lorelei Bunjes**, VP of Digital Services • **Justin Eisinger**, Editorial Director, Graphic Novels and Collections • **Eric Moss**, Sr. Director, Licensing & Business Development

Ted Adams, IDW Founder

Facebook: **facebook.com/idwpublishing** • Twitter: @idwpublishing • YouTube: **youtube.com/idwpublishing**
Tumblr: **tumblr.idwpublishing.com** • Instagram: **instagram.com/idwpublishing**

Originally published as MY LITTLE PONY: NIGHTMARE KNIGHTS issues #1–5.

written by
Jeremy Whitley

art by
Tony Fleecs

colors by
Heather Breckel

letters by
Neil Uyetake & Christa Miesner

series assistant edits by
Megan Brown

series edits by
Bobby Curnow

art by Tony Fleecs

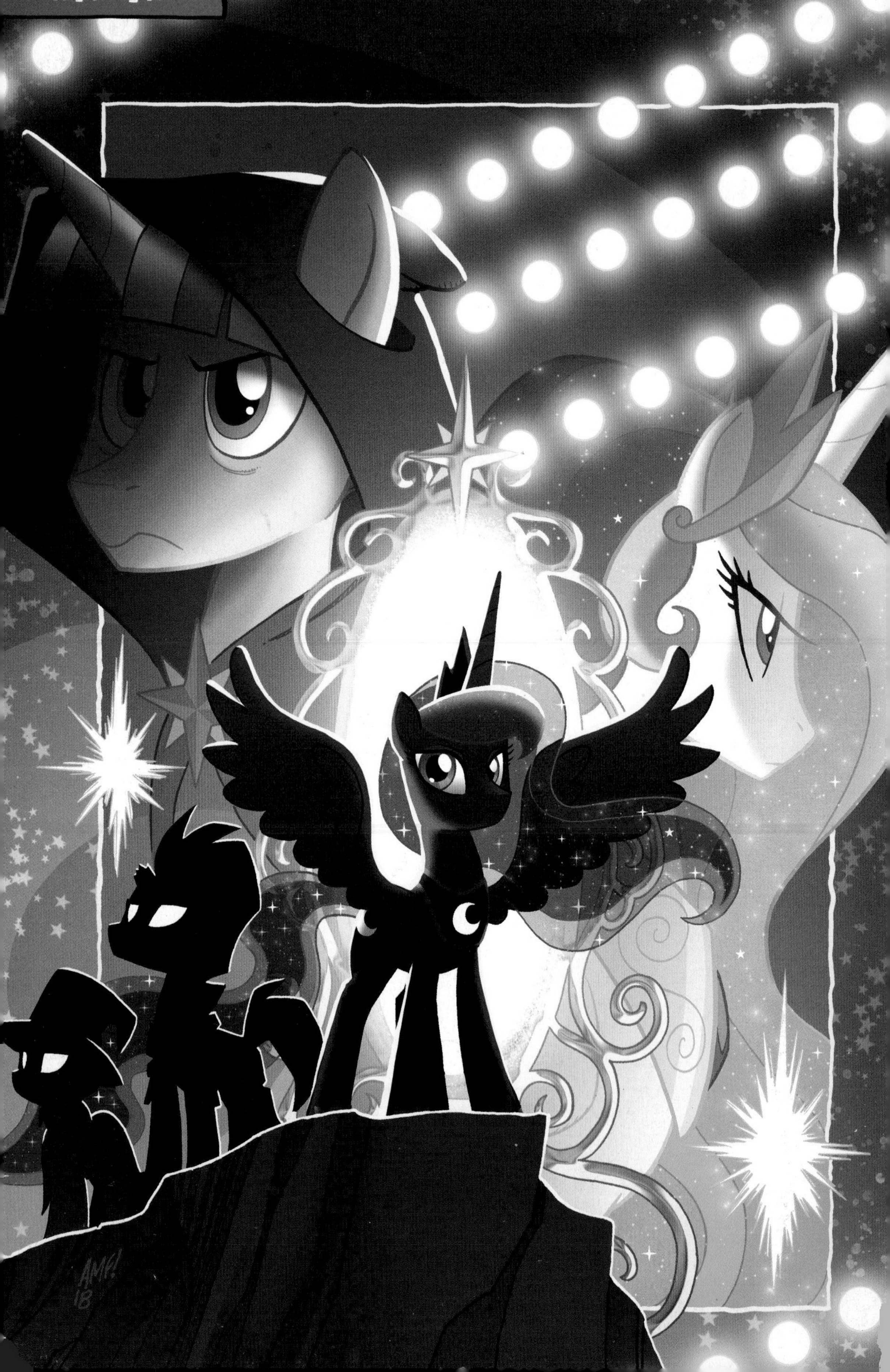
AMP! 18

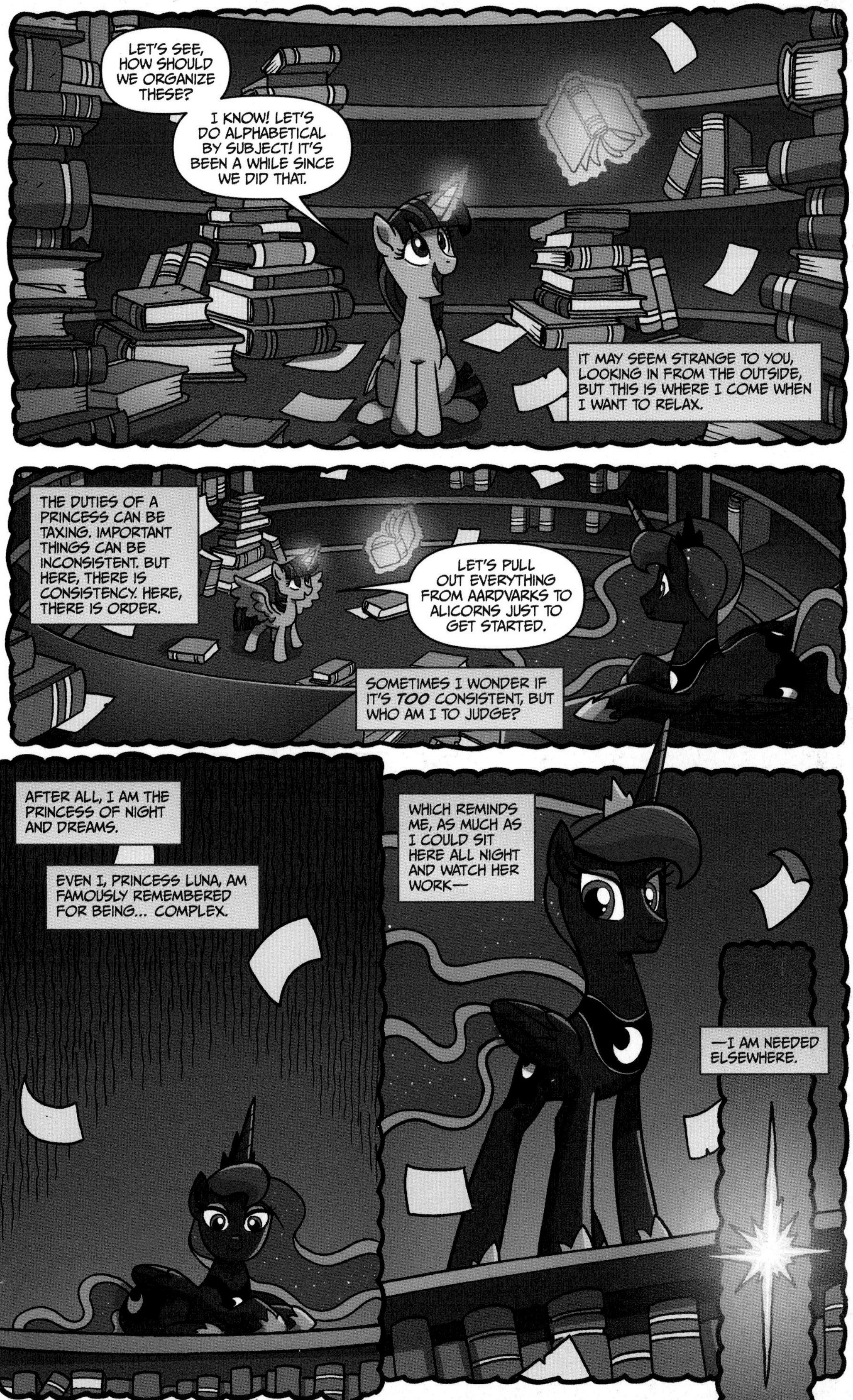
LET'S SEE, HOW SHOULD WE ORGANIZE THESE?
I KNOW! LET'S DO ALPHABETICAL BY SUBJECT! IT'S BEEN A WHILE SINCE WE DID THAT.
IT MAY SEEM STRANGE TO YOU, LOOKING IN FROM THE OUTSIDE, BUT THIS IS WHERE I COME WHEN I WANT TO RELAX.
THE DUTIES OF A PRINCESS CAN BE TAXING. IMPORTANT THINGS CAN BE INCONSISTENT. BUT HERE, THERE IS CONSISTENCY. HERE, THERE IS ORDER.
LET'S PULL OUT EVERYTHING FROM AARDVARKS TO ALICORNS JUST TO GET STARTED.
SOMETIMES I WONDER IF IT'S *TOO* CONSISTENT, BUT WHO AM I TO JUDGE?
AFTER ALL, I AM THE PRINCESS OF NIGHT AND DREAMS.
EVEN I, PRINCESS LUNA, AM FAMOUSLY REMEMBERED FOR BEING... COMPLEX.
WHICH REMINDS ME, AS MUCH AS I COULD SIT HERE ALL NIGHT AND WATCH HER WORK—
—I AM NEEDED ELSEWHERE.

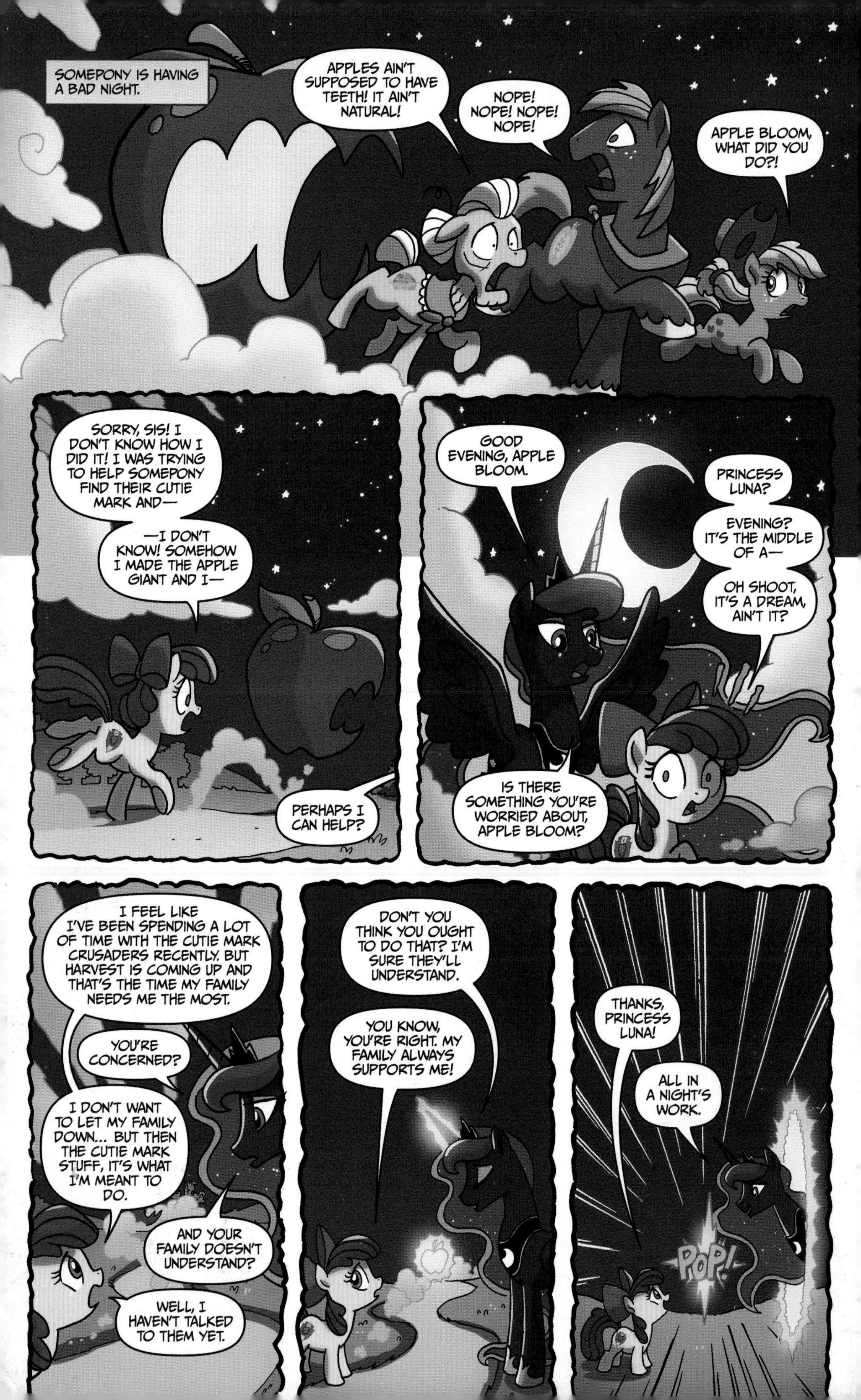
SOMEPONY IS HAVING A BAD NIGHT.
APPLES AIN'T SUPPOSED TO HAVE TEETH! IT AIN'T NATURAL!
NOPE! NOPE! NOPE! NOPE!
APPLE BLOOM, WHAT DID YOU DO?!
SORRY, SIS! I DON'T KNOW HOW I DID IT! I WAS TRYING TO HELP SOMEPONY FIND THEIR CUTIE MARK AND—
—I DON'T KNOW! SOMEHOW I MADE THE APPLE GIANT AND I—
PERHAPS I CAN HELP?
GOOD EVENING, APPLE BLOOM.
PRINCESS LUNA?
EVENING? IT'S THE MIDDLE OF A—
OH SHOOT, IT'S A DREAM, AIN'T IT?
IS THERE SOMETHING YOU'RE WORRIED ABOUT, APPLE BLOOM?
I FEEL LIKE I'VE BEEN SPENDING A LOT OF TIME WITH THE CUTIE MARK CRUSADERS RECENTLY. BUT HARVEST IS COMING UP AND THAT'S THE TIME MY FAMILY NEEDS ME THE MOST.
YOU'RE CONCERNED?
I DON'T WANT TO LET MY FAMILY DOWN... BUT THEN THE CUTIE MARK STUFF, IT'S WHAT I'M MEANT TO DO.
AND YOUR FAMILY DOESN'T UNDERSTAND?
WELL, I HAVEN'T TALKED TO THEM YET.
DON'T YOU THINK YOU OUGHT TO DO THAT? I'M SURE THEY'LL UNDERSTAND.
YOU KNOW, YOU'RE RIGHT. MY FAMILY ALWAYS SUPPORTS ME!
THANKS, PRINCESS LUNA!
ALL IN A NIGHT'S WORK.
POP!

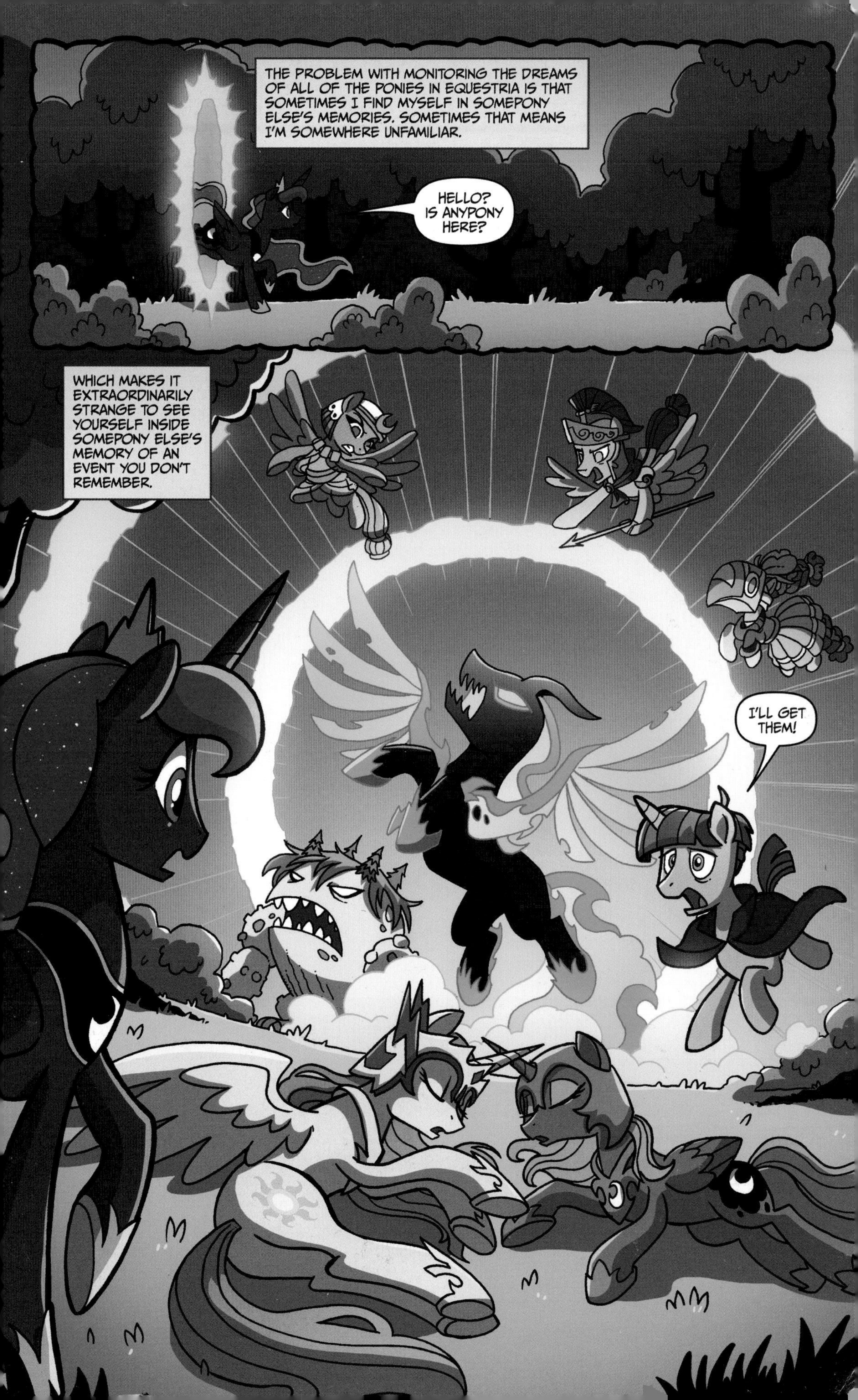
THE PROBLEM WITH MONITORING THE DREAMS OF ALL OF THE PONIES IN EQUESTRIA IS THAT SOMETIMES I FIND MYSELF IN SOMEPONY ELSE'S MEMORIES. SOMETIMES THAT MEANS I'M SOMEWHERE UNFAMILIAR.
HELLO? IS ANYPONY HERE?
WHICH MAKES IT EXTRAORDINARILY STRANGE TO SEE YOURSELF INSIDE SOMEPONY ELSE'S MEMORY OF AN EVENT YOU DON'T REMEMBER.
I'LL GET THEM!

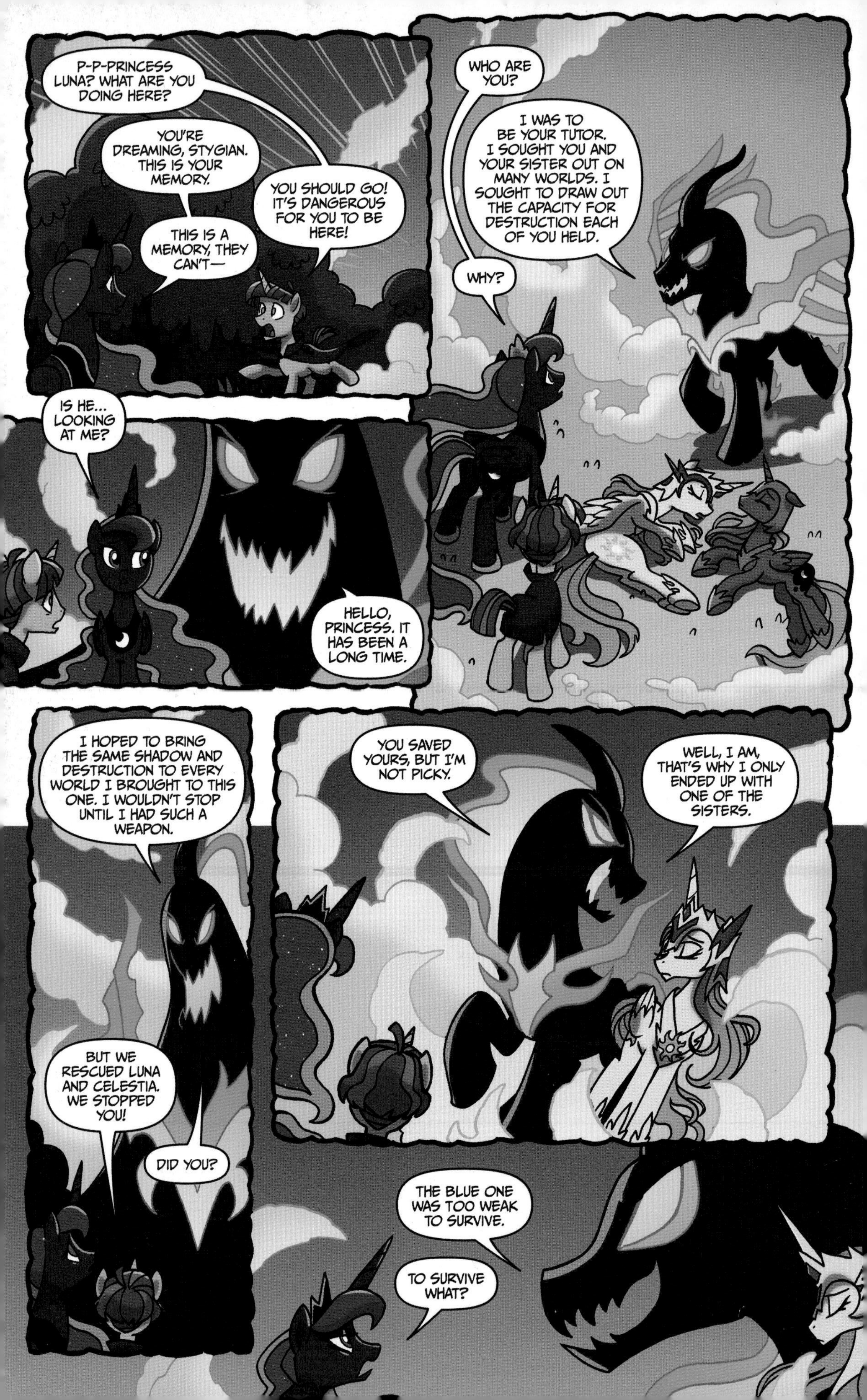
P-P-PRINCESS LUNA? WHAT ARE YOU DOING HERE?
YOU'RE DREAMING, STYGIAN. THIS IS YOUR MEMORY.
YOU SHOULD GO! IT'S DANGEROUS FOR YOU TO BE HERE!
THIS IS A MEMORY, THEY CAN'T—
IS HE... LOOKING AT ME?
HELLO, PRINCESS. IT HAS BEEN A LONG TIME.
WHO ARE YOU?
I WAS TO BE YOUR TUTOR. I SOUGHT YOU AND YOUR SISTER OUT ON MANY WORLDS. I SOUGHT TO DRAW OUT THE CAPACITY FOR DESTRUCTION EACH OF YOU HELD.
WHY?
I HOPED TO BRING THE SAME SHADOW AND DESTRUCTION TO EVERY WORLD I BROUGHT TO THIS ONE. I WOULDN'T STOP UNTIL I HAD SUCH A WEAPON.
BUT WE RESCUED LUNA AND CELESTIA. WE STOPPED YOU!
DID YOU?
YOU SAVED YOURS, BUT I'M NOT PICKY.
WELL, I AM, THAT'S WHY I ONLY ENDED UP WITH ONE OF THE SISTERS.
THE BLUE ONE WAS TOO WEAK TO SURVIVE.
TO SURVIVE WHAT?

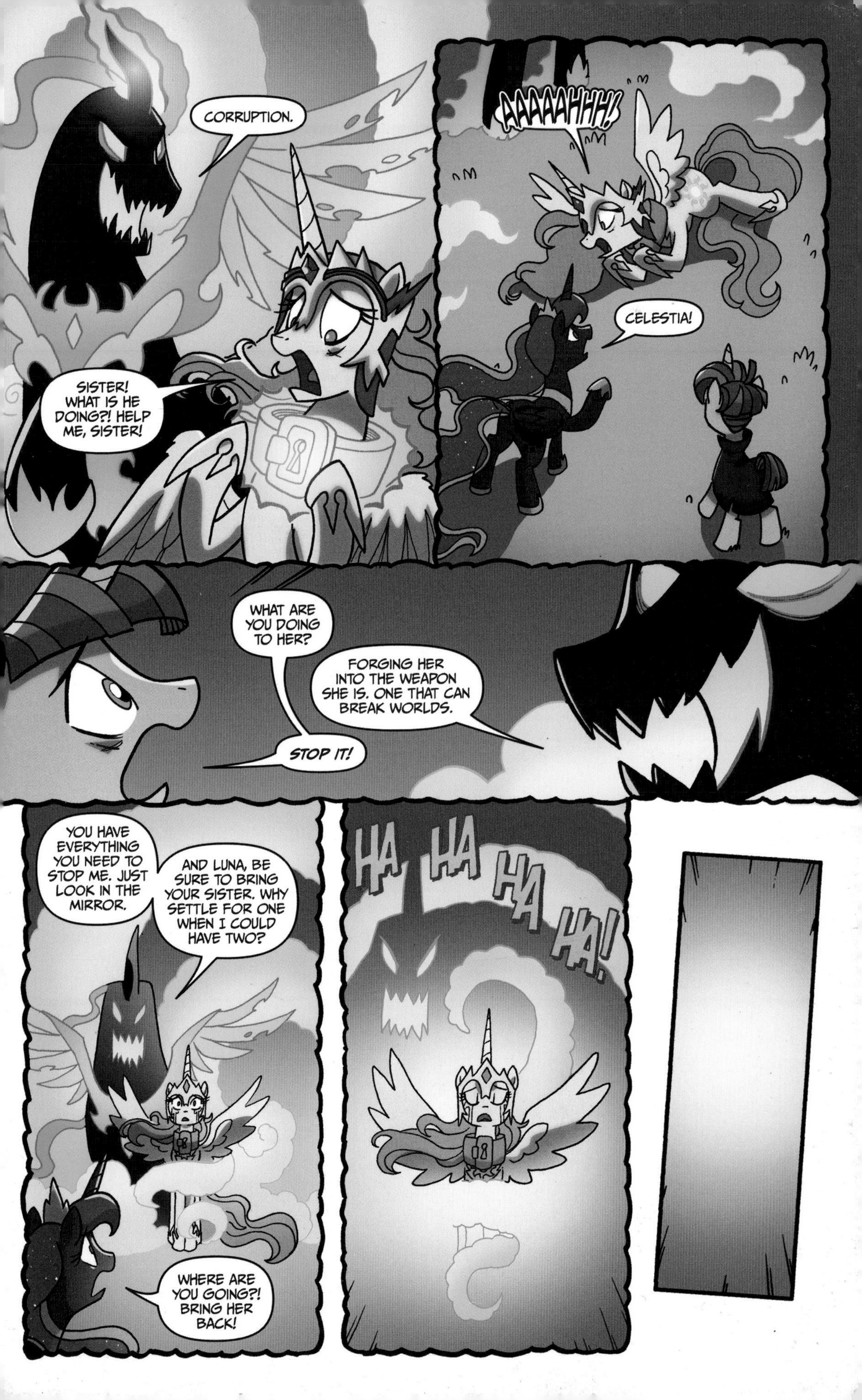
CORRUPTION.
SISTER! WHAT IS HE DOING?! HELP ME, SISTER!
AAAAAHHH!
CELESTIA!
WHAT ARE YOU DOING TO HER?
FORGING HER INTO THE WEAPON SHE IS. ONE THAT CAN BREAK WORLDS.
STOP IT!
YOU HAVE EVERYTHING YOU NEED TO STOP ME. JUST LOOK IN THE MIRROR.
AND LUNA, BE SURE TO BRING YOUR SISTER. WHY SETTLE FOR ONE WHEN I COULD HAVE TWO?
WHERE ARE YOU GOING?! BRING HER BACK!
HA HA HA HA HA!

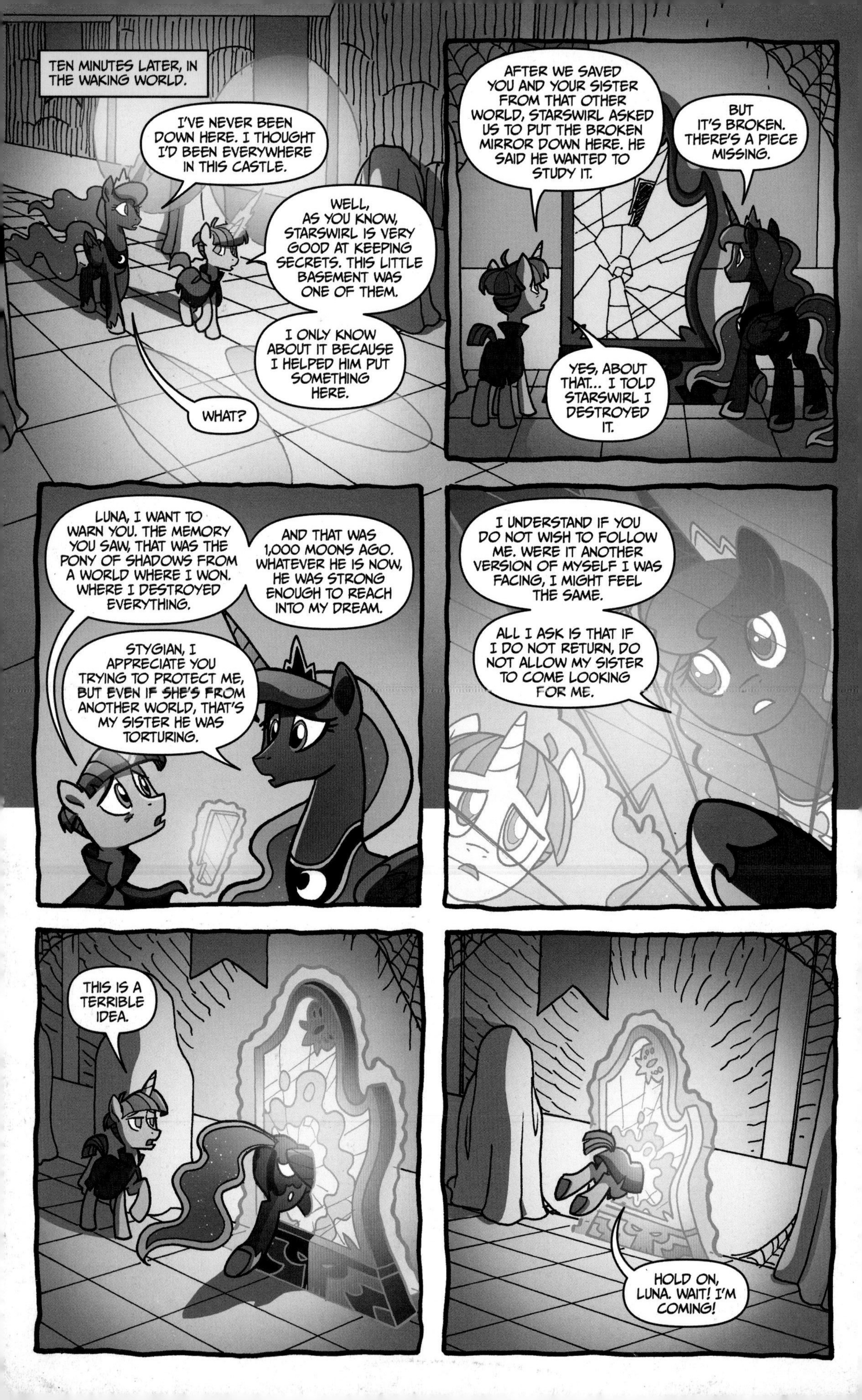
TEN MINUTES LATER, IN THE WAKING WORLD.
I'VE NEVER BEEN DOWN HERE. I THOUGHT I'D BEEN EVERYWHERE IN THIS CASTLE.
WELL, AS YOU KNOW, STARSWIRL IS VERY GOOD AT KEEPING SECRETS. THIS LITTLE BASEMENT WAS ONE OF THEM.
I ONLY KNOW ABOUT IT BECAUSE I HELPED HIM PUT SOMETHING HERE.
WHAT?
AFTER WE SAVED YOU AND YOUR SISTER FROM THAT OTHER WORLD, STARSWIRL ASKED US TO PUT THE BROKEN MIRROR DOWN HERE. HE SAID HE WANTED TO STUDY IT.
BUT IT'S BROKEN. THERE'S A PIECE MISSING.
YES, ABOUT THAT... I TOLD STARSWIRL I DESTROYED IT.
LUNA, I WANT TO WARN YOU. THE MEMORY YOU SAW, THAT WAS THE PONY OF SHADOWS FROM A WORLD WHERE I WON. WHERE I DESTROYED EVERYTHING.
AND THAT WAS 1,000 MOONS AGO. WHATEVER HE IS NOW, HE WAS STRONG ENOUGH TO REACH INTO MY DREAM.
STYGIAN, I APPRECIATE YOU TRYING TO PROTECT ME, BUT EVEN IF SHE'S FROM ANOTHER WORLD, THAT'S MY SISTER HE WAS TORTURING.
I UNDERSTAND IF YOU DO NOT WISH TO FOLLOW ME. WERE IT ANOTHER VERSION OF MYSELF I WAS FACING, I MIGHT FEEL THE SAME.
ALL I ASK IS THAT IF I DO NOT RETURN, DO NOT ALLOW MY SISTER TO COME LOOKING FOR ME.
THIS IS A TERRIBLE IDEA.
HOLD ON, LUNA. WAIT! I'M COMING!

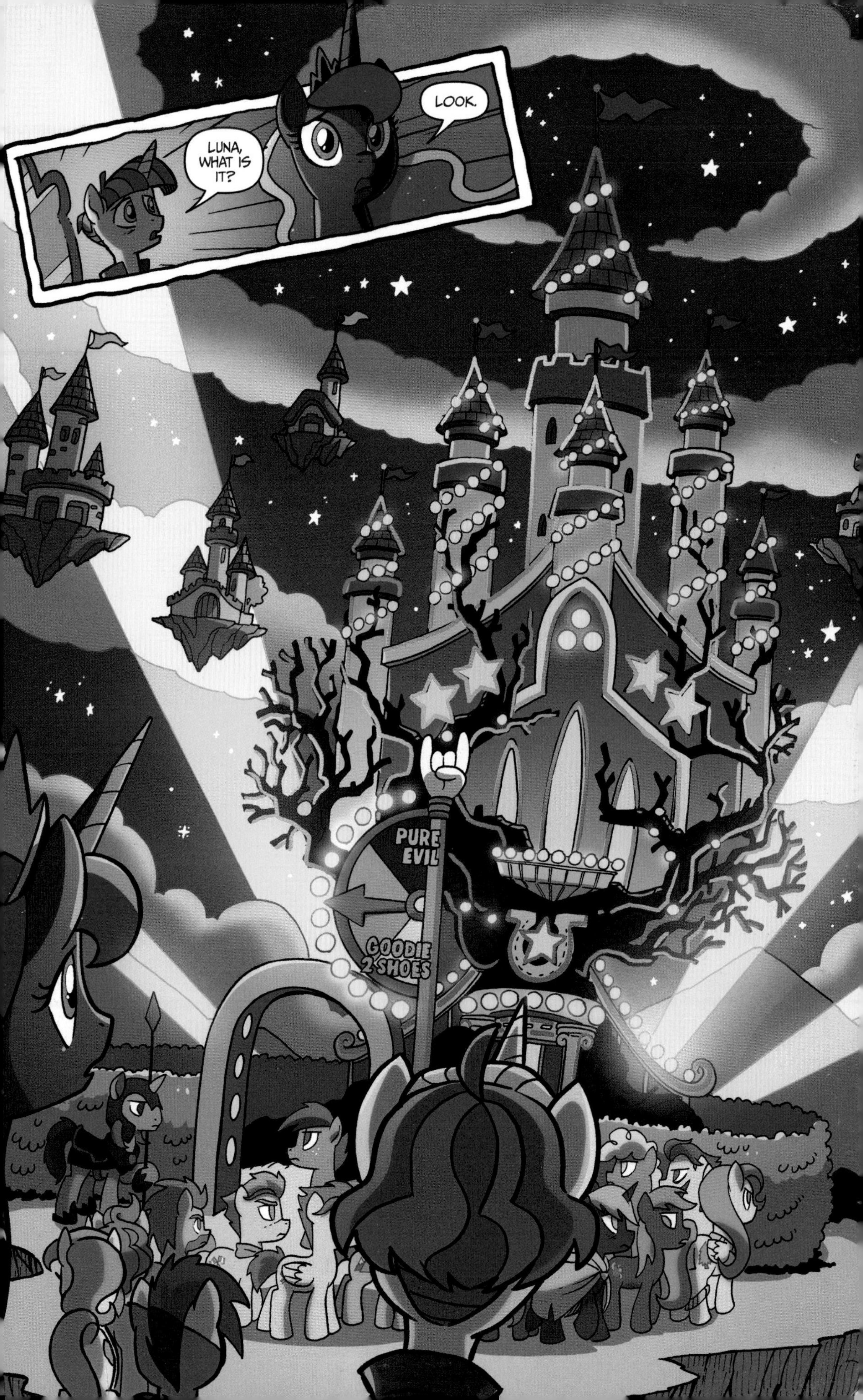
LUNA, WHAT IS IT?
LOOK.
PURE EVIL
GOODIE 2 SHOES

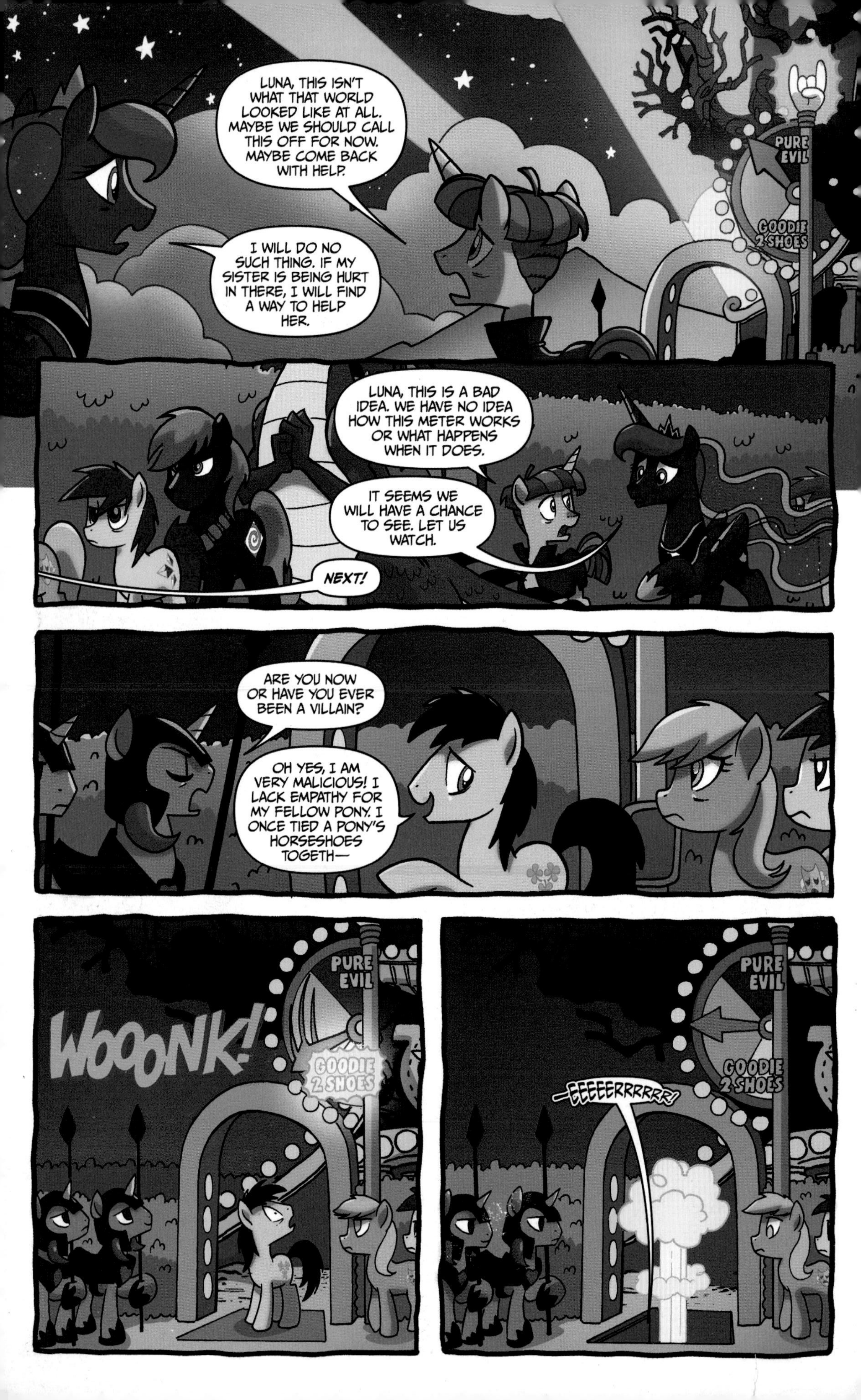
LUNA, THIS ISN'T WHAT THAT WORLD LOOKED LIKE AT ALL. MAYBE WE SHOULD CALL THIS OFF FOR NOW. MAYBE COME BACK WITH HELP.
I WILL DO NO SUCH THING. IF MY SISTER IS BEING HURT IN THERE, I WILL FIND A WAY TO HELP HER.
PURE EVIL
GOODIE 2 SHOES
LUNA, THIS IS A BAD IDEA. WE HAVE NO IDEA HOW THIS METER WORKS OR WHAT HAPPENS WHEN IT DOES.
IT SEEMS WE WILL HAVE A CHANCE TO SEE. LET US WATCH.
NEXT!
ARE YOU NOW OR HAVE YOU EVER BEEN A VILLAIN?
OH YES, I AM VERY MALICIOUS! I LACK EMPATHY FOR MY FELLOW PONY. I ONCE TIED A PONY'S HORSESHOES TOGETH—
WOOONK!
PURE EVIL
GOODIE 2 SHOES
PURE EVIL
GOODIE 2 SHOES
EEEEERRRRRR!

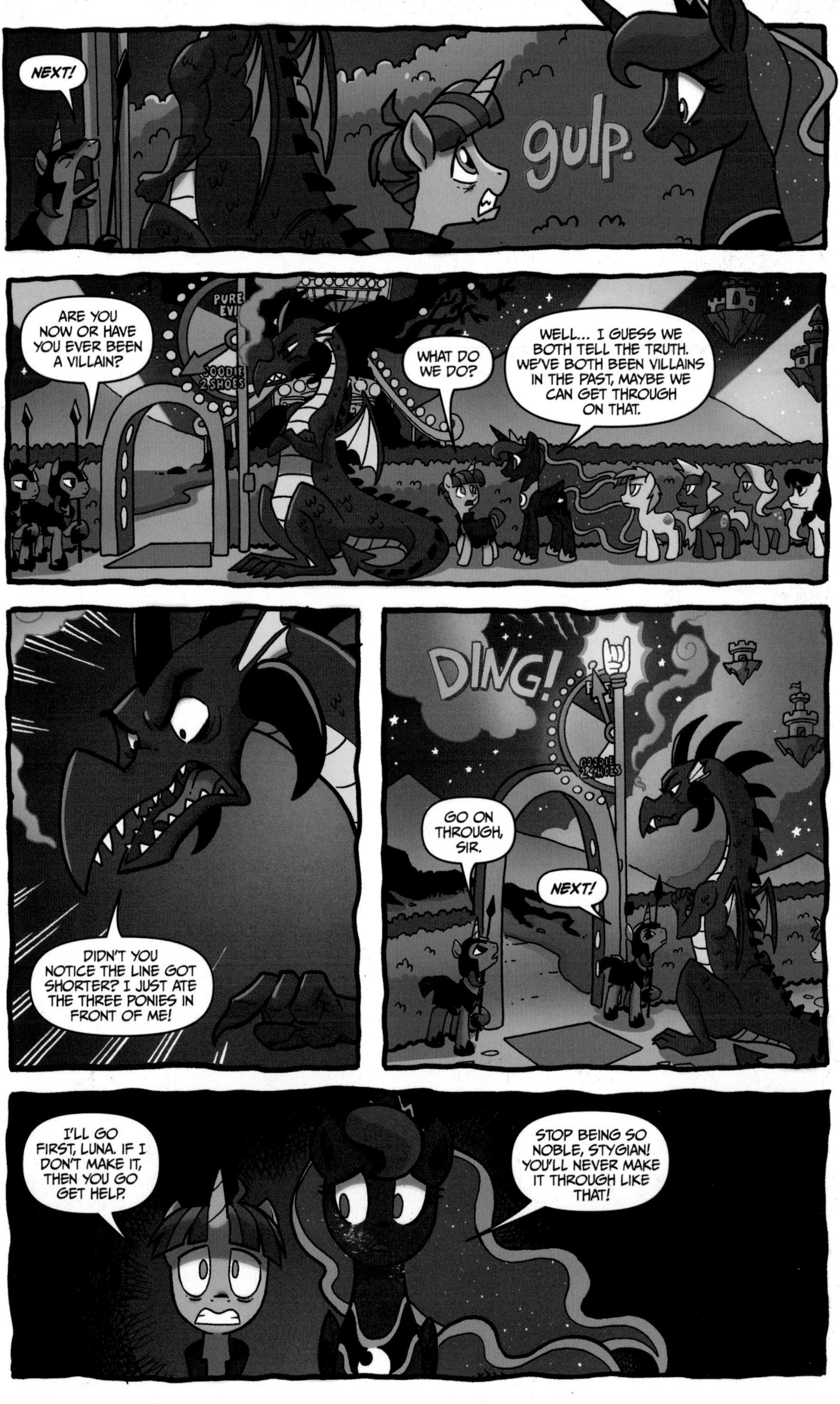
NEXT!
gulp.
ARE YOU NOW OR HAVE YOU EVER BEEN A VILLAIN?
PURE EVIL
GOODIE 2 SHOES
WHAT DO WE DO?
WELL... I GUESS WE BOTH TELL THE TRUTH. WE'VE BOTH BEEN VILLAINS IN THE PAST, MAYBE WE CAN GET THROUGH ON THAT.
DIDN'T YOU NOTICE THE LINE GOT SHORTER? I JUST ATE THE THREE PONIES IN FRONT OF ME!
DING!
GOODIE 2 SHOES
GO ON THROUGH, SIR.
NEXT!
I'LL GO FIRST, LUNA. IF I DON'T MAKE IT, THEN YOU GO GET HELP.
STOP BEING SO NOBLE, STYGIAN! YOU'LL NEVER MAKE IT THROUGH LIKE THAT!

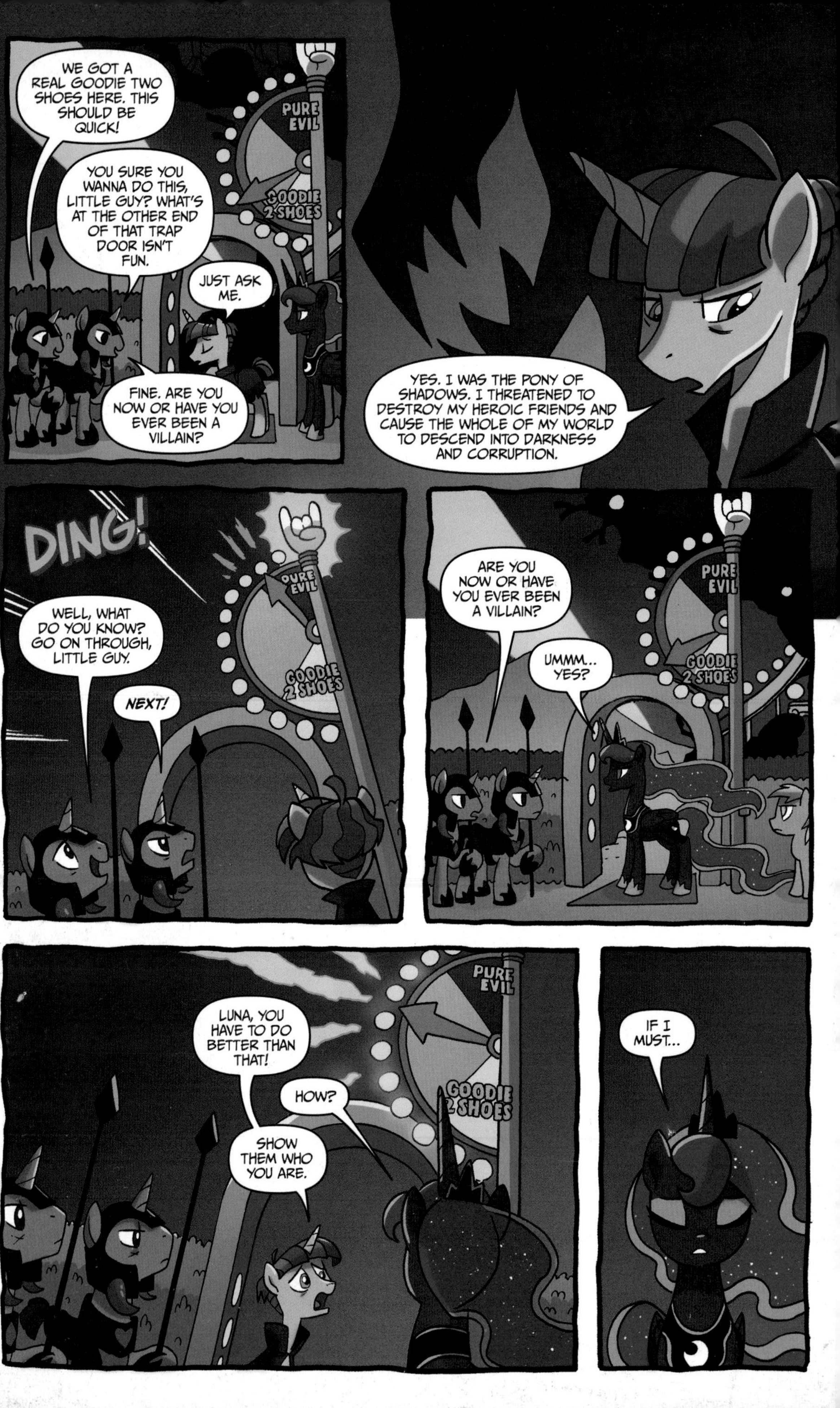
WE GOT A REAL GOODIE TWO SHOES HERE. THIS SHOULD BE QUICK!
PURE EVIL
GOODIE 2 SHOES
YOU SURE YOU WANNA DO THIS, LITTLE GUY? WHAT'S AT THE OTHER END OF THAT TRAP DOOR ISN'T FUN.
JUST ASK ME.
FINE. ARE YOU NOW OR HAVE YOU EVER BEEN A VILLAIN?
YES. I WAS THE PONY OF SHADOWS. I THREATENED TO DESTROY MY HEROIC FRIENDS AND CAUSE THE WHOLE OF MY WORLD TO DESCEND INTO DARKNESS AND CORRUPTION.
DING!
PURE EVIL
GOODIE 2 SHOES
WELL, WHAT DO YOU KNOW? GO ON THROUGH, LITTLE GUY.
NEXT!
PURE EVIL
GOODIE 2 SHOES
ARE YOU NOW OR HAVE YOU EVER BEEN A VILLAIN?
UMMM... YES?
PURE EVIL
GOODIE 2 SHOES
LUNA, YOU HAVE TO DO BETTER THAN THAT!
HOW?
SHOW THEM WHO YOU ARE.
IF I MUST...

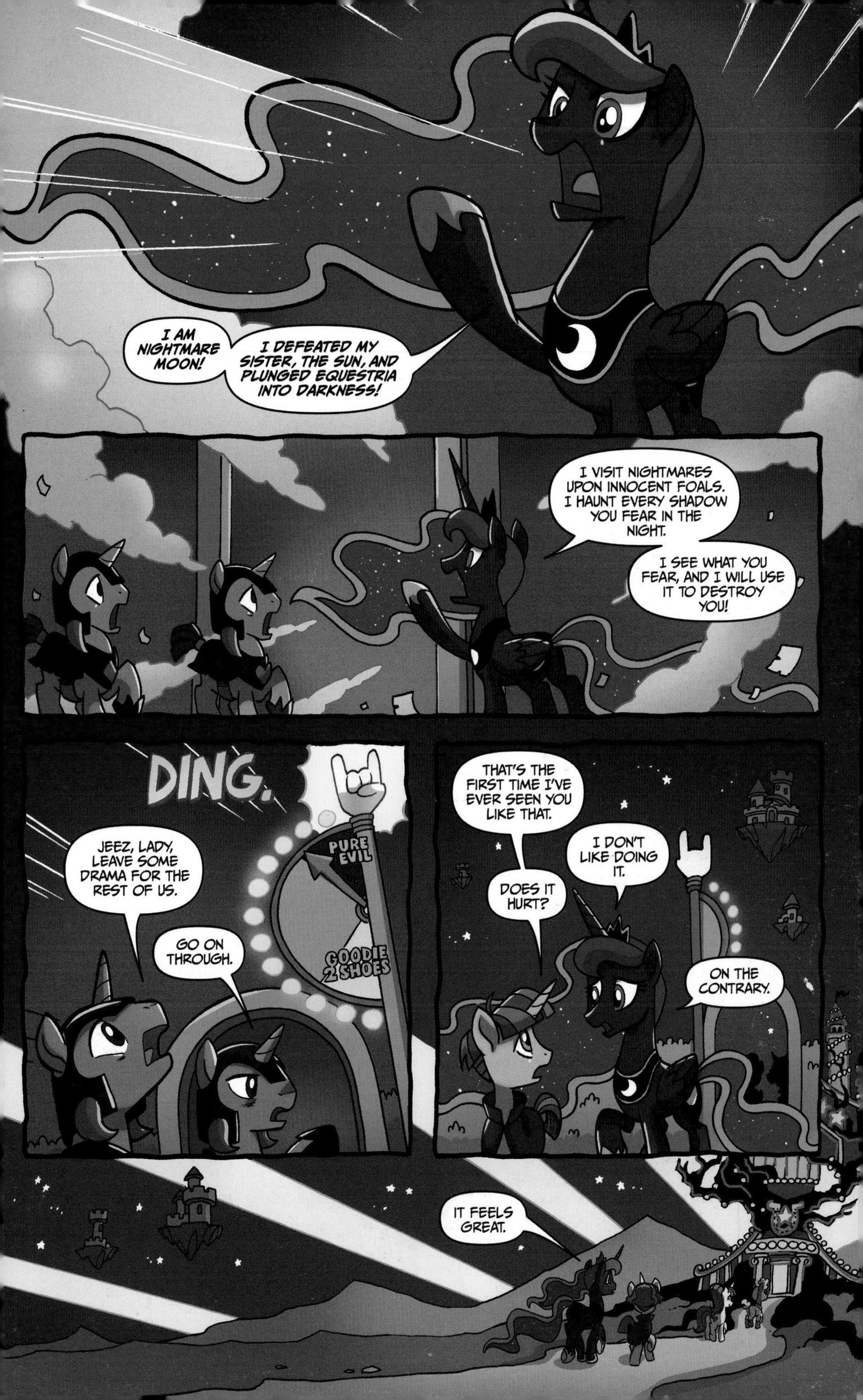
I AM NIGHTMARE MOON!
I DEFEATED MY SISTER, THE SUN, AND PLUNGED EQUESTRIA INTO DARKNESS!
I VISIT NIGHTMARES UPON INNOCENT FOALS. I HAUNT EVERY SHADOW YOU FEAR IN THE NIGHT.
I SEE WHAT YOU FEAR, AND I WILL USE IT TO DESTROY YOU!
DING.
PURE EVIL
GOODIE 2 SHOES
JEEZ, LADY, LEAVE SOME DRAMA FOR THE REST OF US.
GO ON THROUGH.
THAT'S THE FIRST TIME I'VE EVER SEEN YOU LIKE THAT.
DOES IT HURT?
I DON'T LIKE DOING IT.
ON THE CONTRARY.
IT FEELS GREAT.

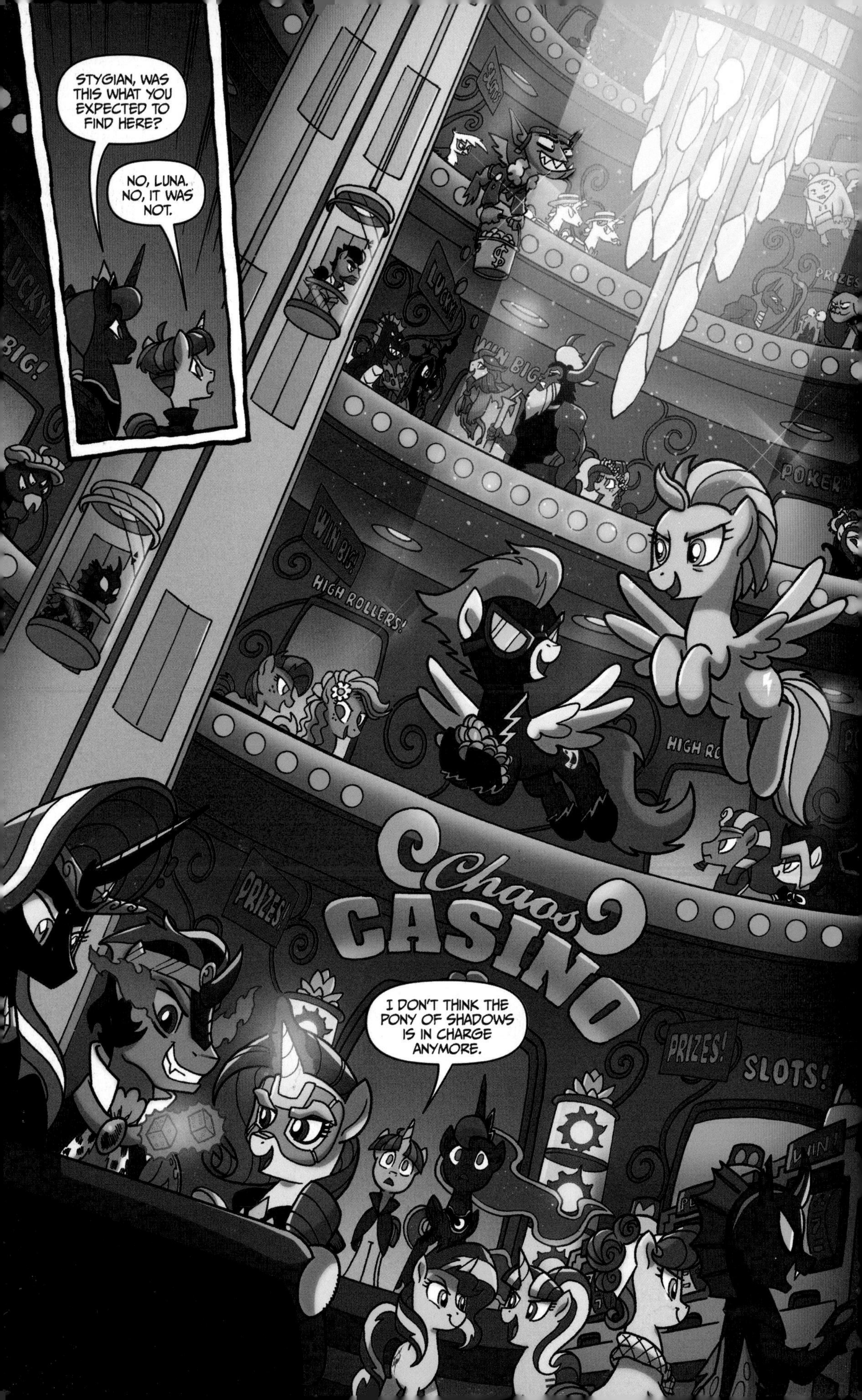
STYGIAN, WAS THIS WHAT YOU EXPECTED TO FIND HERE?
NO, LUNA. NO, IT WAS NOT.
SLOTS
LUCKY
PRIZES
WIN BIG
POKER
WIN BIG!
HIGH ROLLERS!
Chaos CASINO
PRIZES!
I DON'T THINK THE PONY OF SHADOWS IS IN CHARGE ANYMORE.
PRIZES!
SLOTS!

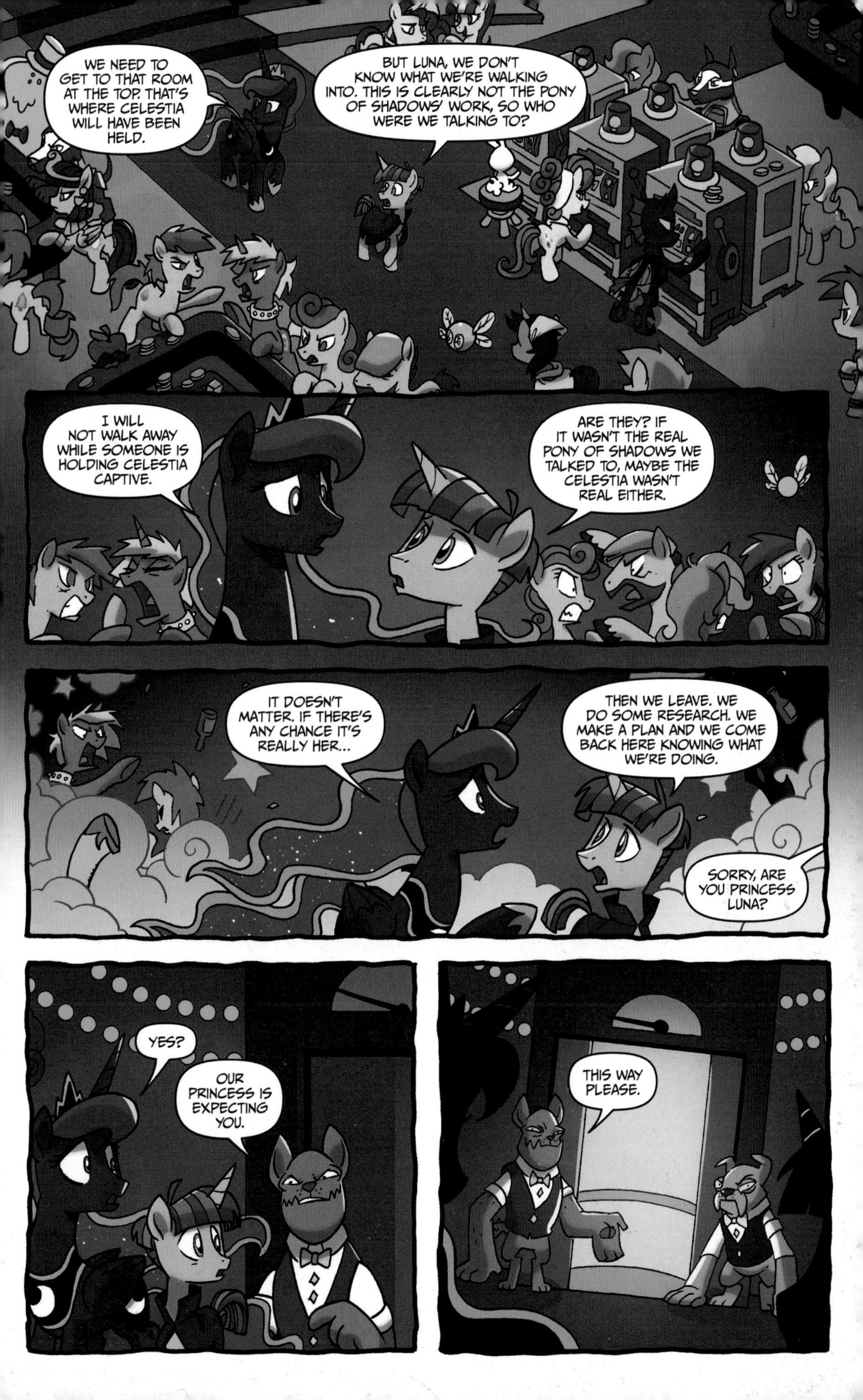
WE NEED TO GET TO THAT ROOM AT THE TOP. THAT'S WHERE CELESTIA WILL HAVE BEEN HELD.
BUT LUNA, WE DON'T KNOW WHAT WE'RE WALKING INTO. THIS IS CLEARLY NOT THE PONY OF SHADOWS' WORK, SO WHO WERE WE TALKING TO?
I WILL NOT WALK AWAY WHILE SOMEONE IS HOLDING CELESTIA CAPTIVE.
ARE THEY? IF IT WASN'T THE REAL PONY OF SHADOWS WE TALKED TO, MAYBE THE CELESTIA WASN'T REAL EITHER.
IT DOESN'T MATTER. IF THERE'S ANY CHANCE IT'S REALLY HER...
THEN WE LEAVE. WE DO SOME RESEARCH. WE MAKE A PLAN AND WE COME BACK HERE KNOWING WHAT WE'RE DOING.
SORRY, ARE YOU PRINCESS LUNA?
YES?
OUR PRINCESS IS EXPECTING YOU.
THIS WAY PLEASE.

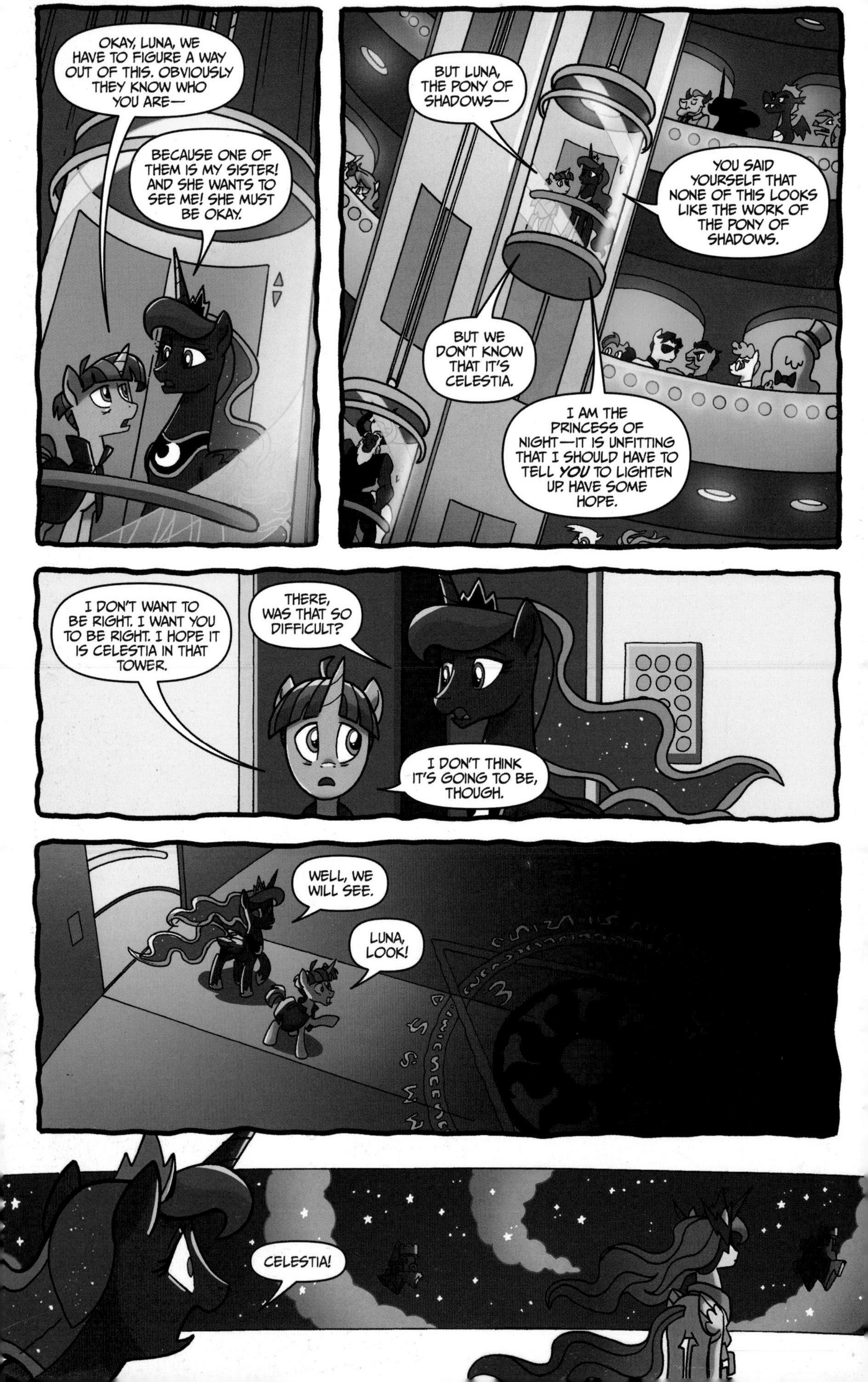
OKAY, LUNA, WE HAVE TO FIGURE A WAY OUT OF THIS. OBVIOUSLY THEY KNOW WHO YOU ARE—
BECAUSE ONE OF THEM IS MY SISTER! AND SHE WANTS TO SEE ME! SHE MUST BE OKAY.
BUT LUNA, THE PONY OF SHADOWS—
YOU SAID YOURSELF THAT NONE OF THIS LOOKS LIKE THE WORK OF THE PONY OF SHADOWS.
BUT WE DON'T KNOW THAT IT'S CELESTIA.
I AM THE PRINCESS OF NIGHT—IT IS UNFITTING THAT I SHOULD HAVE TO TELL *YOU* TO LIGHTEN UP. HAVE SOME HOPE.
I DON'T WANT TO BE RIGHT. I WANT YOU TO BE RIGHT. I HOPE IT IS CELESTIA IN THAT TOWER.
THERE, WAS THAT SO DIFFICULT?
I DON'T THINK IT'S GOING TO BE, THOUGH.
WELL, WE WILL SEE.
LUNA, LOOK!
CELESTIA!

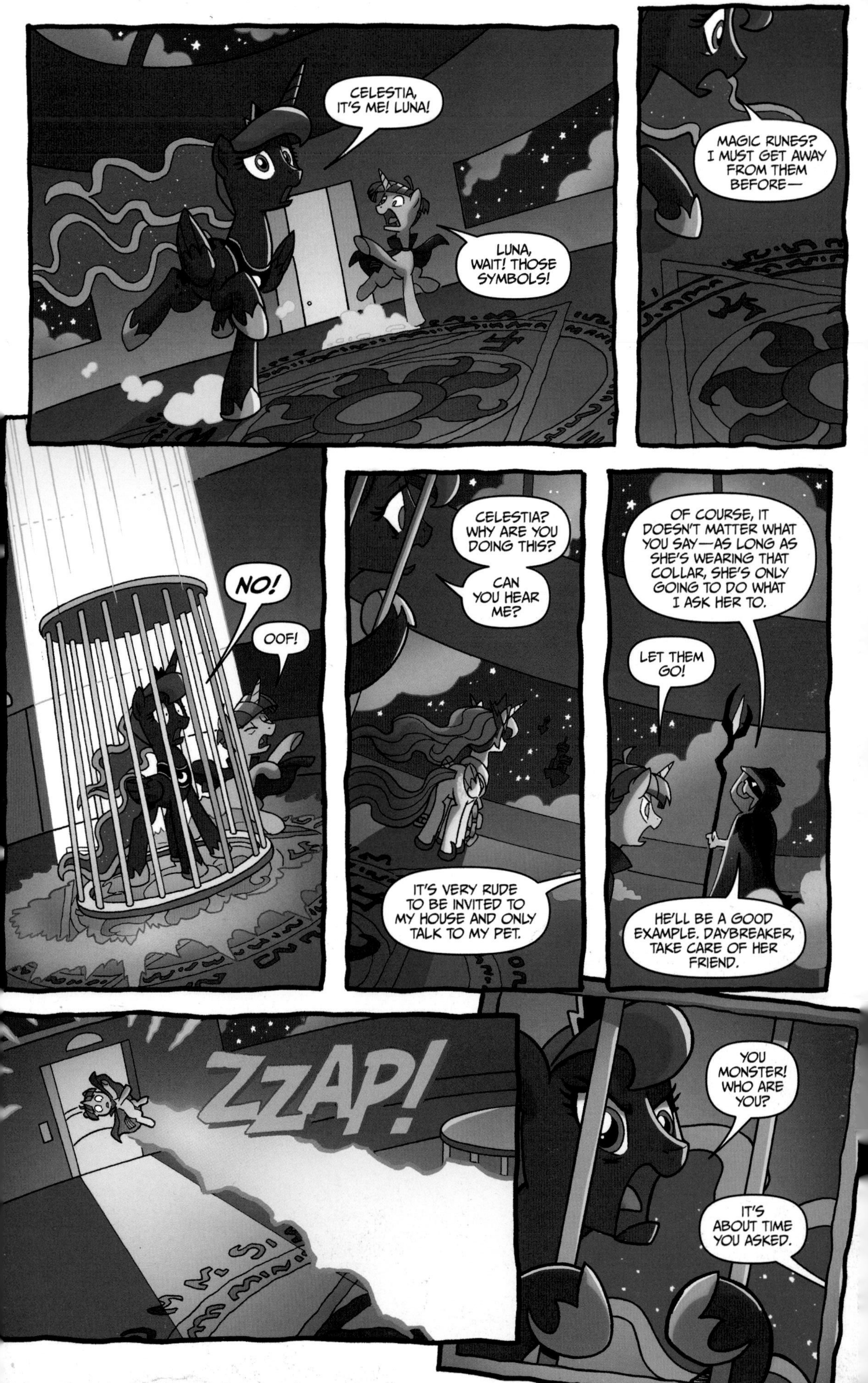
CELESTIA, IT'S ME! LUNA!
LUNA, WAIT! THOSE SYMBOLS!
MAGIC RUNES? I MUST GET AWAY FROM THEM BEFORE—
NO!
OOF!
CELESTIA? WHY ARE YOU DOING THIS?
CAN YOU HEAR ME?
IT'S VERY RUDE TO BE INVITED TO MY HOUSE AND ONLY TALK TO MY PET.
OF COURSE, IT DOESN'T MATTER WHAT YOU SAY—AS LONG AS SHE'S WEARING THAT COLLAR, SHE'S ONLY GOING TO DO WHAT I ASK HER TO.
LET THEM GO!
HE'LL BE A GOOD EXAMPLE. DAYBREAKER, TAKE CARE OF HER FRIEND.
ZZAP!
YOU MONSTER! WHO ARE YOU?
IT'S ABOUT TIME YOU ASKED.

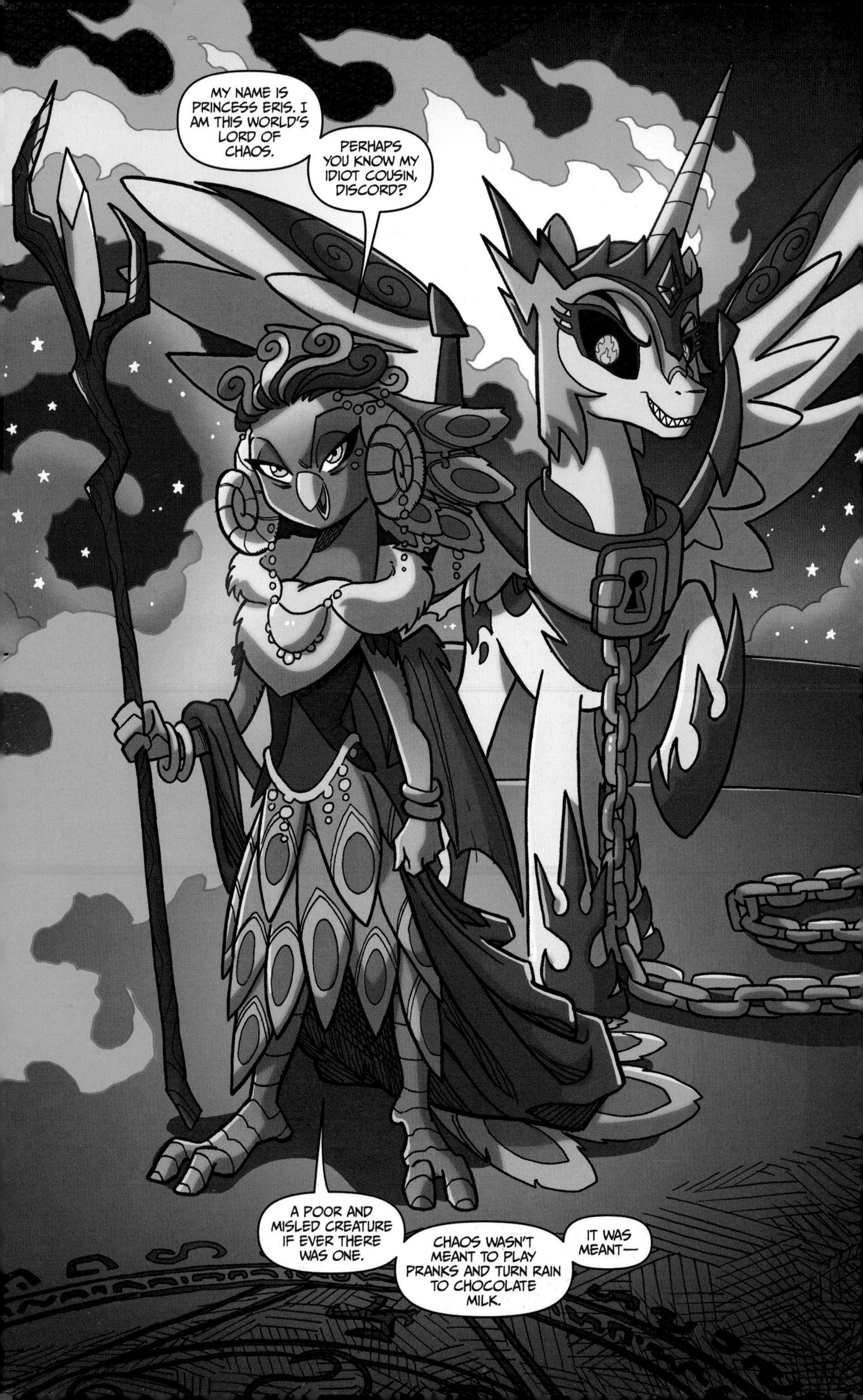
MY NAME IS PRINCESS ERIS. I AM THIS WORLD'S LORD OF CHAOS.
PERHAPS YOU KNOW MY IDIOT COUSIN, DISCORD?
A POOR AND MISLED CREATURE IF EVER THERE WAS ONE.
CHAOS WASN'T MEANT TO PLAY PRANKS AND TURN RAIN TO CHOCOLATE MILK.
IT WAS MEANT—

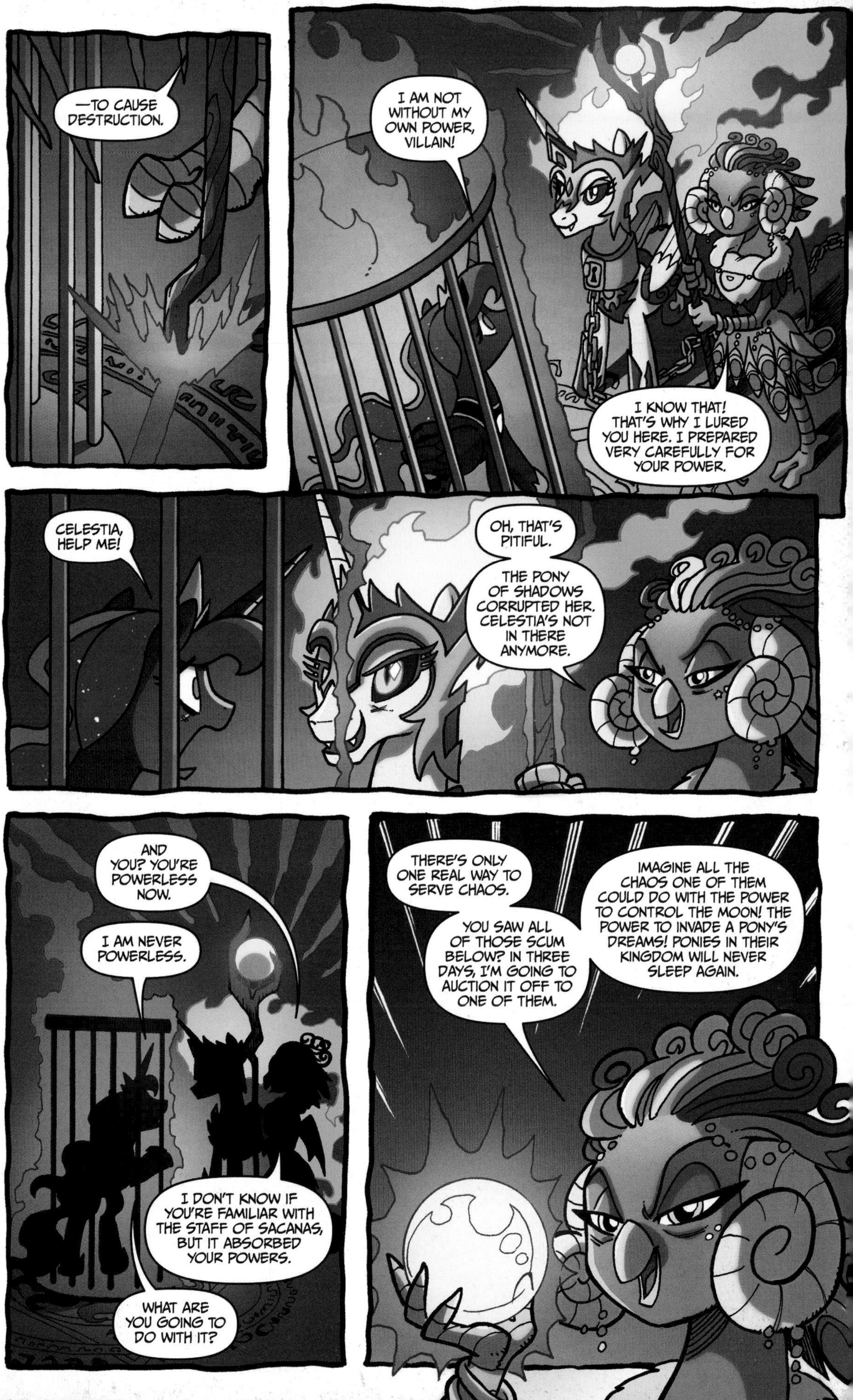
—TO CAUSE DESTRUCTION.
I AM NOT WITHOUT MY OWN POWER, VILLAIN!
I KNOW THAT! THAT'S WHY I LURED YOU HERE. I PREPARED VERY CAREFULLY FOR YOUR POWER.
CELESTIA, HELP ME!
OH, THAT'S PITIFUL.
THE PONY OF SHADOWS CORRUPTED HER. CELESTIA'S NOT IN THERE ANYMORE.
AND YOU? YOU'RE POWERLESS NOW.
I AM NEVER POWERLESS.
I DON'T KNOW IF YOU'RE FAMILIAR WITH THE STAFF OF SACANAS, BUT IT ABSORBED YOUR POWERS.
WHAT ARE YOU GOING TO DO WITH IT?
THERE'S ONLY ONE REAL WAY TO SERVE CHAOS.
YOU SAW ALL OF THOSE SCUM BELOW? IN THREE DAYS, I'M GOING TO AUCTION IT OFF TO ONE OF THEM.
IMAGINE ALL THE CHAOS ONE OF THEM COULD DO WITH THE POWER TO CONTROL THE MOON! THE POWER TO INVADE A PONY'S DREAMS! PONIES IN THEIR KINGDOM WILL NEVER SLEEP AGAIN.

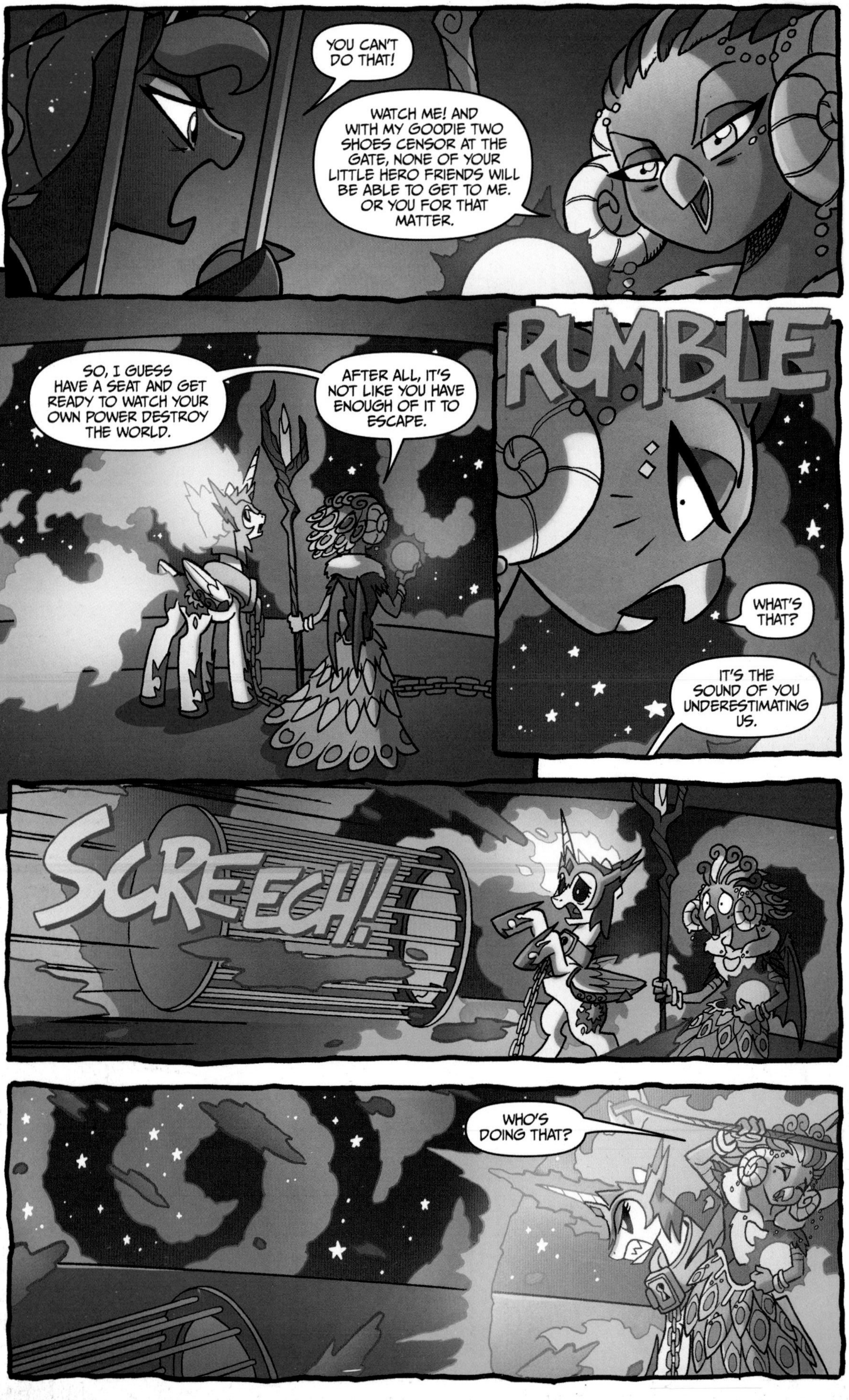
YOU CAN'T DO THAT!
WATCH ME! AND WITH MY GOODIE TWO SHOES CENSOR AT THE GATE, NONE OF YOUR LITTLE HERO FRIENDS WILL BE ABLE TO GET TO ME. OR YOU FOR THAT MATTER.
SO, I GUESS HAVE A SEAT AND GET READY TO WATCH YOUR OWN POWER DESTROY THE WORLD.
AFTER ALL, IT'S NOT LIKE YOU HAVE ENOUGH OF IT TO ESCAPE.
RUMBLE
WHAT'S THAT?
IT'S THE SOUND OF YOU UNDERESTIMATING US.
SCREECH!
WHO'S DOING THAT?

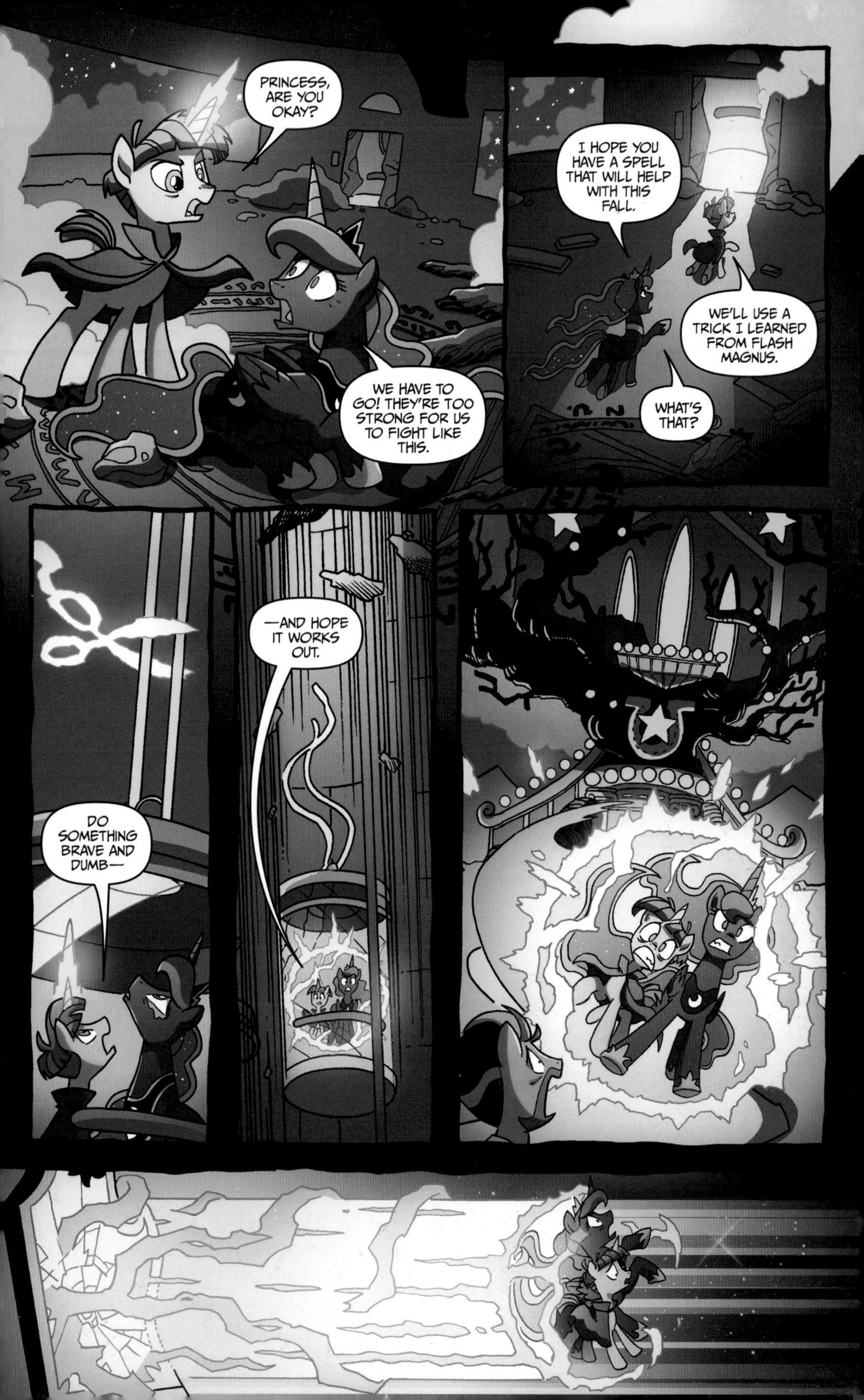
PRINCESS, ARE YOU OKAY?
WE HAVE TO GO! THEY'RE TOO STRONG FOR US TO FIGHT LIKE THIS.
I HOPE YOU HAVE A SPELL THAT WILL HELP WITH THIS FALL.
WE'LL USE A TRICK I LEARNED FROM FLASH MAGNUS.
WHAT'S THAT?
DO SOMETHING BRAVE AND DUMB—
—AND HOPE IT WORKS OUT.

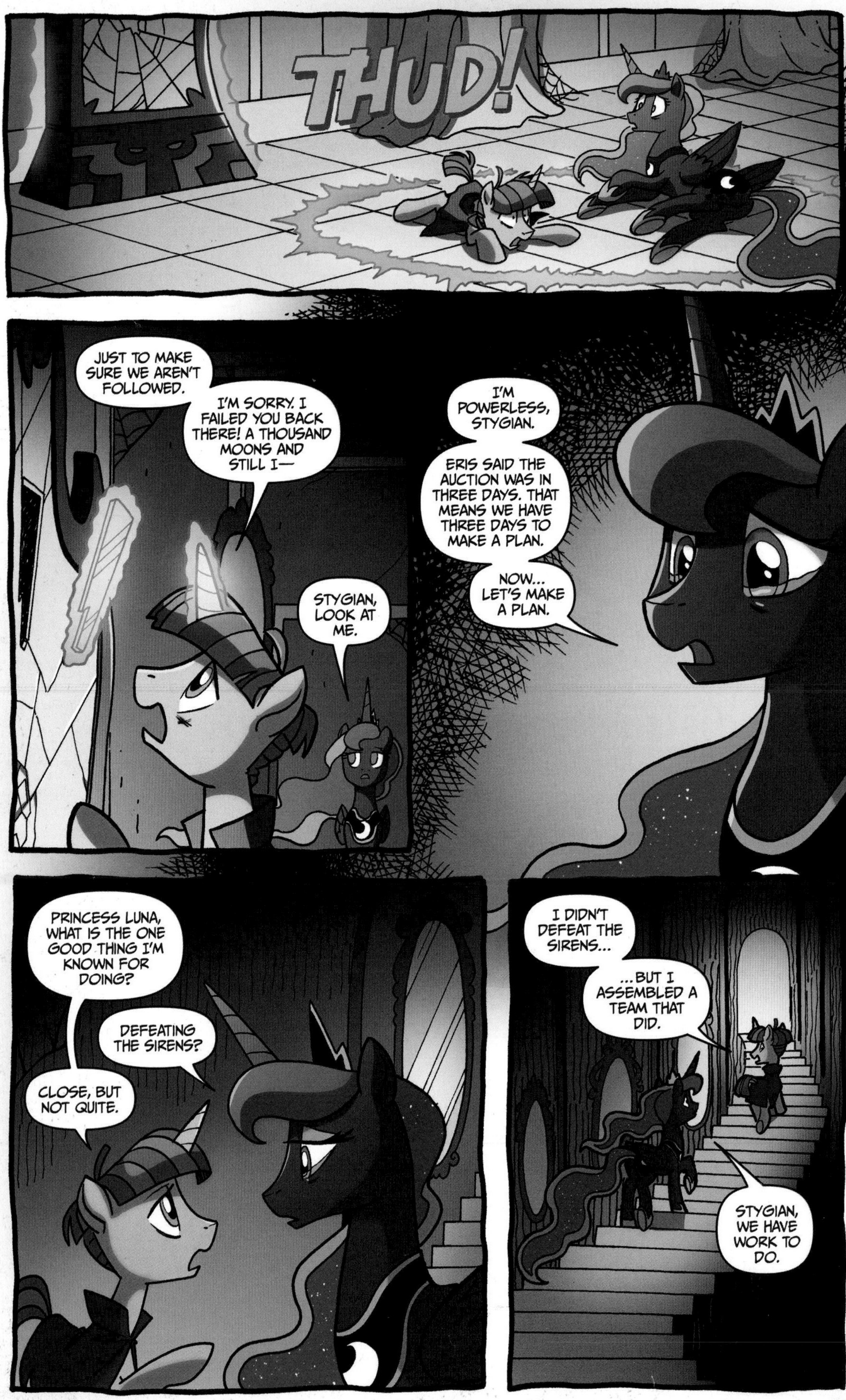
THUD!
JUST TO MAKE SURE WE AREN'T FOLLOWED.
I'M SORRY. I FAILED YOU BACK THERE! A THOUSAND MOONS AND STILL I—
STYGIAN, LOOK AT ME.
I'M POWERLESS, STYGIAN.
ERIS SAID THE AUCTION WAS IN THREE DAYS. THAT MEANS WE HAVE THREE DAYS TO MAKE A PLAN.
NOW... LET'S MAKE A PLAN.
PRINCESS LUNA, WHAT IS THE ONE GOOD THING I'M KNOWN FOR DOING?
DEFEATING THE SIRENS?
CLOSE, BUT NOT QUITE.
I DIDN'T DEFEAT THE SIRENS...
...BUT I ASSEMBLED A TEAM THAT DID.
STYGIAN, WE HAVE WORK TO DO.

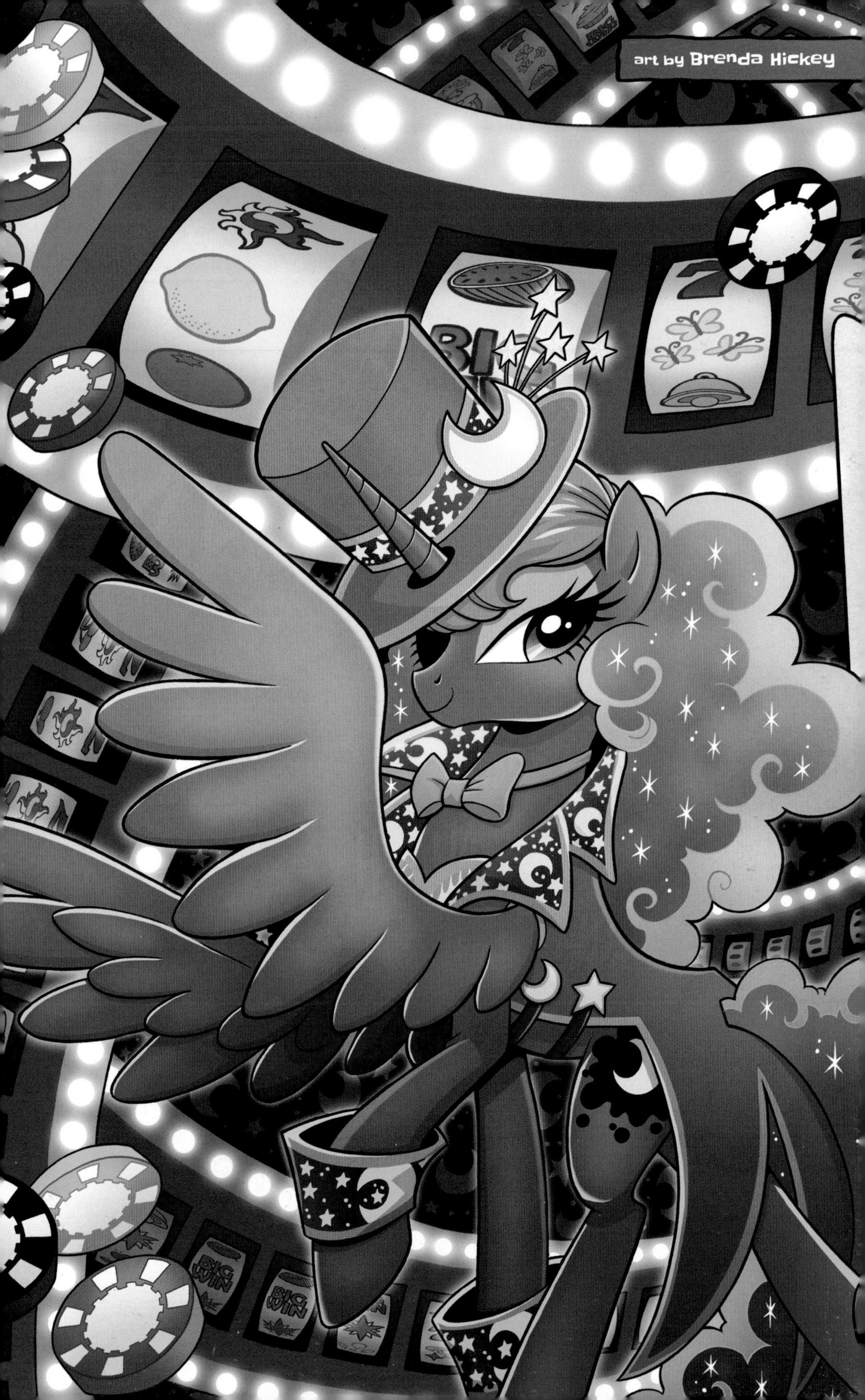
art by Brenda Hickey
BIG WIN
BIG WIN
BIG WIN

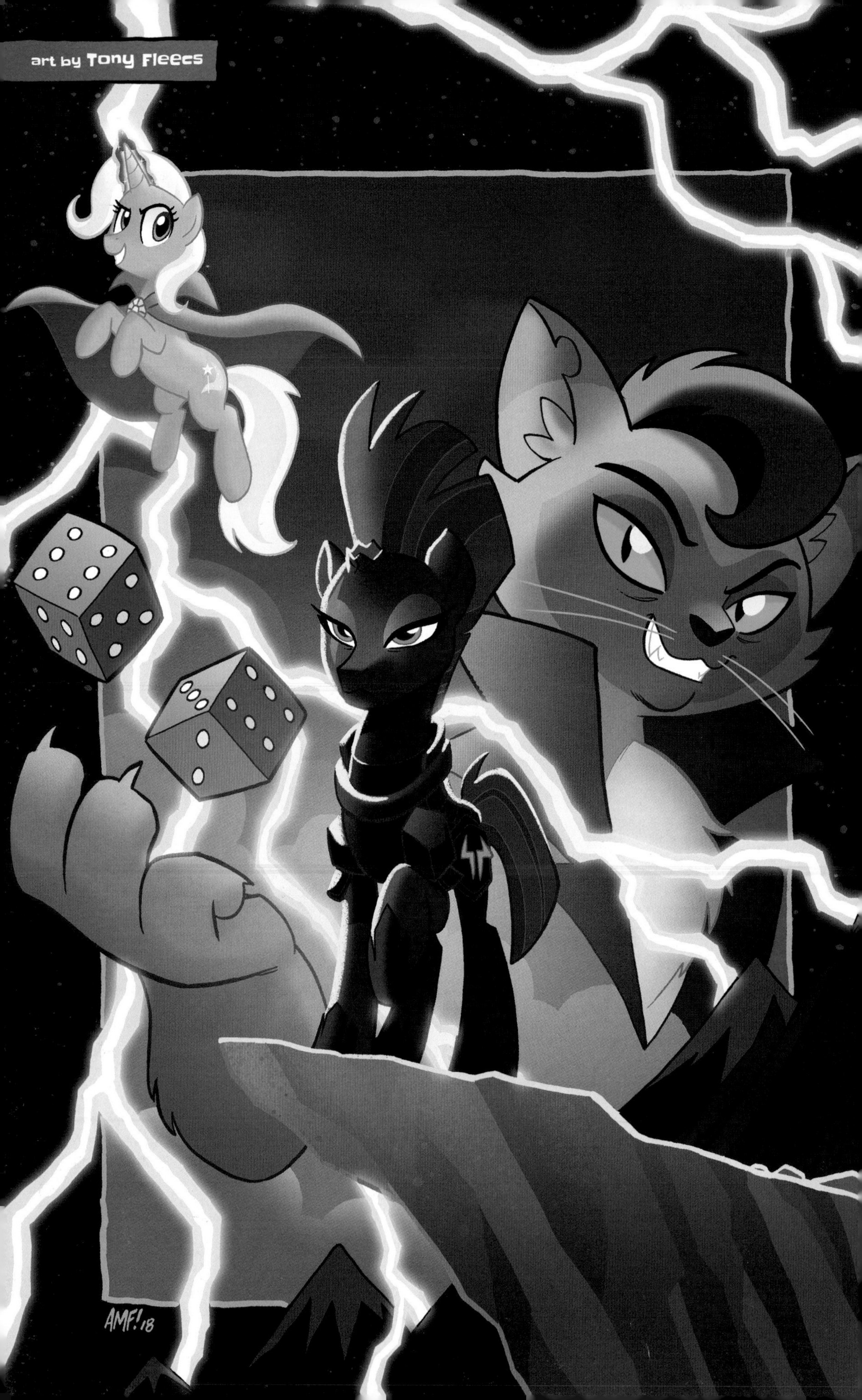
AMF! '18

art by Tony Fleecs

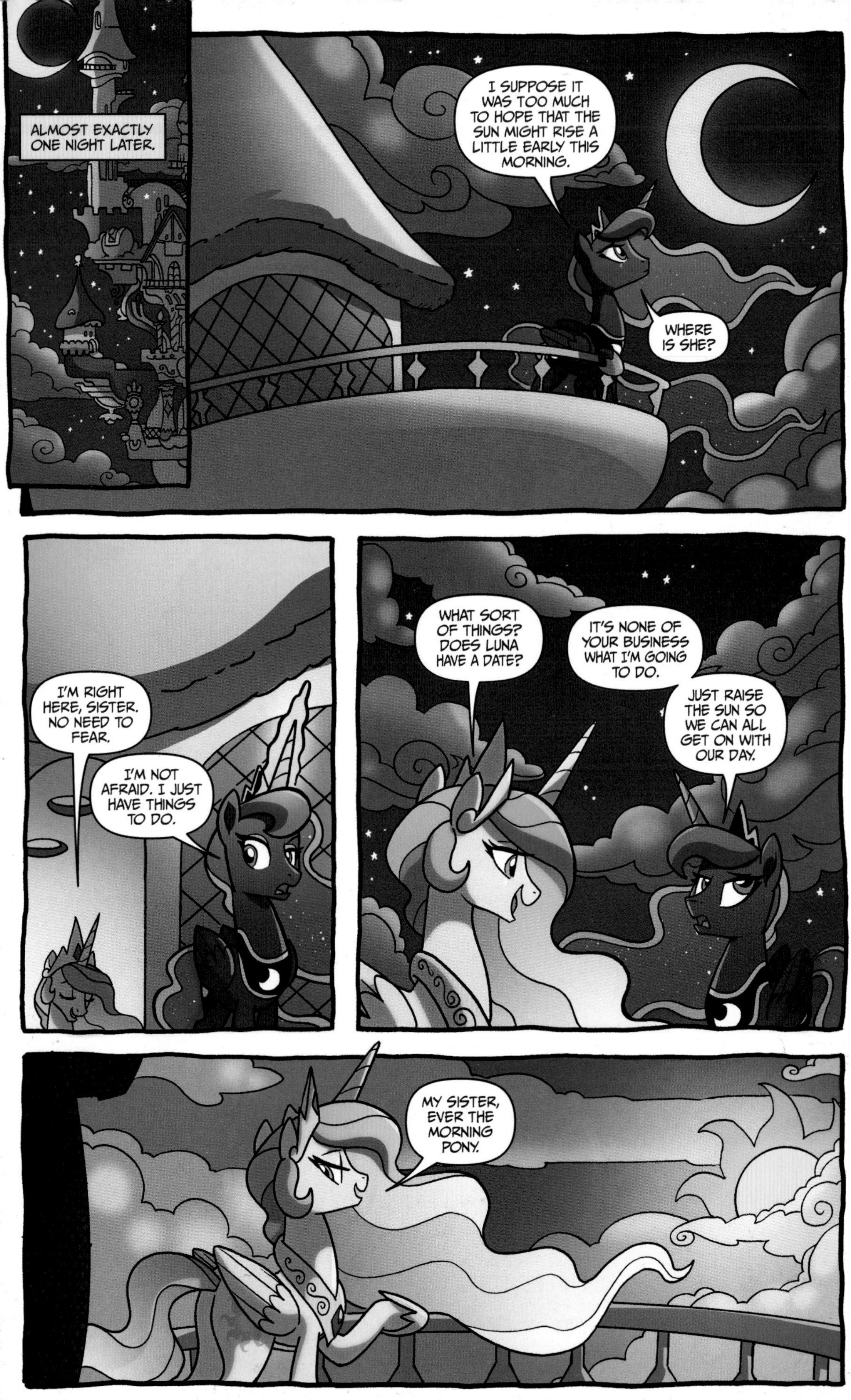
ALMOST EXACTLY ONE NIGHT LATER.
I SUPPOSE IT WAS TOO MUCH TO HOPE THAT THE SUN MIGHT RISE A LITTLE EARLY THIS MORNING.
WHERE IS SHE?
I'M RIGHT HERE, SISTER. NO NEED TO FEAR.
I'M NOT AFRAID. I JUST HAVE THINGS TO DO.
WHAT SORT OF THINGS? DOES LUNA HAVE A DATE?
IT'S NONE OF YOUR BUSINESS WHAT I'M GOING TO DO.
JUST RAISE THE SUN SO WE CAN ALL GET ON WITH OUR DAY.
MY SISTER, EVER THE MORNING PONY.

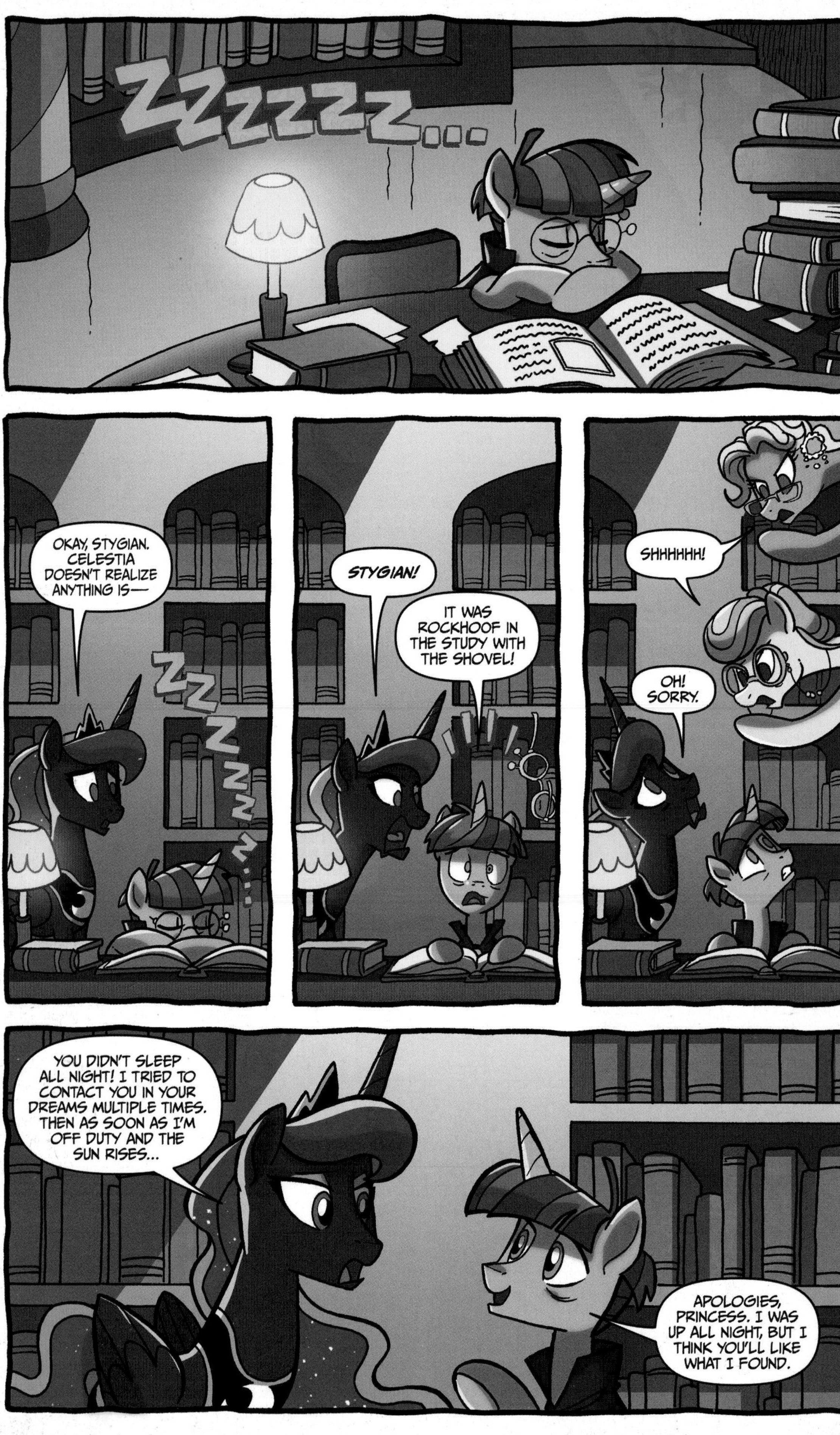
ZZZZZZ...
OKAY, STYGIAN. CELESTIA DOESN'T REALIZE ANYTHING IS—
ZZZZZ...
STYGIAN!
IT WAS ROCKHOOF IN THE STUDY WITH THE SHOVEL!
SHHHHHH!
OH! SORRY.
YOU DIDN'T SLEEP ALL NIGHT! I TRIED TO CONTACT YOU IN YOUR DREAMS MULTIPLE TIMES. THEN AS SOON AS I'M OFF DUTY AND THE SUN RISES...
APOLOGIES, PRINCESS. I WAS UP ALL NIGHT, BUT I THINK YOU'LL LIKE WHAT I FOUND.

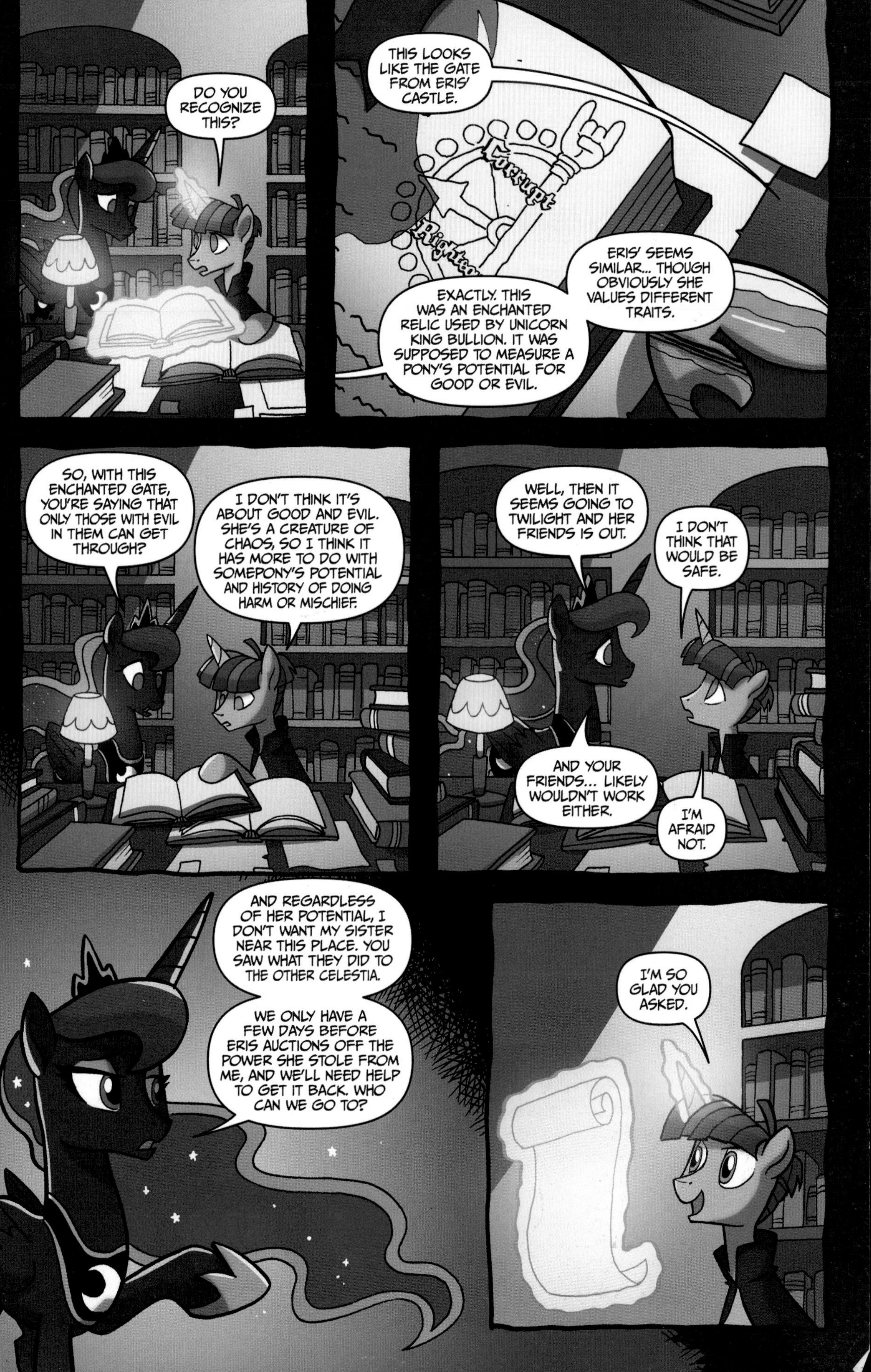
DO YOU RECOGNIZE THIS?
THIS LOOKS LIKE THE GATE FROM ERIS' CASTLE.
Corrupt
EXACTLY. THIS WAS AN ENCHANTED RELIC USED BY UNICORN KING BULLION. IT WAS SUPPOSED TO MEASURE A PONY'S POTENTIAL FOR GOOD OR EVIL.
ERIS' SEEMS SIMILAR... THOUGH OBVIOUSLY SHE VALUES DIFFERENT TRAITS.
SO, WITH THIS ENCHANTED GATE, YOU'RE SAYING THAT ONLY THOSE WITH EVIL IN THEM CAN GET THROUGH?
I DON'T THINK IT'S ABOUT GOOD AND EVIL. SHE'S A CREATURE OF CHAOS, SO I THINK IT HAS MORE TO DO WITH SOMEPONY'S POTENTIAL AND HISTORY OF DOING HARM OR MISCHIEF.
WELL, THEN IT SEEMS GOING TO TWILIGHT AND HER FRIENDS IS OUT.
I DON'T THINK THAT WOULD BE SAFE.
AND YOUR FRIENDS... LIKELY WOULDN'T WORK EITHER.
I'M AFRAID NOT.
AND REGARDLESS OF HER POTENTIAL, I DON'T WANT MY SISTER NEAR THIS PLACE. YOU SAW WHAT THEY DID TO THE OTHER CELESTIA.
WE ONLY HAVE A FEW DAYS BEFORE ERIS AUCTIONS OFF THE POWER SHE STOLE FROM ME, AND WE'LL NEED HELP TO GET IT BACK. WHO CAN WE GO TO?
I'M SO GLAD YOU ASKED.

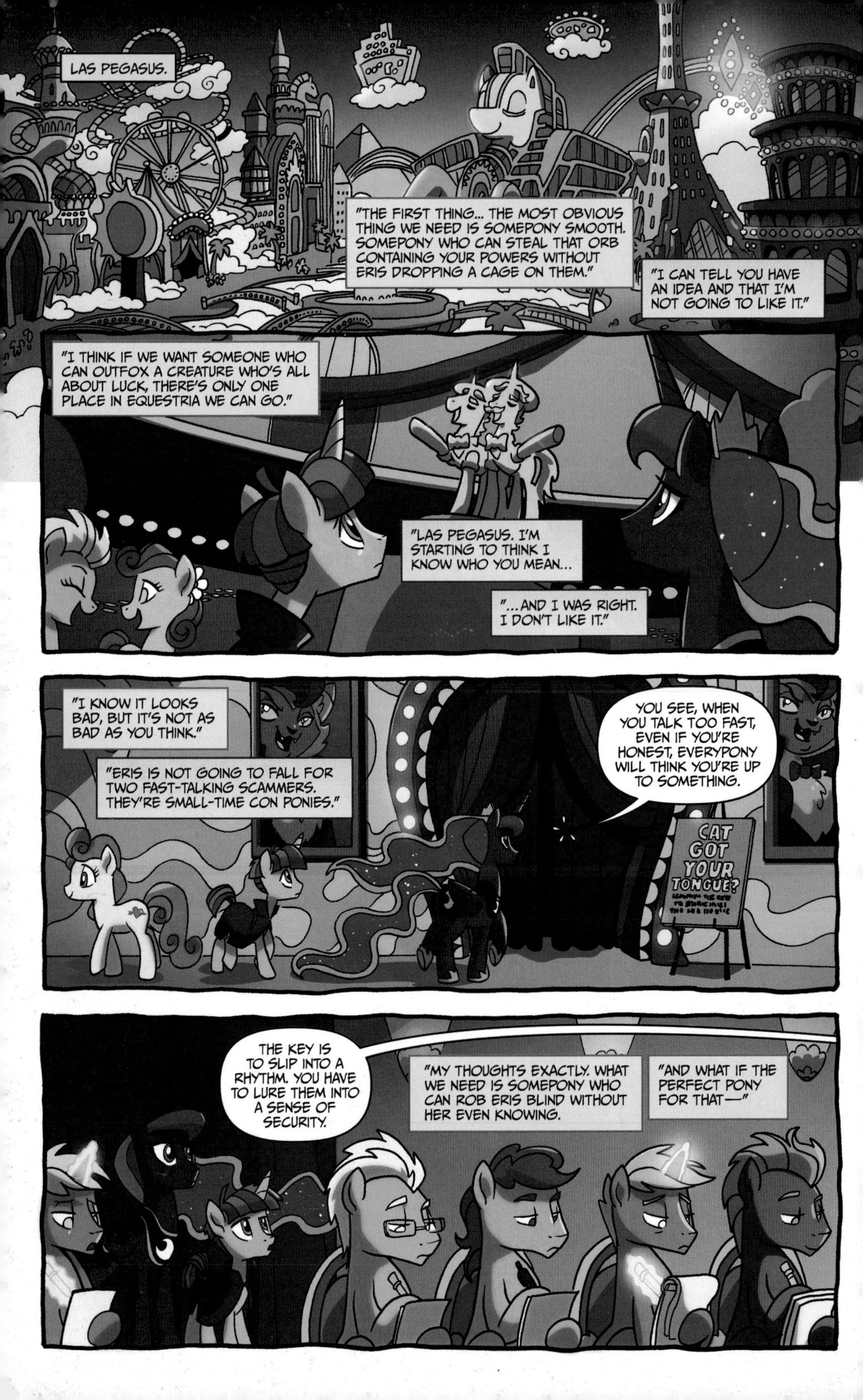
LAS PEGASUS.
"THE FIRST THING... THE MOST OBVIOUS THING WE NEED IS SOMEPONY SMOOTH. SOMEPONY WHO CAN STEAL THAT ORB CONTAINING YOUR POWERS WITHOUT ERIS DROPPING A CAGE ON THEM."
"I CAN TELL YOU HAVE AN IDEA AND THAT I'M NOT GOING TO LIKE IT."
"I THINK IF WE WANT SOMEONE WHO CAN OUTFOX A CREATURE WHO'S ALL ABOUT LUCK, THERE'S ONLY ONE PLACE IN EQUESTRIA WE CAN GO."
"LAS PEGASUS. I'M STARTING TO THINK I KNOW WHO YOU MEAN...
"...AND I WAS RIGHT. I DON'T LIKE IT."
"I KNOW IT LOOKS BAD, BUT IT'S NOT AS BAD AS YOU THINK."
"ERIS IS NOT GOING TO FALL FOR TWO FAST-TALKING SCAMMERS. THEY'RE SMALL-TIME CON PONIES."
YOU SEE, WHEN YOU TALK TOO FAST, EVEN IF YOU'RE HONEST, EVERYPONY WILL THINK YOU'RE UP TO SOMETHING.
CAT GOT YOUR TONGUE?
THE KEY IS TO SLIP INTO A RHYTHM. YOU HAVE TO LURE THEM INTO A SENSE OF SECURITY.
"MY THOUGHTS EXACTLY. WHAT WE NEED IS SOMEPONY WHO CAN ROB ERIS BLIND WITHOUT HER EVEN KNOWING.
"AND WHAT IF THE PERFECT PONY FOR THAT—"

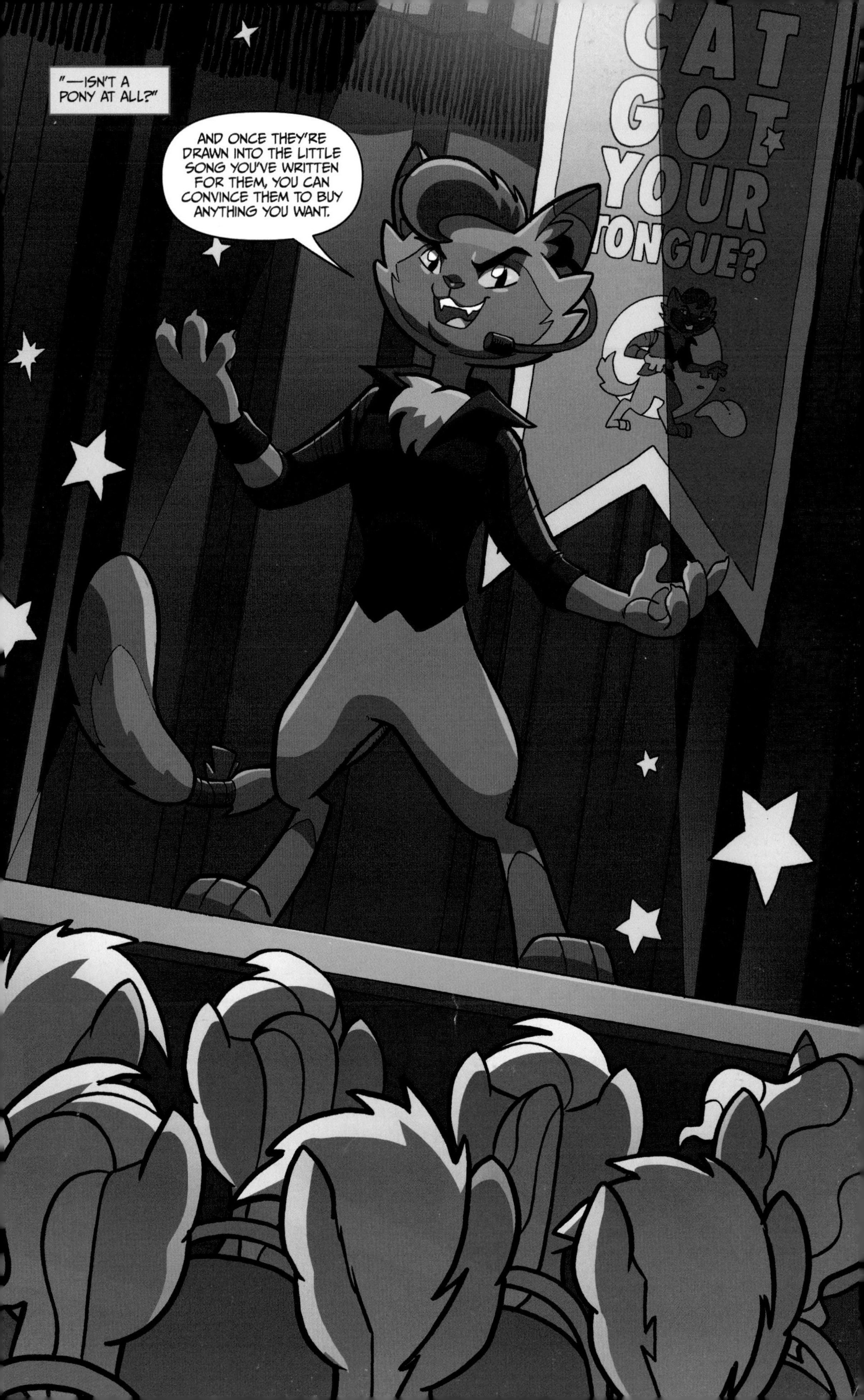
"—ISN'T A PONY AT ALL?"
AND ONCE THEY'RE DRAWN INTO THE LITTLE SONG YOU'VE WRITTEN FOR THEM, YOU CAN CONVINCE THEM TO BUY ANYTHING YOU WANT.
CAT GOT YOUR TONGUE?

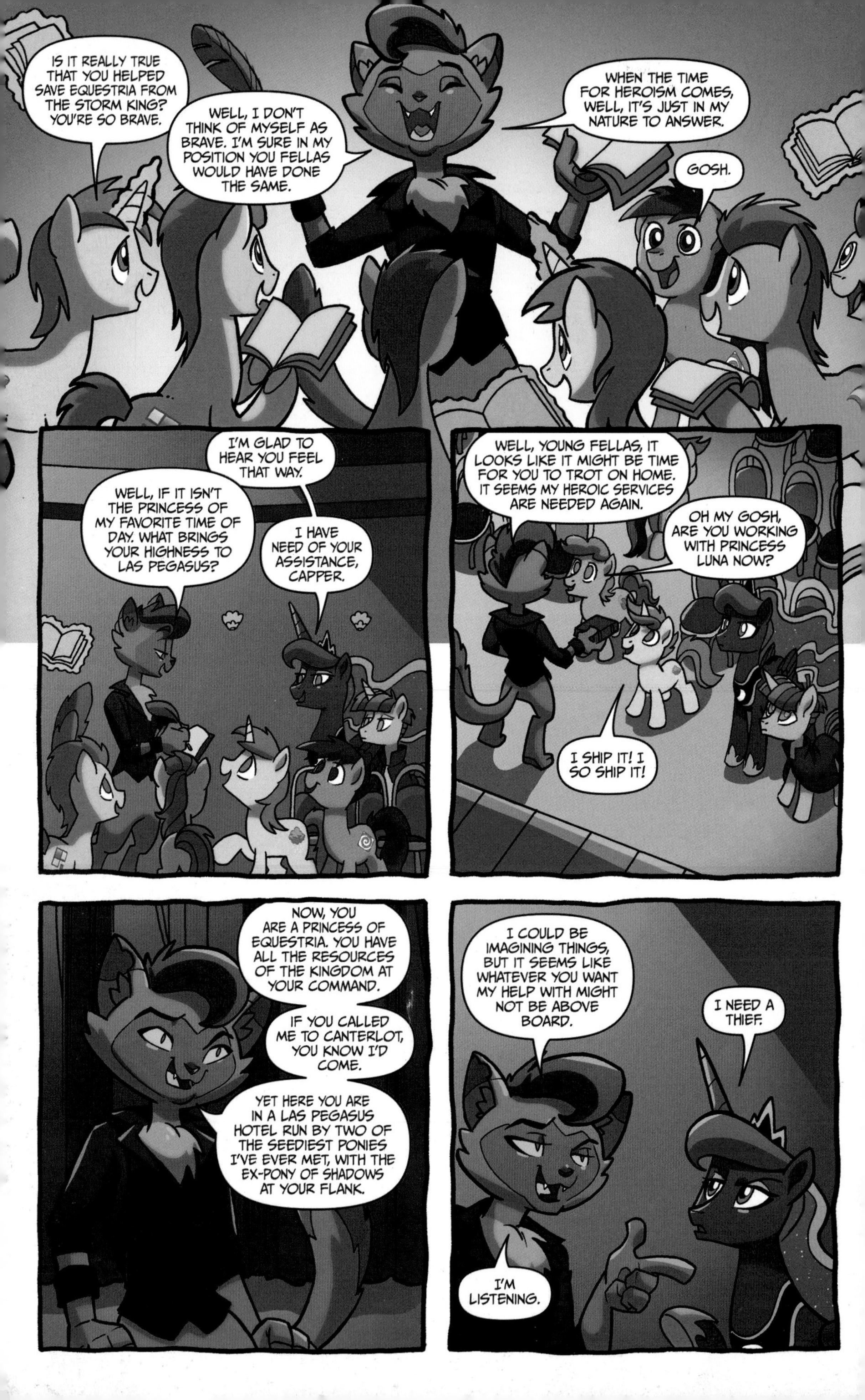
IS IT REALLY TRUE THAT YOU HELPED SAVE EQUESTRIA FROM THE STORM KING? YOU'RE SO BRAVE.
WELL, I DON'T THINK OF MYSELF AS BRAVE. I'M SURE IN MY POSITION YOU FELLAS WOULD HAVE DONE THE SAME.
WHEN THE TIME FOR HEROISM COMES, WELL, IT'S JUST IN MY NATURE TO ANSWER.
GOSH.
I'M GLAD TO HEAR YOU FEEL THAT WAY.
WELL, IF IT ISN'T THE PRINCESS OF MY FAVORITE TIME OF DAY. WHAT BRINGS YOUR HIGHNESS TO LAS PEGASUS?
I HAVE NEED OF YOUR ASSISTANCE, CAPPER.
WELL, YOUNG FELLAS, IT LOOKS LIKE IT MIGHT BE TIME FOR YOU TO TROT ON HOME. IT SEEMS MY HEROIC SERVICES ARE NEEDED AGAIN.
OH MY GOSH, ARE YOU WORKING WITH PRINCESS LUNA NOW?
I SHIP IT! I SO SHIP IT!
NOW, YOU ARE A PRINCESS OF EQUESTRIA. YOU HAVE ALL THE RESOURCES OF THE KINGDOM AT YOUR COMMAND.
IF YOU CALLED ME TO CANTERLOT, YOU KNOW I'D COME.
YET HERE YOU ARE IN A LAS PEGASUS HOTEL RUN BY TWO OF THE SEEDIEST PONIES I'VE EVER MET, WITH THE EX-PONY OF SHADOWS AT YOUR FLANK.
I COULD BE IMAGINING THINGS, BUT IT SEEMS LIKE WHATEVER YOU WANT MY HELP WITH MIGHT NOT BE ABOVE BOARD.
I NEED A THIEF.
I'M LISTENING.

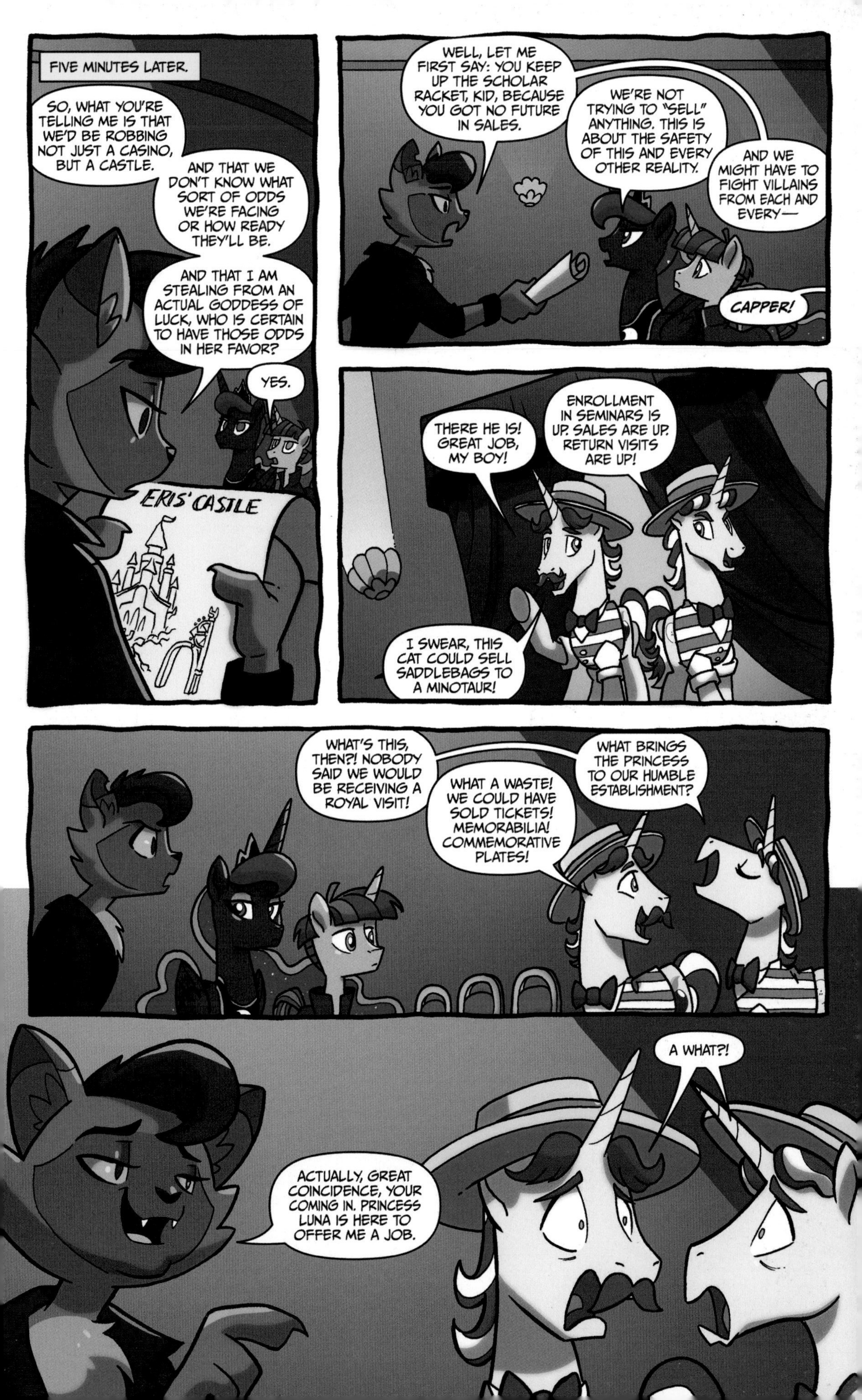
FIVE MINUTES LATER.
SO, WHAT YOU'RE TELLING ME IS THAT WE'D BE ROBBING NOT JUST A CASINO, BUT A CASTLE.
AND THAT WE DON'T KNOW WHAT SORT OF ODDS WE'RE FACING OR HOW READY THEY'LL BE.
AND THAT I AM STEALING FROM AN ACTUAL GODDESS OF LUCK, WHO IS CERTAIN TO HAVE THOSE ODDS IN HER FAVOR?
YES.
ERIS' CASTLE
WELL, LET ME FIRST SAY: YOU KEEP UP THE SCHOLAR RACKET, KID, BECAUSE YOU GOT NO FUTURE IN SALES.
WE'RE NOT TRYING TO "SELL" ANYTHING. THIS IS ABOUT THE SAFETY OF THIS AND EVERY OTHER REALITY.
AND WE MIGHT HAVE TO FIGHT VILLAINS FROM EACH AND EVERY—
CAPPER!
THERE HE IS! GREAT JOB, MY BOY!
ENROLLMENT IN SEMINARS IS UP. SALES ARE UP. RETURN VISITS ARE UP!
I SWEAR, THIS CAT COULD SELL SADDLEBAGS TO A MINOTAUR!
WHAT'S THIS, THEN?! NOBODY SAID WE WOULD BE RECEIVING A ROYAL VISIT!
WHAT A WASTE! WE COULD HAVE SOLD TICKETS! MEMORABILIA! COMMEMORATIVE PLATES!
WHAT BRINGS THE PRINCESS TO OUR HUMBLE ESTABLISHMENT?
ACTUALLY, GREAT COINCIDENCE, YOUR COMING IN. PRINCESS LUNA IS HERE TO OFFER ME A JOB.
A WHAT?!

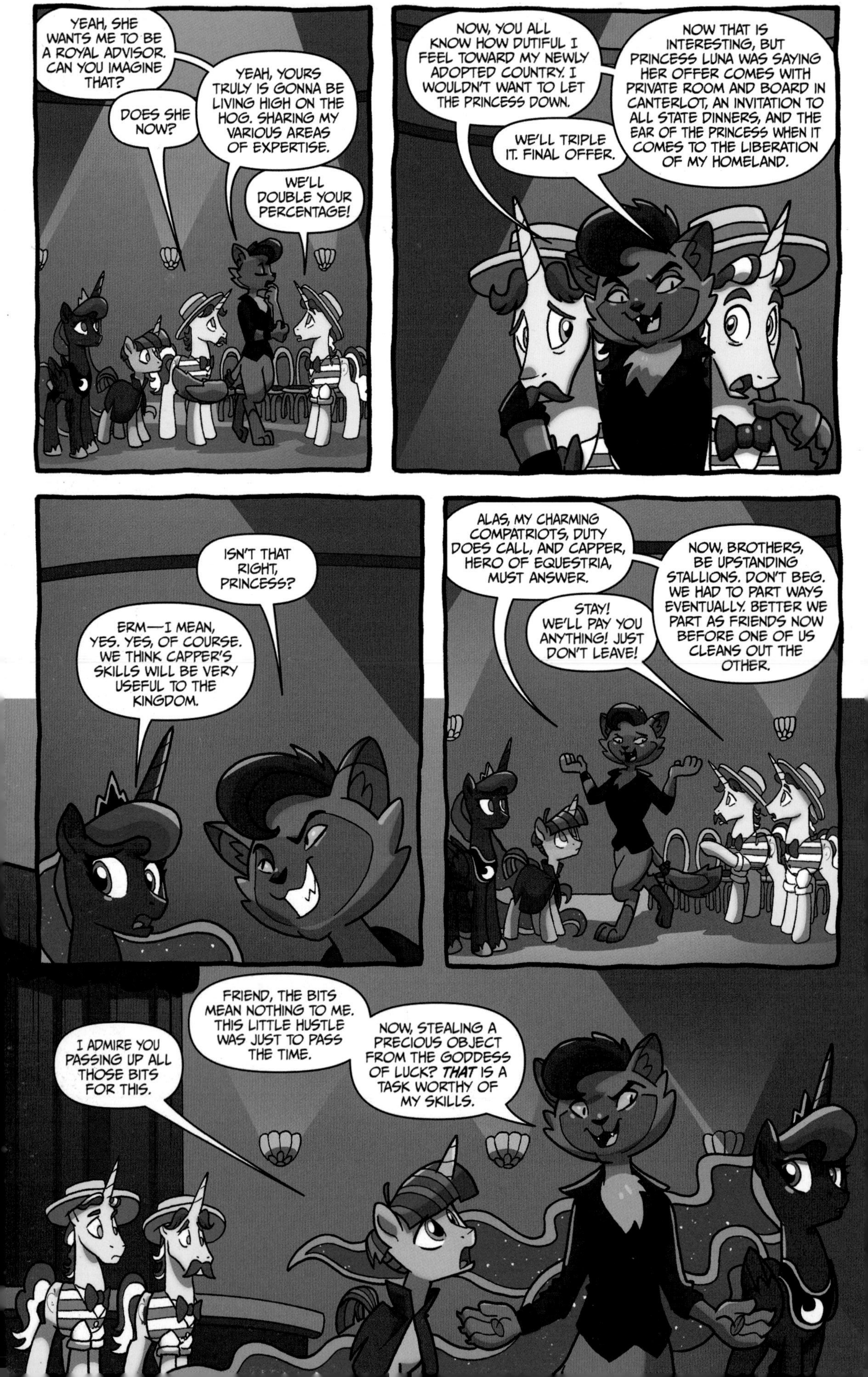
YEAH, SHE WANTS ME TO BE A ROYAL ADVISOR. CAN YOU IMAGINE THAT?
DOES SHE NOW?
YEAH, YOURS TRULY IS GONNA BE LIVING HIGH ON THE HOG. SHARING MY VARIOUS AREAS OF EXPERTISE.
WE'LL DOUBLE YOUR PERCENTAGE!
NOW, YOU ALL KNOW HOW DUTIFUL I FEEL TOWARD MY NEWLY ADOPTED COUNTRY. I WOULDN'T WANT TO LET THE PRINCESS DOWN.
WE'LL TRIPLE IT. FINAL OFFER.
NOW THAT IS INTERESTING, BUT PRINCESS LUNA WAS SAYING HER OFFER COMES WITH PRIVATE ROOM AND BOARD IN CANTERLOT, AN INVITATION TO ALL STATE DINNERS, AND THE EAR OF THE PRINCESS WHEN IT COMES TO THE LIBERATION OF MY HOMELAND.
ISN'T THAT RIGHT, PRINCESS?
ERM—I MEAN, YES. YES, OF COURSE. WE THINK CAPPER'S SKILLS WILL BE VERY USEFUL TO THE KINGDOM.
ALAS, MY CHARMING COMPATRIOTS, DUTY DOES CALL, AND CAPPER, HERO OF EQUESTRIA, MUST ANSWER.
STAY! WE'LL PAY YOU ANYTHING! JUST DON'T LEAVE!
NOW, BROTHERS, BE UPSTANDING STALLIONS. DON'T BEG. WE HAD TO PART WAYS EVENTUALLY. BETTER WE PART AS FRIENDS NOW BEFORE ONE OF US CLEANS OUT THE OTHER.
I ADMIRE YOU PASSING UP ALL THOSE BITS FOR THIS.
FRIEND, THE BITS MEAN NOTHING TO ME. THIS LITTLE HUSTLE WAS JUST TO PASS THE TIME.
NOW, STEALING A PRECIOUS OBJECT FROM THE GODDESS OF LUCK? *THAT* IS A TASK WORTHY OF MY SKILLS.

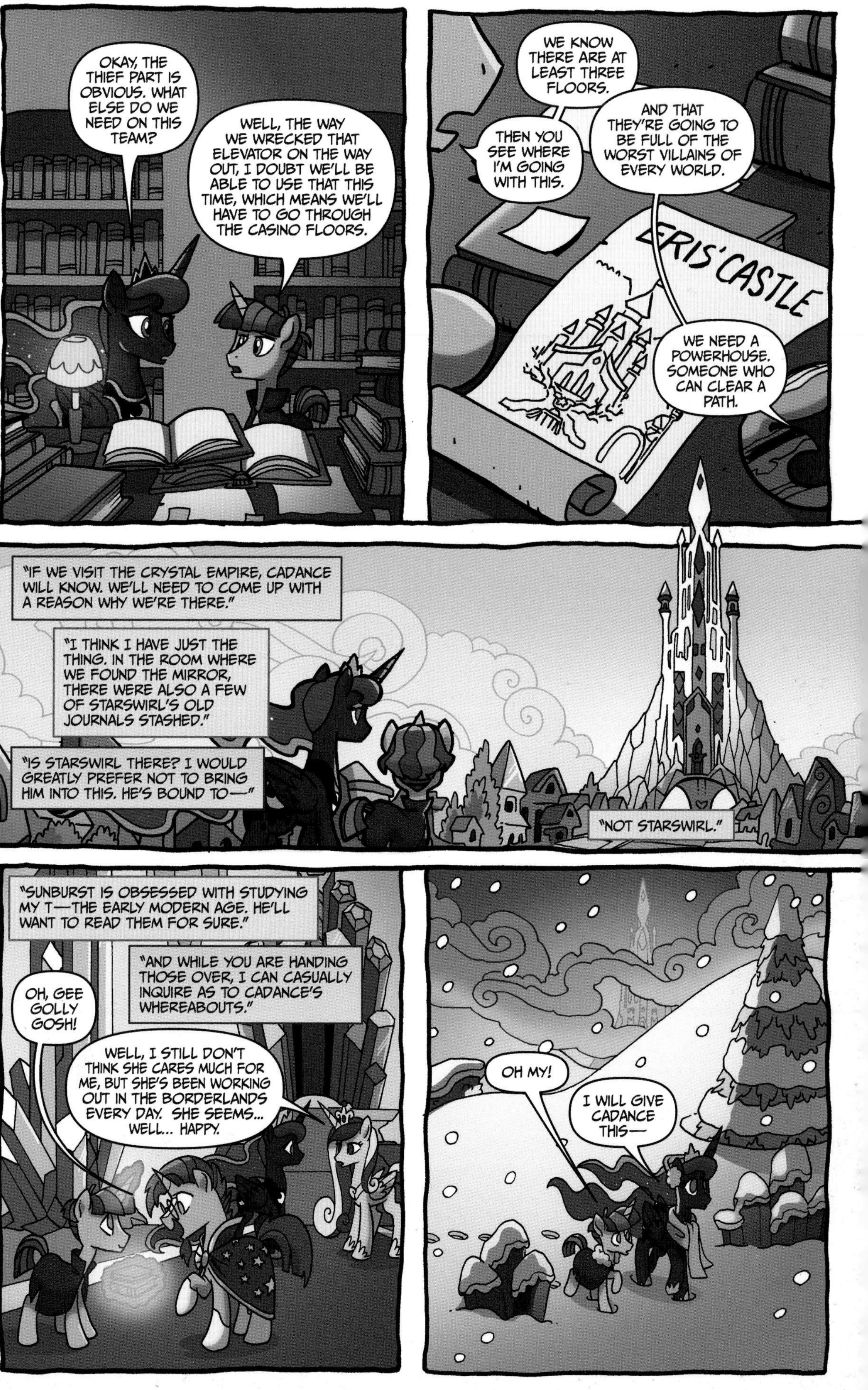
OKAY, THE THIEF PART IS OBVIOUS. WHAT ELSE DO WE NEED ON THIS TEAM?
WELL, THE WAY WE WRECKED THAT ELEVATOR ON THE WAY OUT, I DOUBT WE'LL BE ABLE TO USE THAT THIS TIME, WHICH MEANS WE'LL HAVE TO GO THROUGH THE CASINO FLOORS.
WE KNOW THERE ARE AT LEAST THREE FLOORS.
THEN YOU SEE WHERE I'M GOING WITH THIS.
AND THAT THEY'RE GOING TO BE FULL OF THE WORST VILLAINS OF EVERY WORLD.
ERIS' CASTLE
WE NEED A POWERHOUSE. SOMEONE WHO CAN CLEAR A PATH.
"IF WE VISIT THE CRYSTAL EMPIRE, CADANCE WILL KNOW. WE'LL NEED TO COME UP WITH A REASON WHY WE'RE THERE."
"I THINK I HAVE JUST THE THING. IN THE ROOM WHERE WE FOUND THE MIRROR, THERE WERE ALSO A FEW OF STARSWIRL'S OLD JOURNALS STASHED."
"IS STARSWIRL THERE? I WOULD GREATLY PREFER NOT TO BRING HIM INTO THIS. HE'S BOUND TO—"
"NOT STARSWIRL."
"SUNBURST IS OBSESSED WITH STUDYING MY T—THE EARLY MODERN AGE. HE'LL WANT TO READ THEM FOR SURE."
"AND WHILE YOU ARE HANDING THOSE OVER, I CAN CASUALLY INQUIRE AS TO CADANCE'S WHEREABOUTS."
OH, GEE GOLLY GOSH!
WELL, I STILL DON'T THINK SHE CARES MUCH FOR ME, BUT SHE'S BEEN WORKING OUT IN THE BORDERLANDS EVERY DAY. SHE SEEMS... WELL... HAPPY.
OH MY!
I WILL GIVE CADANCE THIS—

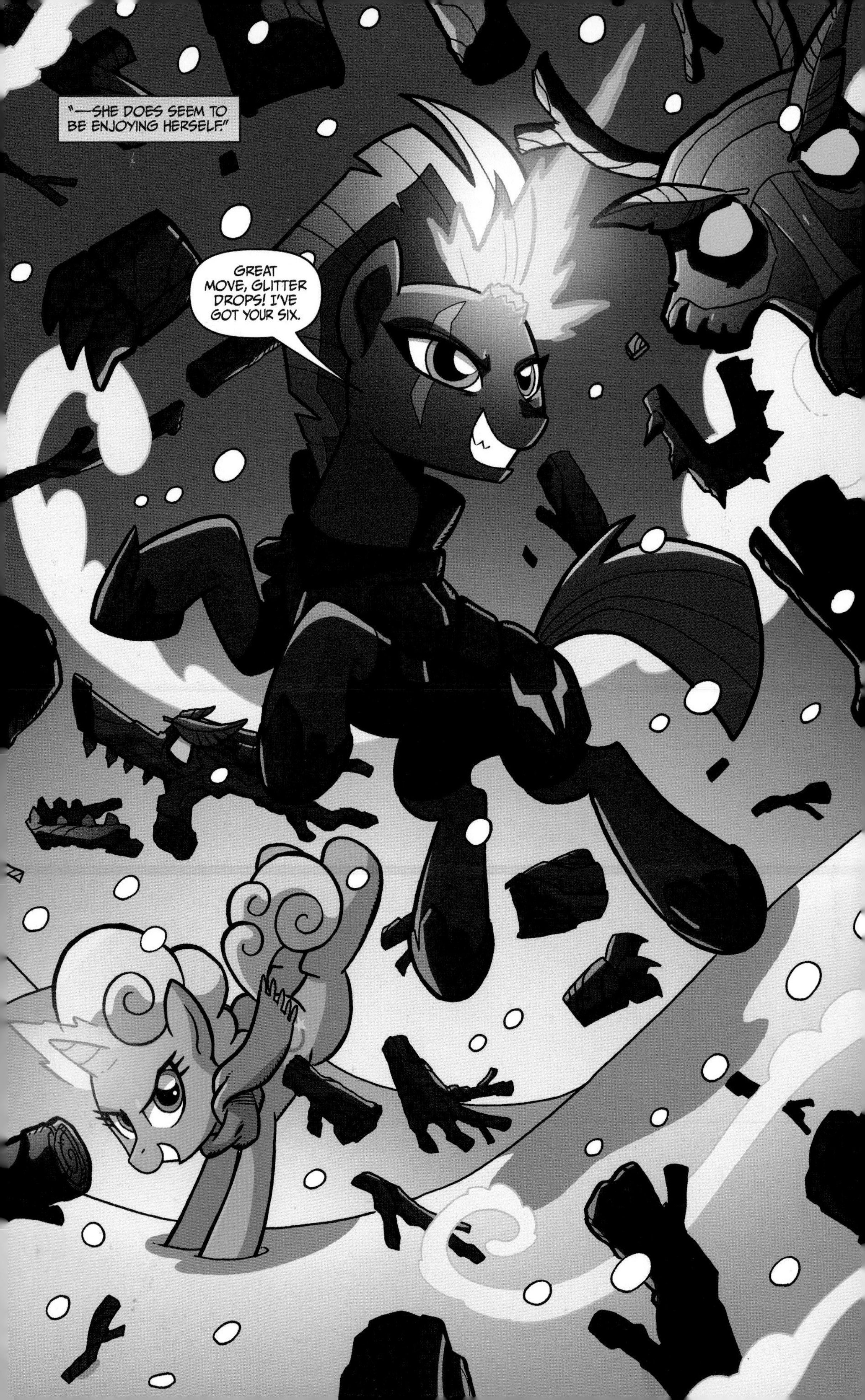
"—SHE DOES SEEM TO BE ENJOYING HERSELF."
GREAT MOVE, GLITTER DROPS! I'VE GOT YOUR SIX.

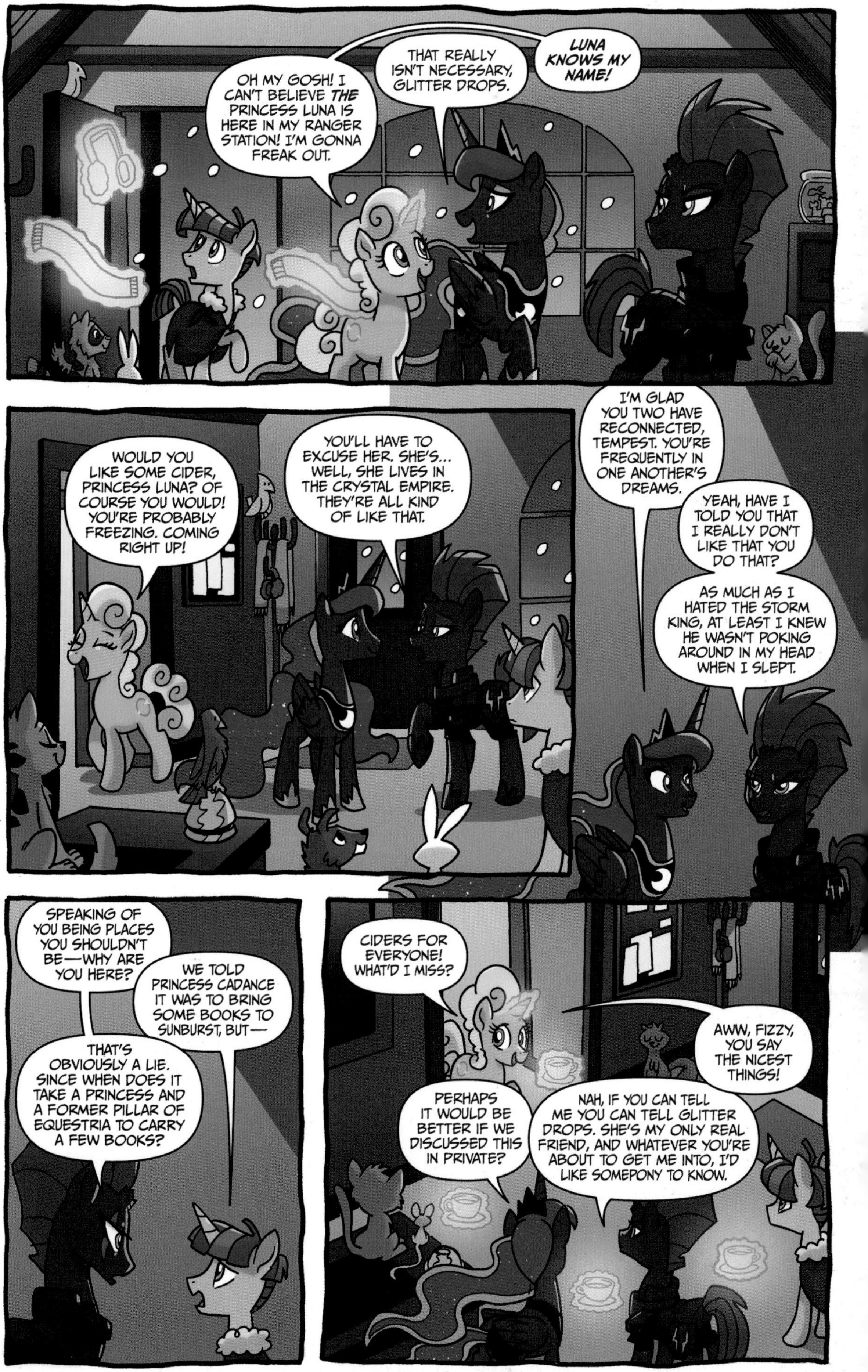
OH MY GOSH! I CAN'T BELIEVE *THE* PRINCESS LUNA IS HERE IN MY RANGER STATION! I'M GONNA FREAK OUT.
THAT REALLY ISN'T NECESSARY, GLITTER DROPS.
LUNA KNOWS MY NAME!
WOULD YOU LIKE SOME CIDER, PRINCESS LUNA? OF COURSE YOU WOULD! YOU'RE PROBABLY FREEZING. COMING RIGHT UP!
YOU'LL HAVE TO EXCUSE HER. SHE'S... WELL, SHE LIVES IN THE CRYSTAL EMPIRE. THEY'RE ALL KIND OF LIKE THAT.
I'M GLAD YOU TWO HAVE RECONNECTED, TEMPEST. YOU'RE FREQUENTLY IN ONE ANOTHER'S DREAMS.
YEAH, HAVE I TOLD YOU THAT I REALLY DON'T LIKE THAT YOU DO THAT?
AS MUCH AS I HATED THE STORM KING, AT LEAST I KNEW HE WASN'T POKING AROUND IN MY HEAD WHEN I SLEPT.
SPEAKING OF YOU BEING PLACES YOU SHOULDN'T BE—WHY ARE YOU HERE?
WE TOLD PRINCESS CADANCE IT WAS TO BRING SOME BOOKS TO SUNBURST, BUT—
THAT'S OBVIOUSLY A LIE. SINCE WHEN DOES IT TAKE A PRINCESS AND A FORMER PILLAR OF EQUESTRIA TO CARRY A FEW BOOKS?
CIDERS FOR EVERYONE! WHAT'D I MISS?
AWW, FIZZY, YOU SAY THE NICEST THINGS!
PERHAPS IT WOULD BE BETTER IF WE DISCUSSED THIS IN PRIVATE?
NAH, IF YOU CAN TELL ME YOU CAN TELL GLITTER DROPS. SHE'S MY ONLY REAL FRIEND, AND WHATEVER YOU'RE ABOUT TO GET ME INTO, I'D LIKE SOMEPONY TO KNOW.

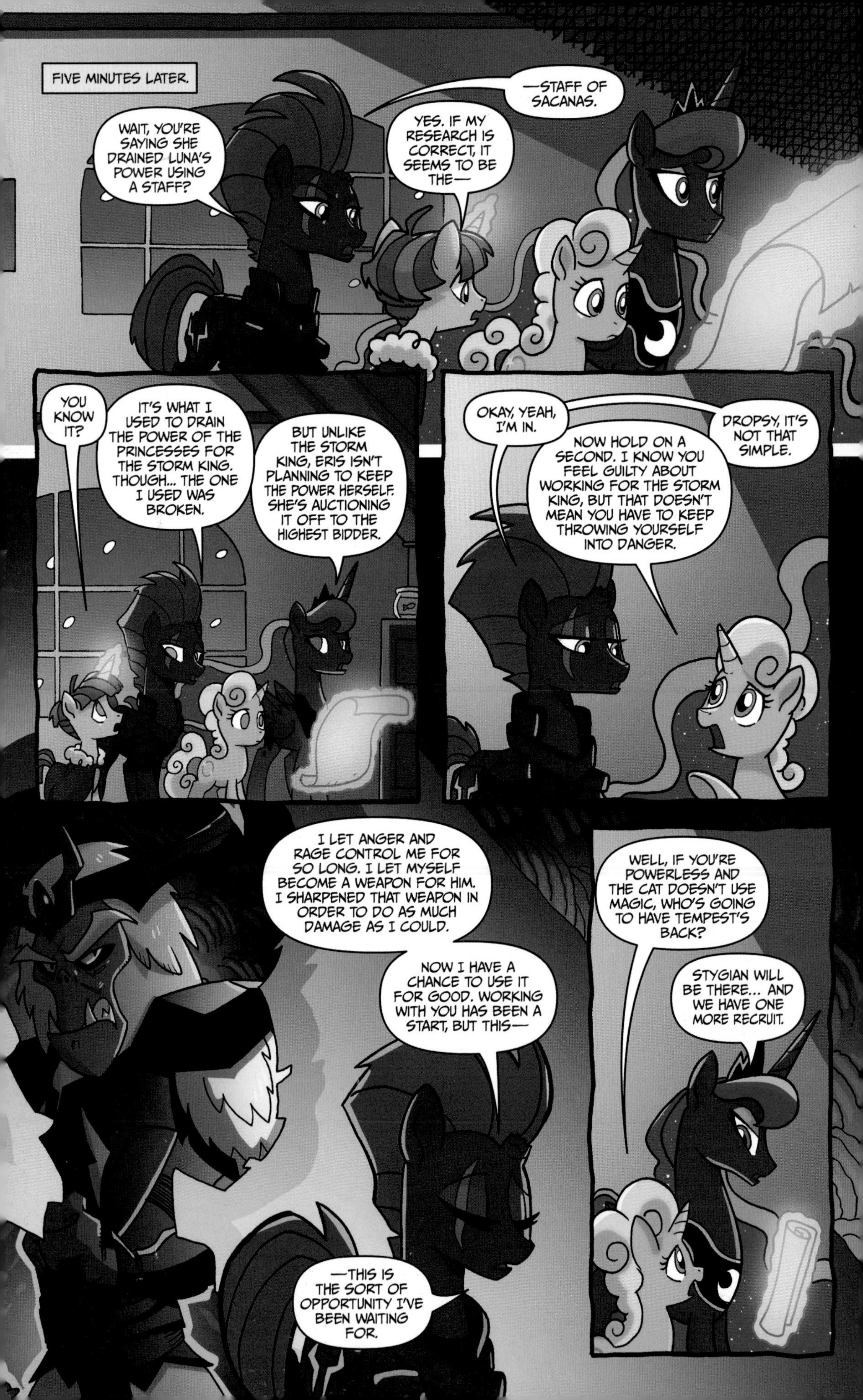
FIVE MINUTES LATER.
WAIT, YOU'RE SAYING SHE DRAINED LUNA'S POWER USING A STAFF?
YES. IF MY RESEARCH IS CORRECT, IT SEEMS TO BE THE—
—STAFF OF SACANAS.
YOU KNOW IT?
IT'S WHAT I USED TO DRAIN THE POWER OF THE PRINCESSES FOR THE STORM KING. THOUGH... THE ONE I USED WAS BROKEN.
BUT UNLIKE THE STORM KING, ERIS ISN'T PLANNING TO KEEP THE POWER HERSELF. SHE'S AUCTIONING IT OFF TO THE HIGHEST BIDDER.
OKAY, YEAH, I'M IN.
DROPSY, IT'S NOT THAT SIMPLE.
NOW HOLD ON A SECOND. I KNOW YOU FEEL GUILTY ABOUT WORKING FOR THE STORM KING, BUT THAT DOESN'T MEAN YOU HAVE TO KEEP THROWING YOURSELF INTO DANGER.
I LET ANGER AND RAGE CONTROL ME FOR SO LONG. I LET MYSELF BECOME A WEAPON FOR HIM. I SHARPENED THAT WEAPON IN ORDER TO DO AS MUCH DAMAGE AS I COULD.
NOW I HAVE A CHANCE TO USE IT FOR GOOD. WORKING WITH YOU HAS BEEN A START, BUT THIS—
—THIS IS THE SORT OF OPPORTUNITY I'VE BEEN WAITING FOR.
WELL, IF YOU'RE POWERLESS AND THE CAT DOESN'T USE MAGIC, WHO'S GOING TO HAVE TEMPEST'S BACK?
STYGIAN WILL BE THERE... AND WE HAVE ONE MORE RECRUIT.

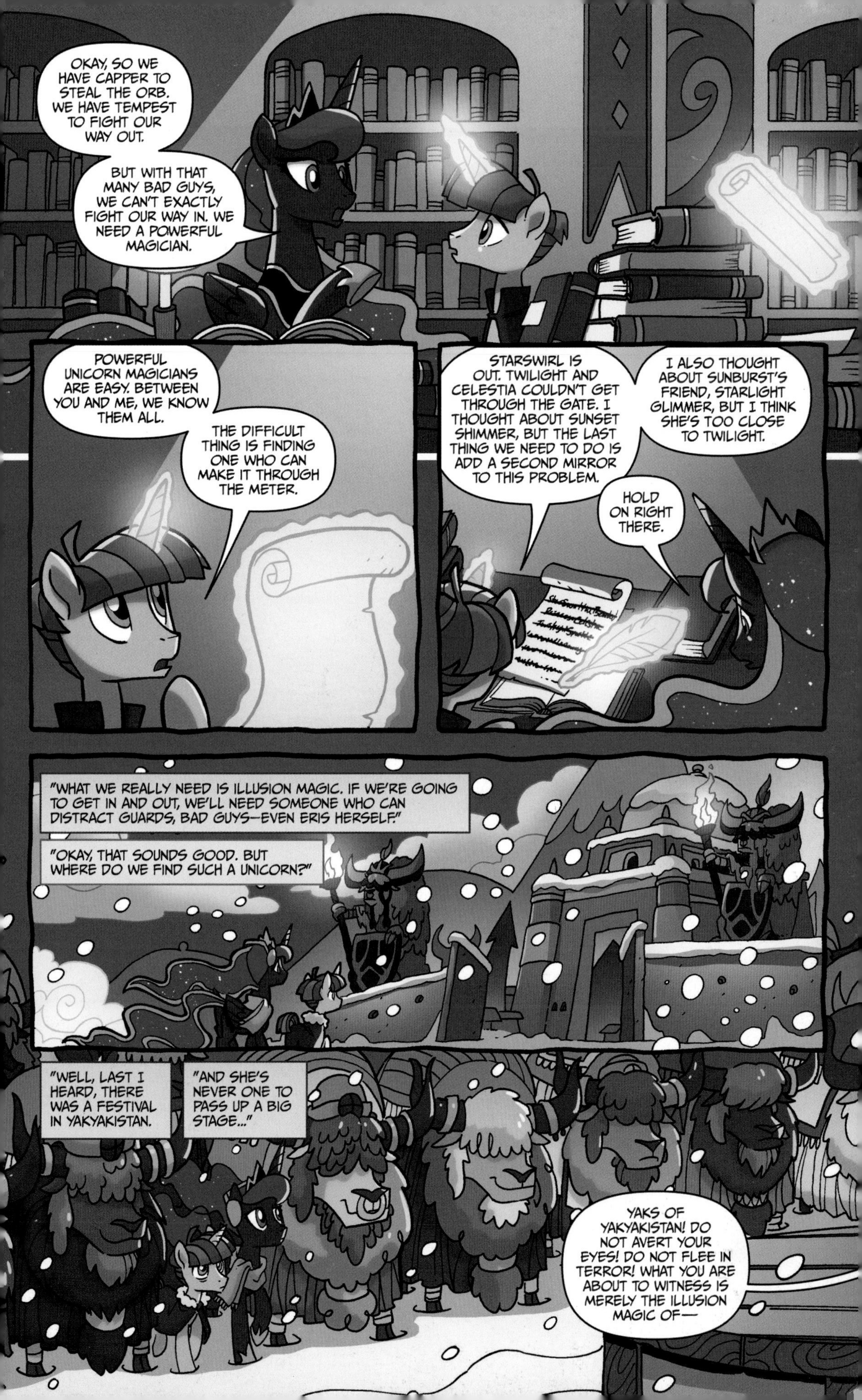
OKAY, SO WE HAVE CAPPER TO STEAL THE ORB. WE HAVE TEMPEST TO FIGHT OUR WAY OUT.
BUT WITH THAT MANY BAD GUYS, WE CAN'T EXACTLY FIGHT OUR WAY IN. WE NEED A POWERFUL MAGICIAN.
POWERFUL UNICORN MAGICIANS ARE EASY. BETWEEN YOU AND ME, WE KNOW THEM ALL.
THE DIFFICULT THING IS FINDING ONE WHO CAN MAKE IT THROUGH THE METER.
STARSWIRL IS OUT. TWILIGHT AND CELESTIA COULDN'T GET THROUGH THE GATE. I THOUGHT ABOUT SUNSET SHIMMER, BUT THE LAST THING WE NEED TO DO IS ADD A SECOND MIRROR TO THIS PROBLEM.
I ALSO THOUGHT ABOUT SUNBURST'S FRIEND, STARLIGHT GLIMMER, BUT I THINK SHE'S TOO CLOSE TO TWILIGHT.
HOLD ON RIGHT THERE.
"WHAT WE REALLY NEED IS ILLUSION MAGIC. IF WE'RE GOING TO GET IN AND OUT, WE'LL NEED SOMEONE WHO CAN DISTRACT GUARDS, BAD GUYS—EVEN ERIS HERSELF."
"OKAY, THAT SOUNDS GOOD. BUT WHERE DO WE FIND SUCH A UNICORN?"
"WELL, LAST I HEARD, THERE WAS A FESTIVAL IN YAKYAKISTAN.
"AND SHE'S NEVER ONE TO PASS UP A BIG STAGE..."
YAKS OF YAKYAKISTAN! DO NOT AVERT YOUR EYES! DO NOT FLEE IN TERROR! WHAT YOU ARE ABOUT TO WITNESS IS MERELY THE ILLUSION MAGIC OF—

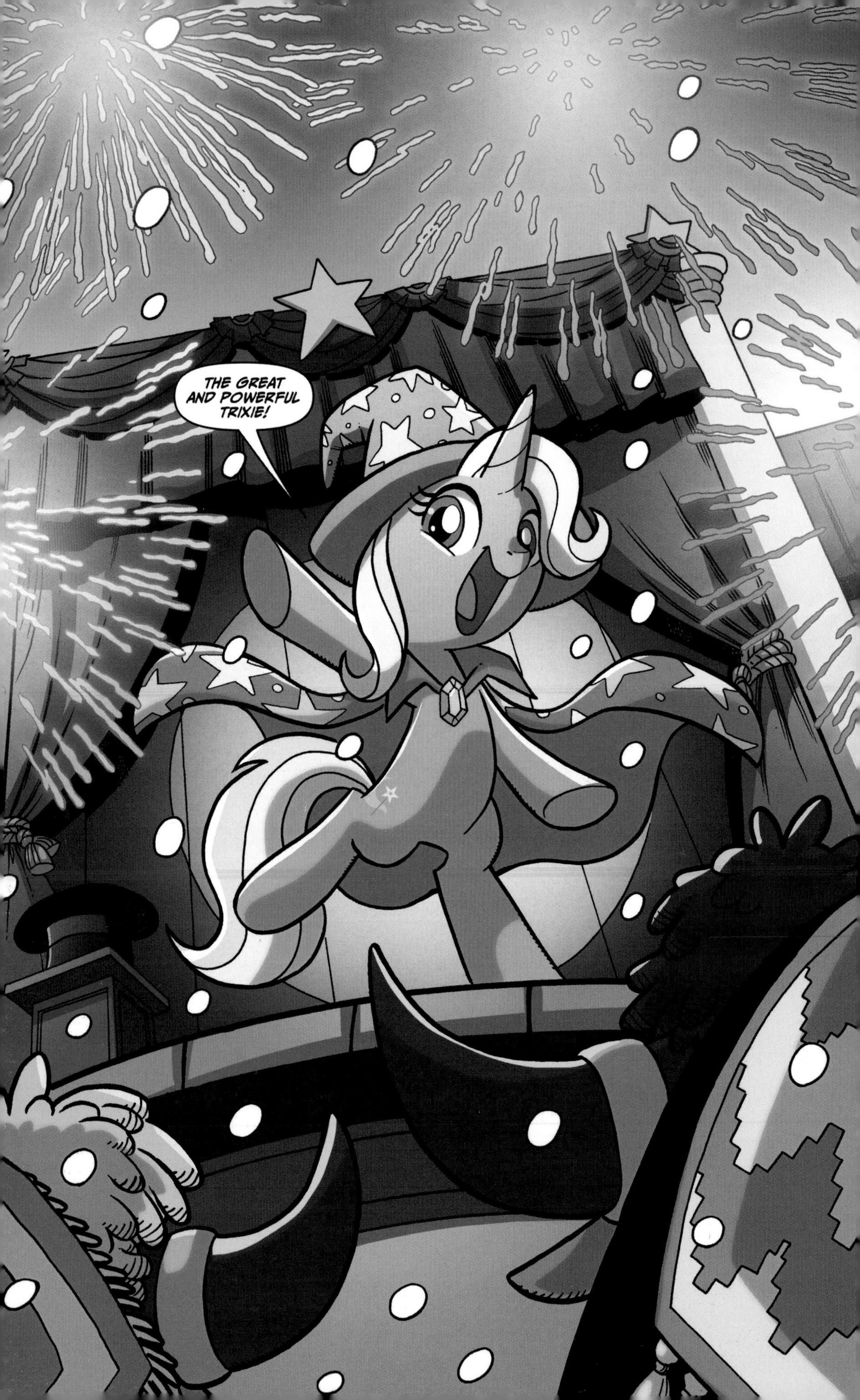
THE GREAT AND POWERFUL TRIXIE!

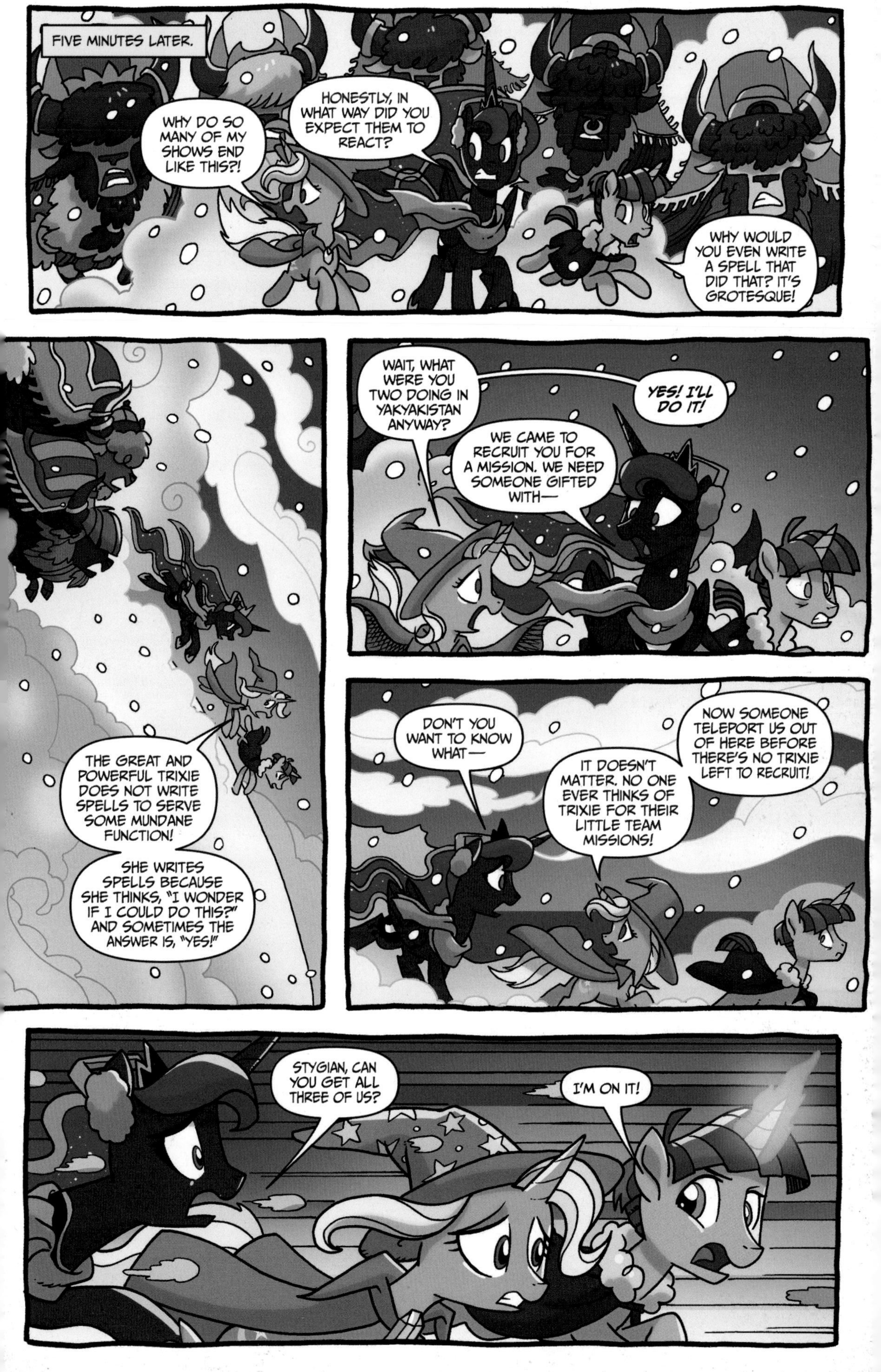
FIVE MINUTES LATER.
WHY DO SO MANY OF MY SHOWS END LIKE THIS?!
HONESTLY, IN WHAT WAY DID YOU EXPECT THEM TO REACT?
WHY WOULD YOU EVEN WRITE A SPELL THAT DID THAT? IT'S GROTESQUE!
THE GREAT AND POWERFUL TRIXIE DOES NOT WRITE SPELLS TO SERVE SOME MUNDANE FUNCTION!
SHE WRITES SPELLS BECAUSE SHE THINKS, "I WONDER IF I COULD DO THIS?" AND SOMETIMES THE ANSWER IS, "YES!"
WAIT, WHAT WERE YOU TWO DOING IN YAKYAKISTAN ANYWAY?
WE CAME TO RECRUIT YOU FOR A MISSION. WE NEED SOMEONE GIFTED WITH—
YES! I'LL DO IT!
DON'T YOU WANT TO KNOW WHAT—
IT DOESN'T MATTER. NO ONE EVER THINKS OF TRIXIE FOR THEIR LITTLE TEAM MISSIONS!
NOW SOMEONE TELEPORT US OUT OF HERE BEFORE THERE'S NO TRIXIE LEFT TO RECRUIT!
STYGIAN, CAN YOU GET ALL THREE OF US?
I'M ON IT!

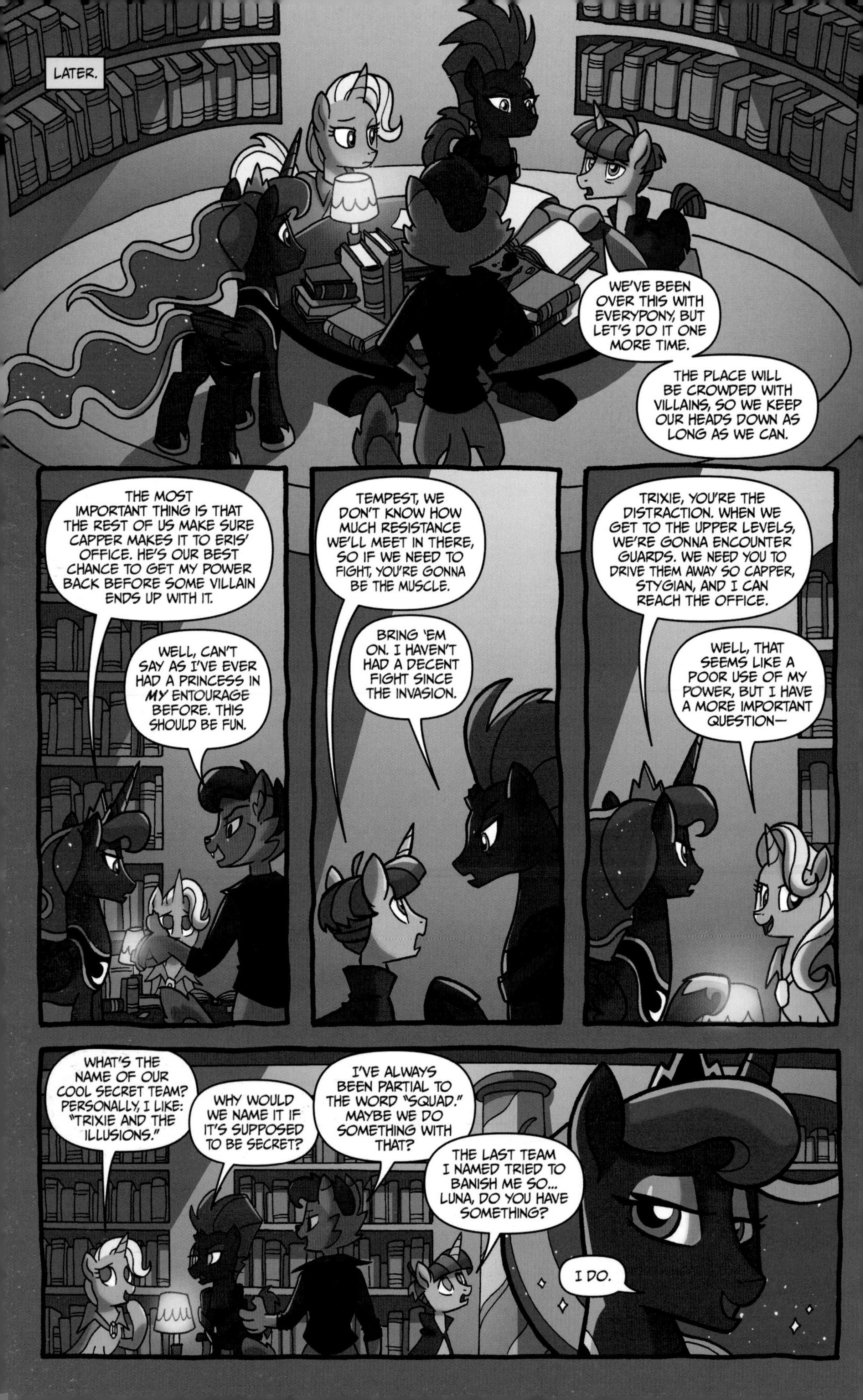
LATER.
WE'VE BEEN OVER THIS WITH EVERYPONY, BUT LET'S DO IT ONE MORE TIME.
THE PLACE WILL BE CROWDED WITH VILLAINS, SO WE KEEP OUR HEADS DOWN AS LONG AS WE CAN.
THE MOST IMPORTANT THING IS THAT THE REST OF US MAKE SURE CAPPER MAKES IT TO ERIS' OFFICE. HE'S OUR BEST CHANCE TO GET MY POWER BACK BEFORE SOME VILLAIN ENDS UP WITH IT.
WELL, CAN'T SAY AS I'VE EVER HAD A PRINCESS IN *MY* ENTOURAGE BEFORE. THIS SHOULD BE FUN.
TEMPEST, WE DON'T KNOW HOW MUCH RESISTANCE WE'LL MEET IN THERE, SO IF WE NEED TO FIGHT, YOU'RE GONNA BE THE MUSCLE.
BRING 'EM ON. I HAVEN'T HAD A DECENT FIGHT SINCE THE INVASION.
TRIXIE, YOU'RE THE DISTRACTION. WHEN WE GET TO THE UPPER LEVELS, WE'RE GONNA ENCOUNTER GUARDS. WE NEED YOU TO DRIVE THEM AWAY SO CAPPER, STYGIAN, AND I CAN REACH THE OFFICE.
WELL, THAT SEEMS LIKE A POOR USE OF MY POWER, BUT I HAVE A MORE IMPORTANT QUESTION—
WHAT'S THE NAME OF OUR COOL SECRET TEAM? PERSONALLY, I LIKE: "TRIXIE AND THE ILLUSIONS."
WHY WOULD WE NAME IT IF IT'S SUPPOSED TO BE SECRET?
I'VE ALWAYS BEEN PARTIAL TO THE WORD "SQUAD." MAYBE WE DO SOMETHING WITH THAT?
THE LAST TEAM I NAMED TRIED TO BANISH ME SO... LUNA, DO YOU HAVE SOMETHING?
I DO.

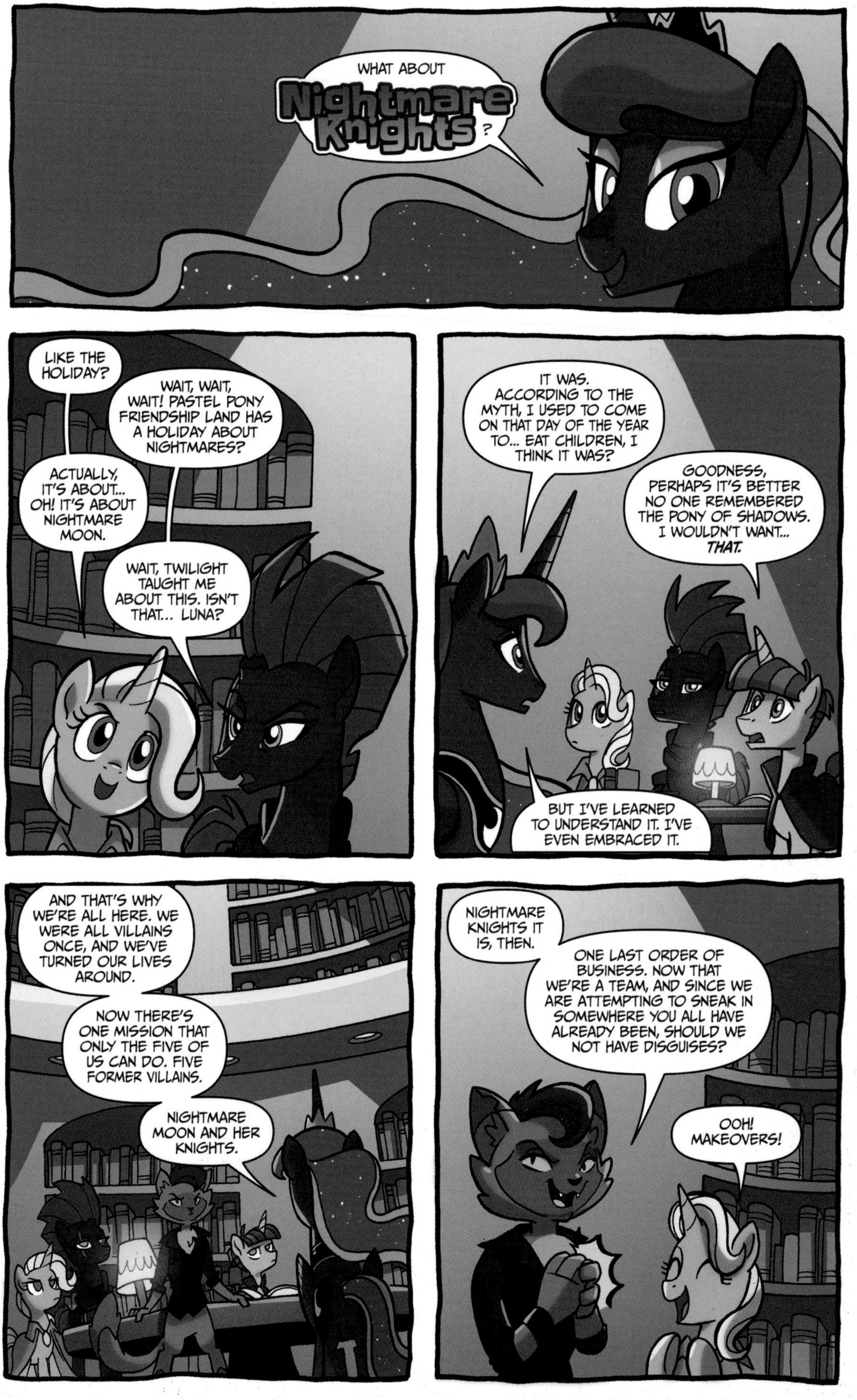

WHAT ABOUT Nightmare Knights?
LIKE THE HOLIDAY?
WAIT, WAIT, WAIT! PASTEL PONY FRIENDSHIP LAND HAS A HOLIDAY ABOUT NIGHTMARES?
ACTUALLY, IT'S ABOUT... OH! IT'S ABOUT NIGHTMARE MOON.
WAIT, TWILIGHT TAUGHT ME ABOUT THIS. ISN'T THAT... LUNA?
IT WAS. ACCORDING TO THE MYTH, I USED TO COME ON THAT DAY OF THE YEAR TO... EAT CHILDREN, I THINK IT WAS?
GOODNESS, PERHAPS IT'S BETTER NO ONE REMEMBERED THE PONY OF SHADOWS. I WOULDN'T WANT... *THAT.*
BUT I'VE LEARNED TO UNDERSTAND IT. I'VE EVEN EMBRACED IT.
AND THAT'S WHY WE'RE ALL HERE. WE WERE ALL VILLAINS ONCE, AND WE'VE TURNED OUR LIVES AROUND.
NOW THERE'S ONE MISSION THAT ONLY THE FIVE OF US CAN DO. FIVE FORMER VILLAINS.
NIGHTMARE MOON AND HER KNIGHTS.
NIGHTMARE KNIGHTS IT IS, THEN.
ONE LAST ORDER OF BUSINESS. NOW THAT WE'RE A TEAM, AND SINCE WE ARE ATTEMPTING TO SNEAK IN SOMEWHERE YOU ALL HAVE ALREADY BEEN, SHOULD WE NOT HAVE DISGUISES?
OOH! MAKEOVERS!

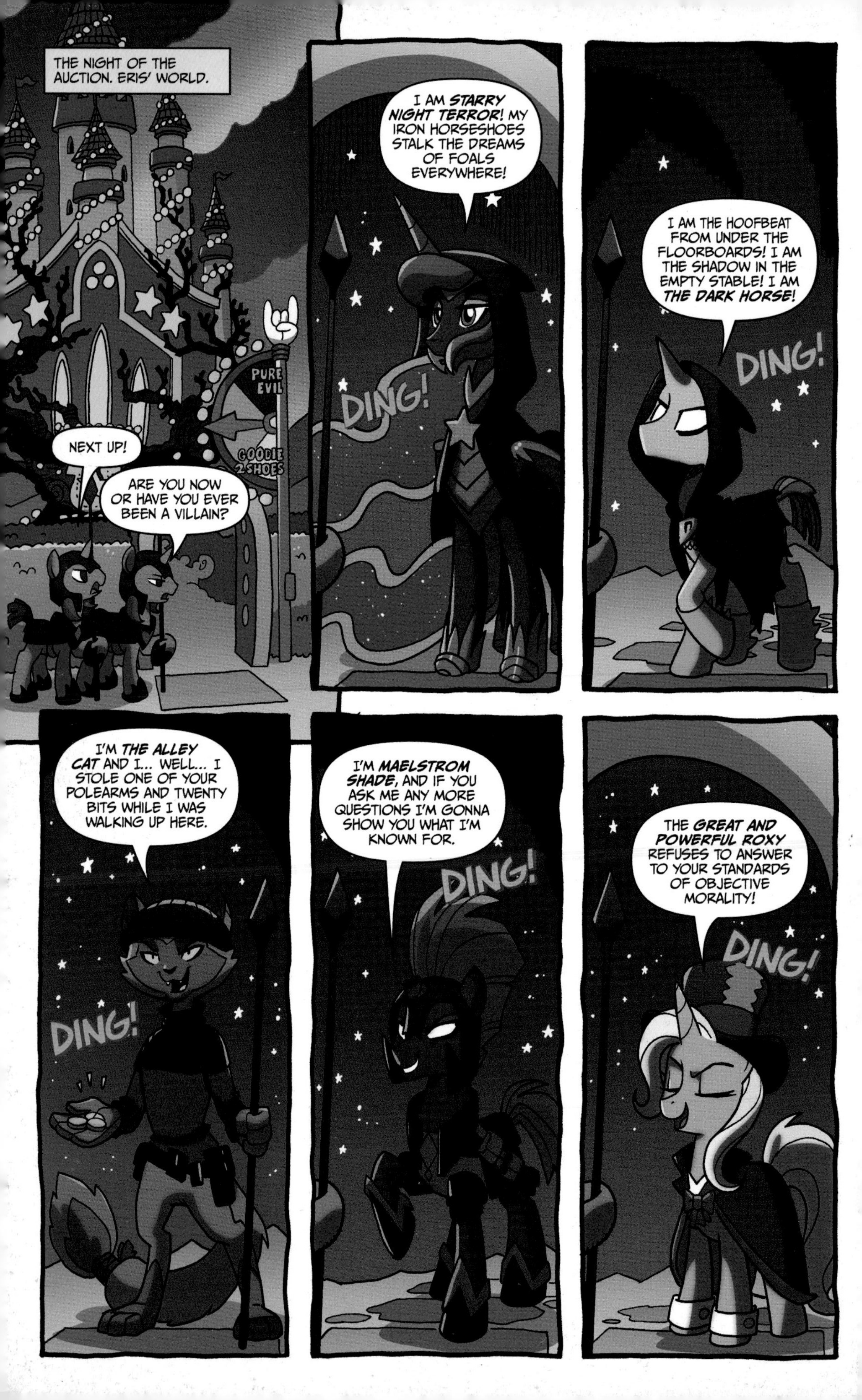
THE NIGHT OF THE AUCTION. ERIS' WORLD.
PURE EVIL
GOODIE 2 SHOES
NEXT UP!
ARE YOU NOW OR HAVE YOU EVER BEEN A VILLAIN?
I AM STARRY NIGHT TERROR! MY IRON HORSESHOES STALK THE DREAMS OF FOALS EVERYWHERE!
DING!
I AM THE HOOFBEAT FROM UNDER THE FLOORBOARDS! I AM THE SHADOW IN THE EMPTY STABLE! I AM THE DARK HORSE!
DING!
I'M THE ALLEY CAT AND I... WELL... I STOLE ONE OF YOUR POLEARMS AND TWENTY BITS WHILE I WAS WALKING UP HERE.
DING!
I'M MAELSTROM SHADE, AND IF YOU ASK ME ANY MORE QUESTIONS I'M GONNA SHOW YOU WHAT I'M KNOWN FOR.
DING!
THE GREAT AND POWERFUL ROXY REFUSES TO ANSWER TO YOUR STANDARDS OF OBJECTIVE MORALITY!
DING!

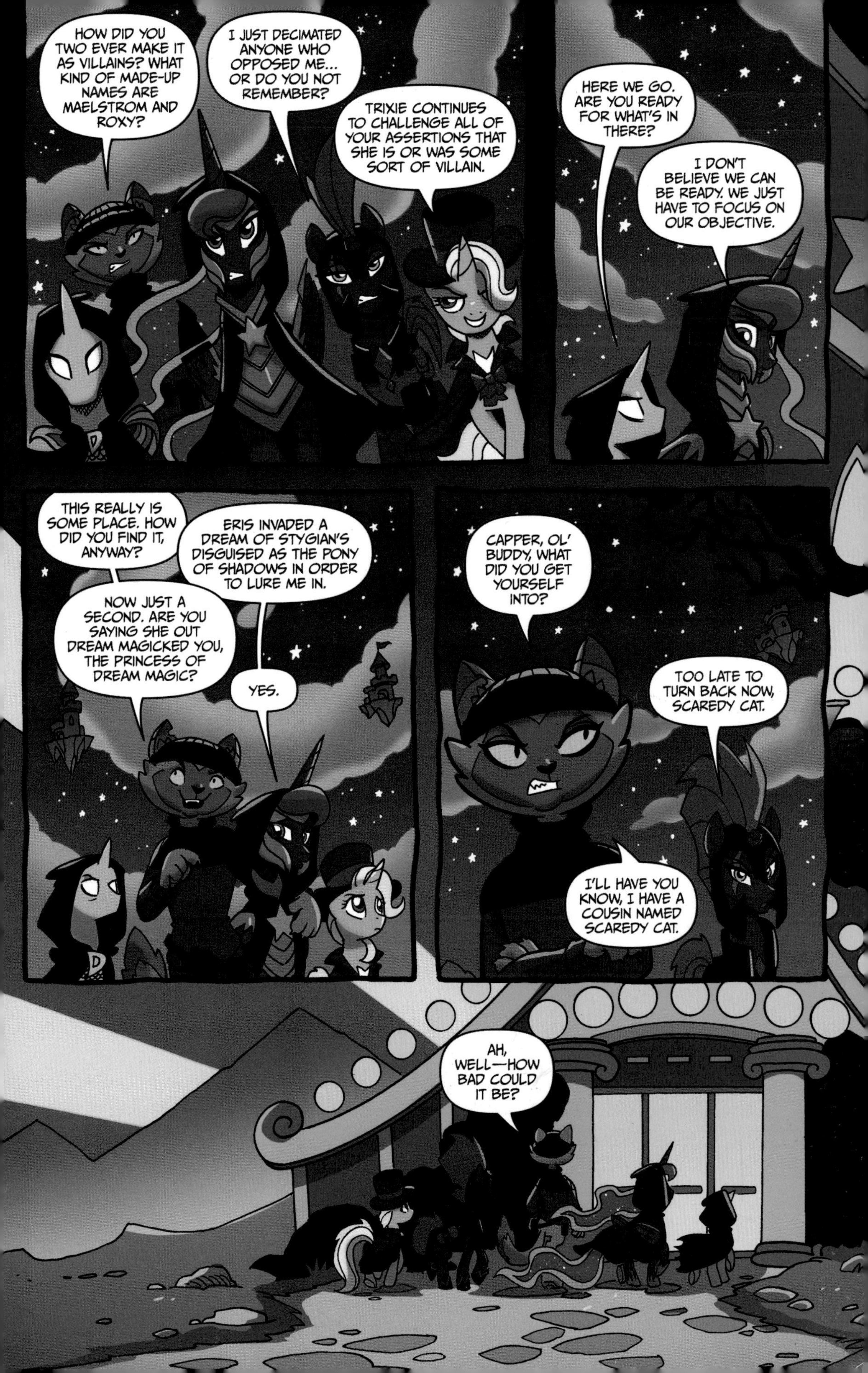
HOW DID YOU TWO EVER MAKE IT AS VILLAINS? WHAT KIND OF MADE-UP NAMES ARE MAELSTROM AND ROXY?
I JUST DECIMATED ANYONE WHO OPPOSED ME... OR DO YOU NOT REMEMBER?
TRIXIE CONTINUES TO CHALLENGE ALL OF YOUR ASSERTIONS THAT SHE IS OR WAS SOME SORT OF VILLAIN.
HERE WE GO. ARE YOU READY FOR WHAT'S IN THERE?
I DON'T BELIEVE WE CAN BE READY. WE JUST HAVE TO FOCUS ON OUR OBJECTIVE.
THIS REALLY IS SOME PLACE. HOW DID YOU FIND IT, ANYWAY?
ERIS INVADED A DREAM OF STYGIAN'S DISGUISED AS THE PONY OF SHADOWS IN ORDER TO LURE ME IN.
NOW JUST A SECOND. ARE YOU SAYING SHE OUT DREAM MAGICKED YOU, THE PRINCESS OF DREAM MAGIC?
YES.
CAPPER, OL' BUDDY, WHAT DID YOU GET YOURSELF INTO?
TOO LATE TO TURN BACK NOW, SCAREDY CAT.
I'LL HAVE YOU KNOW, I HAVE A COUSIN NAMED SCAREDY CAT.
AH, WELL—HOW BAD COULD IT BE?

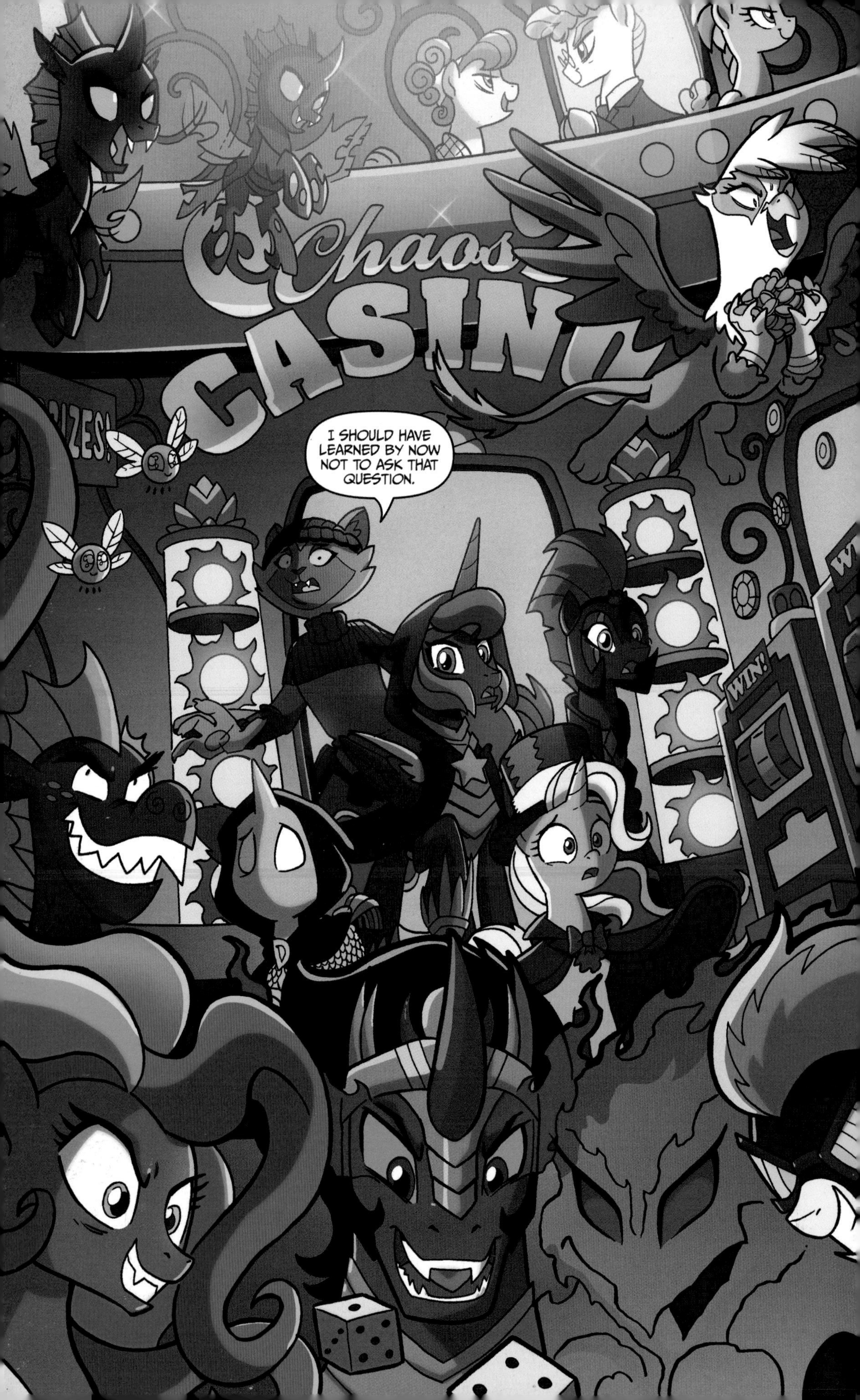
Chaos CASINO
I SHOULD HAVE LEARNED BY NOW NOT TO ASK THAT QUESTION.
WIN!

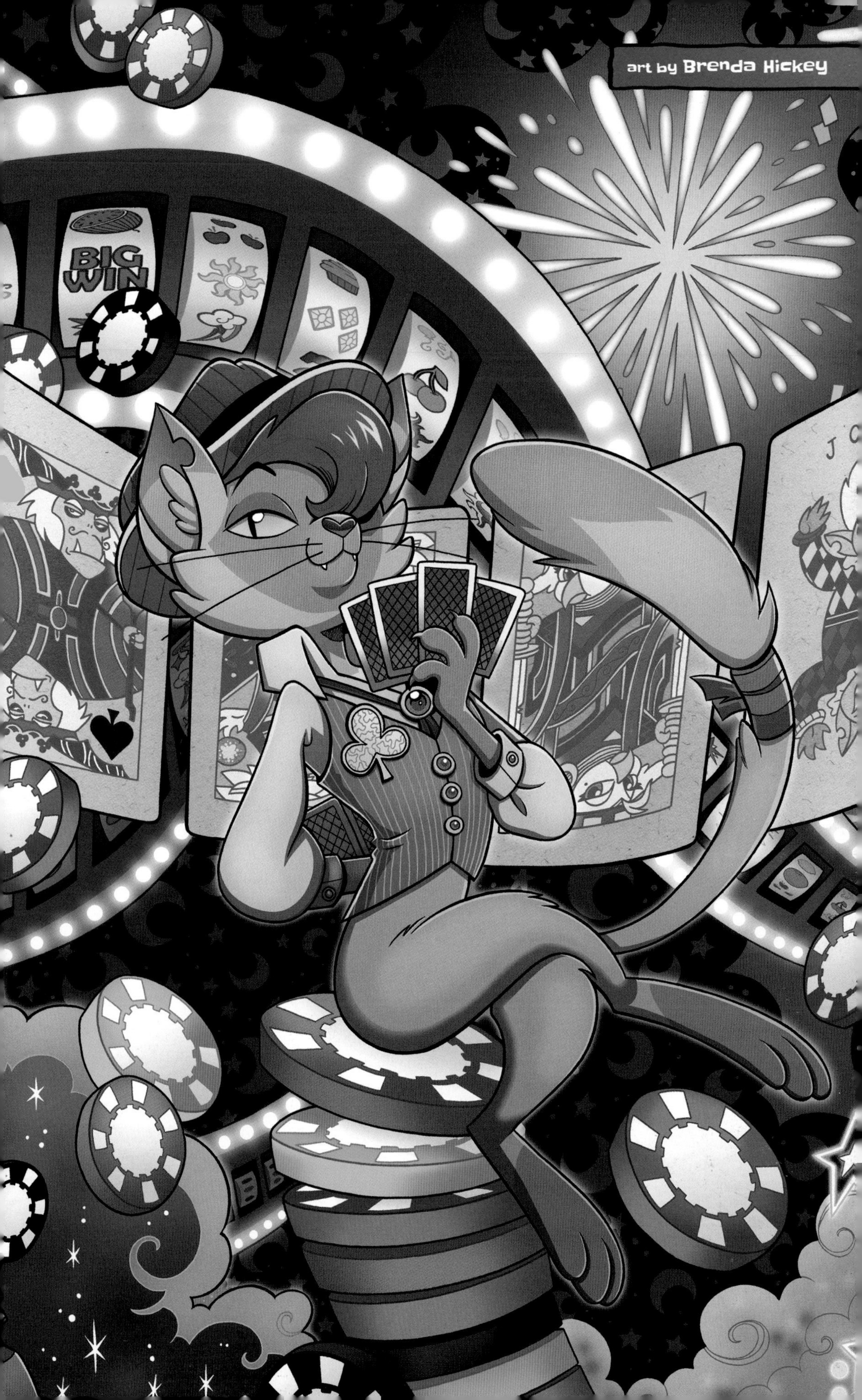
art by Brenda Hickey
BIG WIN

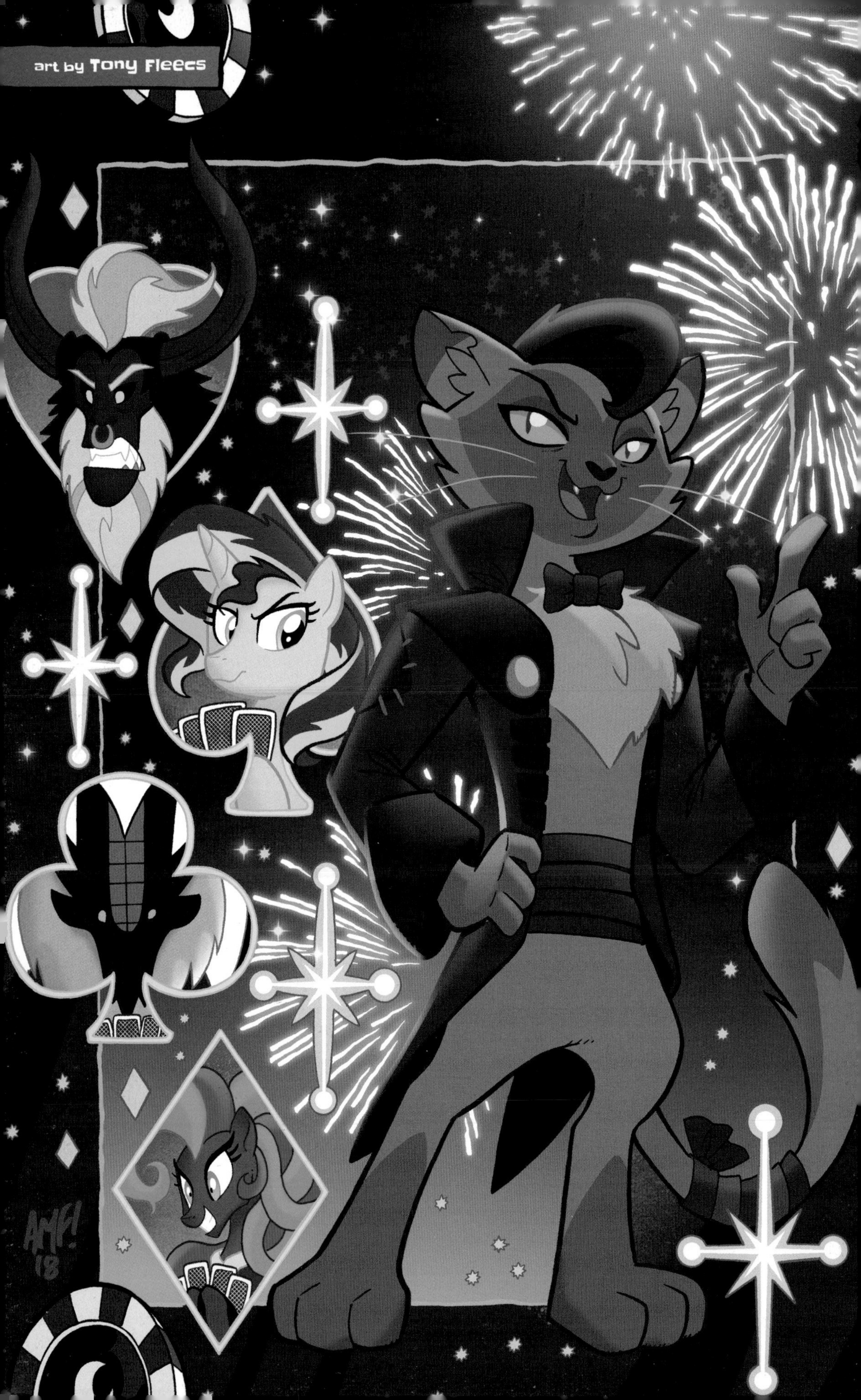
art by Tony Fleecs
AMF! '18

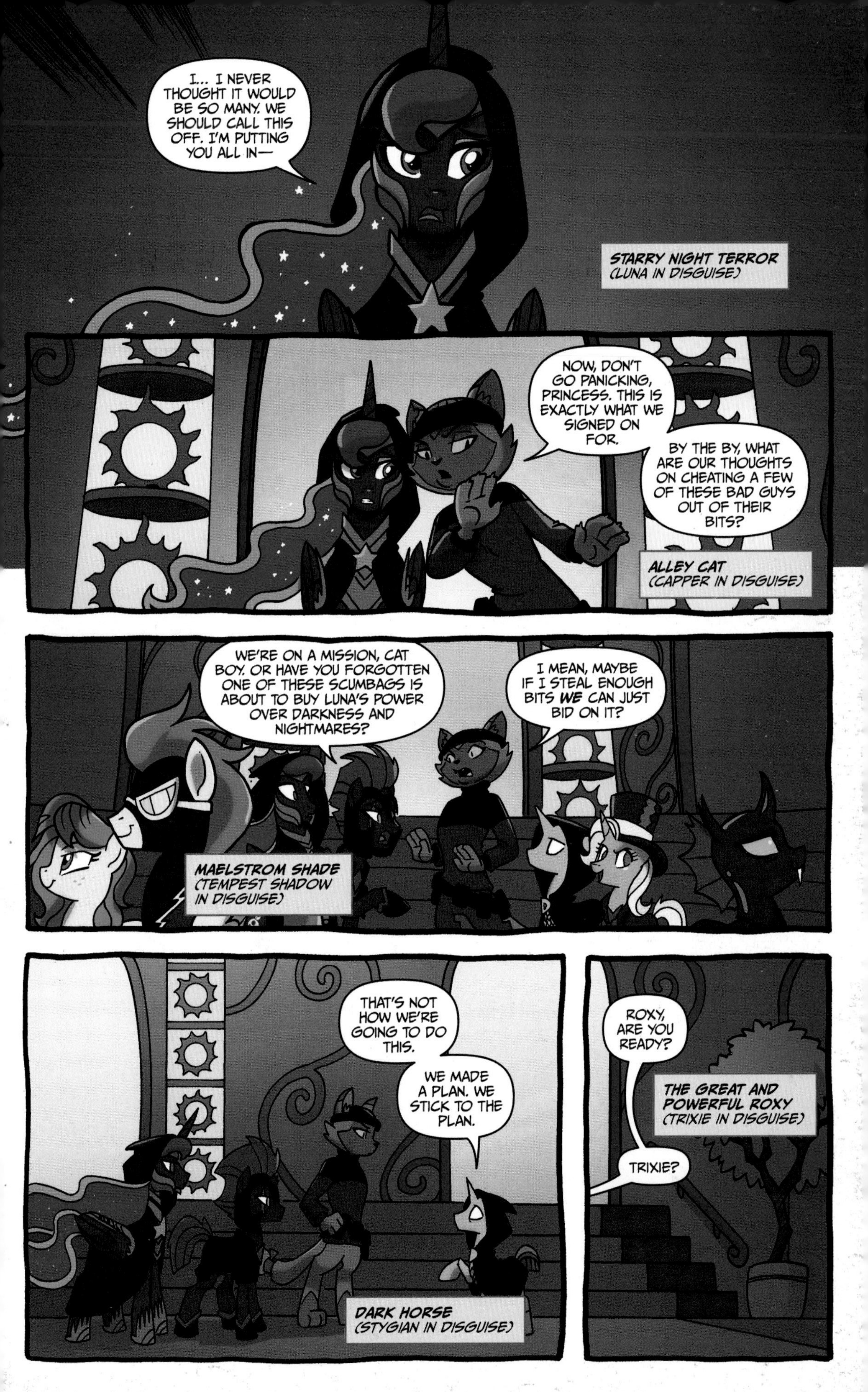
I... I NEVER THOUGHT IT WOULD BE SO MANY. WE SHOULD CALL THIS OFF. I'M PUTTING YOU ALL IN—
STARRY NIGHT TERROR (LUNA IN DISGUISE)
NOW, DON'T GO PANICKING, PRINCESS. THIS IS EXACTLY WHAT WE SIGNED ON FOR.
BY THE BY, WHAT ARE OUR THOUGHTS ON CHEATING A FEW OF THESE BAD GUYS OUT OF THEIR BITS?
ALLEY CAT (CAPPER IN DISGUISE)
WE'RE ON A MISSION, CAT BOY. OR HAVE YOU FORGOTTEN ONE OF THESE SCUMBAGS IS ABOUT TO BUY LUNA'S POWER OVER DARKNESS AND NIGHTMARES?
I MEAN, MAYBE IF I STEAL ENOUGH BITS WE CAN JUST BID ON IT?
MAELSTROM SHADE (TEMPEST SHADOW IN DISGUISE)
THAT'S NOT HOW WE'RE GOING TO DO THIS.
WE MADE A PLAN. WE STICK TO THE PLAN.
DARK HORSE (STYGIAN IN DISGUISE)
ROXY, ARE YOU READY?
THE GREAT AND POWERFUL ROXY (TRIXIE IN DISGUISE)
TRIXIE?

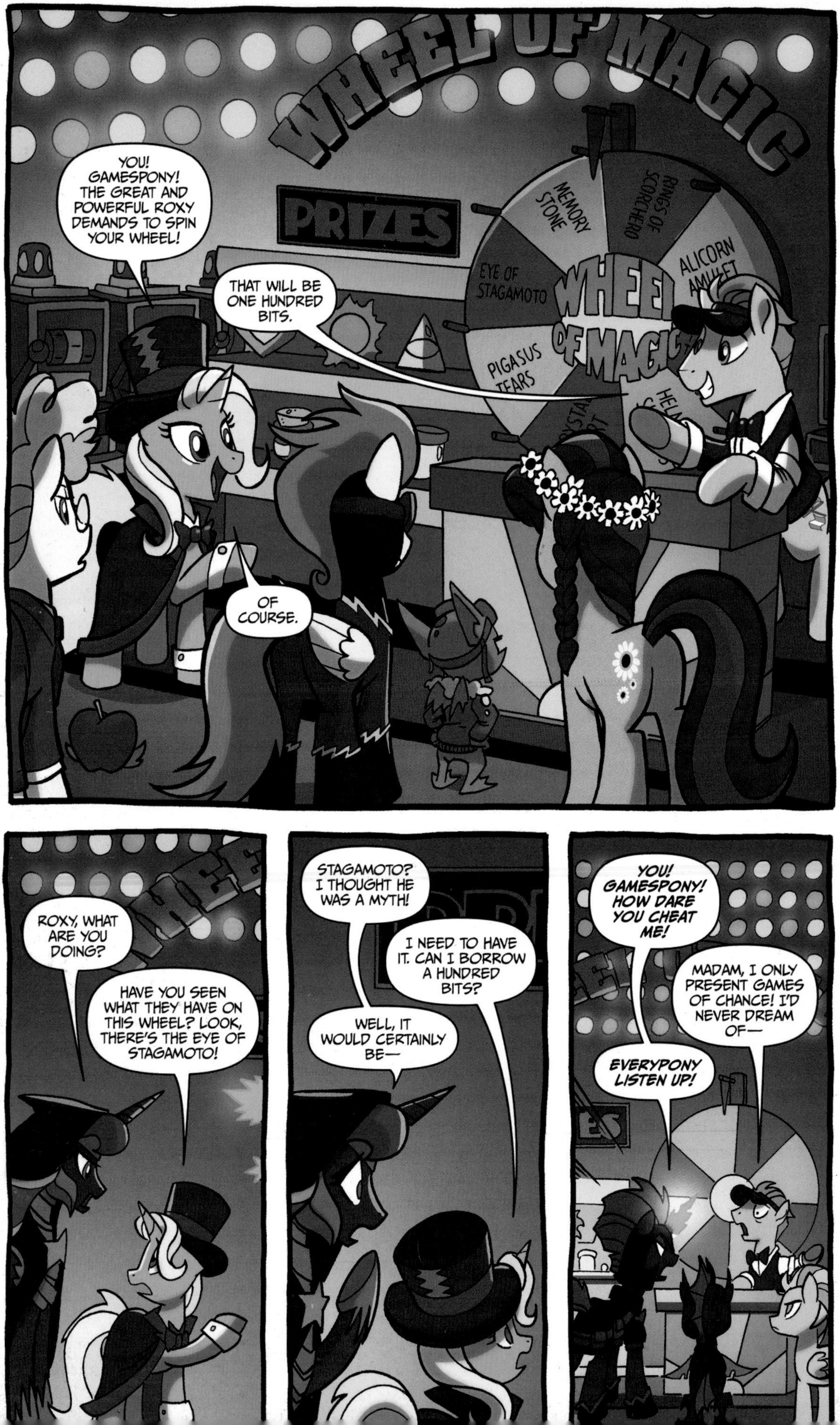
WHEEL OF MAGIC
PRIZES
MEMORY STONE
RINGS OF SCORCHERO
ALICORN AMULET
EYE OF STAGAMOTO
WHEEL OF MAGIC
PIGASUS TEARS
YOU! GAMESPONY! THE GREAT AND POWERFUL ROXY DEMANDS TO SPIN YOUR WHEEL!
THAT WILL BE ONE HUNDRED BITS.
OF COURSE.
ROXY, WHAT ARE YOU DOING?
HAVE YOU SEEN WHAT THEY HAVE ON THIS WHEEL? LOOK, THERE'S THE EYE OF STAGAMOTO!
STAGAMOTO? I THOUGHT HE WAS A MYTH!
I NEED TO HAVE IT. CAN I BORROW A HUNDRED BITS?
WELL, IT WOULD CERTAINLY BE—
YOU! GAMESPONY! HOW DARE YOU CHEAT ME!
MADAM, I ONLY PRESENT GAMES OF CHANCE! I'D NEVER DREAM OF—
EVERYPONY LISTEN UP!

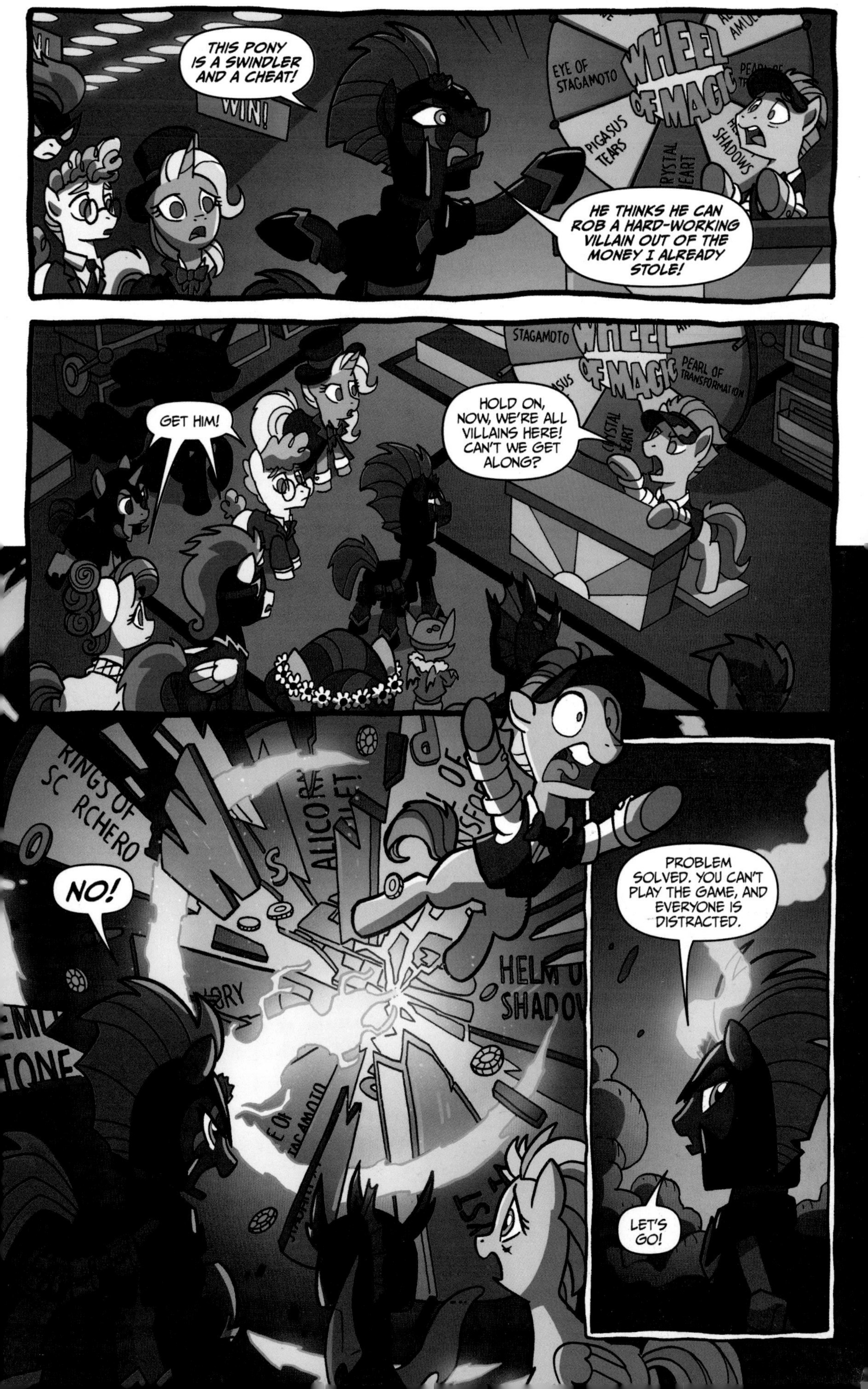
WIN!
THIS PONY IS A SWINDLER AND A CHEAT!
WHEEL OF MAGIC
EYE OF STAGAMOTO
PIGASUS TEARS
SHADOWS
HE THINKS HE CAN ROB A HARD-WORKING VILLAIN OUT OF THE MONEY I ALREADY STOLE!
STAGAMOTO
WHEEL OF MAGIC
PEARL OF TRANSFORMATION
GET HIM!
HOLD ON, NOW, WE'RE ALL VILLAINS HERE! CAN'T WE GET ALONG?
NO!
PROBLEM SOLVED. YOU CAN'T PLAY THE GAME, AND EVERYONE IS DISTRACTED.
LET'S GO!

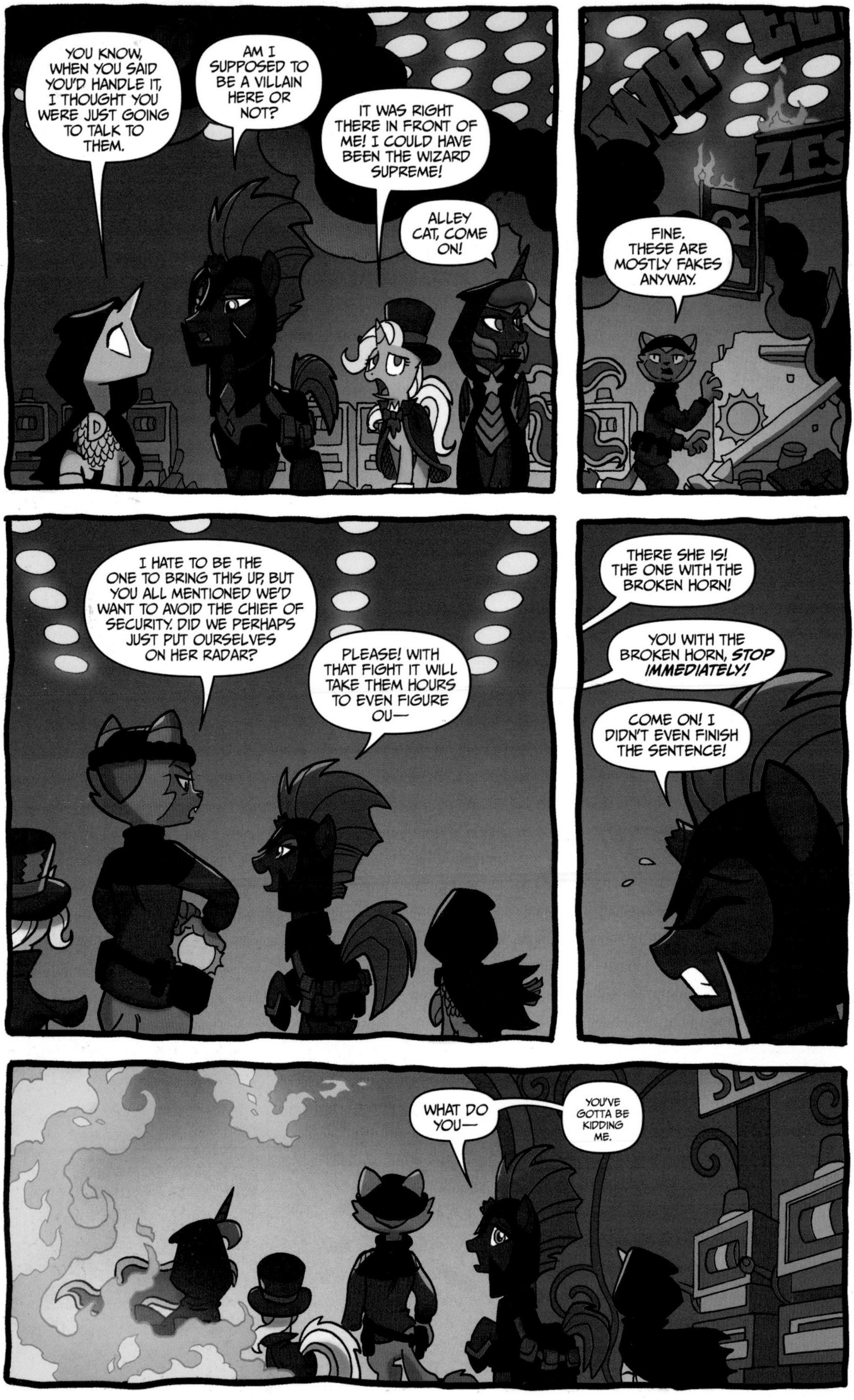
YOU KNOW, WHEN YOU SAID YOU'D HANDLE IT, I THOUGHT YOU WERE JUST GOING TO TALK TO THEM.
AM I SUPPOSED TO BE A VILLAIN HERE OR NOT?
IT WAS RIGHT THERE IN FRONT OF ME! I COULD HAVE BEEN THE WIZARD SUPREME!
ALLEY CAT, COME ON!
WH
ZES
FINE. THESE ARE MOSTLY FAKES ANYWAY.
I HATE TO BE THE ONE TO BRING THIS UP, BUT YOU ALL MENTIONED WE'D WANT TO AVOID THE CHIEF OF SECURITY. DID WE PERHAPS JUST PUT OURSELVES ON HER RADAR?
PLEASE! WITH THAT FIGHT IT WILL TAKE THEM HOURS TO EVEN FIGURE OU—
THERE SHE IS! THE ONE WITH THE BROKEN HORN!
YOU WITH THE BROKEN HORN, ***STOP IMMEDIATELY!***
COME ON! I DIDN'T EVEN FINISH THE SENTENCE!
WHAT DO YOU—
YOU'VE GOTTA BE KIDDING ME.

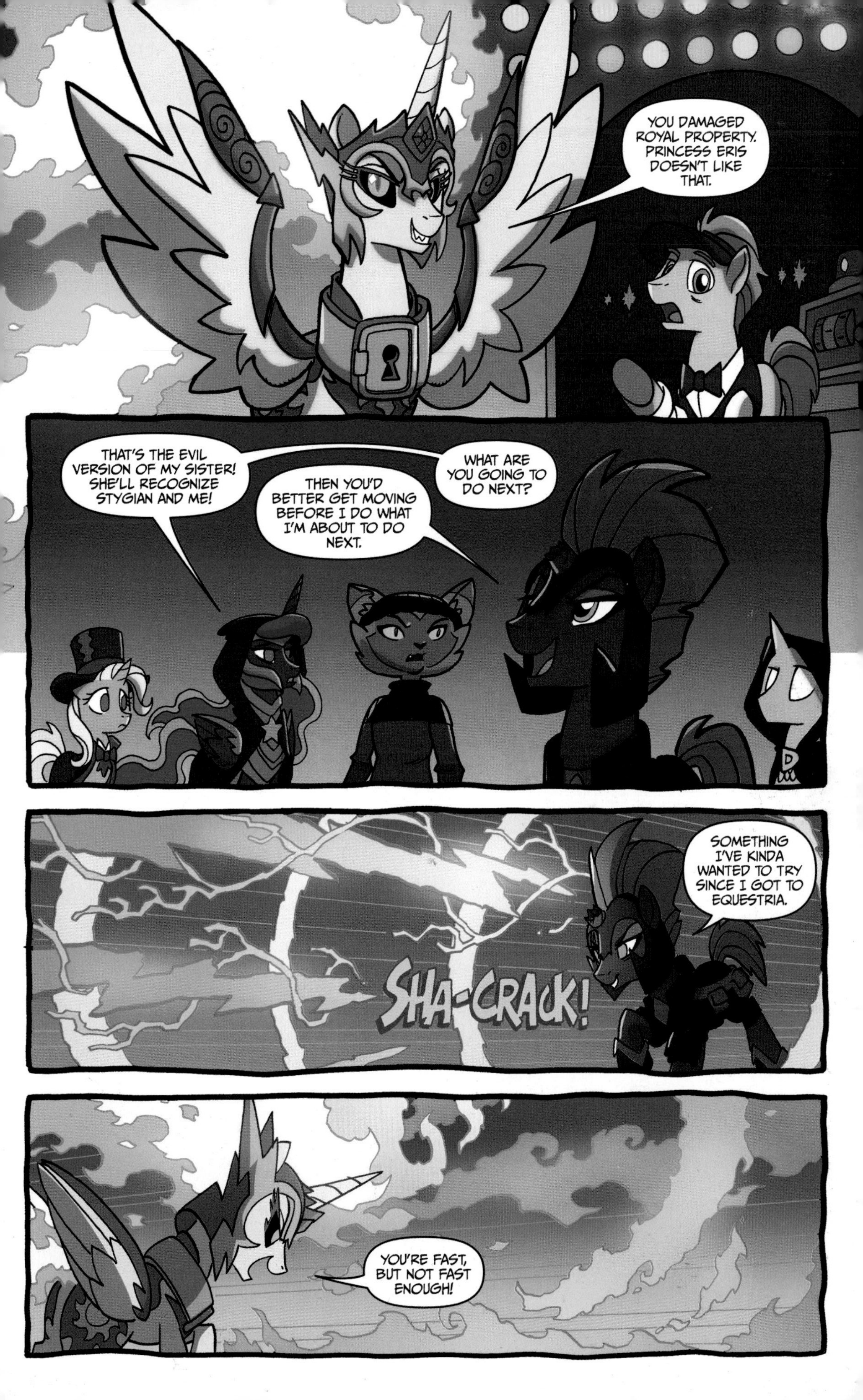
YOU DAMAGED ROYAL PROPERTY. PRINCESS ERIS DOESN'T LIKE THAT.
THAT'S THE EVIL VERSION OF MY SISTER! SHE'LL RECOGNIZE STYGIAN AND ME!
WHAT ARE YOU GOING TO DO NEXT?
THEN YOU'D BETTER GET MOVING BEFORE I DO WHAT I'M ABOUT TO DO NEXT.
SOMETHING I'VE KINDA WANTED TO TRY SINCE I GOT TO EQUESTRIA.
SHA-CRACK!
YOU'RE FAST, BUT NOT FAST ENOUGH!

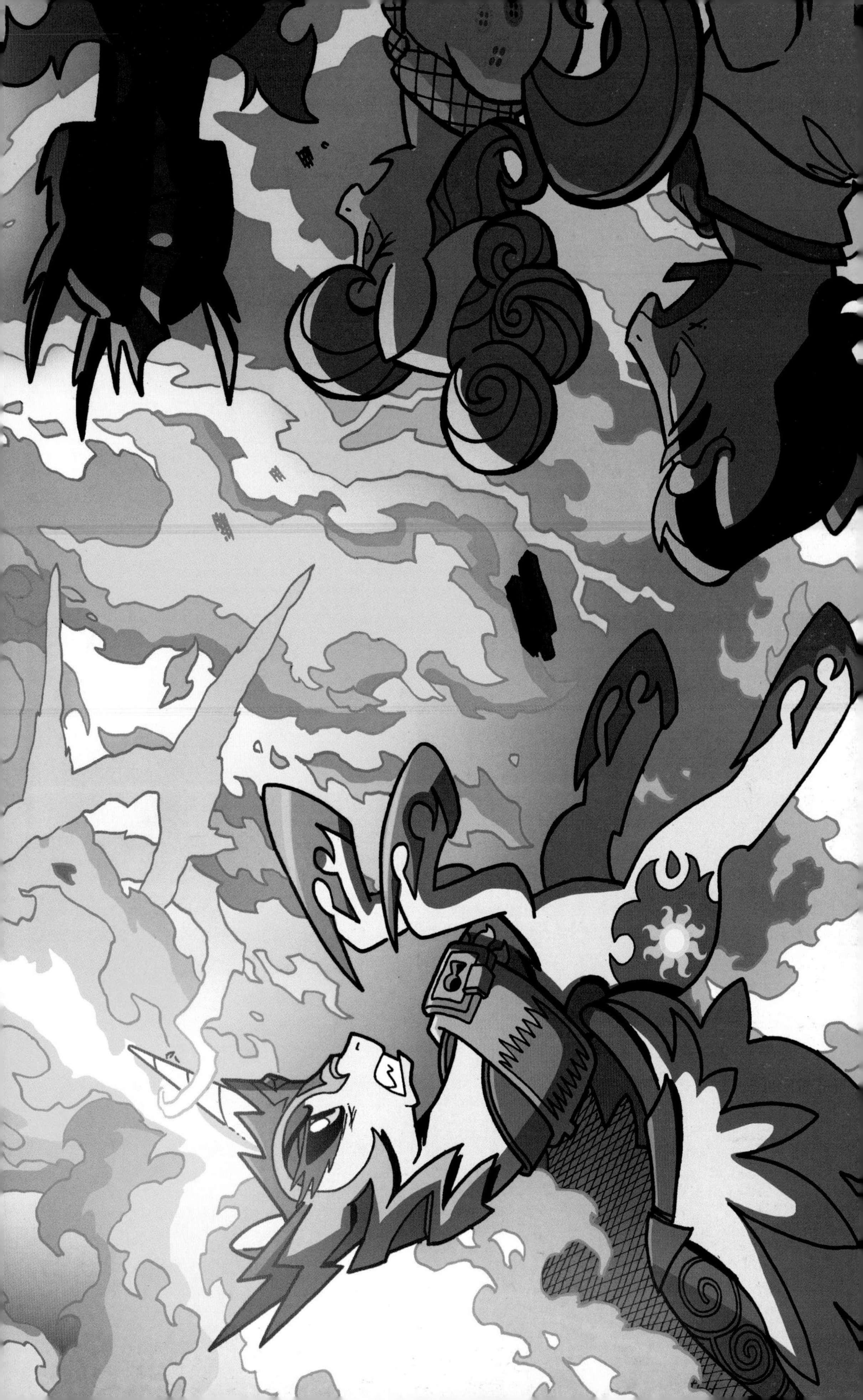

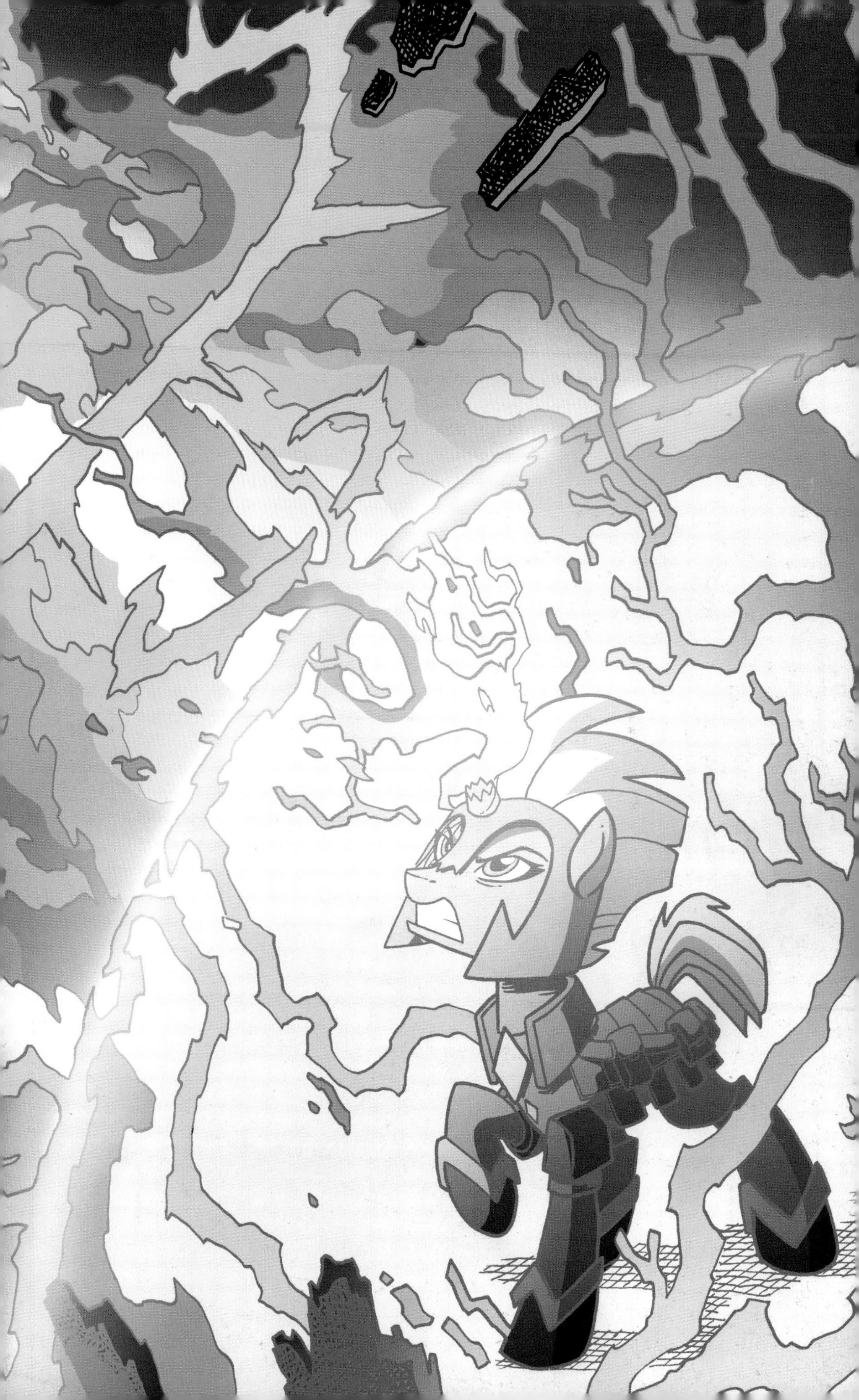

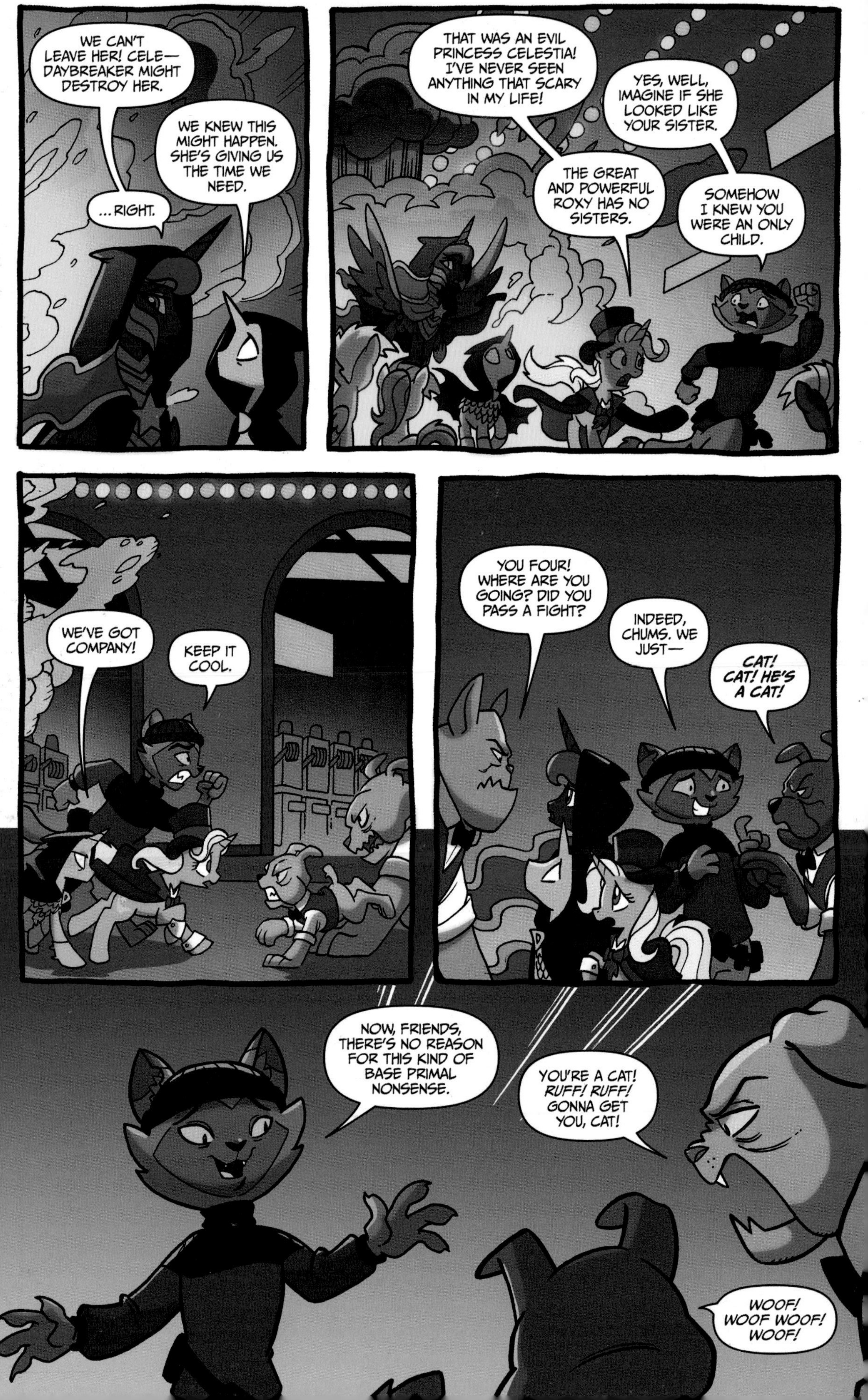
WE CAN'T LEAVE HER! CELE— DAYBREAKER MIGHT DESTROY HER.
WE KNEW THIS MIGHT HAPPEN. SHE'S GIVING US THE TIME WE NEED.
...RIGHT.
THAT WAS AN EVIL PRINCESS CELESTIA! I'VE NEVER SEEN ANYTHING THAT SCARY IN MY LIFE!
YES, WELL, IMAGINE IF SHE LOOKED LIKE YOUR SISTER.
THE GREAT AND POWERFUL ROXY HAS NO SISTERS.
SOMEHOW I KNEW YOU WERE AN ONLY CHILD.
WE'VE GOT COMPANY!
KEEP IT COOL.
YOU FOUR! WHERE ARE YOU GOING? DID YOU PASS A FIGHT?
INDEED, CHUMS. WE JUST—
CAT! CAT! HE'S A CAT!
NOW, FRIENDS, THERE'S NO REASON FOR THIS KIND OF BASE PRIMAL NONSENSE.
YOU'RE A CAT! *RUFF! RUFF!* GONNA GET YOU, CAT!
WOOF! WOOF WOOF! WOOF!

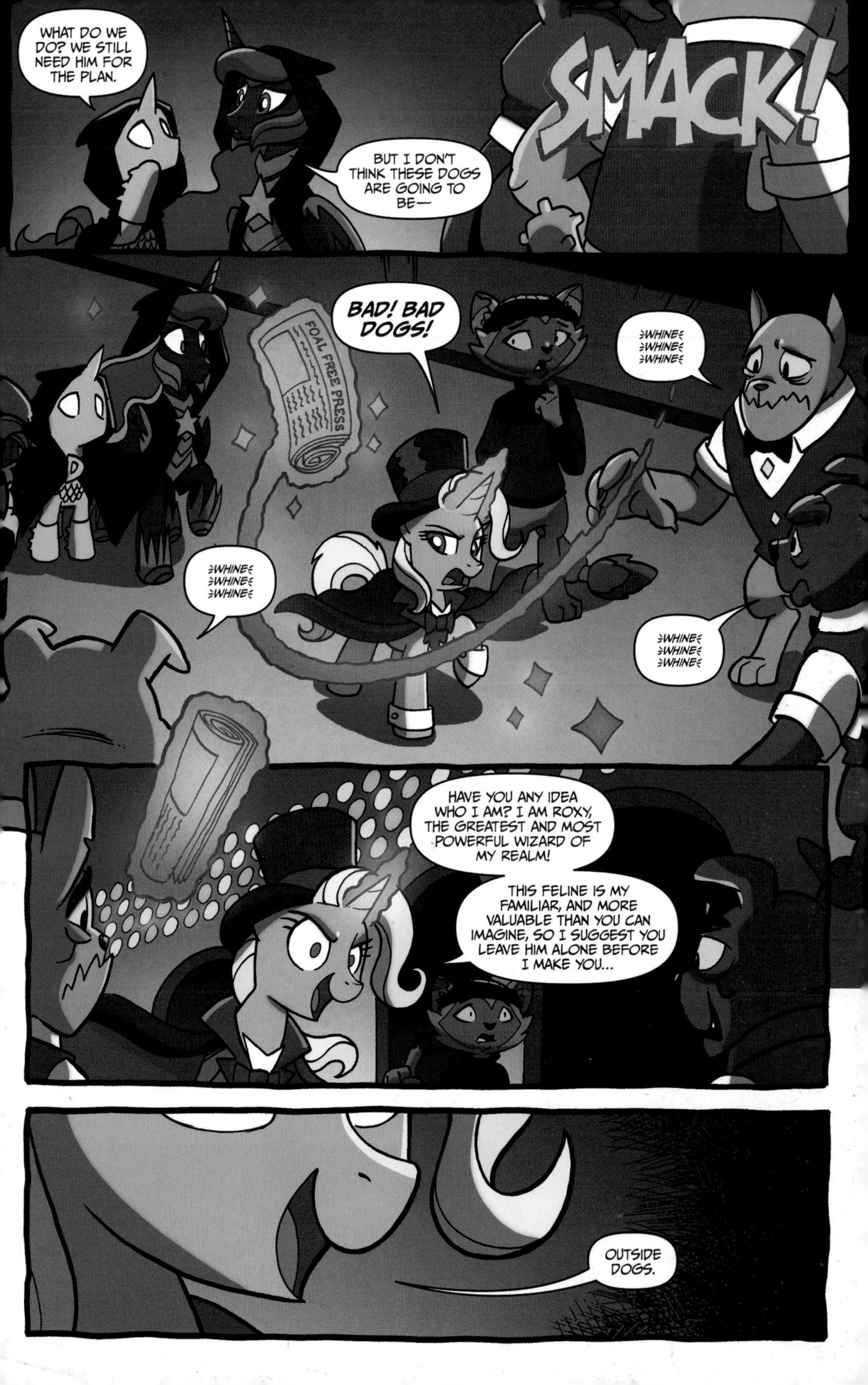
WHAT DO WE DO? WE STILL NEED HIM FOR THE PLAN.
BUT I DON'T THINK THESE DOGS ARE GOING TO BE—
SMACK!
BAD! BAD DOGS!
FOAL FREE PRESS
WHINE WHINE WHINE
WHINE WHINE WHINE
WHINE WHINE WHINE
HAVE YOU ANY IDEA WHO I AM? I AM ROXY, THE GREATEST AND MOST POWERFUL WIZARD OF MY REALM!
THIS FELINE IS MY FAMILIAR, AND MORE VALUABLE THAN YOU CAN IMAGINE, SO I SUGGEST YOU LEAVE HIM ALONE BEFORE I MAKE YOU...
OUTSIDE DOGS.

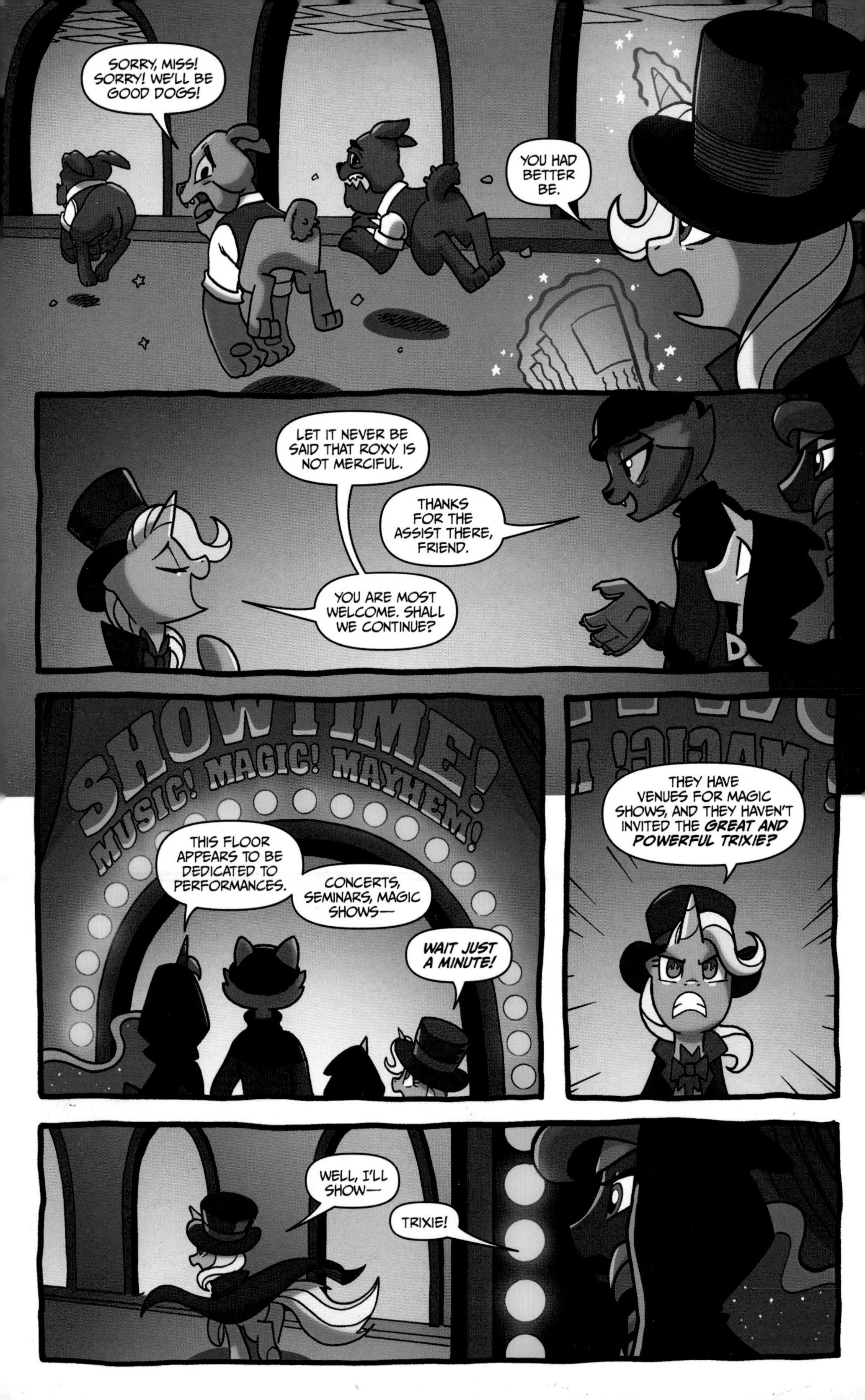
SORRY, MISS! SORRY! WE'LL BE GOOD DOGS!
YOU HAD BETTER BE.
LET IT NEVER BE SAID THAT ROXY IS NOT MERCIFUL.
THANKS FOR THE ASSIST THERE, FRIEND.
YOU ARE MOST WELCOME. SHALL WE CONTINUE?
SHOWTIME! MUSIC! MAGIC! MAYHEM!
THIS FLOOR APPEARS TO BE DEDICATED TO PERFORMANCES.
CONCERTS, SEMINARS, MAGIC SHOWS—
WAIT JUST A MINUTE!
THEY HAVE VENUES FOR MAGIC SHOWS, AND THEY HAVEN'T INVITED THE ***GREAT AND POWERFUL TRIXIE?***
WELL, I'LL SHOW—
TRIXIE!

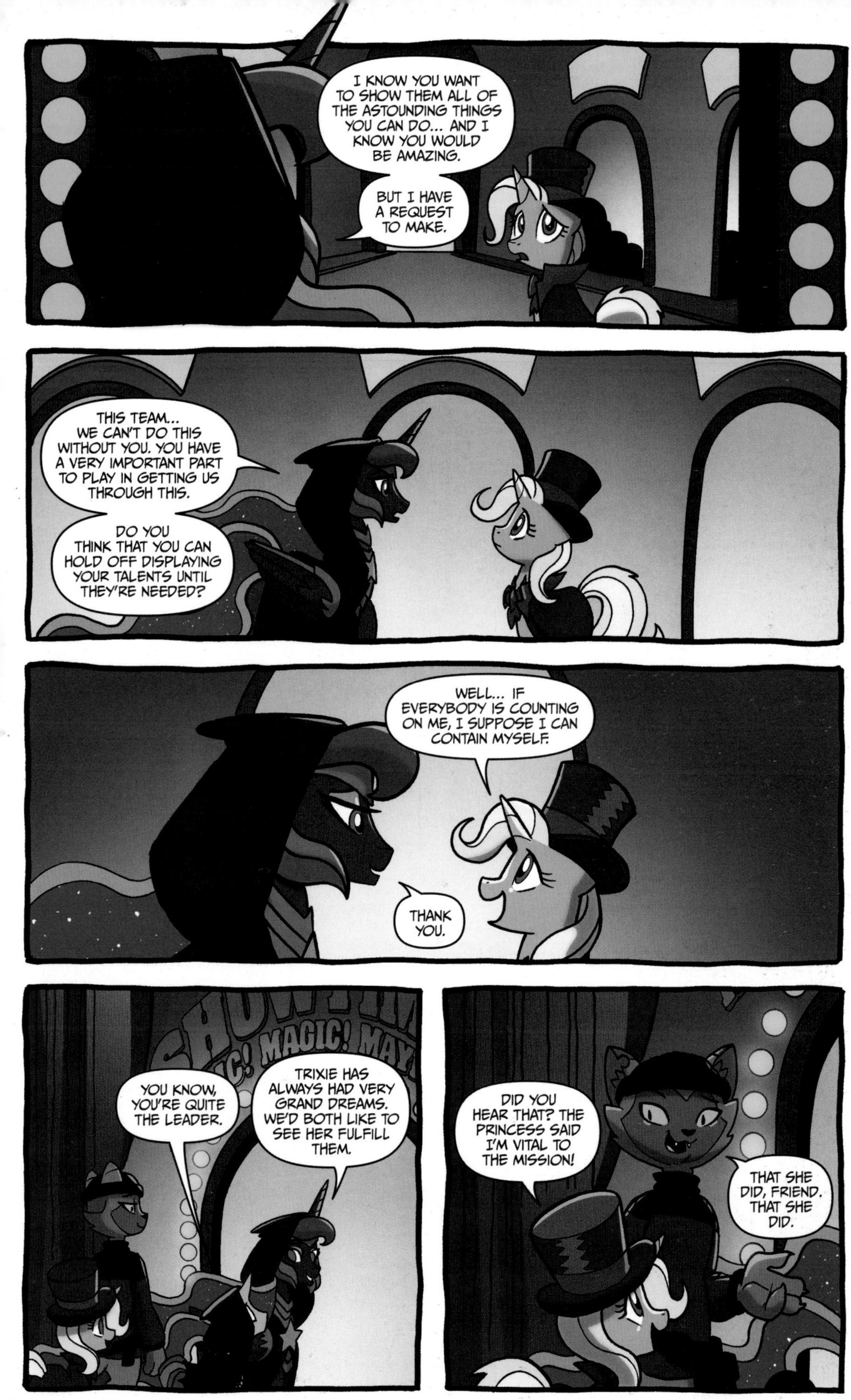
I KNOW YOU WANT TO SHOW THEM ALL OF THE ASTOUNDING THINGS YOU CAN DO... AND I KNOW YOU WOULD BE AMAZING.
BUT I HAVE A REQUEST TO MAKE.
THIS TEAM... WE CAN'T DO THIS WITHOUT YOU. YOU HAVE A VERY IMPORTANT PART TO PLAY IN GETTING US THROUGH THIS.
DO YOU THINK THAT YOU CAN HOLD OFF DISPLAYING YOUR TALENTS UNTIL THEY'RE NEEDED?
WELL... IF EVERYBODY IS COUNTING ON ME, I SUPPOSE I CAN CONTAIN MYSELF.
THANK YOU.
YOU KNOW, YOU'RE QUITE THE LEADER.
TRIXIE HAS ALWAYS HAD VERY GRAND DREAMS. WE'D BOTH LIKE TO SEE HER FULFILL THEM.
DID YOU HEAR THAT? THE PRINCESS SAID I'M VITAL TO THE MISSION!
THAT SHE DID, FRIEND. THAT SHE DID.

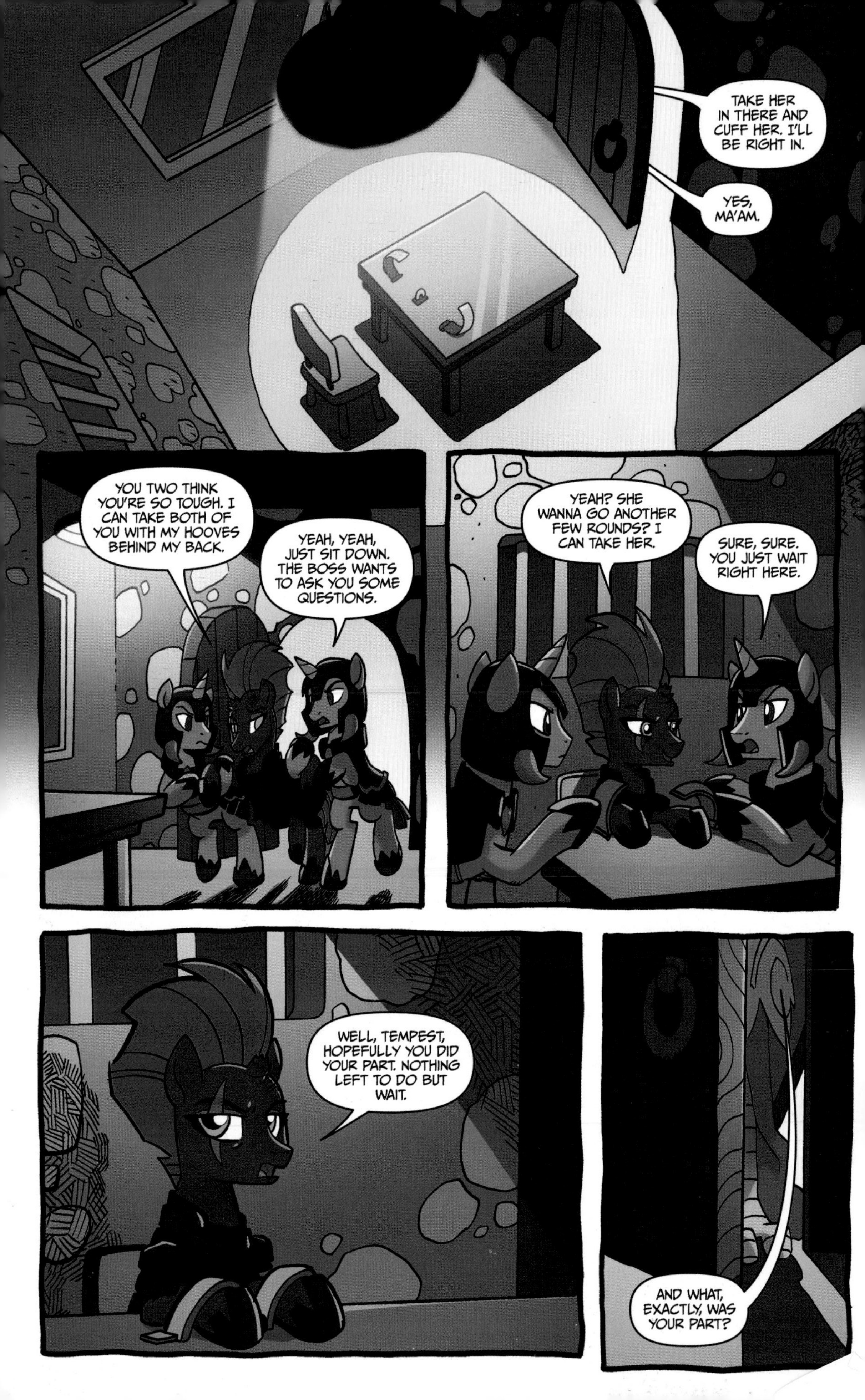
TAKE HER IN THERE AND CUFF HER. I'LL BE RIGHT IN.
YES, MA'AM.
YOU TWO THINK YOU'RE SO TOUGH. I CAN TAKE BOTH OF YOU WITH MY HOOVES BEHIND MY BACK.
YEAH, YEAH, JUST SIT DOWN. THE BOSS WANTS TO ASK YOU SOME QUESTIONS.
YEAH? SHE WANNA GO ANOTHER FEW ROUNDS? I CAN TAKE HER.
SURE, SURE. YOU JUST WAIT RIGHT HERE.
WELL, TEMPEST, HOPEFULLY YOU DID YOUR PART. NOTHING LEFT TO DO BUT WAIT.
AND WHAT, EXACTLY, WAS YOUR PART?

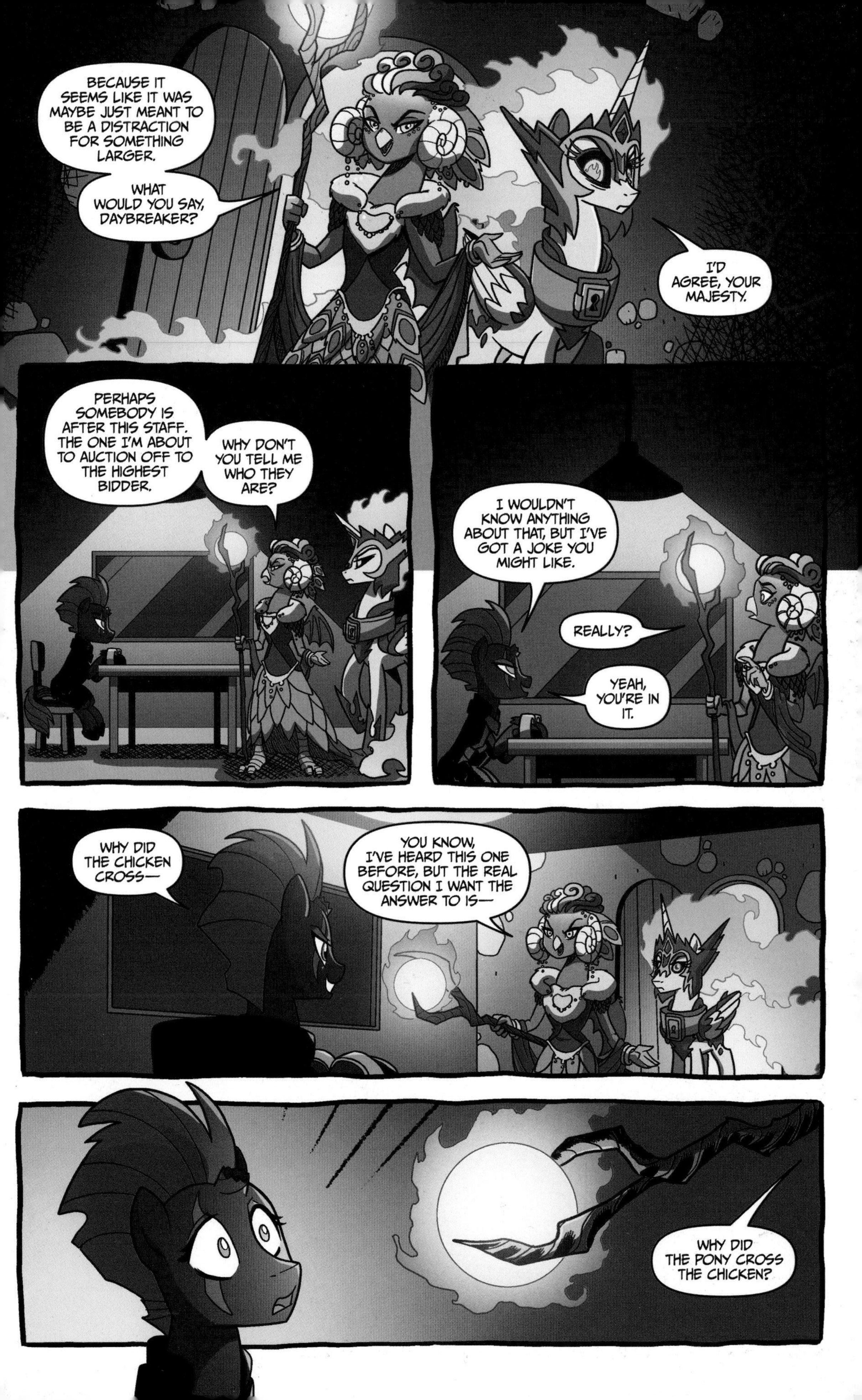
BECAUSE IT SEEMS LIKE IT WAS MAYBE JUST MEANT TO BE A DISTRACTION FOR SOMETHING LARGER.
WHAT WOULD YOU SAY, DAYBREAKER?
I'D AGREE, YOUR MAJESTY.
PERHAPS SOMEBODY IS AFTER THIS STAFF. THE ONE I'M ABOUT TO AUCTION OFF TO THE HIGHEST BIDDER.
WHY DON'T YOU TELL ME WHO THEY ARE?
I WOULDN'T KNOW ANYTHING ABOUT THAT, BUT I'VE GOT A JOKE YOU MIGHT LIKE.
REALLY?
YEAH, YOU'RE IN IT.
WHY DID THE CHICKEN CROSS—
YOU KNOW, I'VE HEARD THIS ONE BEFORE, BUT THE REAL QUESTION I WANT THE ANSWER TO IS—
WHY DID THE PONY CROSS THE CHICKEN?

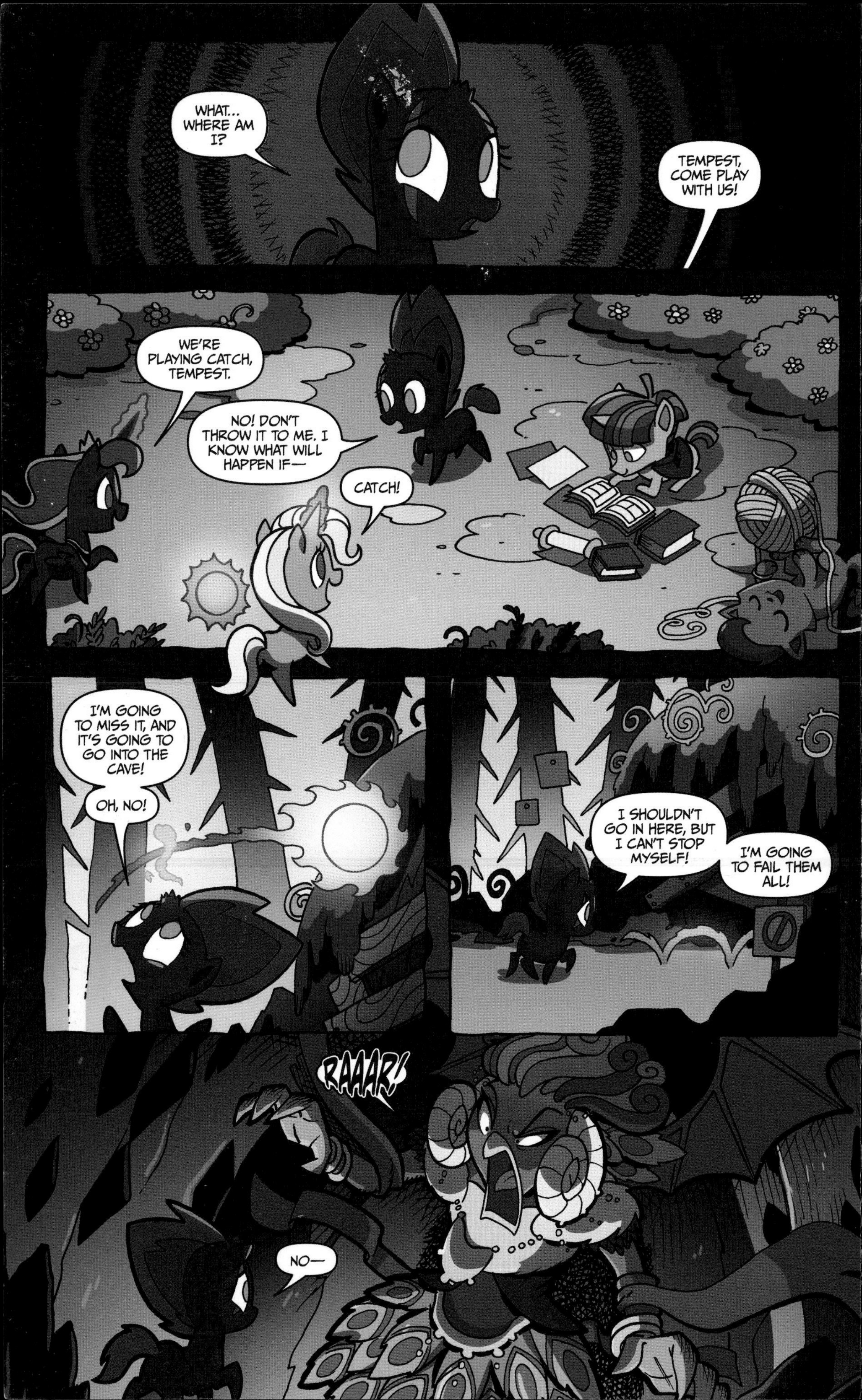
WHAT... WHERE AM I?
TEMPEST, COME PLAY WITH US!
WE'RE PLAYING CATCH, TEMPEST.
NO! DON'T THROW IT TO ME. I KNOW WHAT WILL HAPPEN IF—
CATCH!
I'M GOING TO MISS IT, AND IT'S GOING TO GO INTO THE CAVE!
OH, NO!
I SHOULDN'T GO IN HERE, BUT I CAN'T STOP MYSELF!
I'M GOING TO FAIL THEM ALL!
RAAAR!
NO—

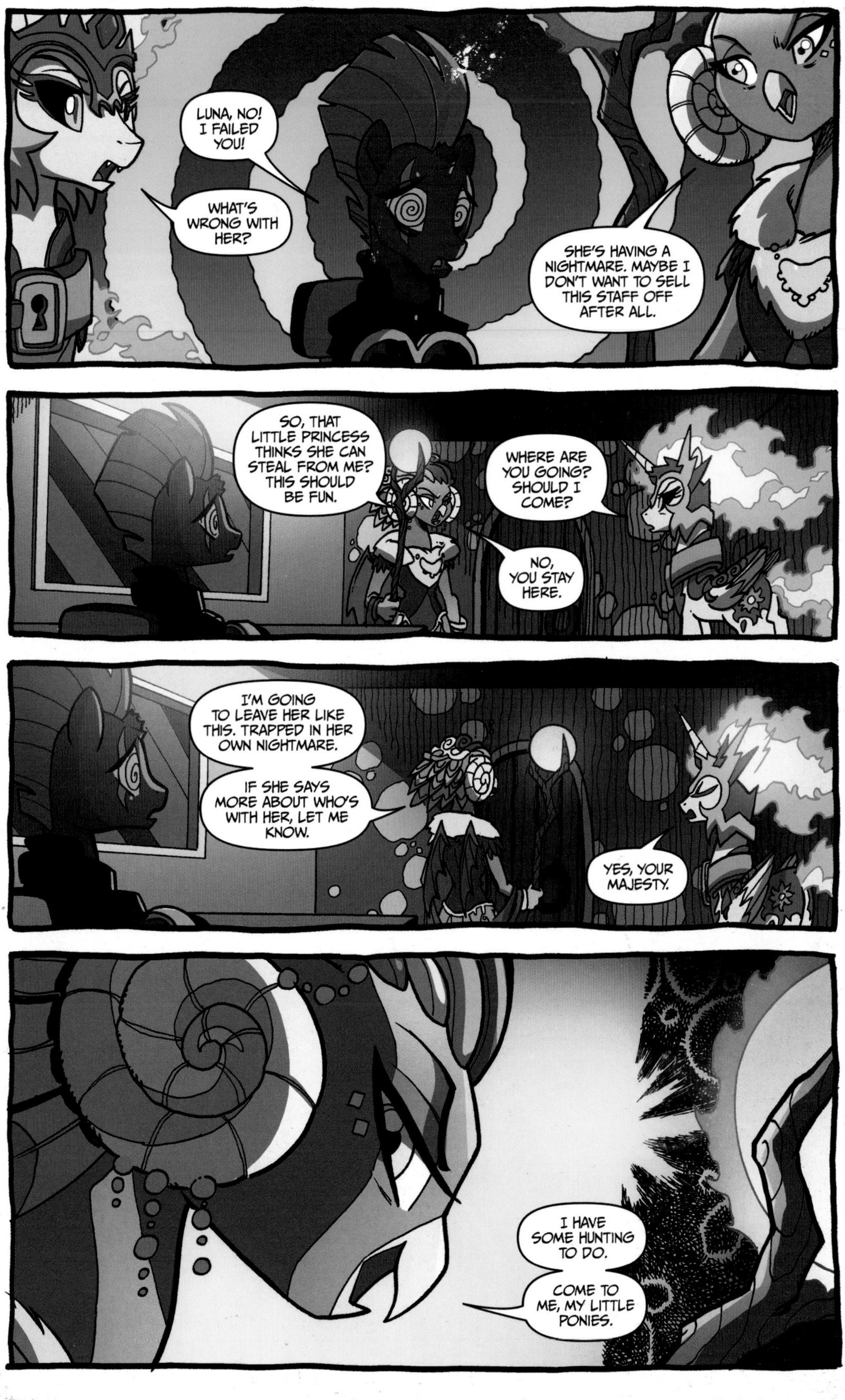
LUNA, NO! I FAILED YOU!
WHAT'S WRONG WITH HER?
SHE'S HAVING A NIGHTMARE. MAYBE I DON'T WANT TO SELL THIS STAFF OFF AFTER ALL.
SO, THAT LITTLE PRINCESS THINKS SHE CAN STEAL FROM ME? THIS SHOULD BE FUN.
WHERE ARE YOU GOING? SHOULD I COME?
NO, YOU STAY HERE.
I'M GOING TO LEAVE HER LIKE THIS. TRAPPED IN HER OWN NIGHTMARE.
IF SHE SAYS MORE ABOUT WHO'S WITH HER, LET ME KNOW.
YES, YOUR MAJESTY.
I HAVE SOME HUNTING TO DO.
COME TO ME, MY LITTLE PONIES.

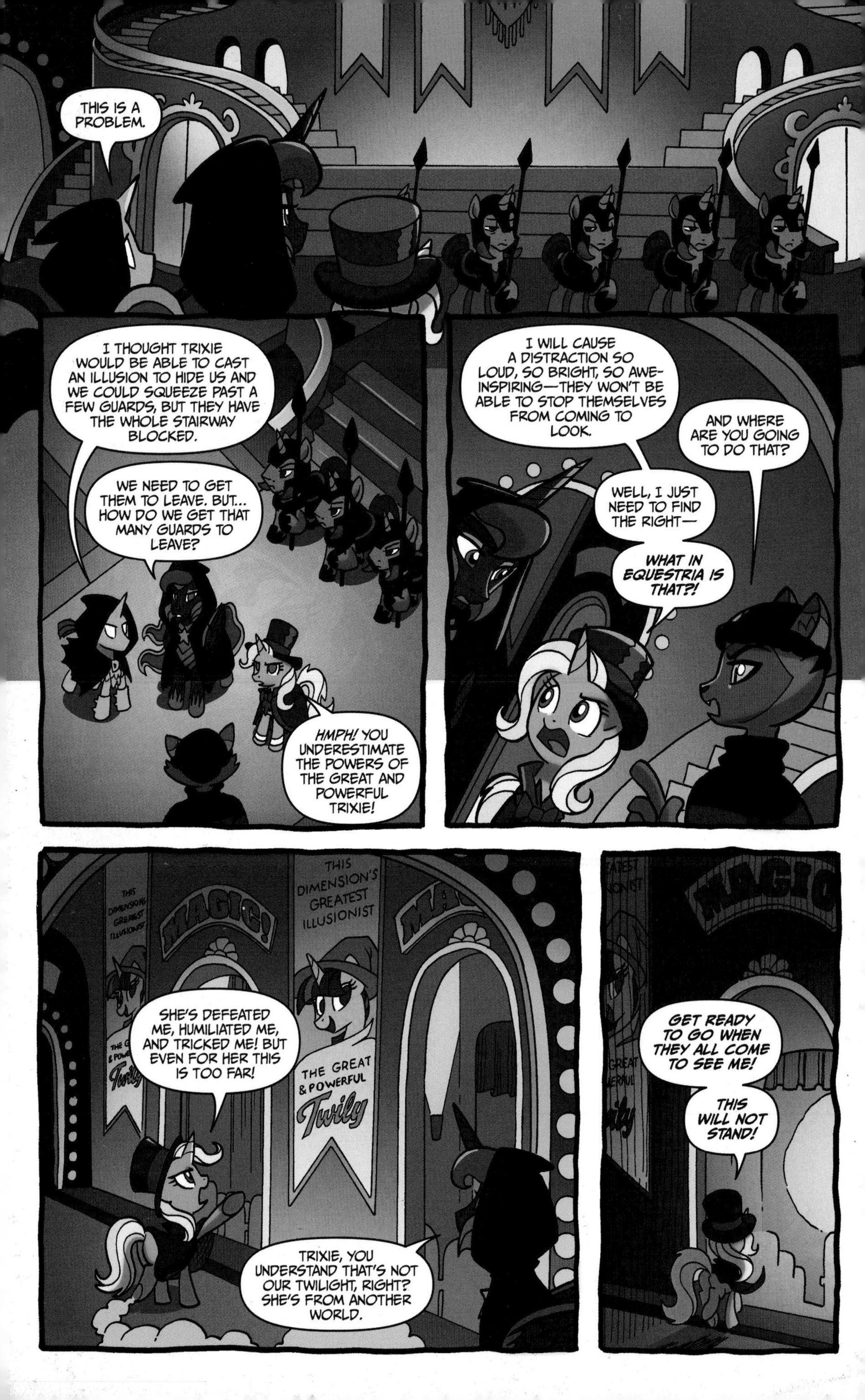
THIS IS A PROBLEM.
I THOUGHT TRIXIE WOULD BE ABLE TO CAST AN ILLUSION TO HIDE US AND WE COULD SQUEEZE PAST A FEW GUARDS, BUT THEY HAVE THE WHOLE STAIRWAY BLOCKED.
WE NEED TO GET THEM TO LEAVE. BUT... HOW DO WE GET THAT MANY GUARDS TO LEAVE?
HMPH! YOU UNDERESTIMATE THE POWERS OF THE GREAT AND POWERFUL TRIXIE!
I WILL CAUSE A DISTRACTION SO LOUD, SO BRIGHT, SO AWE-INSPIRING—THEY WON'T BE ABLE TO STOP THEMSELVES FROM COMING TO LOOK.
AND WHERE ARE YOU GOING TO DO THAT?
WELL, I JUST NEED TO FIND THE RIGHT—
WHAT IN EQUESTRIA IS THAT?!
THIS DIMENSION'S GREATEST ILLUSIONIST
MAGIC!
THE GREAT & POWERFUL Twily
SHE'S DEFEATED ME, HUMILIATED ME, AND TRICKED ME! BUT EVEN FOR HER THIS IS TOO FAR!
TRIXIE, YOU UNDERSTAND THAT'S NOT OUR TWILIGHT, RIGHT? SHE'S FROM ANOTHER WORLD.
GET READY TO GO WHEN THEY ALL COME TO SEE ME!
THIS WILL NOT STAND!

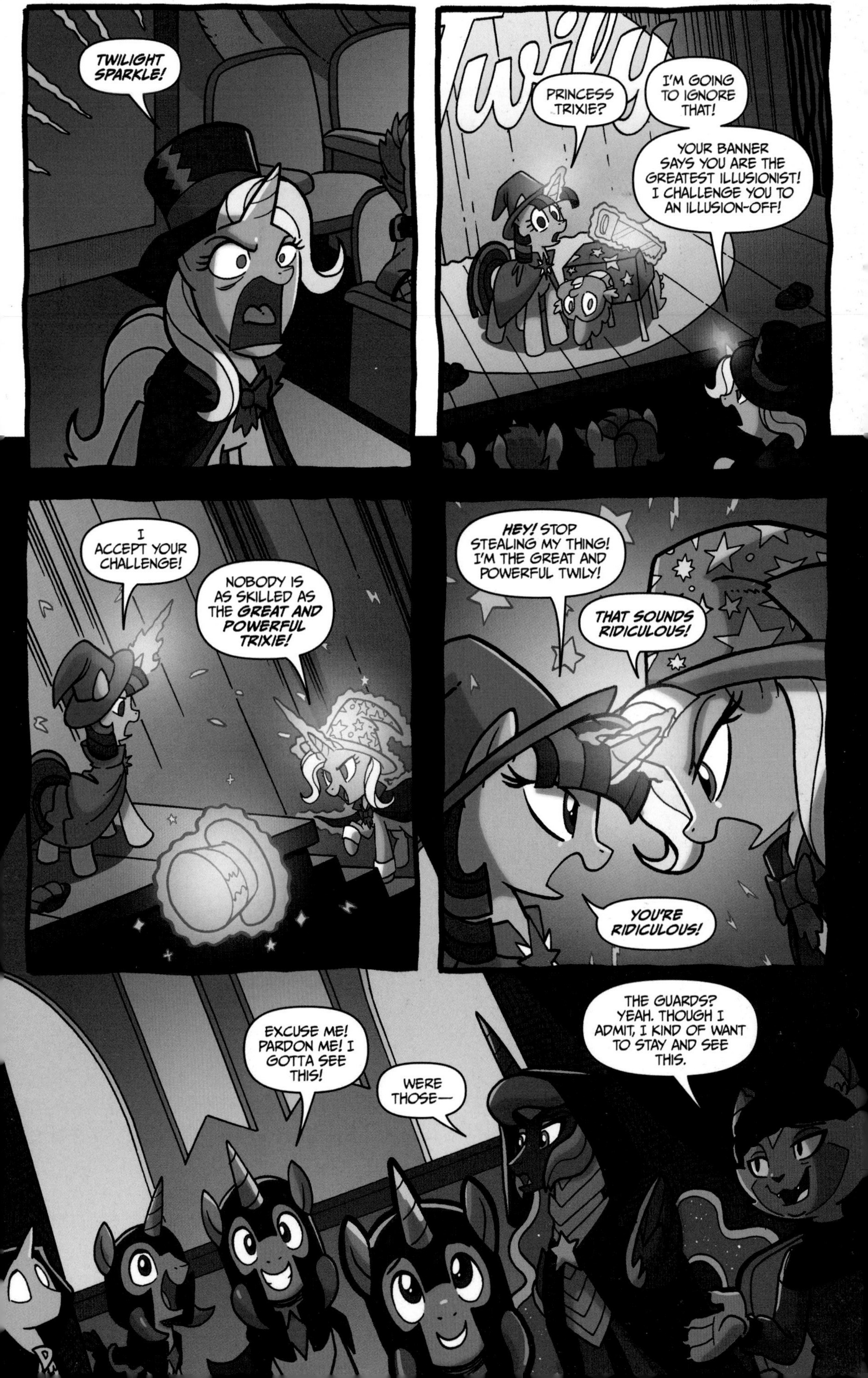
TWILIGHT SPARKLE!
Twily
PRINCESS TRIXIE?
I'M GOING TO IGNORE THAT!
YOUR BANNER SAYS YOU ARE THE GREATEST ILLUSIONIST! I CHALLENGE YOU TO AN ILLUSION-OFF!
I ACCEPT YOUR CHALLENGE!
NOBODY IS AS SKILLED AS THE GREAT AND POWERFUL TRIXIE!
HEY! STOP STEALING MY THING! I'M THE GREAT AND POWERFUL TWILY!
THAT SOUNDS RIDICULOUS!
YOU'RE RIDICULOUS!
EXCUSE ME! PARDON ME! I GOTTA SEE THIS!
WERE THOSE—
THE GUARDS? YEAH. THOUGH I ADMIT, I KIND OF WANT TO STAY AND SEE THIS.

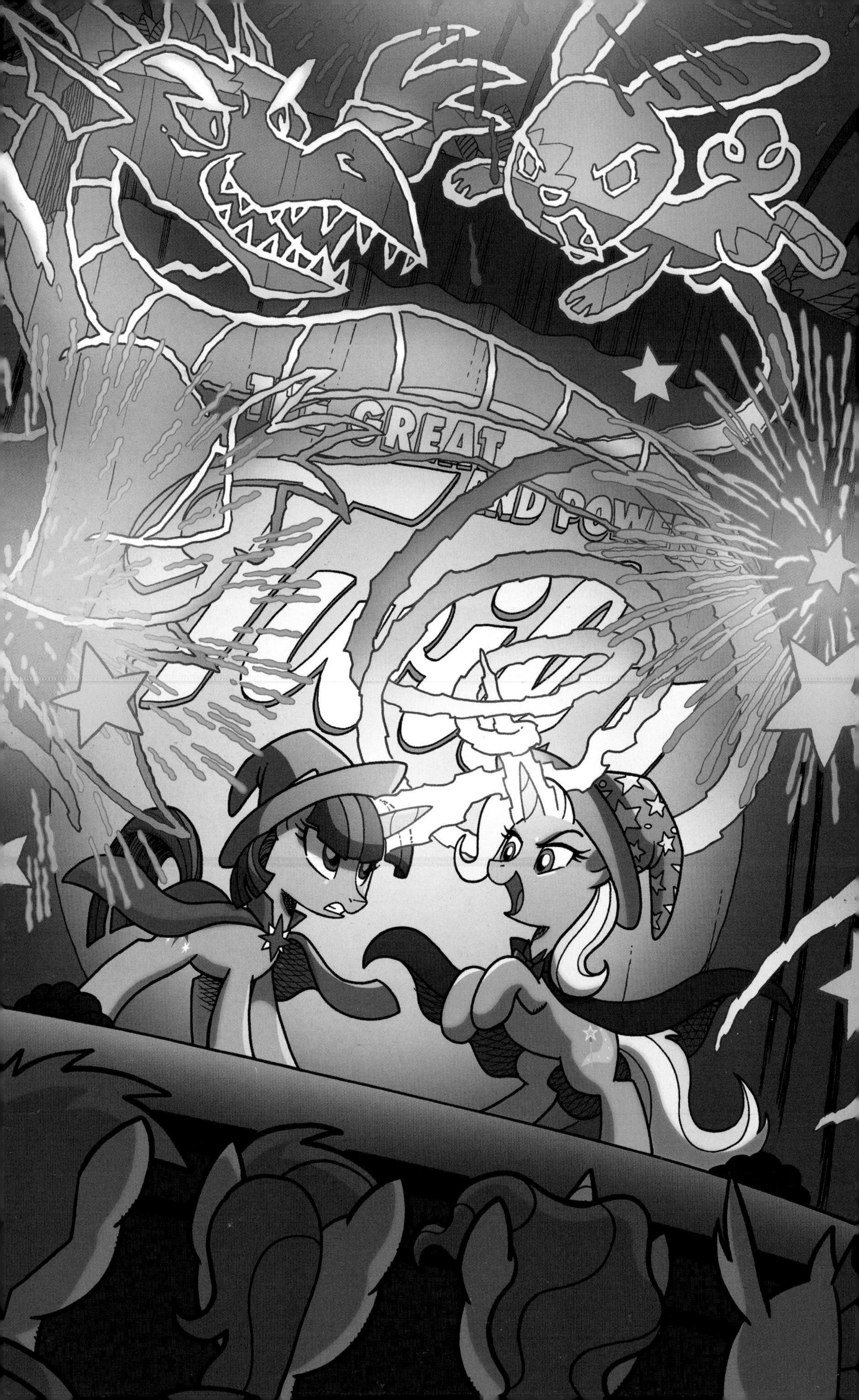
GREAT

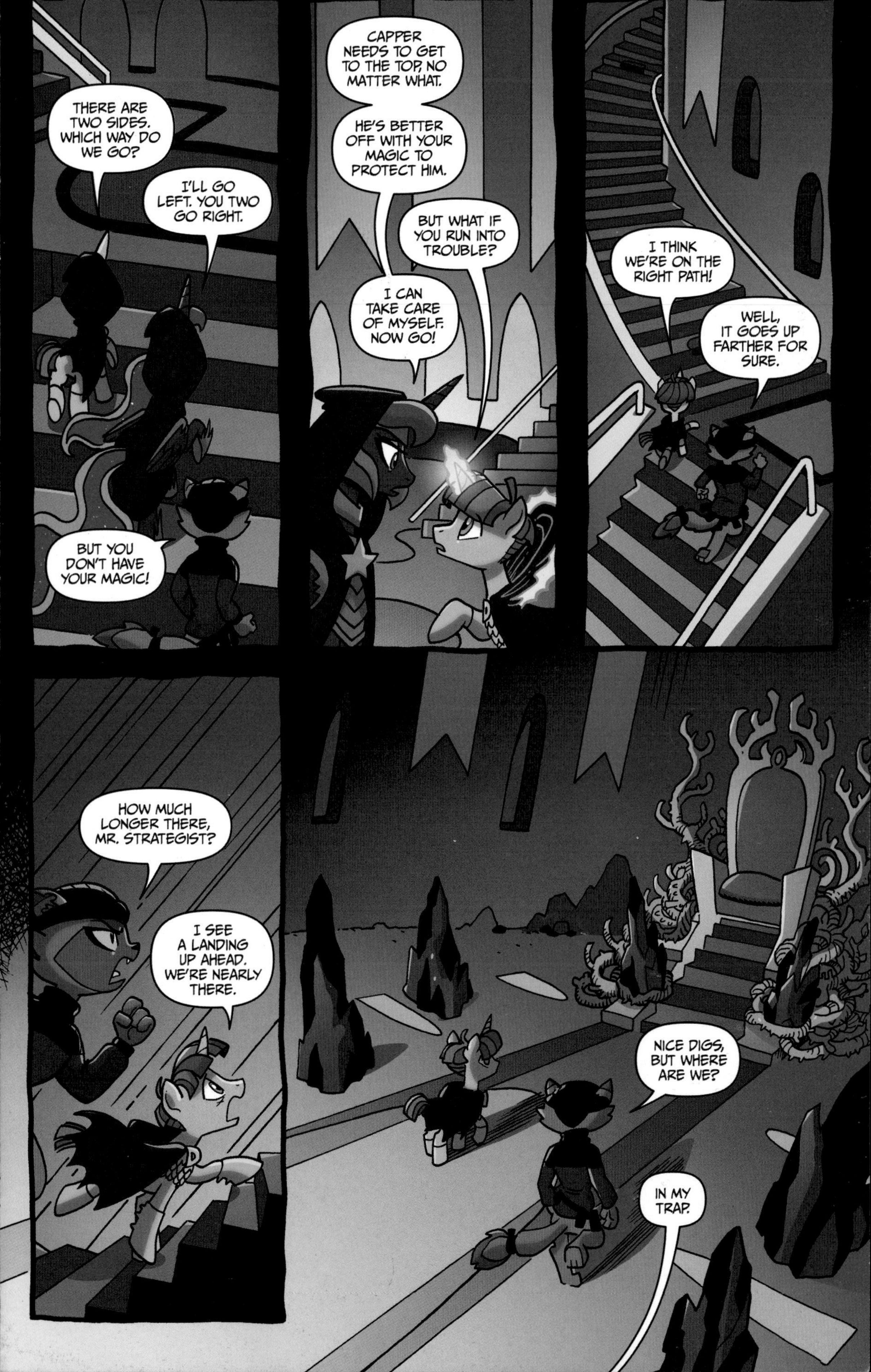
THERE ARE TWO SIDES. WHICH WAY DO WE GO?
I'LL GO LEFT. YOU TWO GO RIGHT.
BUT YOU DON'T HAVE YOUR MAGIC!
CAPPER NEEDS TO GET TO THE TOP, NO MATTER WHAT.
HE'S BETTER OFF WITH YOUR MAGIC TO PROTECT HIM.
BUT WHAT IF YOU RUN INTO TROUBLE?
I CAN TAKE CARE OF MYSELF. NOW GO!
I THINK WE'RE ON THE RIGHT PATH!
WELL, IT GOES UP FARTHER FOR SURE.
HOW MUCH LONGER THERE, MR. STRATEGIST?
I SEE A LANDING UP AHEAD. WE'RE NEARLY THERE.
NICE DIGS, BUT WHERE ARE WE?
IN MY TRAP.

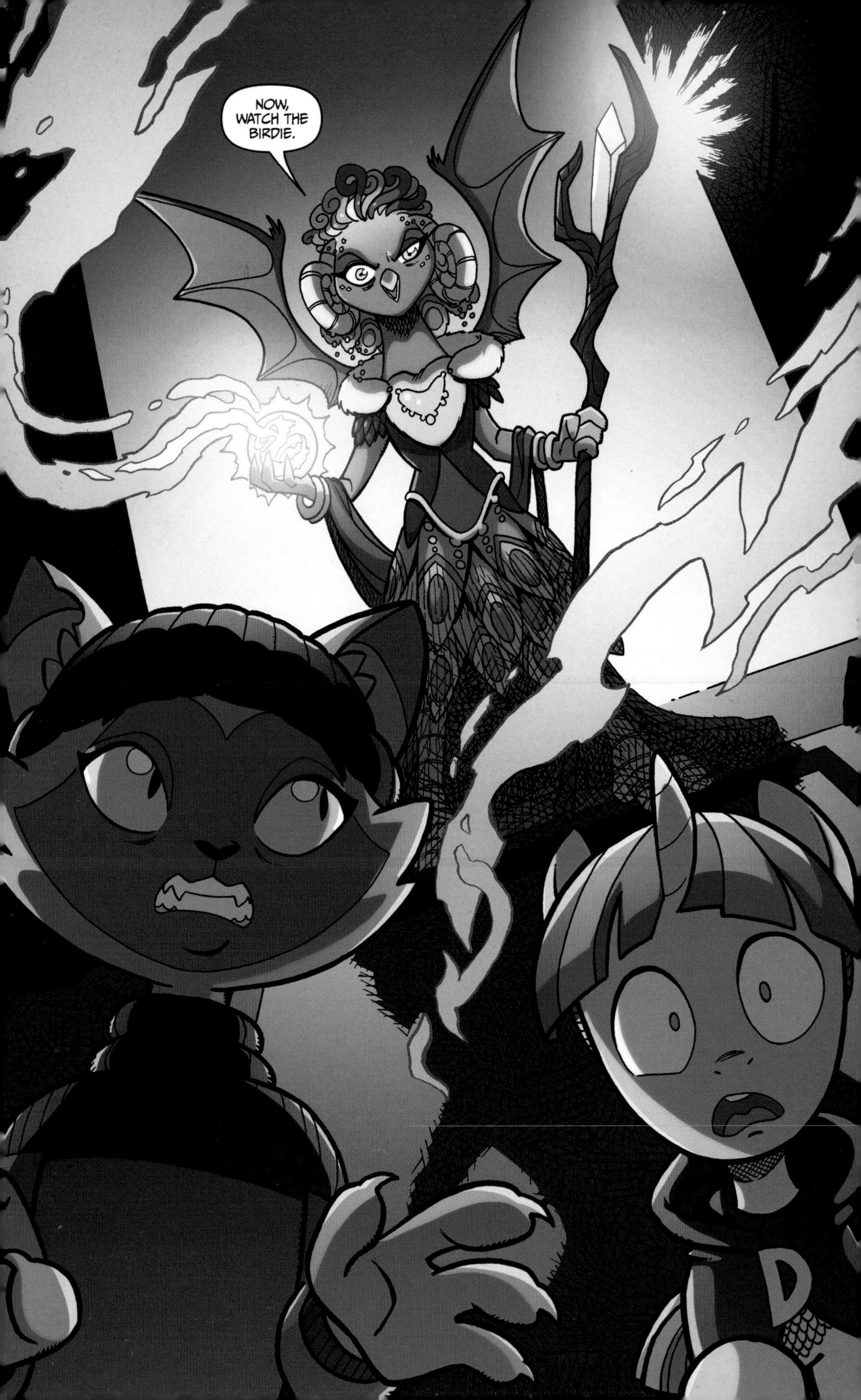
NOW, WATCH THE BIRDIE.

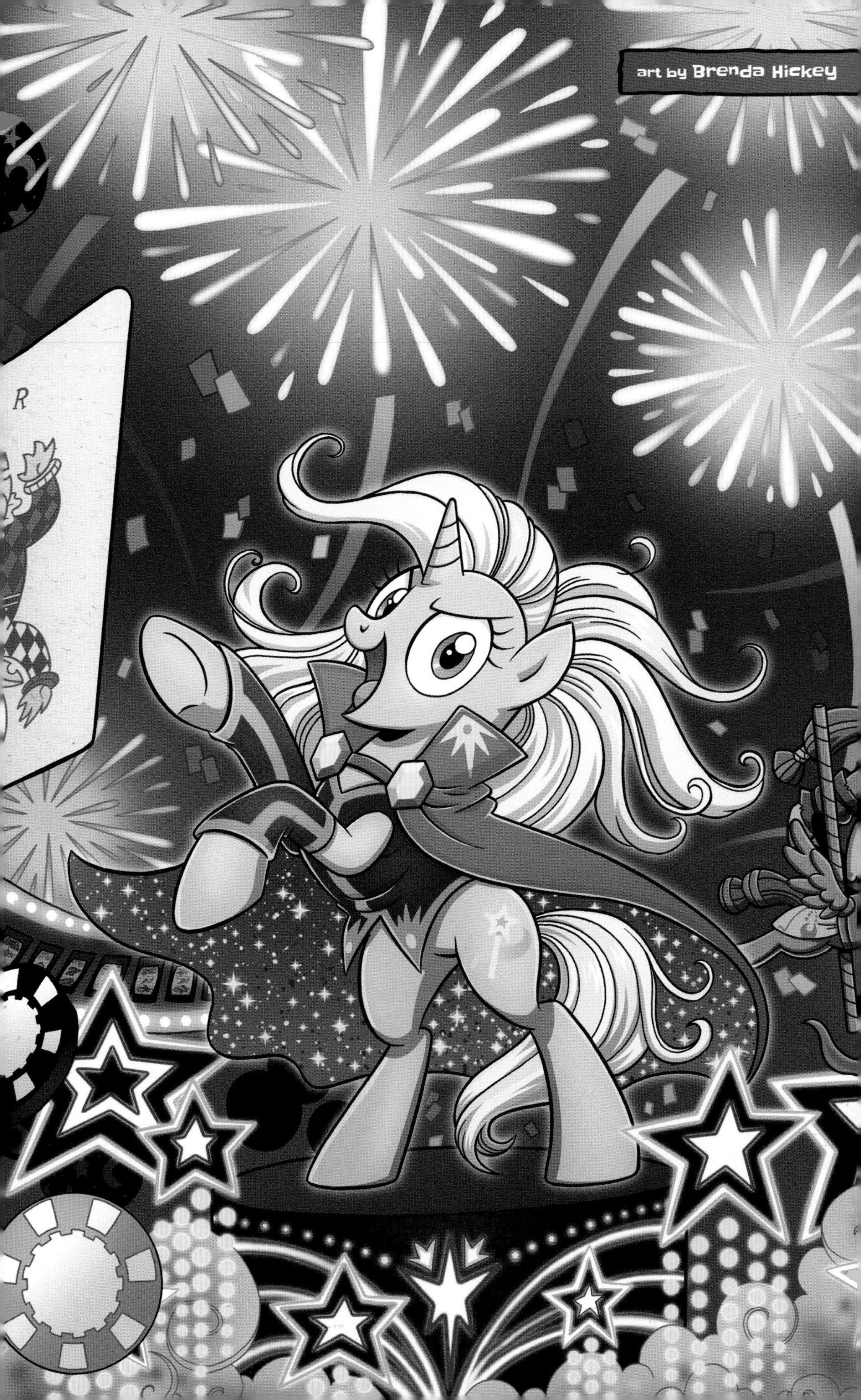
art by Brenda Hickey

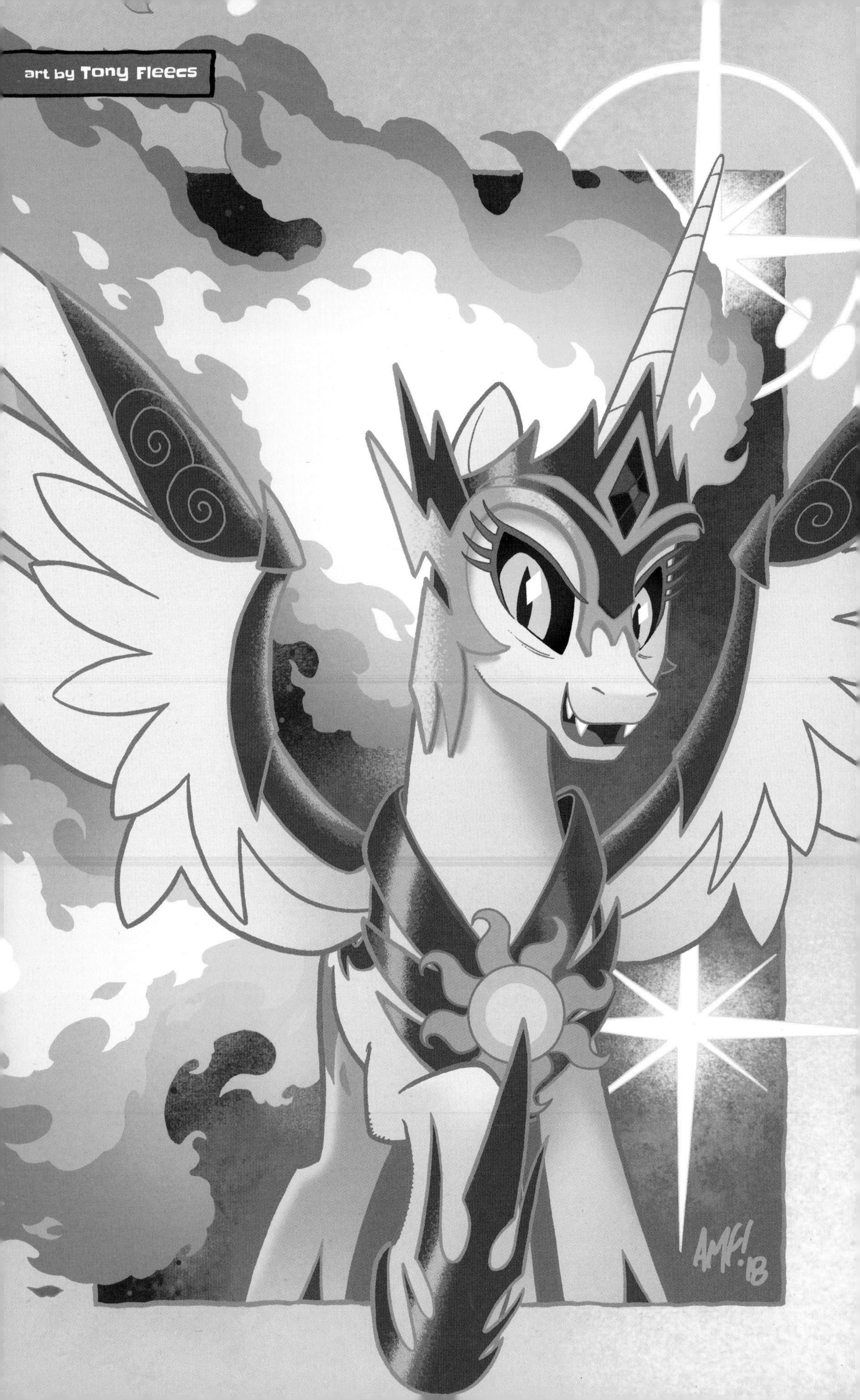

art by Tony Fleecs

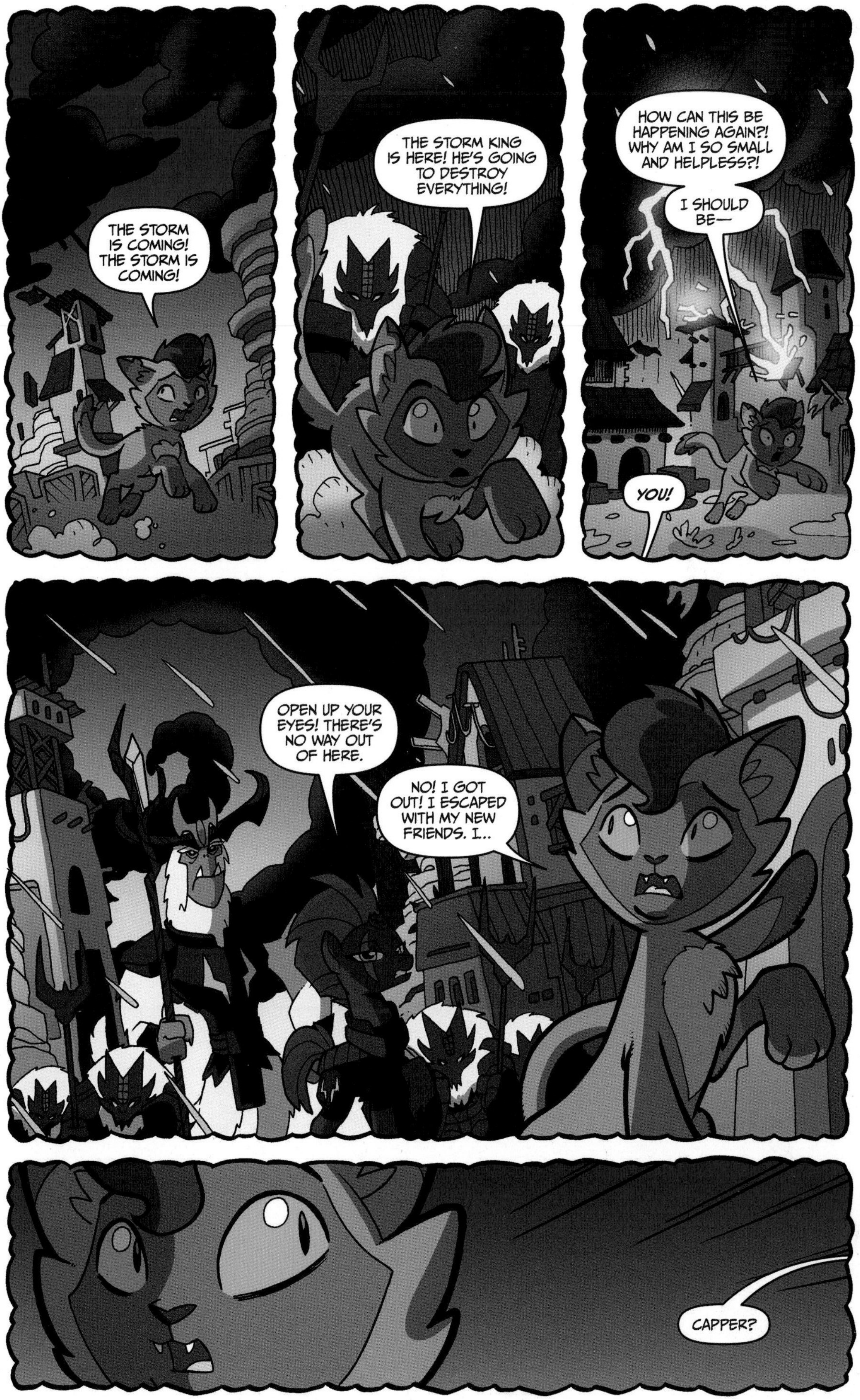
THE STORM IS COMING! THE STORM IS COMING!
THE STORM KING IS HERE! HE'S GOING TO DESTROY EVERYTHING!
HOW CAN THIS BE HAPPENING AGAIN?! WHY AM I SO SMALL AND HELPLESS?!
I SHOULD BE—
YOU!
OPEN UP YOUR EYES! THERE'S NO WAY OUT OF HERE.
NO! I GOT OUT! I ESCAPED WITH MY NEW FRIENDS. I...
CAPPER?

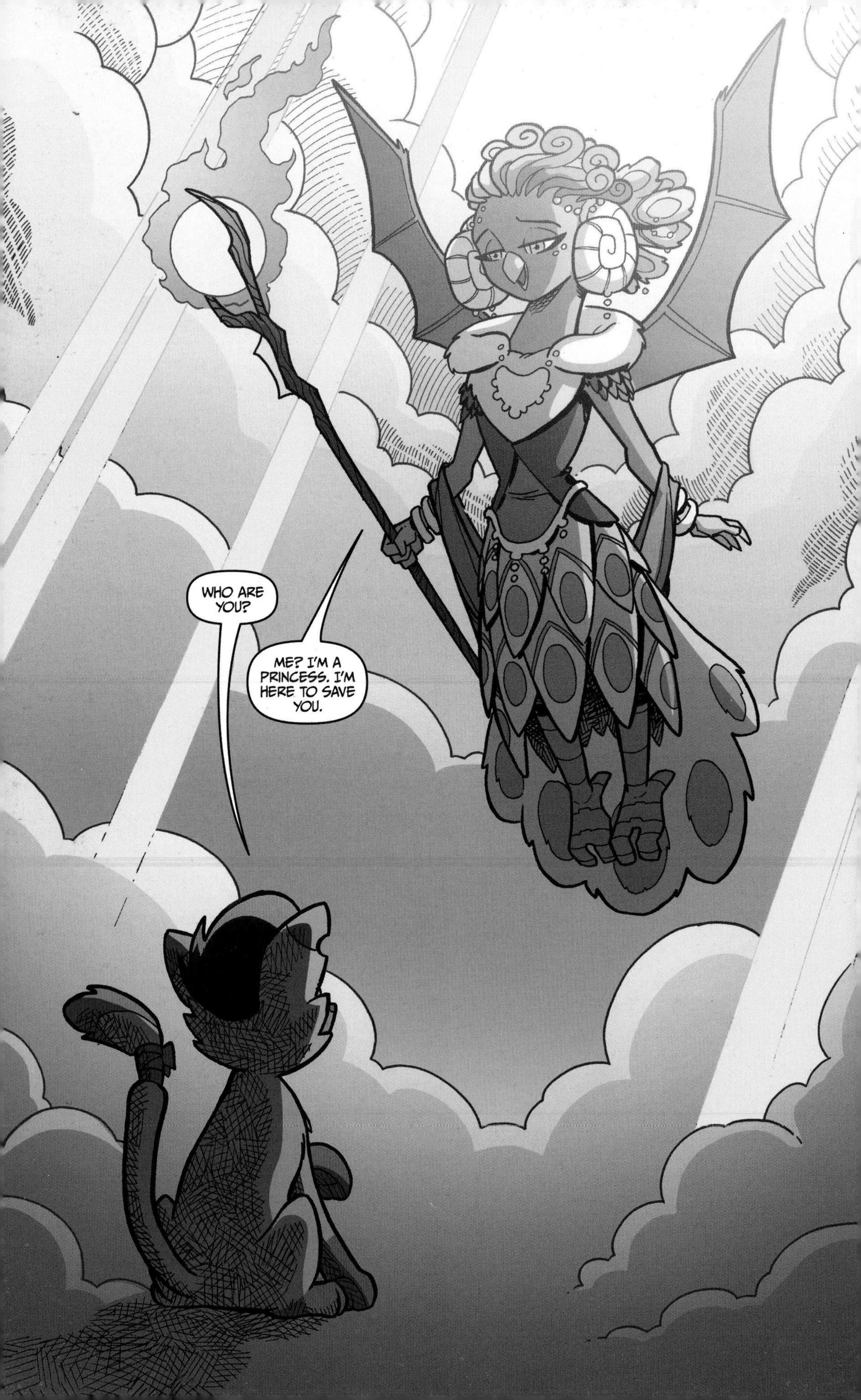
WHO ARE YOU?
ME? I'M A PRINCESS. I'M HERE TO SAVE YOU.

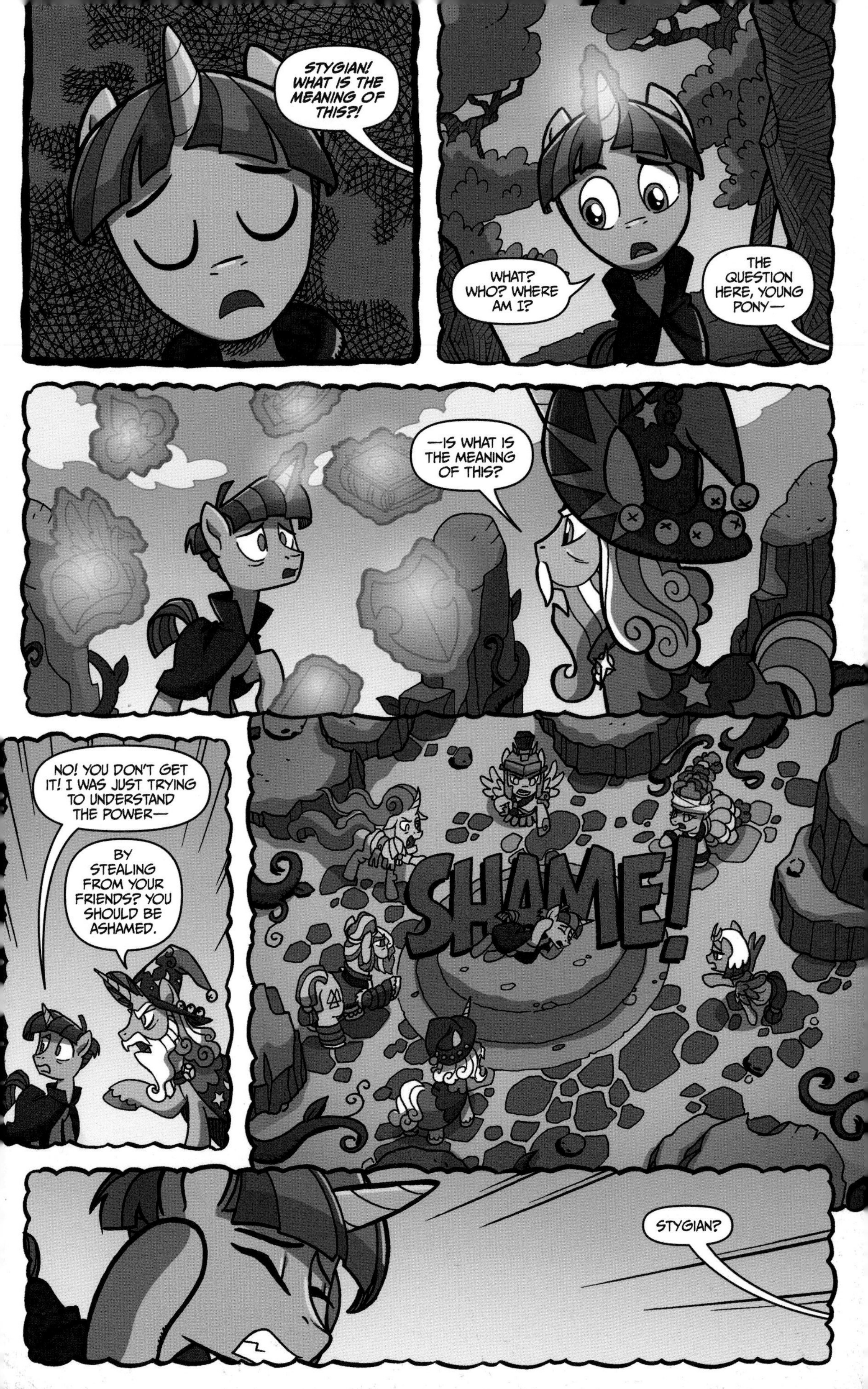
STYGIAN! WHAT IS THE MEANING OF THIS?!
WHAT? WHO? WHERE AM I?
THE QUESTION HERE, YOUNG PONY—
—IS WHAT IS THE MEANING OF THIS?
NO! YOU DON'T GET IT! I WAS JUST TRYING TO UNDERSTAND THE POWER—
BY STEALING FROM YOUR FRIENDS? YOU SHOULD BE ASHAMED.
SHAME!
STYGIAN?

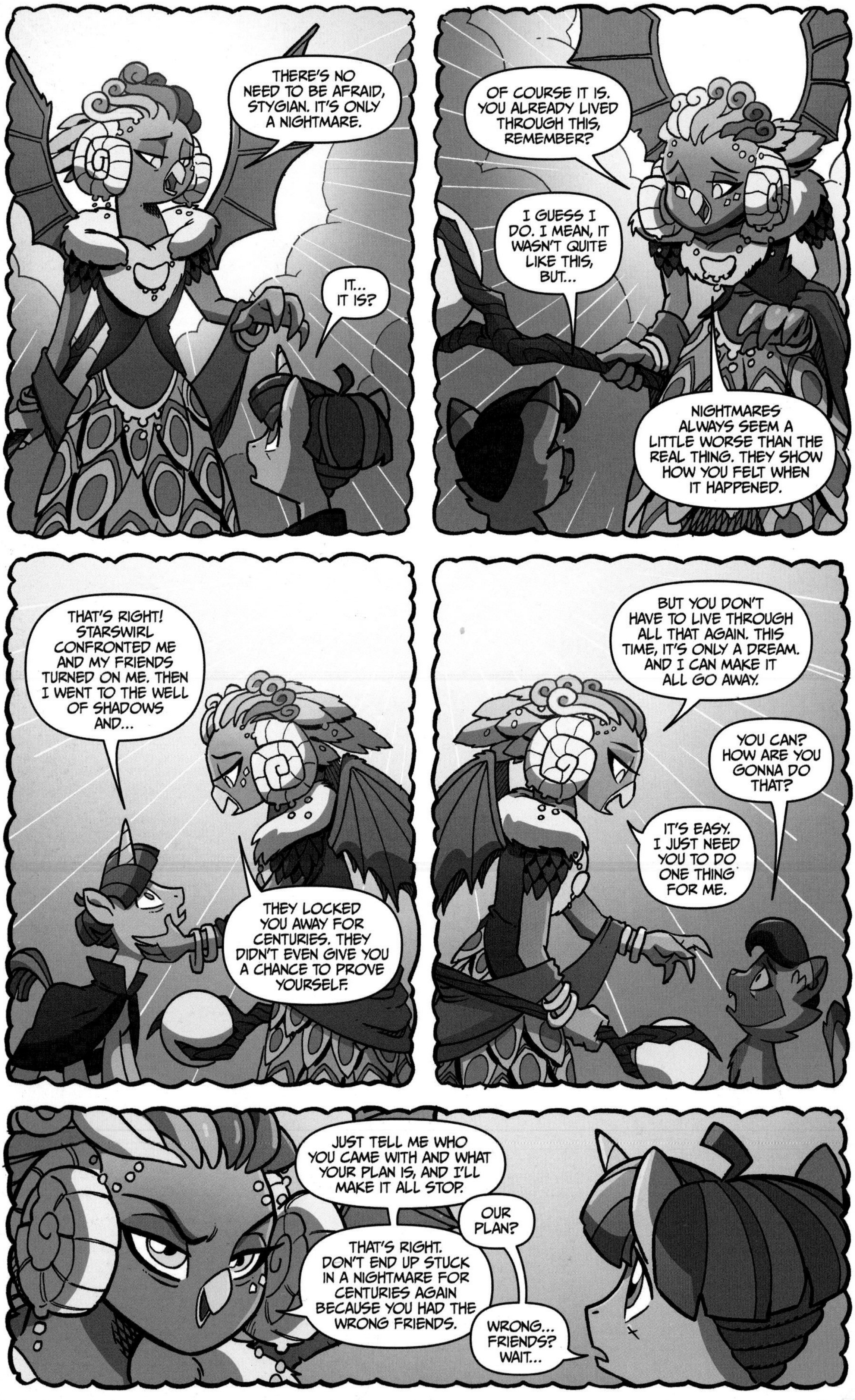
THERE'S NO NEED TO BE AFRAID, STYGIAN. IT'S ONLY A NIGHTMARE.
IT... IT IS?
OF COURSE IT IS. YOU ALREADY LIVED THROUGH THIS, REMEMBER?
I GUESS I DO. I MEAN, IT WASN'T QUITE LIKE THIS, BUT...
NIGHTMARES ALWAYS SEEM A LITTLE WORSE THAN THE REAL THING. THEY SHOW HOW YOU FELT WHEN IT HAPPENED.
THAT'S RIGHT! STARSWIRL CONFRONTED ME AND MY FRIENDS TURNED ON ME. THEN I WENT TO THE WELL OF SHADOWS AND...
THEY LOCKED YOU AWAY FOR CENTURIES. THEY DIDN'T EVEN GIVE YOU A CHANCE TO PROVE YOURSELF.
BUT YOU DON'T HAVE TO LIVE THROUGH ALL THAT AGAIN. THIS TIME, IT'S ONLY A DREAM. AND I CAN MAKE IT ALL GO AWAY.
YOU CAN? HOW ARE YOU GONNA DO THAT?
IT'S EASY. I JUST NEED YOU TO DO ONE THING FOR ME.
JUST TELL ME WHO YOU CAME WITH AND WHAT YOUR PLAN IS, AND I'LL MAKE IT ALL STOP.
OUR PLAN?
THAT'S RIGHT. DON'T END UP STUCK IN A NIGHTMARE FOR CENTURIES AGAIN BECAUSE YOU HAD THE WRONG FRIENDS.
WRONG... FRIENDS? WAIT...

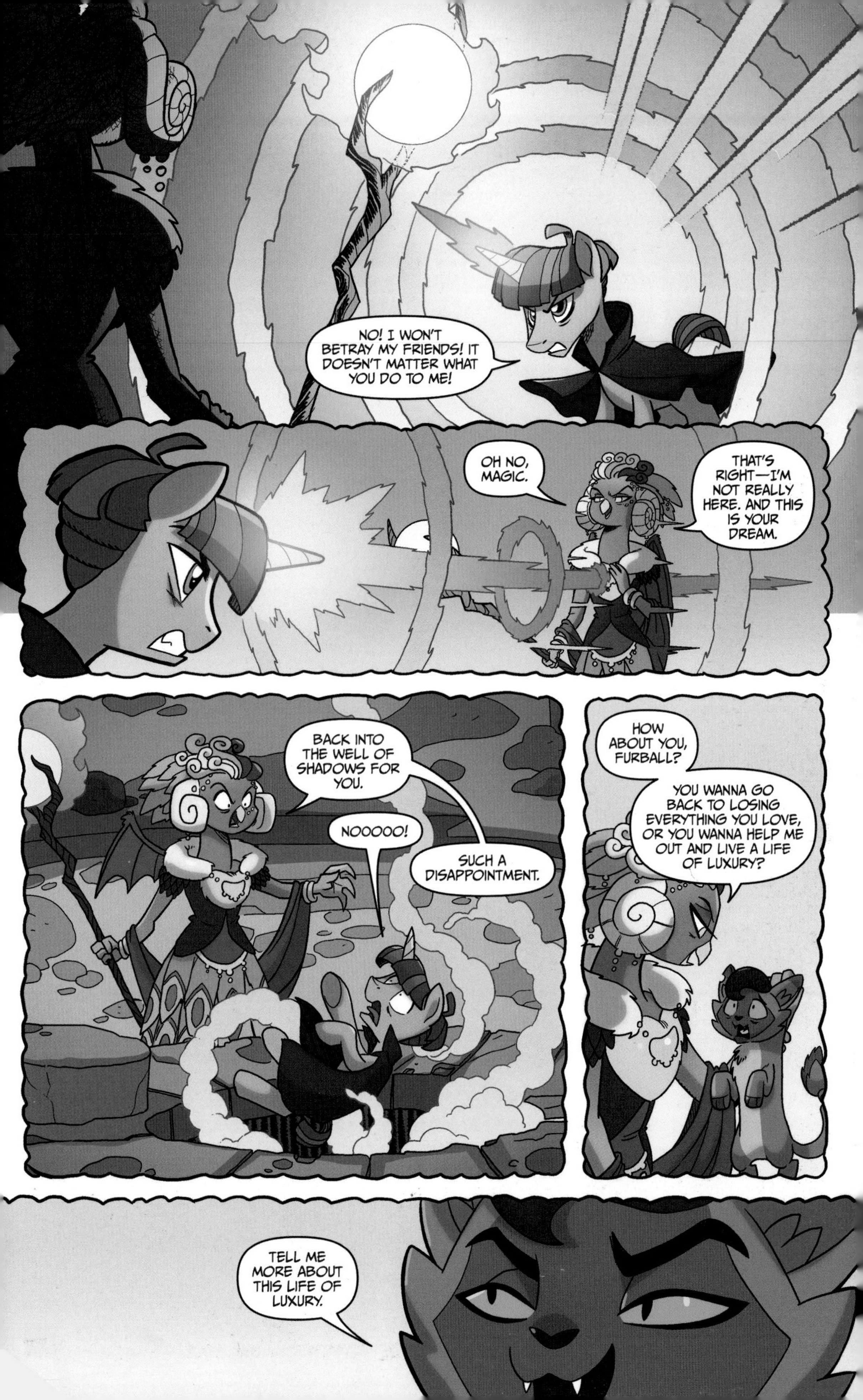
NO! I WON'T BETRAY MY FRIENDS! IT DOESN'T MATTER WHAT YOU DO TO ME!
OH NO, MAGIC.
THAT'S RIGHT—I'M NOT REALLY HERE. AND THIS IS YOUR DREAM.
BACK INTO THE WELL OF SHADOWS FOR YOU.
NOOOOO!
SUCH A DISAPPOINTMENT.
HOW ABOUT YOU, FURBALL?
YOU WANNA GO BACK TO LOSING EVERYTHING YOU LOVE, OR YOU WANNA HELP ME OUT AND LIVE A LIFE OF LUXURY?
TELL ME MORE ABOUT THIS LIFE OF LUXURY.

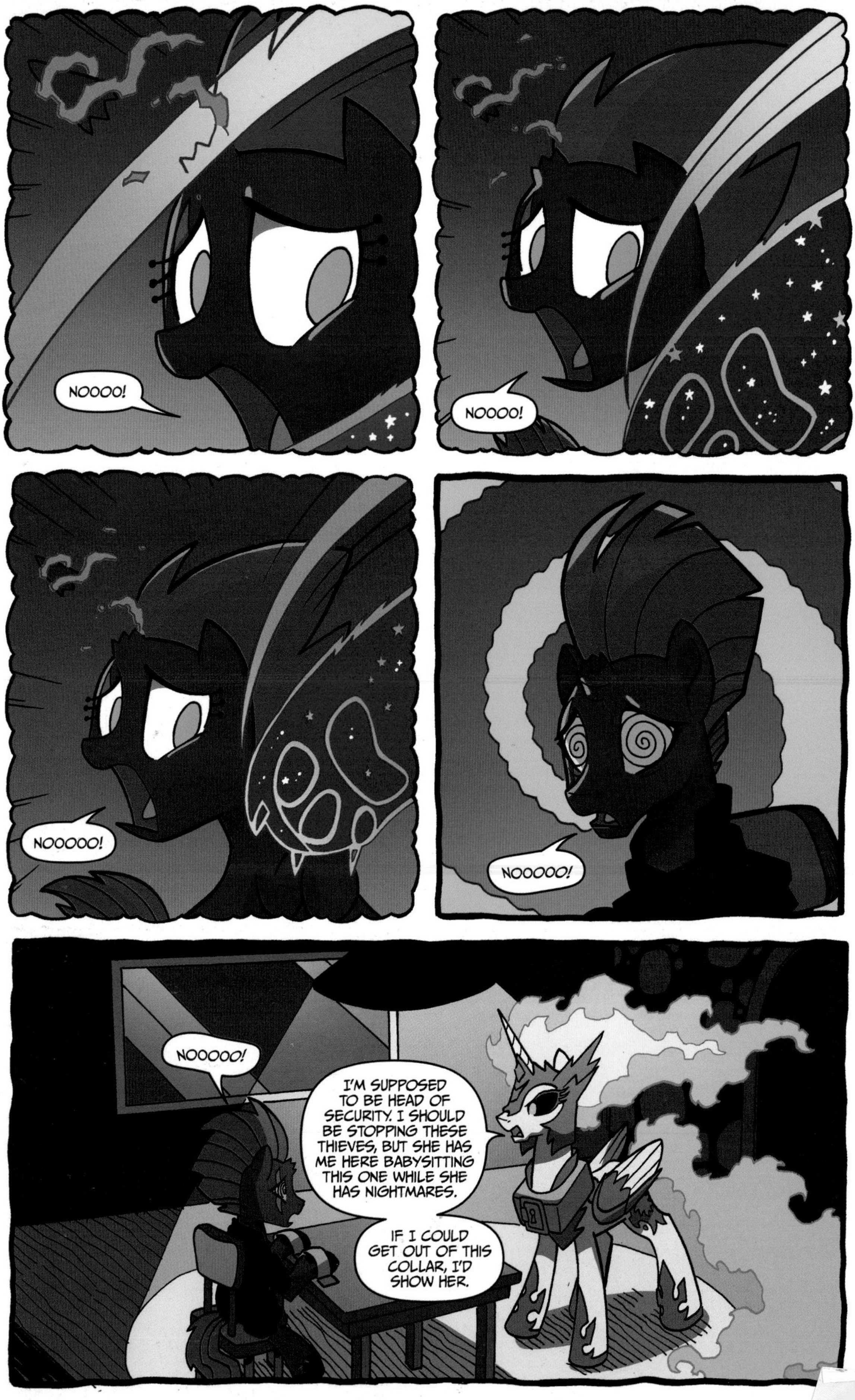
NOOOO!
NOOOO!
NOOOOO!
NOOOOO!
NOOOOO!
I'M SUPPOSED TO BE HEAD OF SECURITY. I SHOULD BE STOPPING THESE THIEVES, BUT SHE HAS ME HERE BABYSITTING THIS ONE WHILE SHE HAS NIGHTMARES.
IF I COULD GET OUT OF THIS COLLAR, I'D SHOW HER.

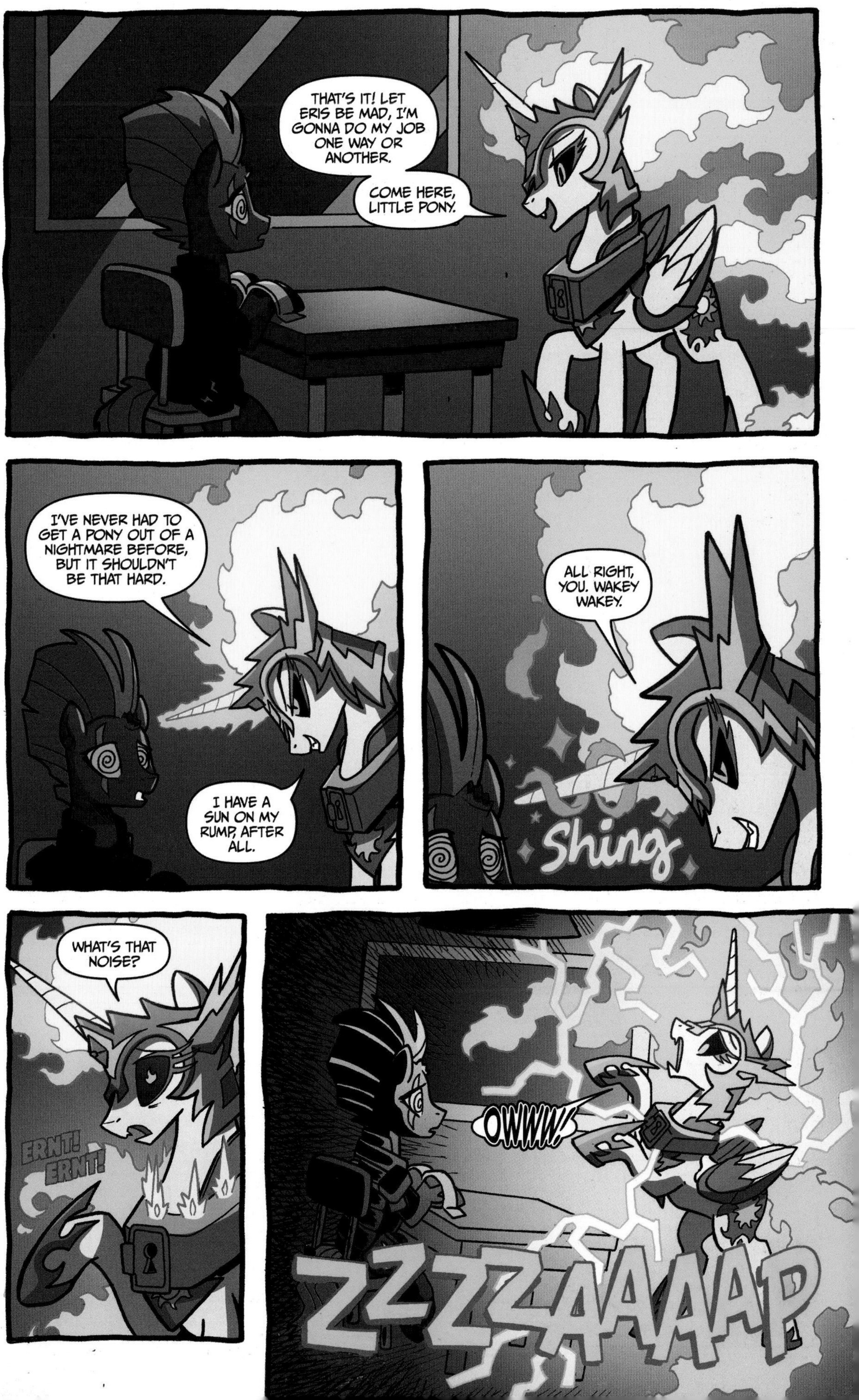
THAT'S IT! LET ERIS BE MAD, I'M GONNA DO MY JOB ONE WAY OR ANOTHER.
COME HERE, LITTLE PONY.
I'VE NEVER HAD TO GET A PONY OUT OF A NIGHTMARE BEFORE, BUT IT SHOULDN'T BE THAT HARD.
I HAVE A SUN ON MY RUMP, AFTER ALL.
ALL RIGHT, YOU. WAKEY WAKEY.
Shing
WHAT'S THAT NOISE?
ERNT! ERNT!
OWWW!
ZZZZAAAAP

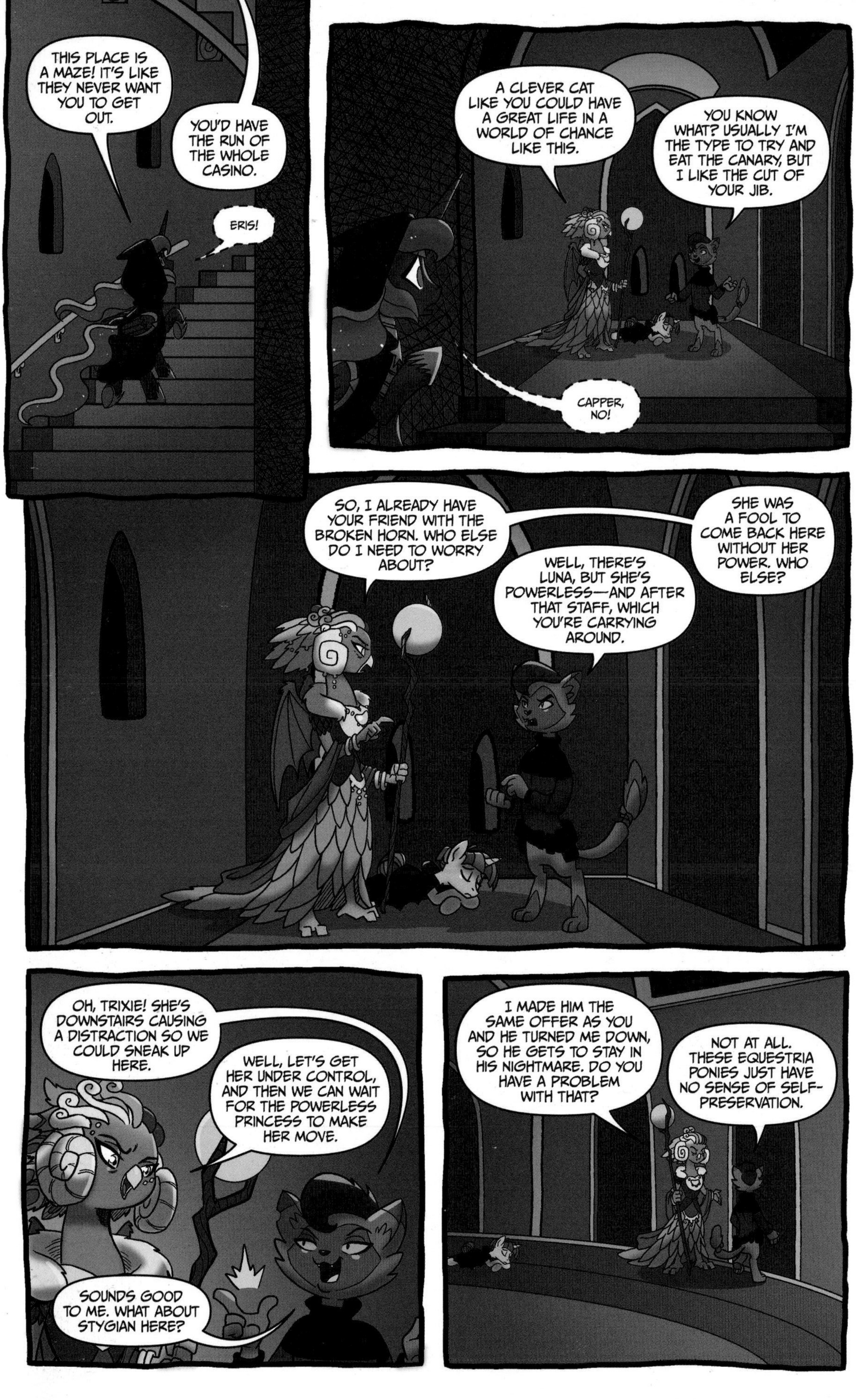
THIS PLACE IS A MAZE! IT'S LIKE THEY NEVER WANT YOU TO GET OUT.
YOU'D HAVE THE RUN OF THE WHOLE CASINO.
ERIS!
A CLEVER CAT LIKE YOU COULD HAVE A GREAT LIFE IN A WORLD OF CHANCE LIKE THIS.
YOU KNOW WHAT? USUALLY I'M THE TYPE TO TRY AND EAT THE CANARY, BUT I LIKE THE CUT OF YOUR JIB.
CAPPER, NO!
SO, I ALREADY HAVE YOUR FRIEND WITH THE BROKEN HORN. WHO ELSE DO I NEED TO WORRY ABOUT?
SHE WAS A FOOL TO COME BACK HERE WITHOUT HER POWER. WHO ELSE?
WELL, THERE'S LUNA, BUT SHE'S POWERLESS—AND AFTER THAT STAFF, WHICH YOU'RE CARRYING AROUND.
OH, TRIXIE! SHE'S DOWNSTAIRS CAUSING A DISTRACTION SO WE COULD SNEAK UP HERE.
WELL, LET'S GET HER UNDER CONTROL, AND THEN WE CAN WAIT FOR THE POWERLESS PRINCESS TO MAKE HER MOVE.
SOUNDS GOOD TO ME. WHAT ABOUT STYGIAN HERE?
I MADE HIM THE SAME OFFER AS YOU AND HE TURNED ME DOWN, SO HE GETS TO STAY IN HIS NIGHTMARE. DO YOU HAVE A PROBLEM WITH THAT?
NOT AT ALL. THESE EQUESTRIA PONIES JUST HAVE NO SENSE OF SELF-PRESERVATION.

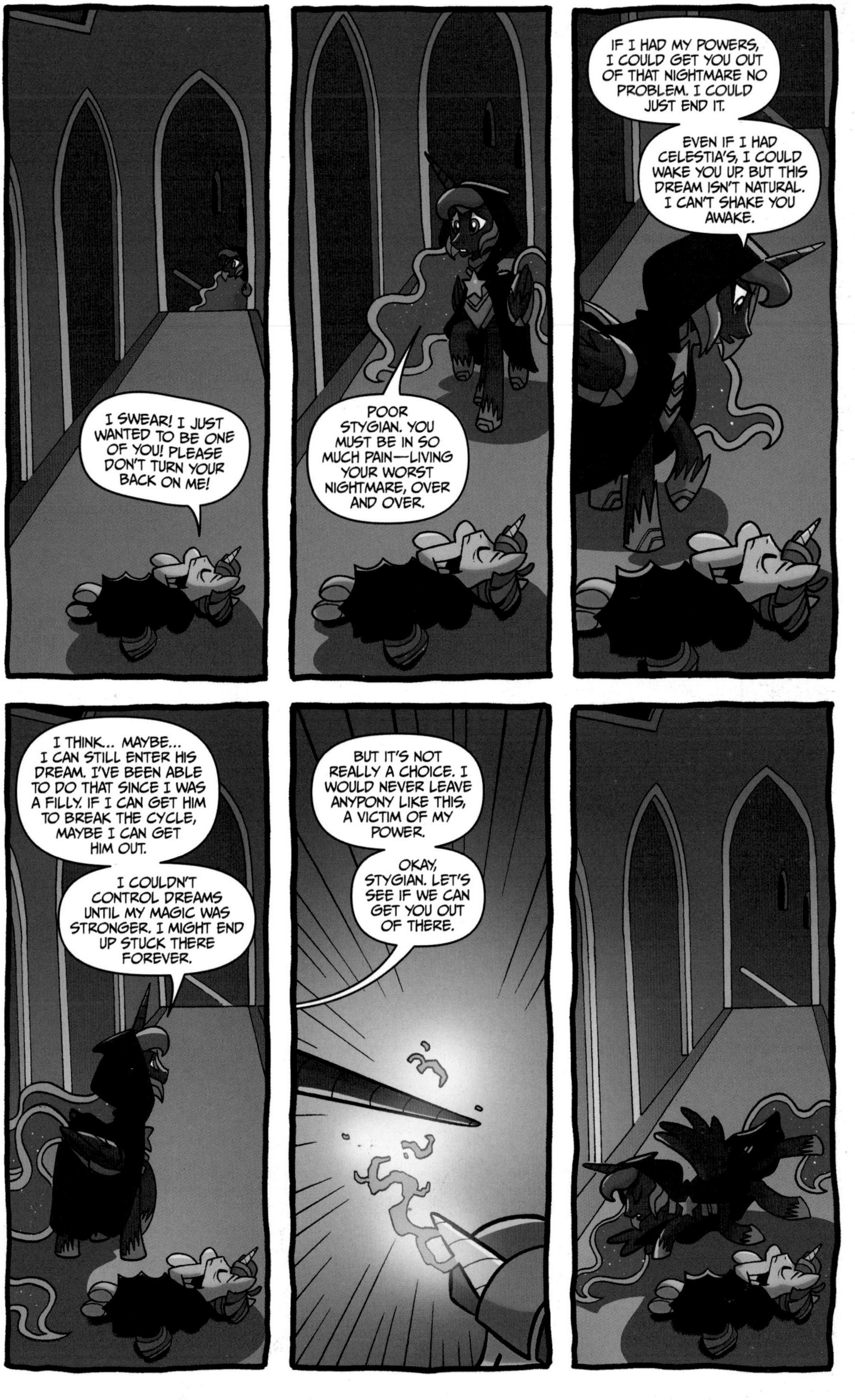
I SWEAR! I JUST WANTED TO BE ONE OF YOU! PLEASE DON'T TURN YOUR BACK ON ME!
POOR STYGIAN. YOU MUST BE IN SO MUCH PAIN—LIVING YOUR WORST NIGHTMARE, OVER AND OVER.
IF I HAD MY POWERS, I COULD GET YOU OUT OF THAT NIGHTMARE NO PROBLEM. I COULD JUST END IT.
EVEN IF I HAD CELESTIA'S, I COULD WAKE YOU UP. BUT THIS DREAM ISN'T NATURAL. I CAN'T SHAKE YOU AWAKE.
I THINK... MAYBE... I CAN STILL ENTER HIS DREAM. I'VE BEEN ABLE TO DO THAT SINCE I WAS A FILLY. IF I CAN GET HIM TO BREAK THE CYCLE, MAYBE I CAN GET HIM OUT.
I COULDN'T CONTROL DREAMS UNTIL MY MAGIC WAS STRONGER. I MIGHT END UP STUCK THERE FOREVER.
BUT IT'S NOT REALLY A CHOICE. I WOULD NEVER LEAVE ANYPONY LIKE THIS, A VICTIM OF MY POWER.
OKAY, STYGIAN. LET'S SEE IF WE CAN GET YOU OUT OF THERE.

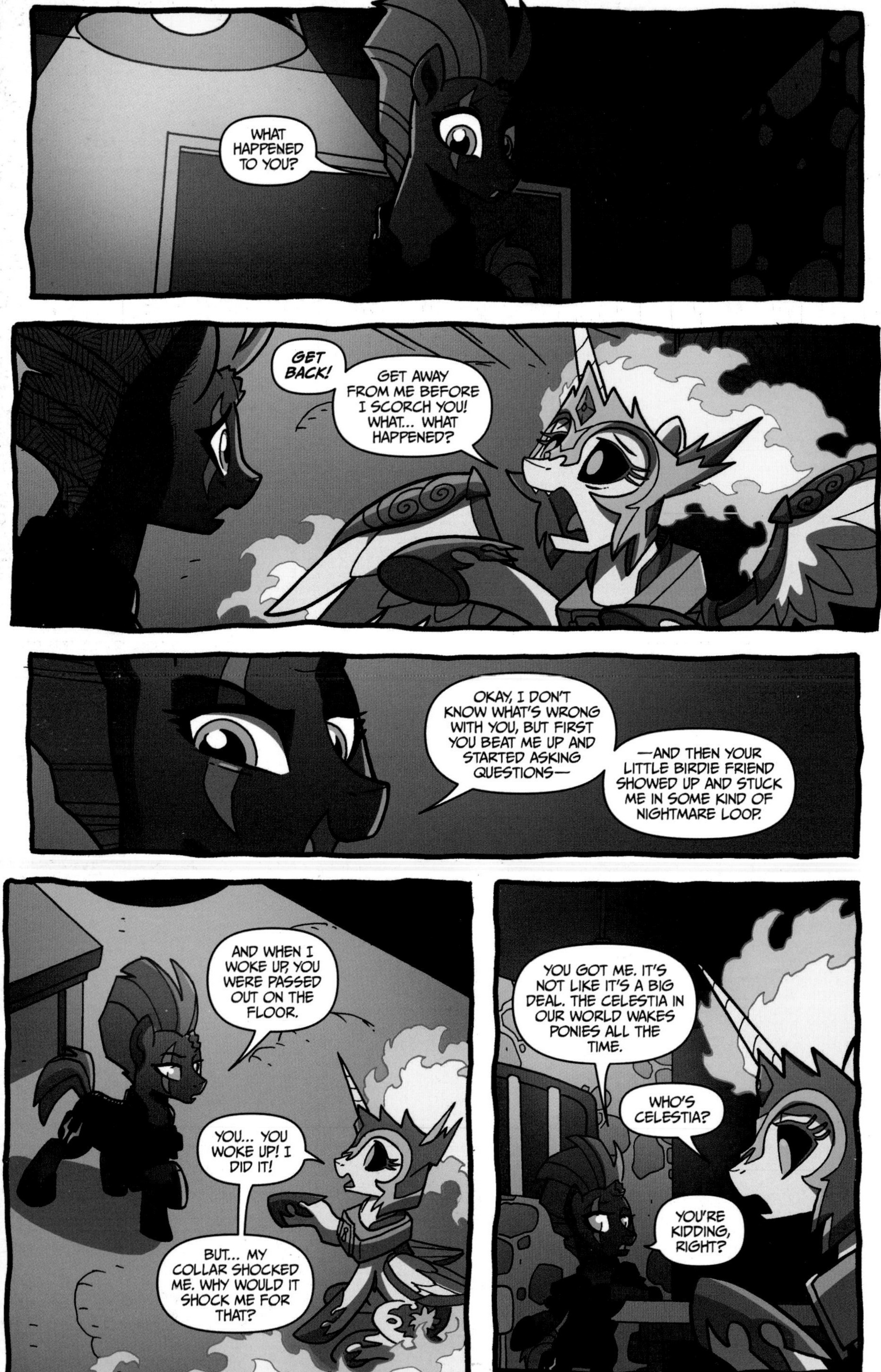
WHAT HAPPENED TO YOU?
GET BACK!
GET AWAY FROM ME BEFORE I SCORCH YOU! WHAT... WHAT HAPPENED?
OKAY, I DON'T KNOW WHAT'S WRONG WITH YOU, BUT FIRST YOU BEAT ME UP AND STARTED ASKING QUESTIONS—
—AND THEN YOUR LITTLE BIRDIE FRIEND SHOWED UP AND STUCK ME IN SOME KIND OF NIGHTMARE LOOP.
AND WHEN I WOKE UP, YOU WERE PASSED OUT ON THE FLOOR.
YOU... YOU WOKE UP! I DID IT!
BUT... MY COLLAR SHOCKED ME. WHY WOULD IT SHOCK ME FOR THAT?
YOU GOT ME. IT'S NOT LIKE IT'S A BIG DEAL. THE CELESTIA IN OUR WORLD WAKES PONIES ALL THE TIME.
WHO'S CELESTIA?
YOU'RE KIDDING, RIGHT?

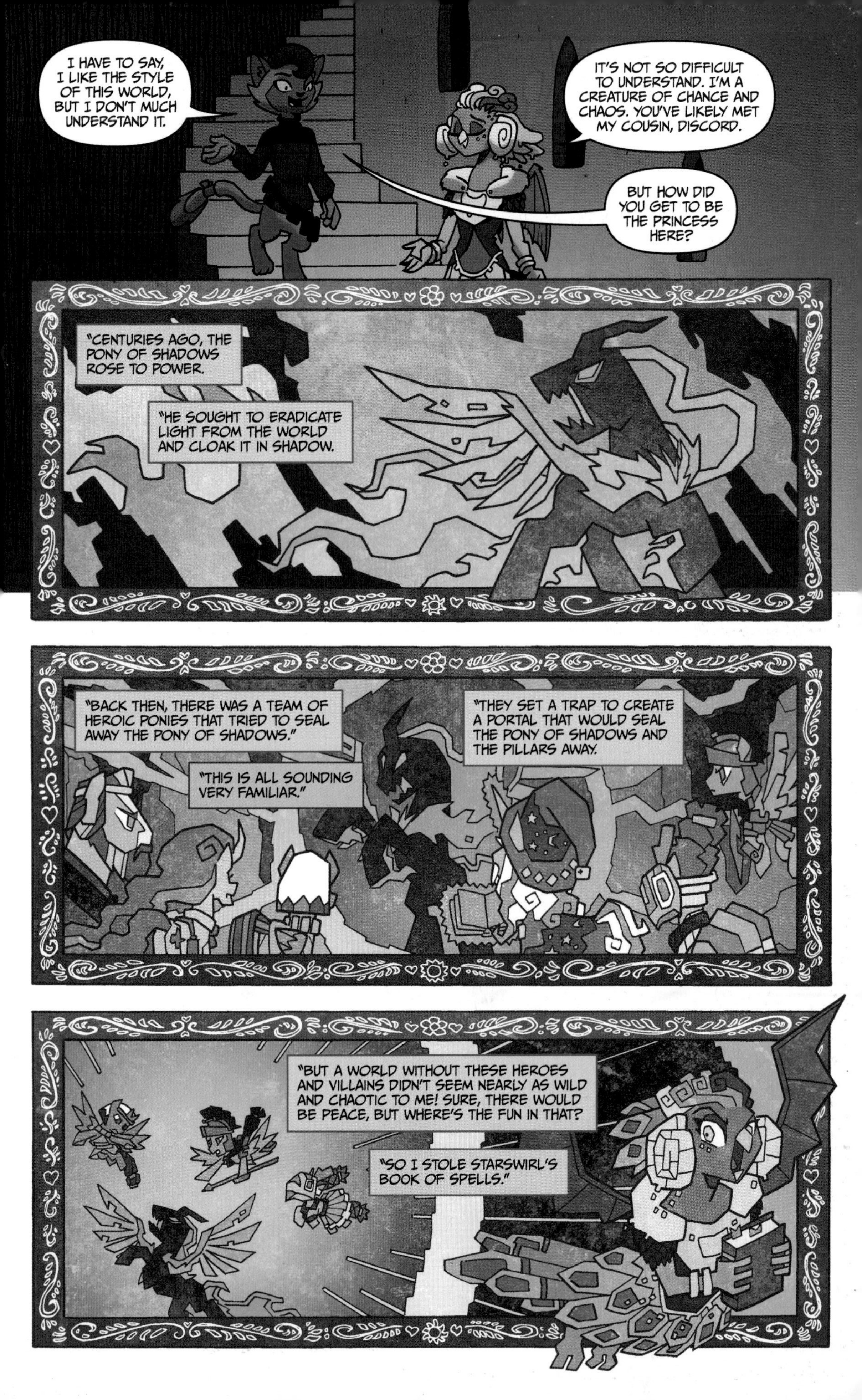
I HAVE TO SAY, I LIKE THE STYLE OF THIS WORLD, BUT I DON'T MUCH UNDERSTAND IT.
IT'S NOT SO DIFFICULT TO UNDERSTAND. I'M A CREATURE OF CHANCE AND CHAOS. YOU'VE LIKELY MET MY COUSIN, DISCORD.
BUT HOW DID YOU GET TO BE THE PRINCESS HERE?
"CENTURIES AGO, THE PONY OF SHADOWS ROSE TO POWER.
"HE SOUGHT TO ERADICATE LIGHT FROM THE WORLD AND CLOAK IT IN SHADOW.
"BACK THEN, THERE WAS A TEAM OF HEROIC PONIES THAT TRIED TO SEAL AWAY THE PONY OF SHADOWS."
"THIS IS ALL SOUNDING VERY FAMILIAR."
"THEY SET A TRAP TO CREATE A PORTAL THAT WOULD SEAL THE PONY OF SHADOWS AND THE PILLARS AWAY.
"BUT A WORLD WITHOUT THESE HEROES AND VILLAINS DIDN'T SEEM NEARLY AS WILD AND CHAOTIC TO ME! SURE, THERE WOULD BE PEACE, BUT WHERE'S THE FUN IN THAT?
"SO I STOLE STARSWIRL'S BOOK OF SPELLS."

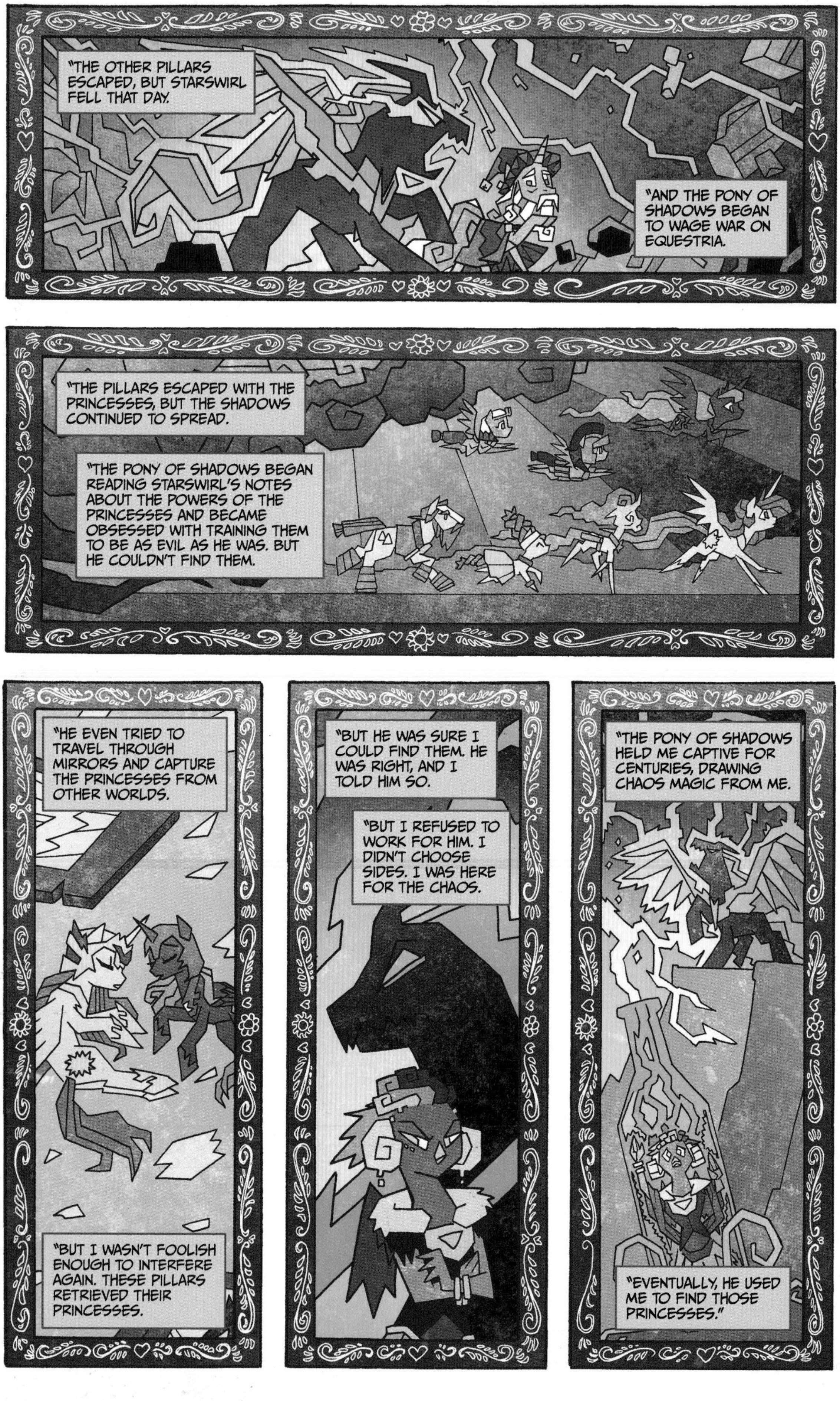
"THE OTHER PILLARS ESCAPED, BUT STARSWIRL FELL THAT DAY.
"AND THE PONY OF SHADOWS BEGAN TO WAGE WAR ON EQUESTRIA.
"THE PILLARS ESCAPED WITH THE PRINCESSES, BUT THE SHADOWS CONTINUED TO SPREAD.
"THE PONY OF SHADOWS BEGAN READING STARSWIRL'S NOTES ABOUT THE POWERS OF THE PRINCESSES AND BECAME OBSESSED WITH TRAINING THEM TO BE AS EVIL AS HE WAS. BUT HE COULDN'T FIND THEM.
"HE EVEN TRIED TO TRAVEL THROUGH MIRRORS AND CAPTURE THE PRINCESSES FROM OTHER WORLDS.
"BUT I WASN'T FOOLISH ENOUGH TO INTERFERE AGAIN. THESE PILLARS RETRIEVED THEIR PRINCESSES.
"BUT HE WAS SURE I COULD FIND THEM. HE WAS RIGHT, AND I TOLD HIM SO.
"BUT I REFUSED TO WORK FOR HIM. I DIDN'T CHOOSE SIDES. I WAS HERE FOR THE CHAOS.
"THE PONY OF SHADOWS HELD ME CAPTIVE FOR CENTURIES, DRAWING CHAOS MAGIC FROM ME.
"EVENTUALLY, HE USED ME TO FIND THOSE PRINCESSES."

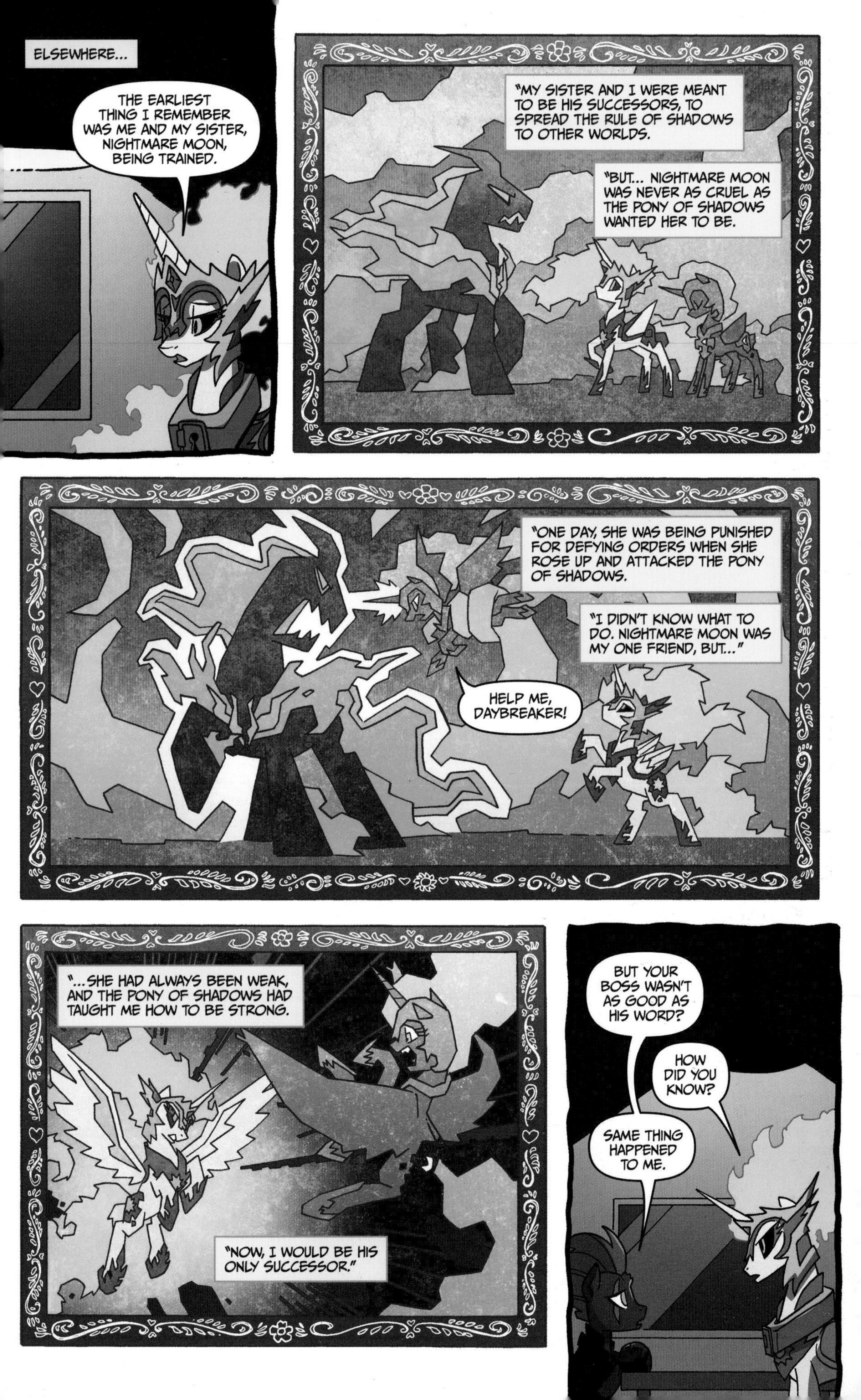
ELSEWHERE...
THE EARLIEST THING I REMEMBER WAS ME AND MY SISTER, NIGHTMARE MOON, BEING TRAINED.
"MY SISTER AND I WERE MEANT TO BE HIS SUCCESSORS, TO SPREAD THE RULE OF SHADOWS TO OTHER WORLDS.
"BUT... NIGHTMARE MOON WAS NEVER AS CRUEL AS THE PONY OF SHADOWS WANTED HER TO BE.
"ONE DAY, SHE WAS BEING PUNISHED FOR DEFYING ORDERS WHEN SHE ROSE UP AND ATTACKED THE PONY OF SHADOWS.
"I DIDN'T KNOW WHAT TO DO. NIGHTMARE MOON WAS MY ONE FRIEND, BUT..."
HELP ME, DAYBREAKER!
"...SHE HAD ALWAYS BEEN WEAK, AND THE PONY OF SHADOWS HAD TAUGHT ME HOW TO BE STRONG.
"NOW, I WOULD BE HIS ONLY SUCCESSOR."
BUT YOUR BOSS WASN'T AS GOOD AS HIS WORD?
HOW DID YOU KNOW?
SAME THING HAPPENED TO ME.

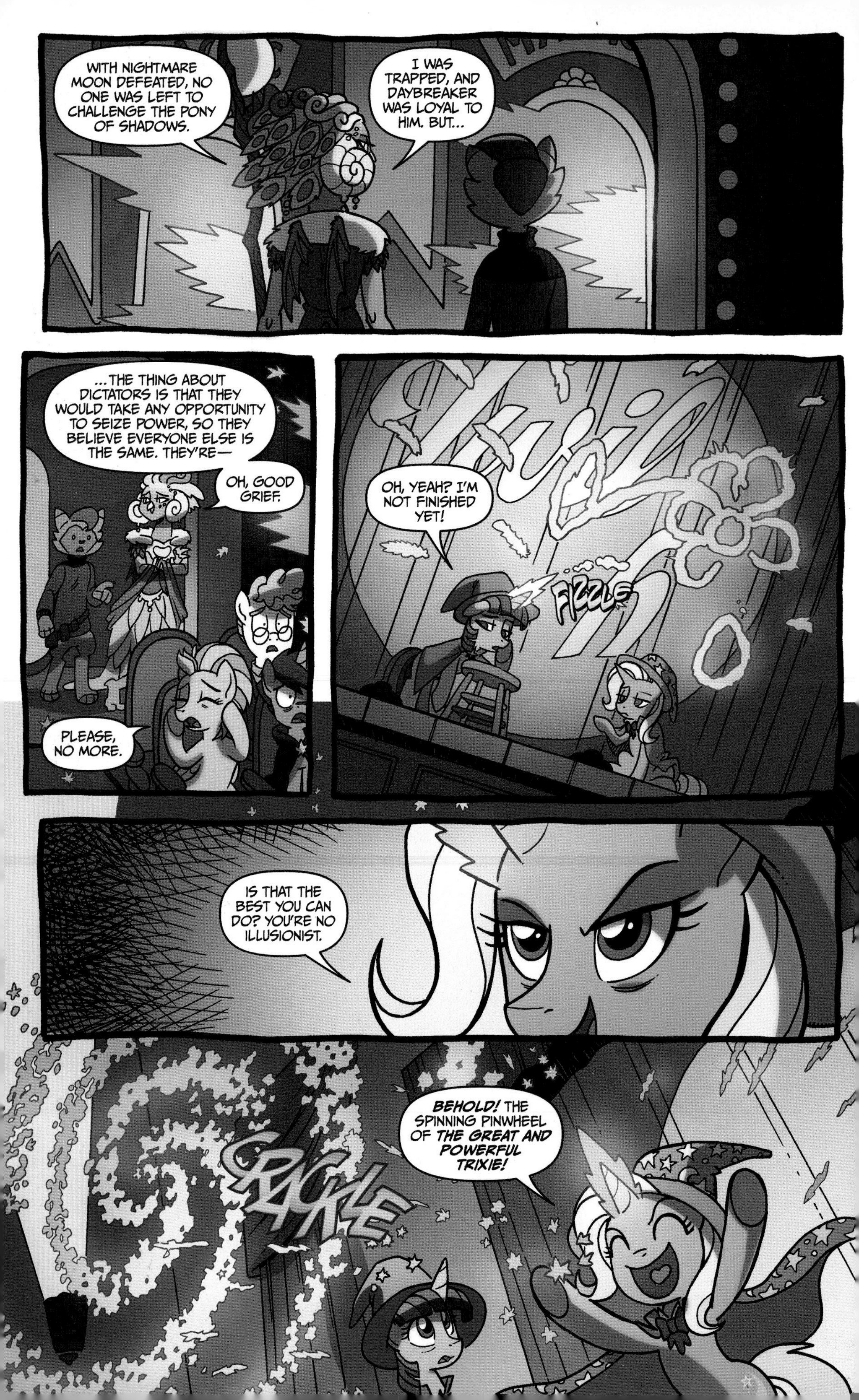
WITH NIGHTMARE MOON DEFEATED, NO ONE WAS LEFT TO CHALLENGE THE PONY OF SHADOWS.
I WAS TRAPPED, AND DAYBREAKER WAS LOYAL TO HIM. BUT...
...THE THING ABOUT DICTATORS IS THAT THEY WOULD TAKE ANY OPPORTUNITY TO SEIZE POWER, SO THEY BELIEVE EVERYONE ELSE IS THE SAME. THEY'RE—
OH, GOOD GRIEF.
PLEASE, NO MORE.
OH, YEAH? I'M NOT FINISHED YET!
FIZZLE
IS THAT THE BEST YOU CAN DO? YOU'RE NO ILLUSIONIST.
BEHOLD! THE SPINNING PINWHEEL OF ***THE GREAT AND POWERFUL TRIXIE!***
CRACKLE

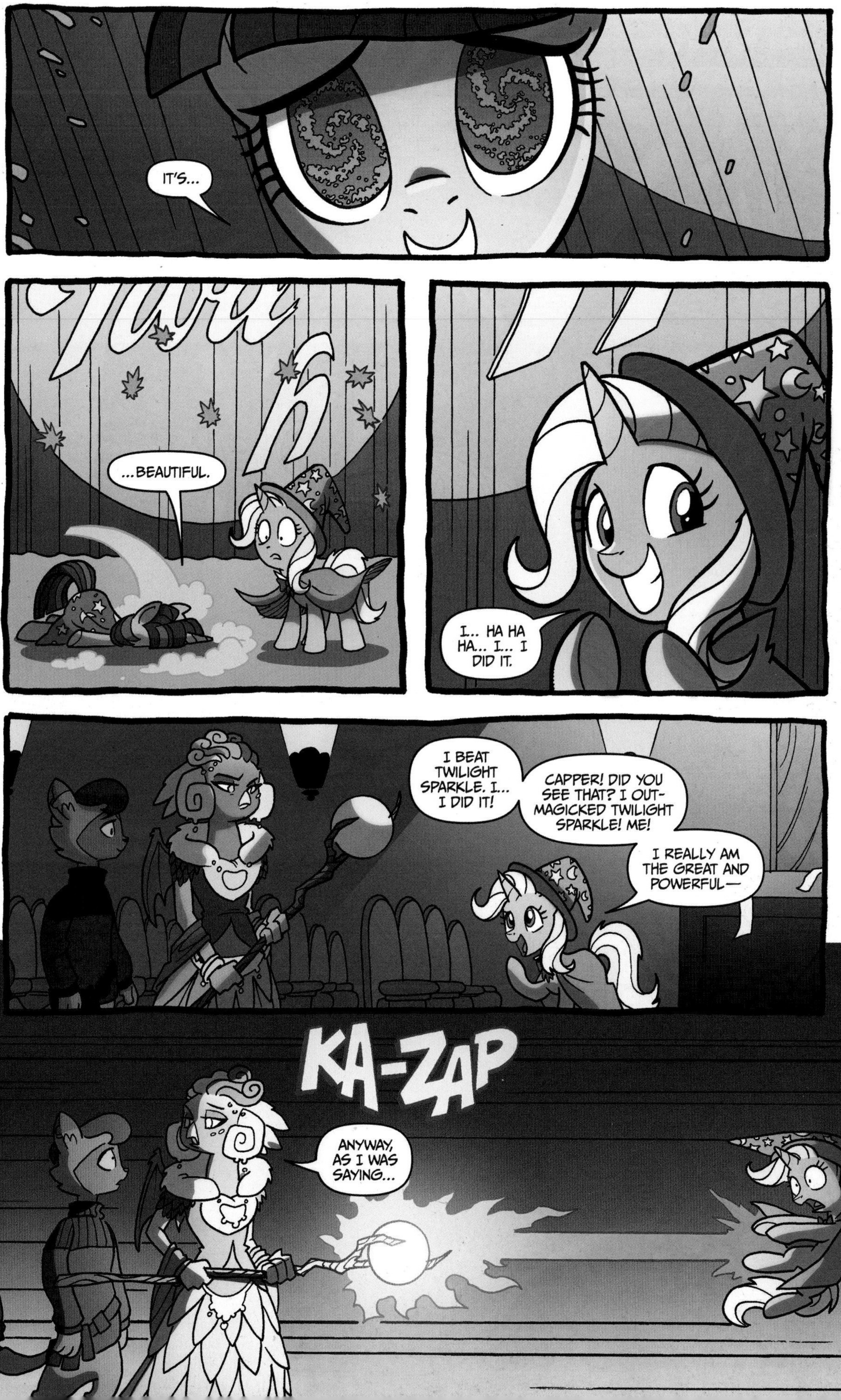

IT'S...
...BEAUTIFUL.
I... HA HA HA... I... I DID IT.
I BEAT TWILIGHT SPARKLE. I... I DID IT!
CAPPER! DID YOU SEE THAT? I OUT-MAGICKED TWILIGHT SPARKLE! ME!
I REALLY AM THE GREAT AND POWERFUL—
KA-ZAP
ANYWAY, AS I WAS SAYING...

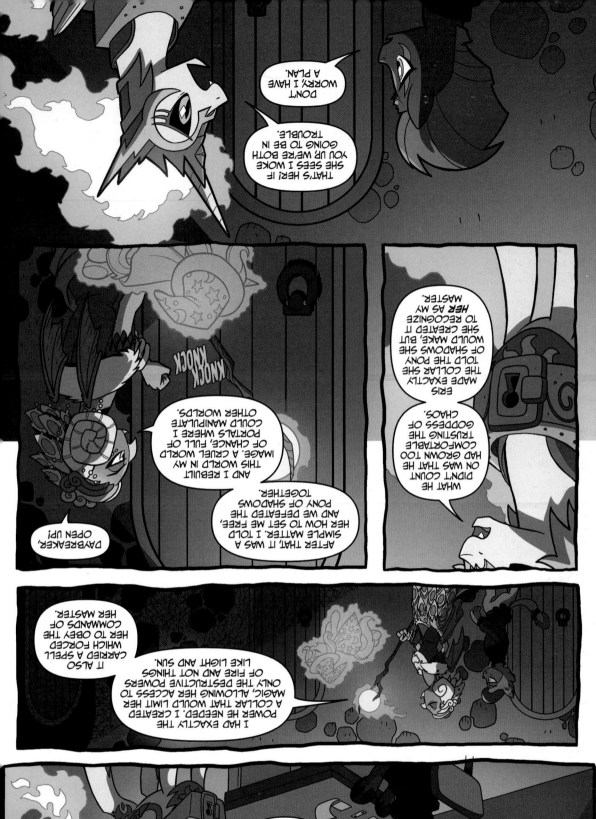

DON'T WORRY, I HAVE A PLAN.

THAT'S HER! IF SHE SEES I WOKE YOU UP, WE'RE BOTH GOING TO BE IN TROUBLE.

DAYBREAKER, OPEN UP!

KNOCK KNOCK

AFTER THAT, IT WAS A SIMPLE MATTER. I TOLD HER HOW TO SET ME FREE, AND WE DEFEATED THE PONY OF SHADOWS TOGETHER.

AND I REBUILT THIS WORLD IN MY IMAGE. A CRUEL WORLD OF CHANCE, FULL OF PORTALS WHERE I COULD MANIPULATE OTHER WORLDS.

ERIS MADE EXACTLY THE COLLAR SHE TOLD THE PONY OF SHADOWS SHE WOULD MAKE, BUT SHE CREATED IT TO RECOGNIZE HER AS MY MASTER.

WHAT HE DIDN'T COUNT ON WAS THAT HE HAD GROWN TOO COMFORTABLE TRUSTING THE GODDESS OF CHAOS.

I HAD EXACTLY THE POWER HE NEEDED. I CREATED A COLLAR THAT WOULD LIMIT HER MAGIC, ALLOWING HER ACCESS TO ONLY THE DESTRUCTIVE POWERS OF FIRE AND NOT THINGS LIKE LIGHT AND SUN.

IT ALSO CARRIED A SPELL WHICH FORCED HER TO OBEY THE COMMANDS OF HER MASTER.

THE PONY OF SHADOWS WANTED A WAY TO CONTAIN MY POWERS, BUT HE DIDN'T THINK HE COULD DO IT WITH HIS OWN MAGIC.

SO HE TURNED TO ERIS.

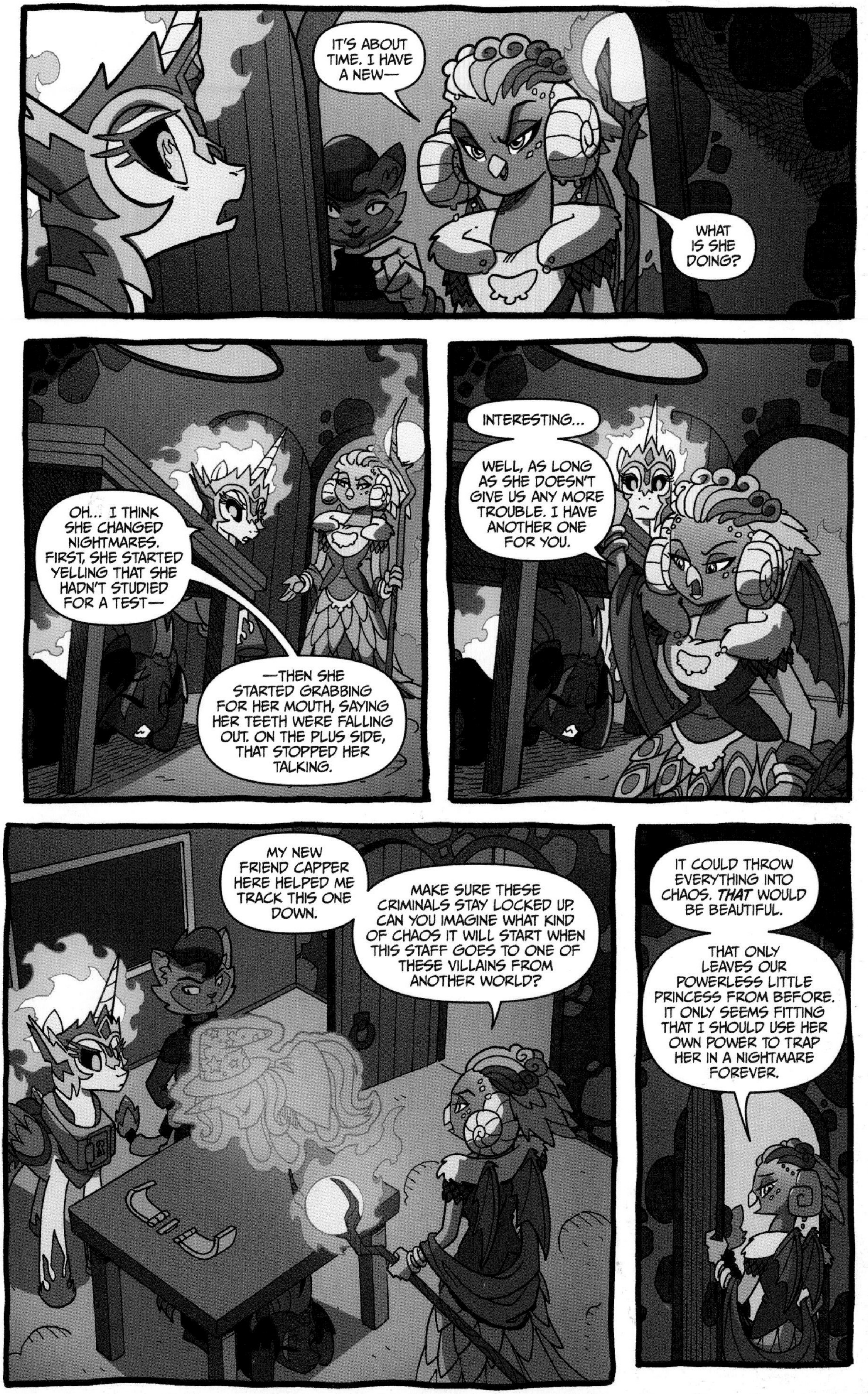
IT'S ABOUT TIME. I HAVE A NEW—
WHAT IS SHE DOING?
OH... I THINK SHE CHANGED NIGHTMARES. FIRST, SHE STARTED YELLING THAT SHE HADN'T STUDIED FOR A TEST—
—THEN SHE STARTED GRABBING FOR HER MOUTH, SAYING HER TEETH WERE FALLING OUT. ON THE PLUS SIDE, THAT STOPPED HER TALKING.
INTERESTING...
WELL, AS LONG AS SHE DOESN'T GIVE US ANY MORE TROUBLE. I HAVE ANOTHER ONE FOR YOU.
MY NEW FRIEND CAPPER HERE HELPED ME TRACK THIS ONE DOWN.
MAKE SURE THESE CRIMINALS STAY LOCKED UP. CAN YOU IMAGINE WHAT KIND OF CHAOS IT WILL START WHEN THIS STAFF GOES TO ONE OF THESE VILLAINS FROM ANOTHER WORLD?
IT COULD THROW EVERYTHING INTO CHAOS. THAT WOULD BE BEAUTIFUL.
THAT ONLY LEAVES OUR POWERLESS LITTLE PRINCESS FROM BEFORE. IT ONLY SEEMS FITTING THAT I SHOULD USE HER OWN POWER TO TRAP HER IN A NIGHTMARE FOREVER.

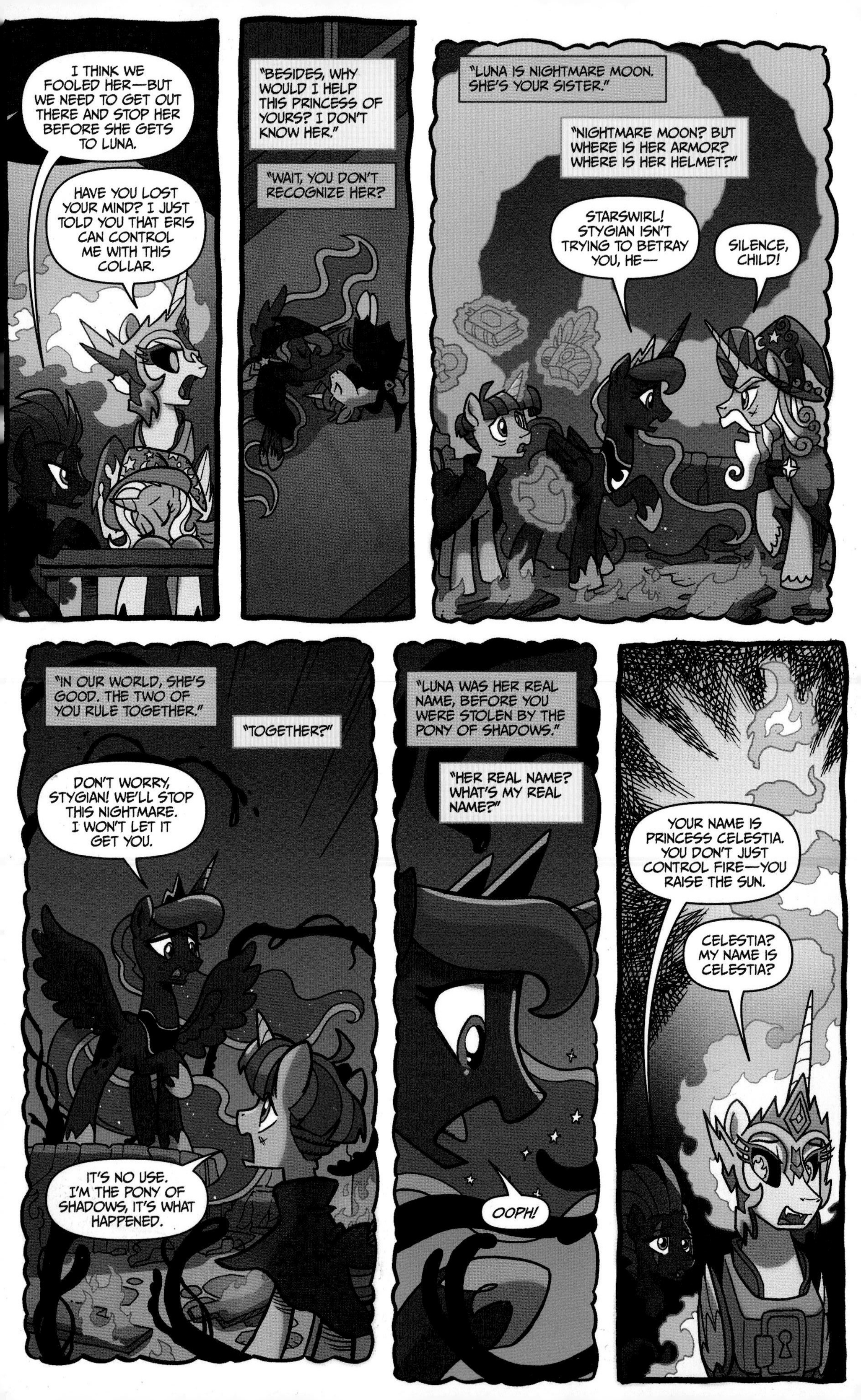
I THINK WE FOOLED HER—BUT WE NEED TO GET OUT THERE AND STOP HER BEFORE SHE GETS TO LUNA.
HAVE YOU LOST YOUR MIND? I JUST TOLD YOU THAT ERIS CAN CONTROL ME WITH THIS COLLAR.
"BESIDES, WHY WOULD I HELP THIS PRINCESS OF YOURS? I DON'T KNOW HER."
"WAIT, YOU DON'T RECOGNIZE HER?
"LUNA IS NIGHTMARE MOON. SHE'S YOUR SISTER."
"NIGHTMARE MOON? BUT WHERE IS HER ARMOR? WHERE IS HER HELMET?"
STARSWIRL! STYGIAN ISN'T TRYING TO BETRAY YOU, HE—
SILENCE, CHILD!
"IN OUR WORLD, SHE'S GOOD. THE TWO OF YOU RULE TOGETHER."
"TOGETHER?"
DON'T WORRY, STYGIAN! WE'LL STOP THIS NIGHTMARE. I WON'T LET IT GET YOU.
IT'S NO USE. I'M THE PONY OF SHADOWS, IT'S WHAT HAPPENED.
"LUNA WAS HER REAL NAME, BEFORE YOU WERE STOLEN BY THE PONY OF SHADOWS."
"HER REAL NAME? WHAT'S MY REAL NAME?"
OOPH!
YOUR NAME IS PRINCESS CELESTIA. YOU DON'T JUST CONTROL FIRE—YOU RAISE THE SUN.
CELESTIA? MY NAME IS CELESTIA?

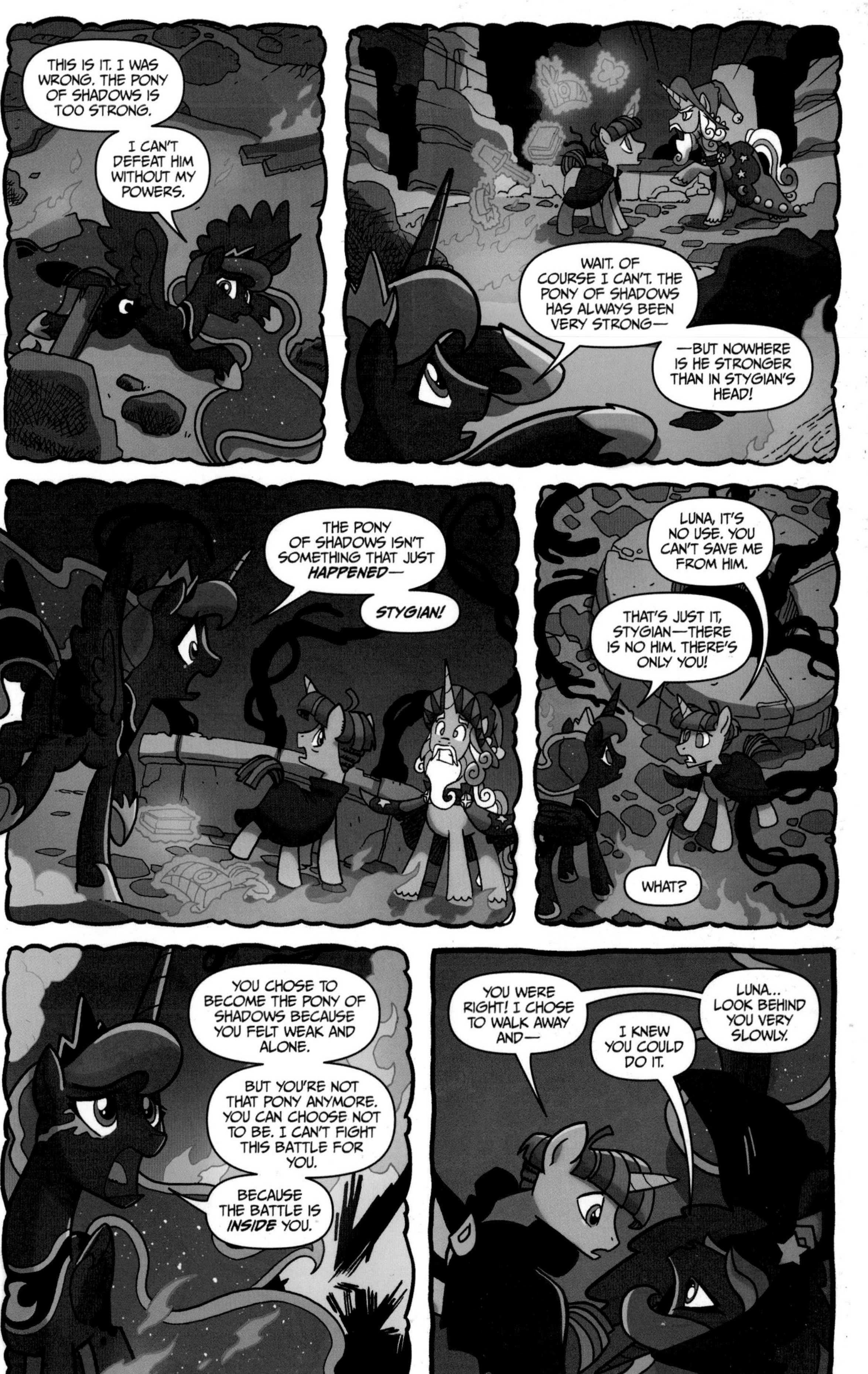
THIS IS IT. I WAS WRONG. THE PONY OF SHADOWS IS TOO STRONG.
I CAN'T DEFEAT HIM WITHOUT MY POWERS.
WAIT. OF COURSE I CAN'T. THE PONY OF SHADOWS HAS ALWAYS BEEN VERY STRONG—
—BUT NOWHERE IS HE STRONGER THAN IN STYGIAN'S HEAD!
THE PONY OF SHADOWS ISN'T SOMETHING THAT JUST *HAPPENED*—
STYGIAN!
LUNA, IT'S NO USE. YOU CAN'T SAVE ME FROM HIM.
THAT'S JUST IT, STYGIAN—THERE IS NO HIM. THERE'S ONLY YOU!
WHAT?
YOU CHOSE TO BECOME THE PONY OF SHADOWS BECAUSE YOU FELT WEAK AND ALONE.
BUT YOU'RE NOT THAT PONY ANYMORE. YOU CAN CHOOSE NOT TO BE. I CAN'T FIGHT THIS BATTLE FOR YOU.
BECAUSE THE BATTLE IS *INSIDE* YOU.
YOU WERE RIGHT! I CHOSE TO WALK AWAY AND—
I KNEW YOU COULD DO IT.
LUNA... LOOK BEHIND YOU VERY SLOWLY.

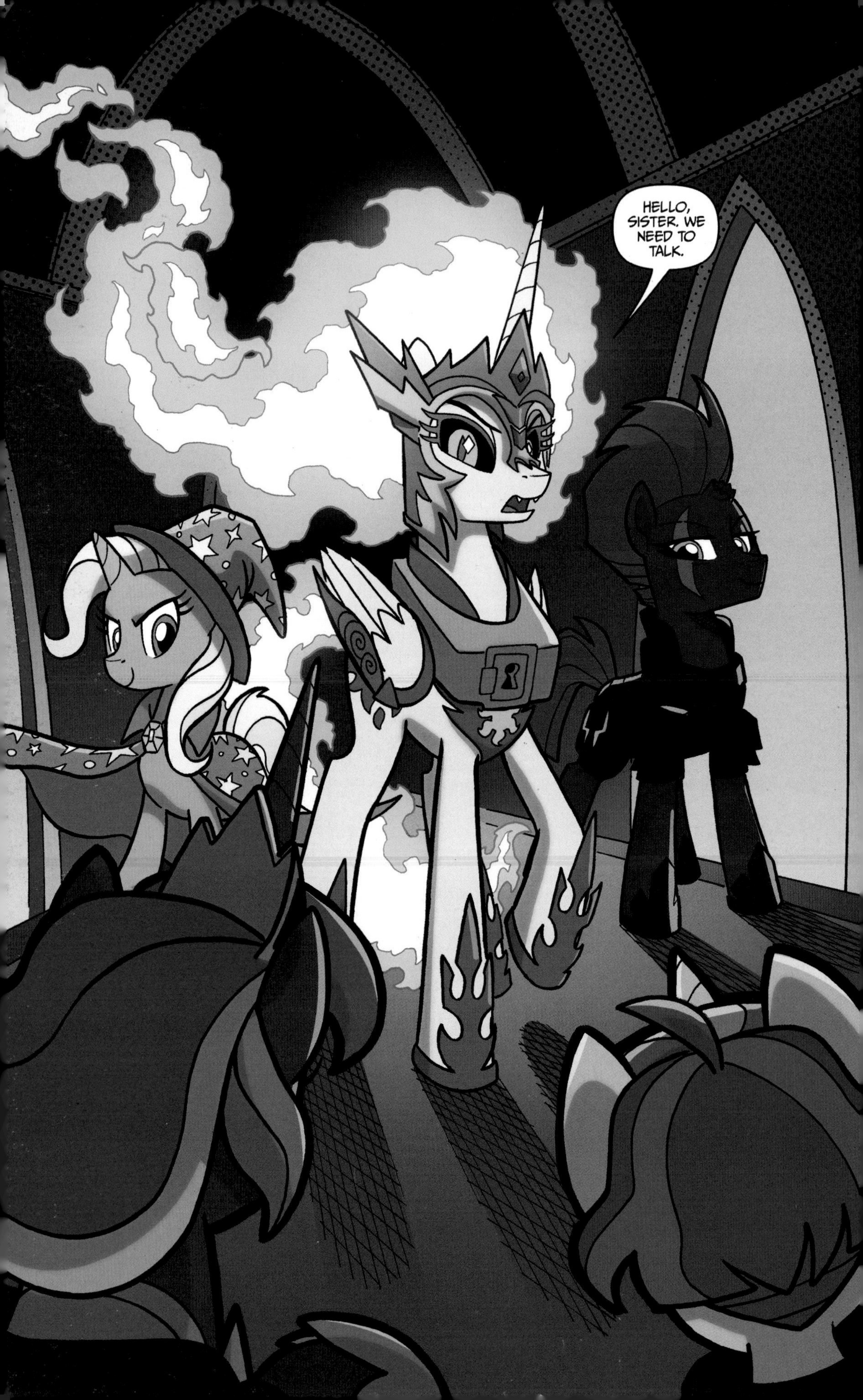
HELLO, SISTER. WE NEED TO TALK.

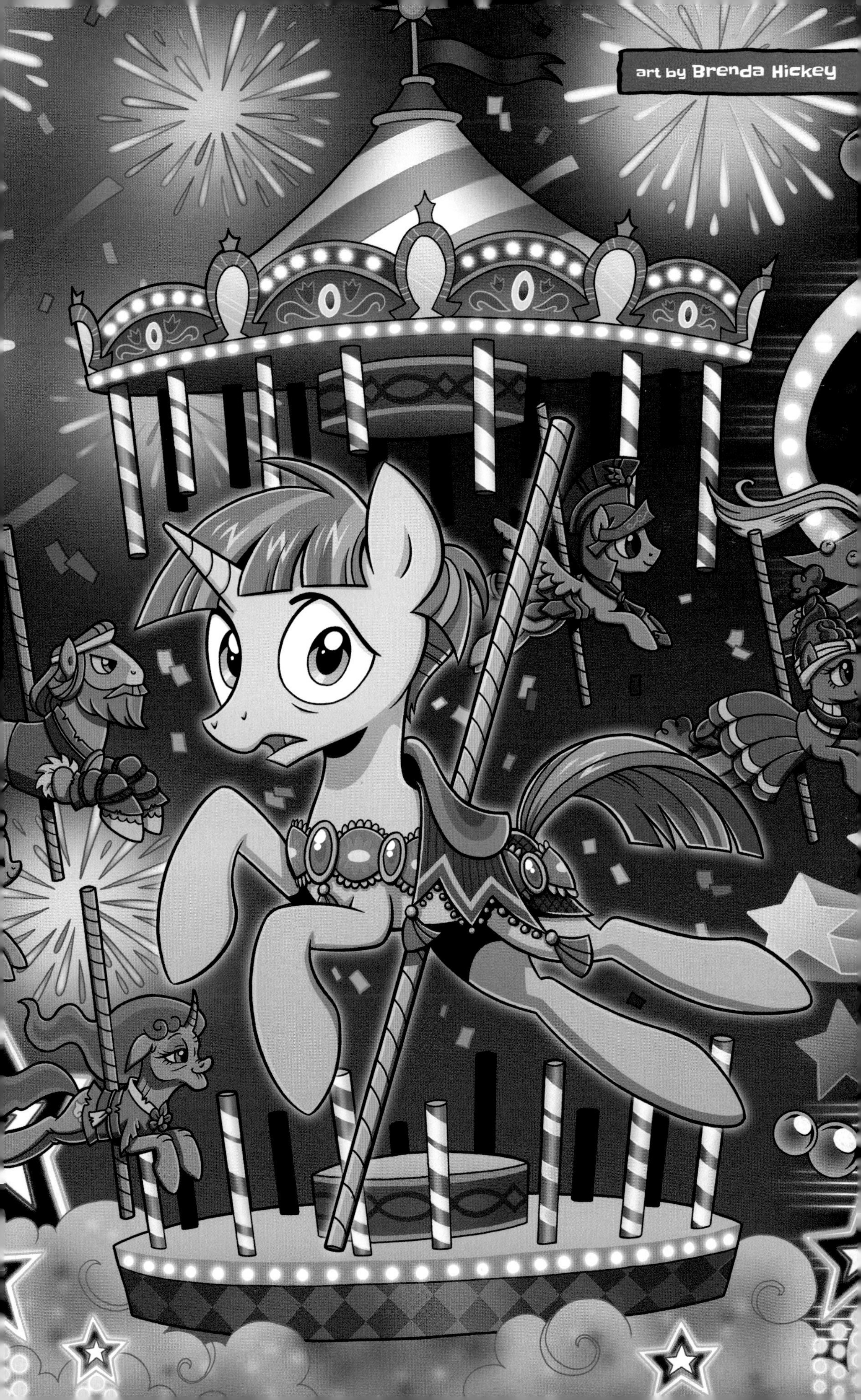
art by Brenda Hickey

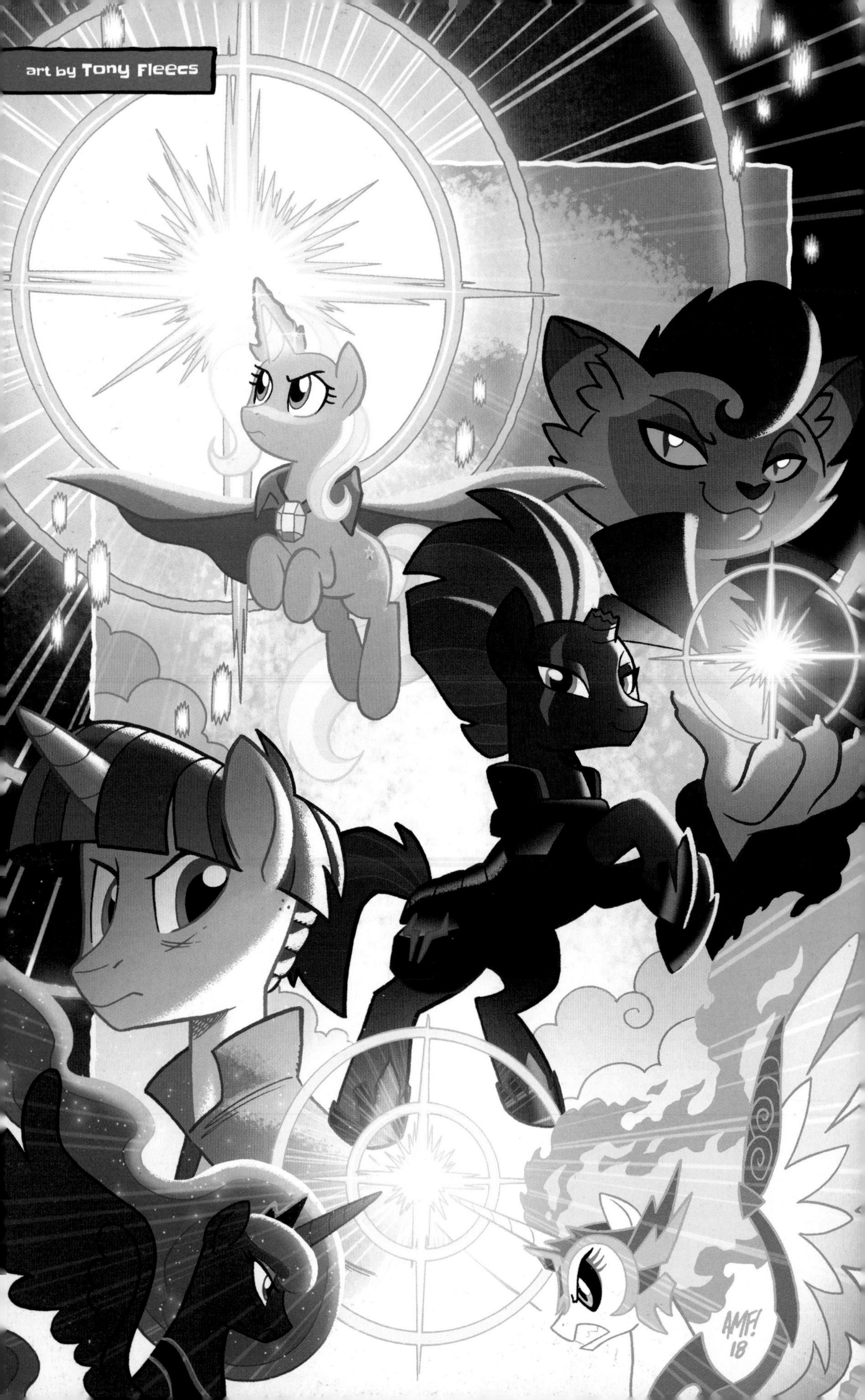
art by Tony Fleecs
AMF! 18

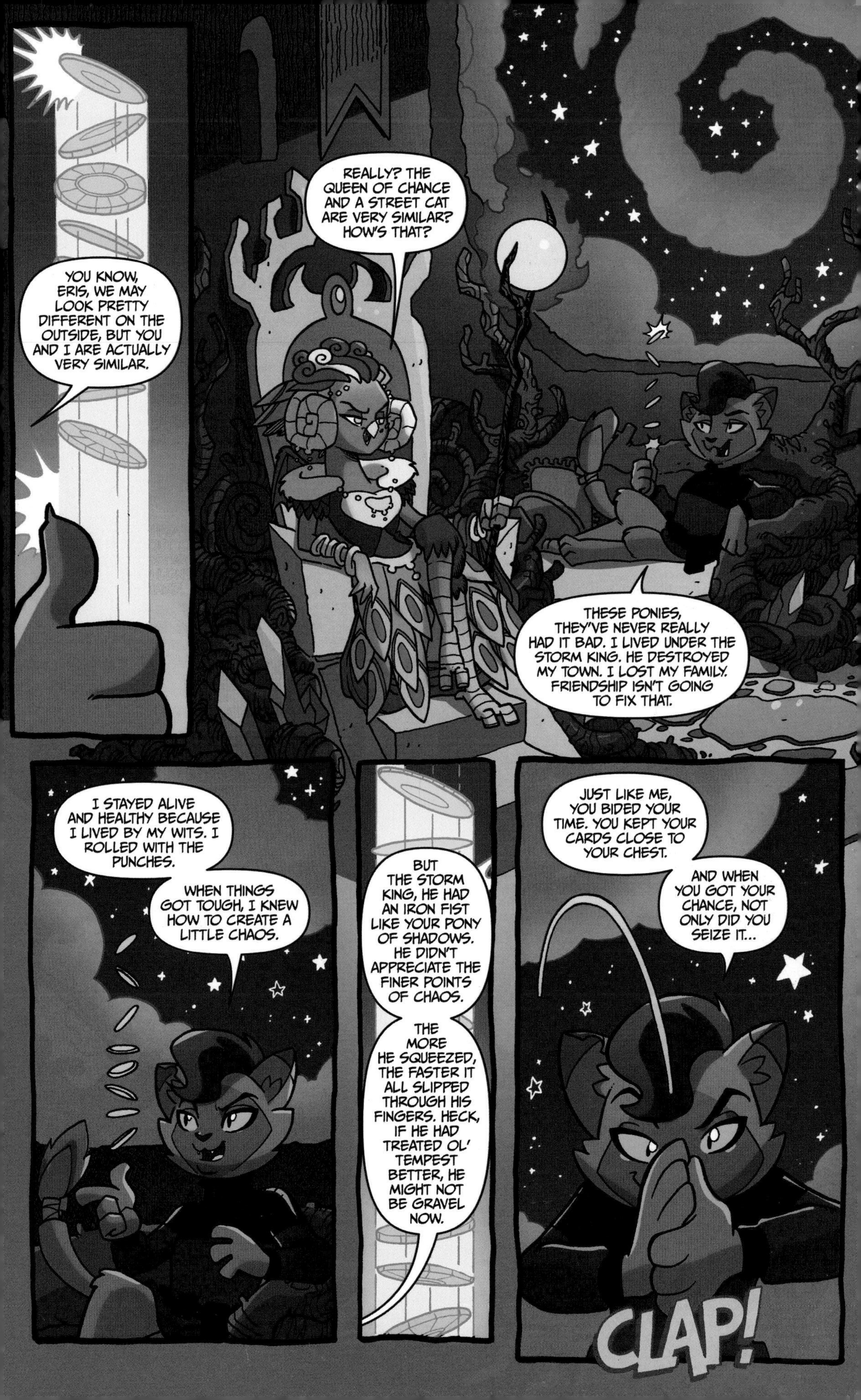
YOU KNOW, ERIS, WE MAY LOOK PRETTY DIFFERENT ON THE OUTSIDE, BUT YOU AND I ARE ACTUALLY VERY SIMILAR.
REALLY? THE QUEEN OF CHANCE AND A STREET CAT ARE VERY SIMILAR? HOW'S THAT?
THESE PONIES, THEY'VE NEVER REALLY HAD IT BAD. I LIVED UNDER THE STORM KING. HE DESTROYED MY TOWN. I LOST MY FAMILY. FRIENDSHIP ISN'T GOING TO FIX THAT.
I STAYED ALIVE AND HEALTHY BECAUSE I LIVED BY MY WITS. I ROLLED WITH THE PUNCHES.
WHEN THINGS GOT TOUGH, I KNEW HOW TO CREATE A LITTLE CHAOS.
BUT THE STORM KING, HE HAD AN IRON FIST LIKE YOUR PONY OF SHADOWS. HE DIDN'T APPRECIATE THE FINER POINTS OF CHAOS.
THE MORE HE SQUEEZED, THE FASTER IT ALL SLIPPED THROUGH HIS FINGERS. HECK, IF HE HAD TREATED OL' TEMPEST BETTER, HE MIGHT NOT BE GRAVEL NOW.
JUST LIKE ME, YOU BIDED YOUR TIME. YOU KEPT YOUR CARDS CLOSE TO YOUR CHEST.
AND WHEN YOU GOT YOUR CHANCE, NOT ONLY DID YOU SEIZE IT...
CLAP!

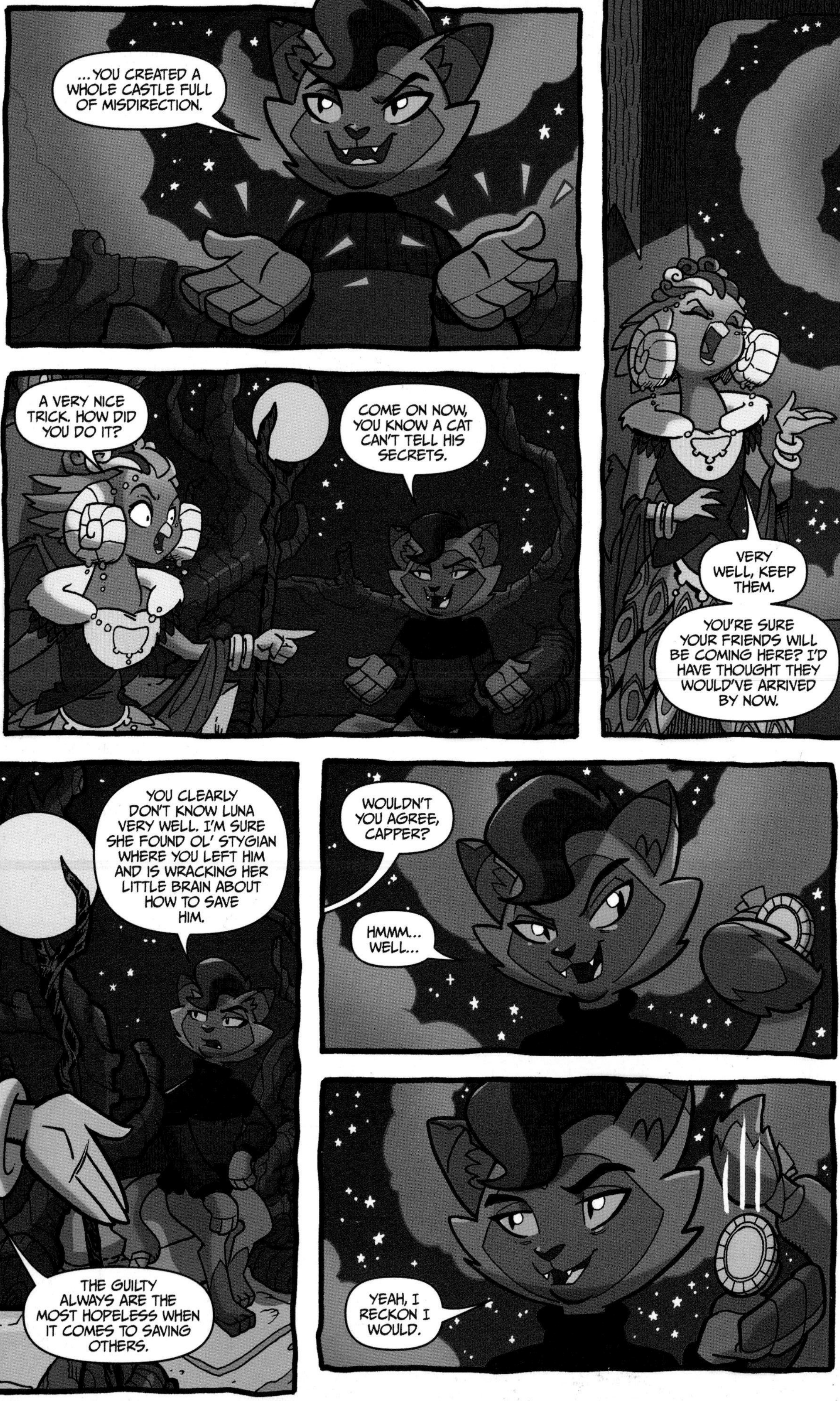
...YOU CREATED A WHOLE CASTLE FULL OF MISDIRECTION.
A VERY NICE TRICK. HOW DID YOU DO IT?
COME ON NOW, YOU KNOW A CAT CAN'T TELL HIS SECRETS.
VERY WELL, KEEP THEM.
YOU'RE SURE YOUR FRIENDS WILL BE COMING HERE? I'D HAVE THOUGHT THEY WOULD'VE ARRIVED BY NOW.
YOU CLEARLY DON'T KNOW LUNA VERY WELL. I'M SURE SHE FOUND OL' STYGIAN WHERE YOU LEFT HIM AND IS WRACKING HER LITTLE BRAIN ABOUT HOW TO SAVE HIM.
THE GUILTY ALWAYS ARE THE MOST HOPELESS WHEN IT COMES TO SAVING OTHERS.
WOULDN'T YOU AGREE, CAPPER?
HMMM... WELL...
YEAH, I RECKON I WOULD.

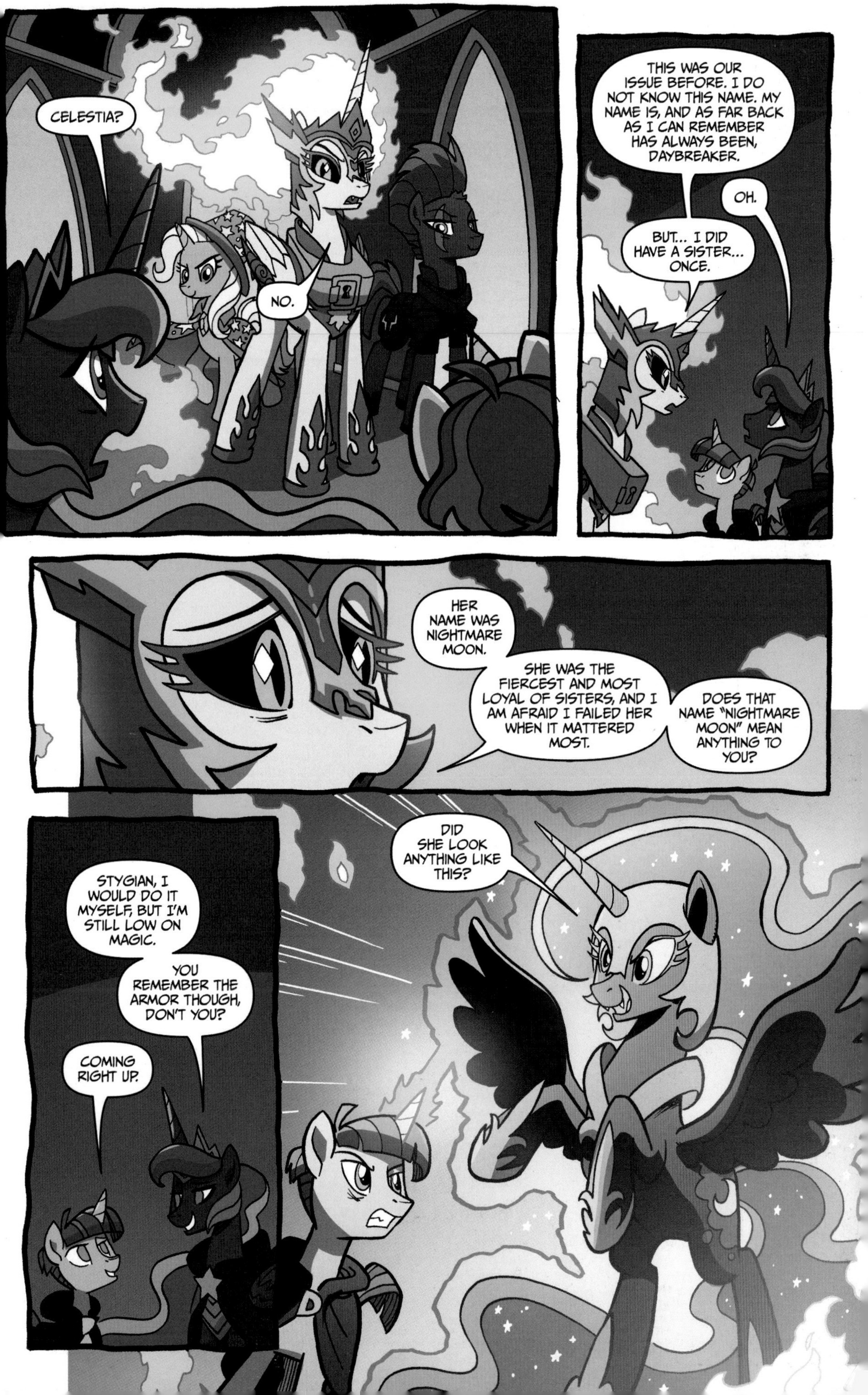
CELESTIA?
NO.
THIS WAS OUR ISSUE BEFORE. I DO NOT KNOW THIS NAME. MY NAME IS, AND AS FAR BACK AS I CAN REMEMBER HAS ALWAYS BEEN, DAYBREAKER.
BUT... I DID HAVE A SISTER... ONCE.
OH.
HER NAME WAS NIGHTMARE MOON.
SHE WAS THE FIERCEST AND MOST LOYAL OF SISTERS, AND I AM AFRAID I FAILED HER WHEN IT MATTERED MOST.
DOES THAT NAME "NIGHTMARE MOON" MEAN ANYTHING TO YOU?
STYGIAN, I WOULD DO IT MYSELF, BUT I'M STILL LOW ON MAGIC.
YOU REMEMBER THE ARMOR THOUGH, DON'T YOU?
COMING RIGHT UP.
DID SHE LOOK ANYTHING LIKE THIS?

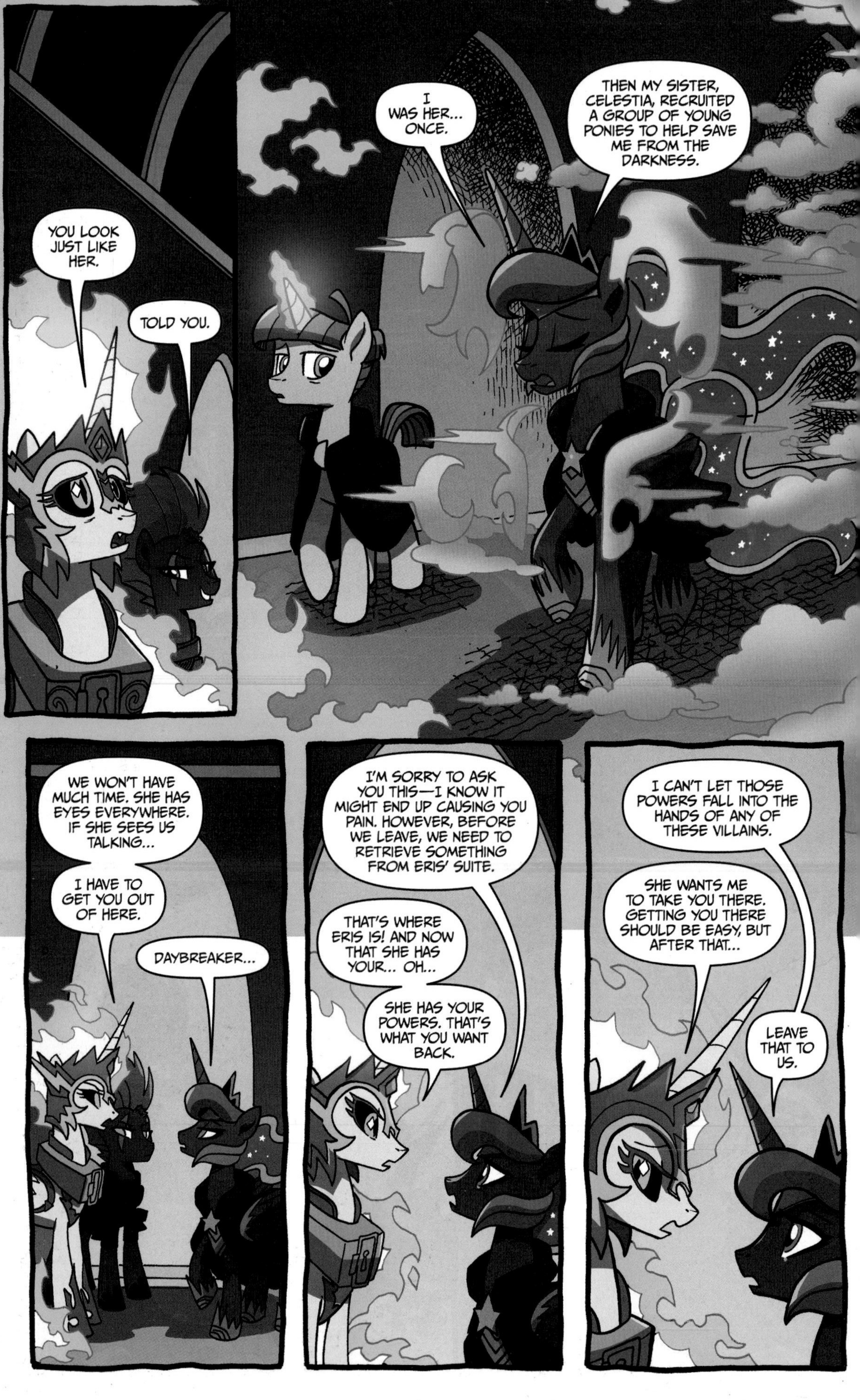
YOU LOOK JUST LIKE HER.
TOLD YOU.
I WAS HER... ONCE.
THEN MY SISTER, CELESTIA, RECRUITED A GROUP OF YOUNG PONIES TO HELP SAVE ME FROM THE DARKNESS.
WE WON'T HAVE MUCH TIME. SHE HAS EYES EVERYWHERE. IF SHE SEES US TALKING...
I HAVE TO GET YOU OUT OF HERE.
DAYBREAKER...
I'M SORRY TO ASK YOU THIS—I KNOW IT MIGHT END UP CAUSING YOU PAIN. HOWEVER, BEFORE WE LEAVE, WE NEED TO RETRIEVE SOMETHING FROM ERIS' SUITE.
THAT'S WHERE ERIS IS! AND NOW THAT SHE HAS YOUR... OH...
SHE HAS YOUR POWERS. THAT'S WHAT YOU WANT BACK.
I CAN'T LET THOSE POWERS FALL INTO THE HANDS OF ANY OF THESE VILLAINS.
SHE WANTS ME TO TAKE YOU THERE. GETTING YOU THERE SHOULD BE EASY, BUT AFTER THAT...
LEAVE THAT TO US.

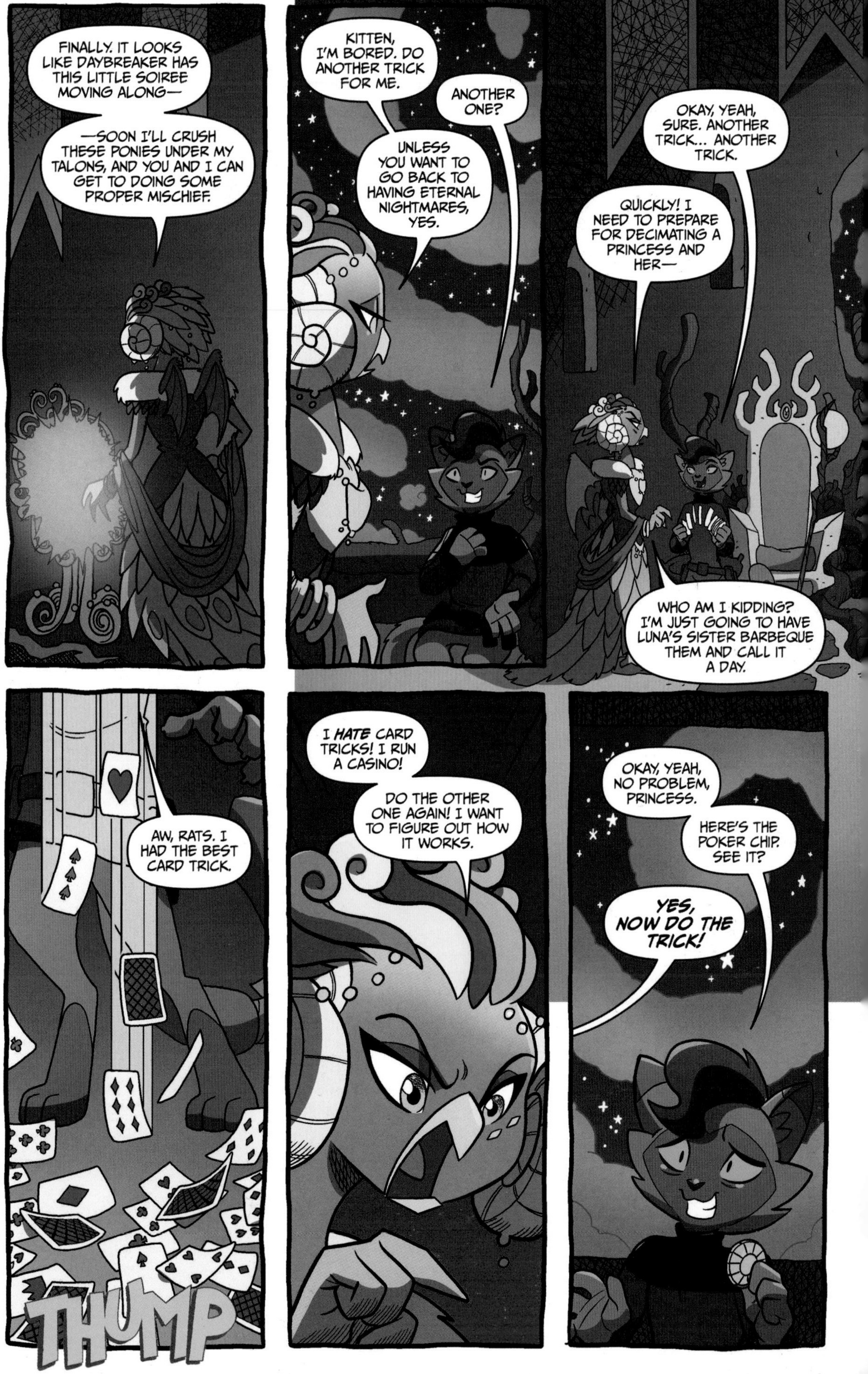
FINALLY. IT LOOKS LIKE DAYBREAKER HAS THIS LITTLE SOIREE MOVING ALONG—
—SOON I'LL CRUSH THESE PONIES UNDER MY TALONS, AND YOU AND I CAN GET TO DOING SOME PROPER MISCHIEF.
KITTEN, I'M BORED. DO ANOTHER TRICK FOR ME.
ANOTHER ONE?
UNLESS YOU WANT TO GO BACK TO HAVING ETERNAL NIGHTMARES, YES.
OKAY, YEAH, SURE. ANOTHER TRICK... ANOTHER TRICK.
QUICKLY! I NEED TO PREPARE FOR DECIMATING A PRINCESS AND HER—
WHO AM I KIDDING? I'M JUST GOING TO HAVE LUNA'S SISTER BARBEQUE THEM AND CALL IT A DAY.
AW, RATS. I HAD THE BEST CARD TRICK.
THUMP
I *HATE* CARD TRICKS! I RUN A CASINO!
DO THE OTHER ONE AGAIN! I WANT TO FIGURE OUT HOW IT WORKS.
OKAY, YEAH, NO PROBLEM, PRINCESS.
HERE'S THE POKER CHIP. SEE IT?
YES, NOW DO THE TRICK!

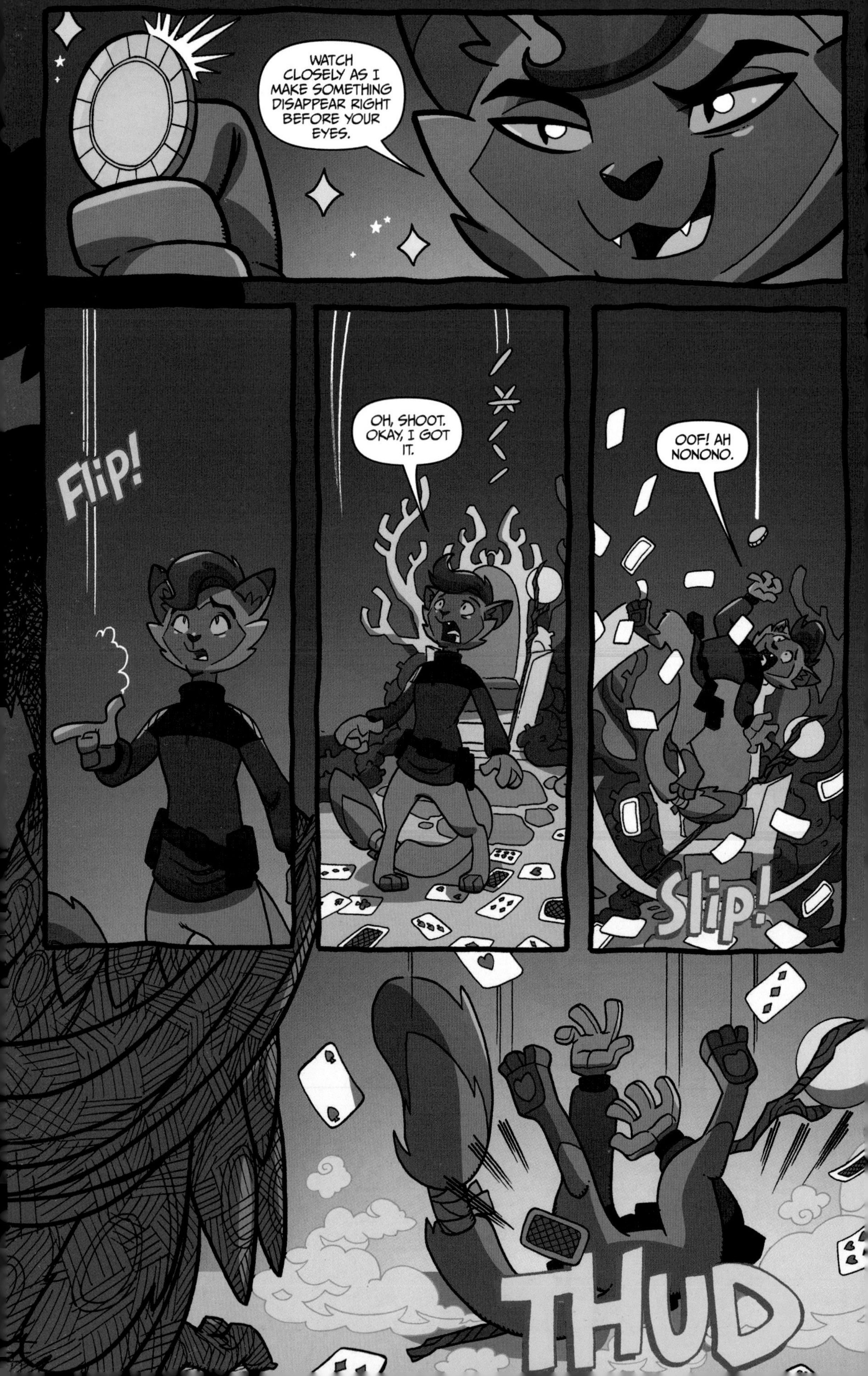
WATCH CLOSELY AS I MAKE SOMETHING DISAPPEAR RIGHT BEFORE YOUR EYES.
Flip!
OH, SHOOT. OKAY, I GOT IT.
OOF! AH NONONO.
Slip!
THUD

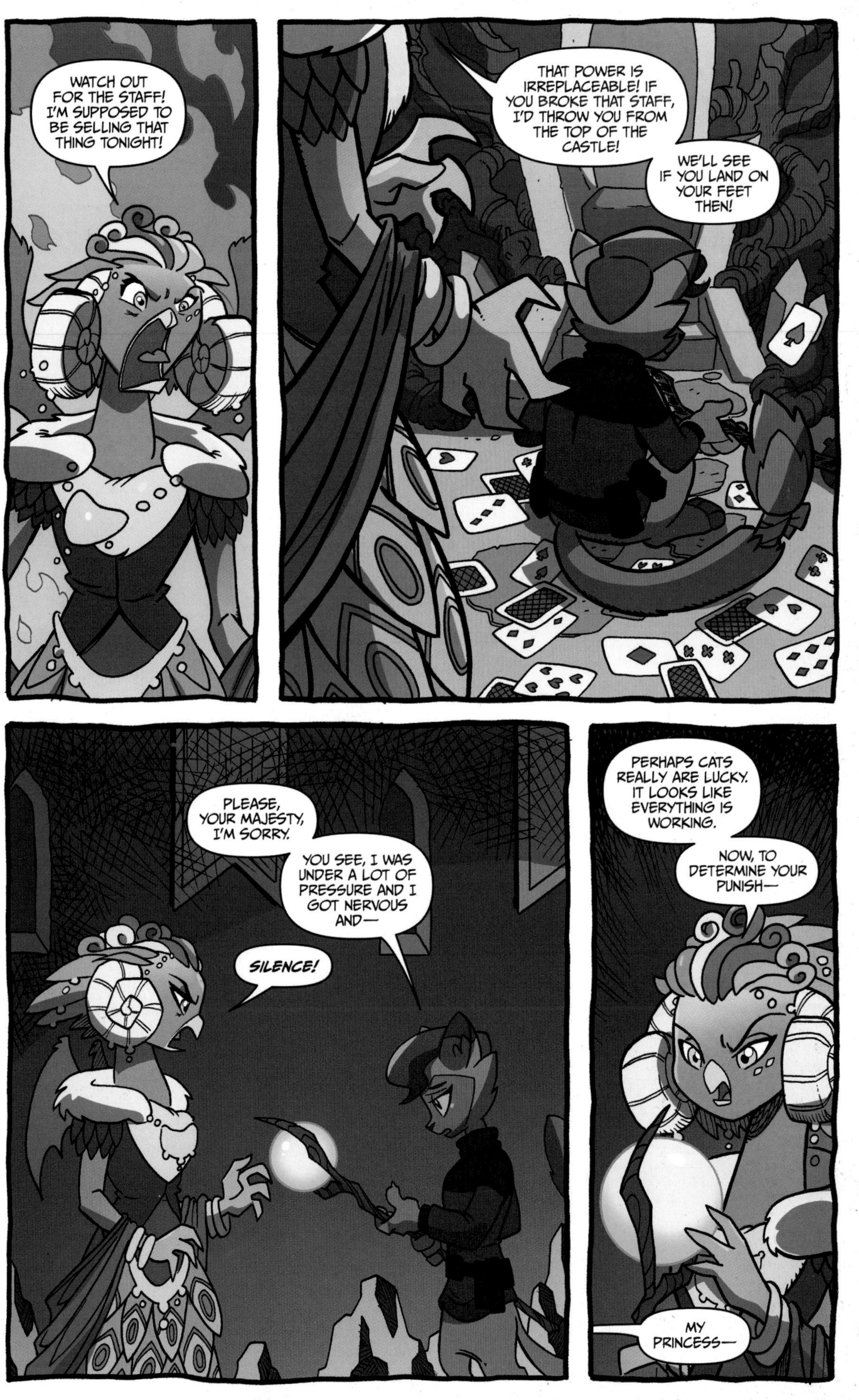
WATCH OUT FOR THE STAFF! I'M SUPPOSED TO BE SELLING THAT THING TONIGHT!
THAT POWER IS IRREPLACEABLE! IF YOU BROKE THAT STAFF, I'D THROW YOU FROM THE TOP OF THE CASTLE!
WE'LL SEE IF YOU LAND ON YOUR FEET THEN!
PLEASE, YOUR MAJESTY, I'M SORRY.
YOU SEE, I WAS UNDER A LOT OF PRESSURE AND I GOT NERVOUS AND—
SILENCE!
PERHAPS CATS REALLY ARE LUCKY. IT LOOKS LIKE EVERYTHING IS WORKING.
NOW, TO DETERMINE YOUR PUNISH—
MY PRINCESS—

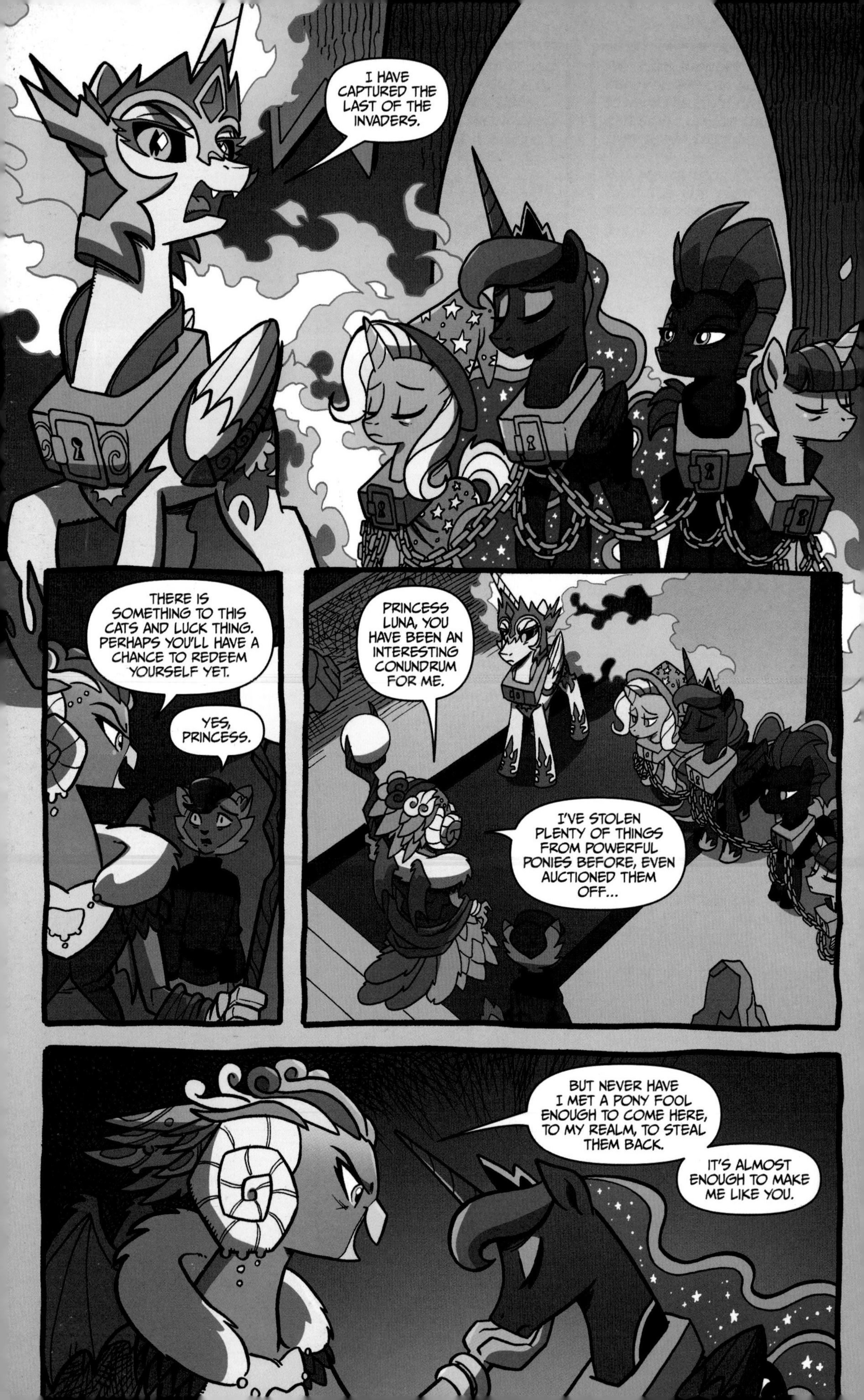
I HAVE CAPTURED THE LAST OF THE INVADERS.
THERE IS SOMETHING TO THIS CATS AND LUCK THING. PERHAPS YOU'LL HAVE A CHANCE TO REDEEM YOURSELF YET.
YES, PRINCESS.
PRINCESS LUNA, YOU HAVE BEEN AN INTERESTING CONUNDRUM FOR ME.
I'VE STOLEN PLENTY OF THINGS FROM POWERFUL PONIES BEFORE, EVEN AUCTIONED THEM OFF...
BUT NEVER HAVE I MET A PONY FOOL ENOUGH TO COME HERE, TO MY REALM, TO STEAL THEM BACK.
IT'S ALMOST ENOUGH TO MAKE ME LIKE YOU.

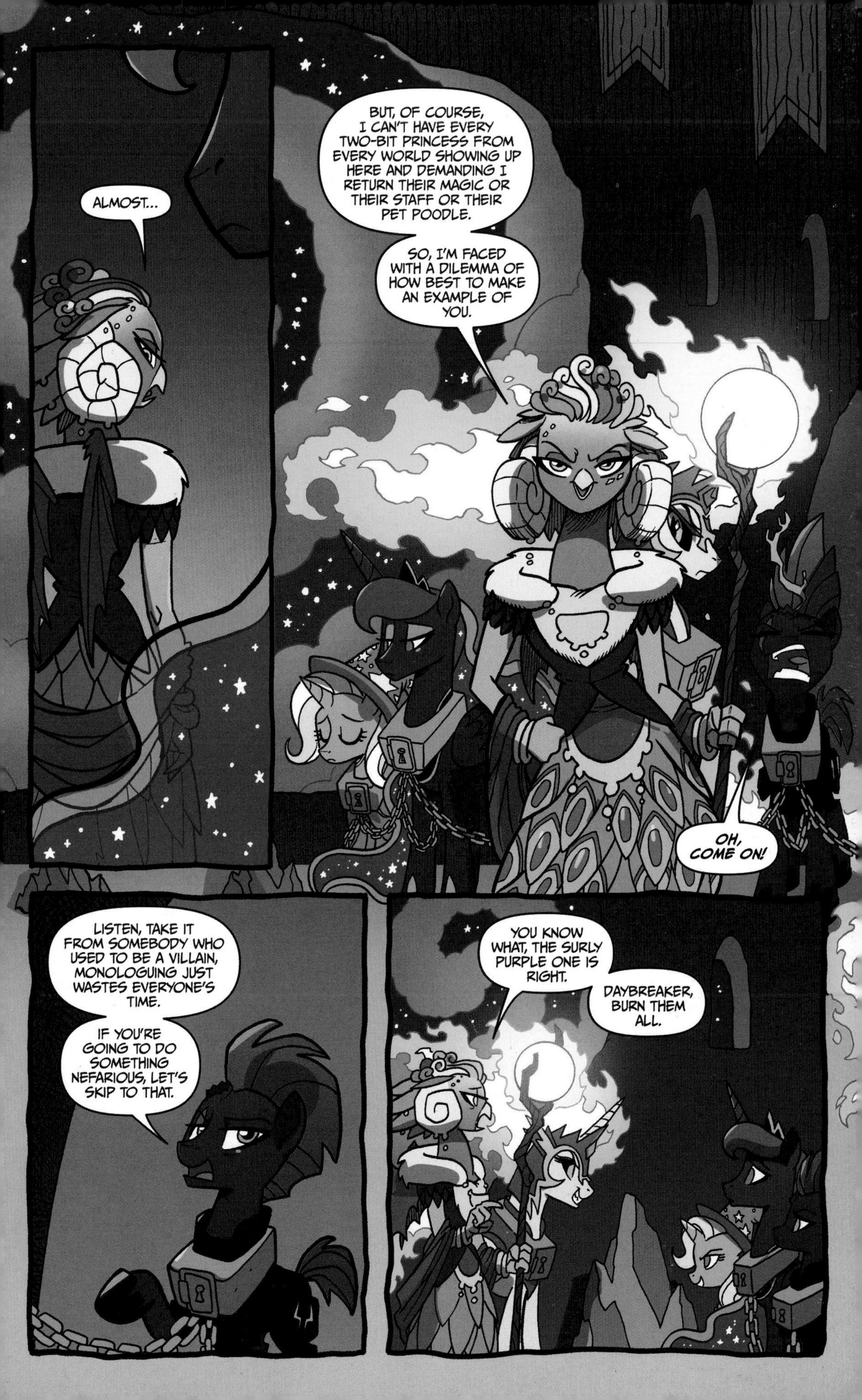
ALMOST...
BUT, OF COURSE, I CAN'T HAVE EVERY TWO-BIT PRINCESS FROM EVERY WORLD SHOWING UP HERE AND DEMANDING I RETURN THEIR MAGIC OR THEIR STAFF OR THEIR PET POODLE.
SO, I'M FACED WITH A DILEMMA OF HOW BEST TO MAKE AN EXAMPLE OF YOU.
OH, COME ON!
LISTEN, TAKE IT FROM SOMEBODY WHO USED TO BE A VILLAIN, MONOLOGUING JUST WASTES EVERYONE'S TIME.
IF YOU'RE GOING TO DO SOMETHING NEFARIOUS, LET'S SKIP TO THAT.
YOU KNOW WHAT, THE SURLY PURPLE ONE IS RIGHT.
DAYBREAKER, BURN THEM ALL.

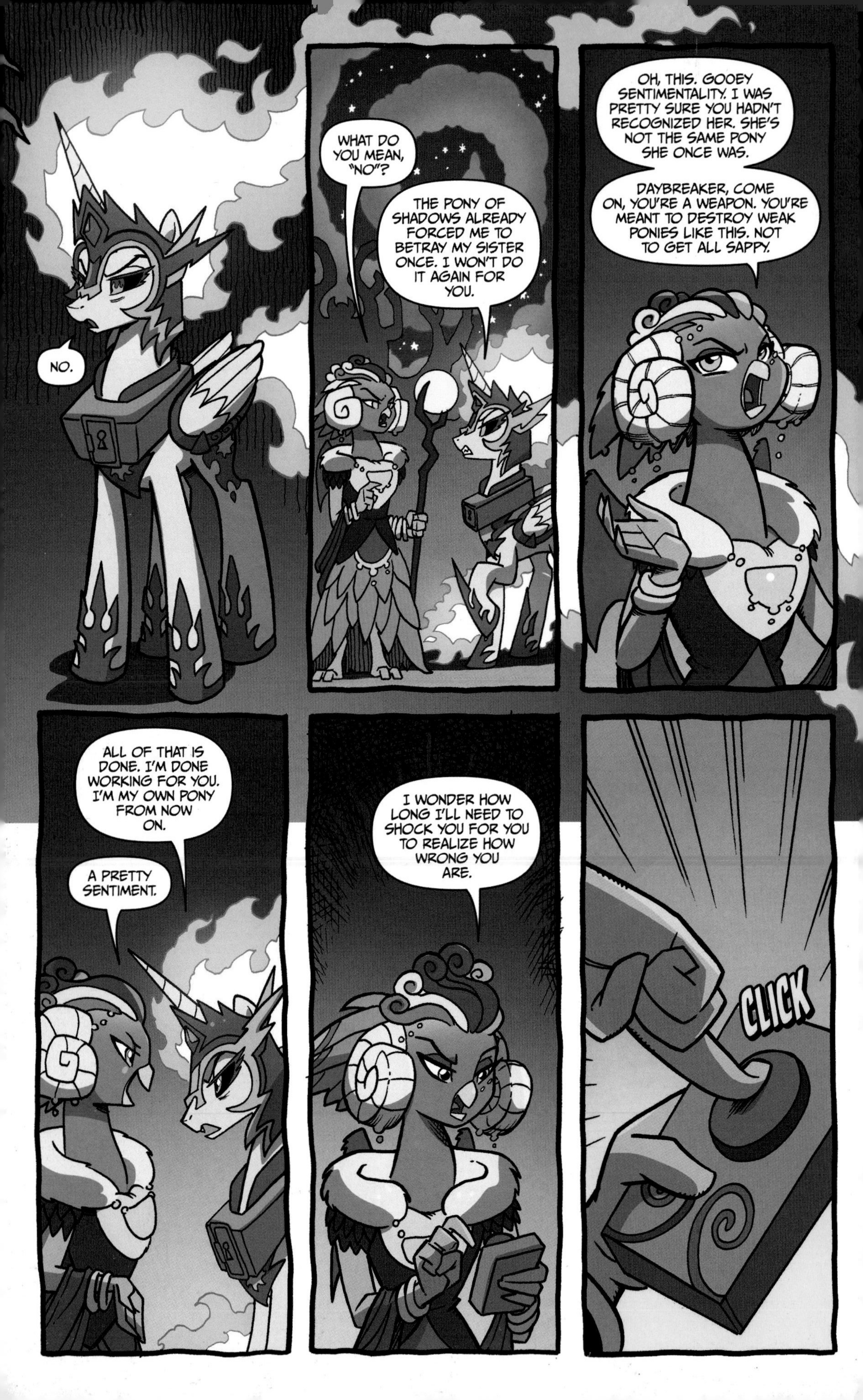
NO.
WHAT DO YOU MEAN, "NO"?
THE PONY OF SHADOWS ALREADY FORCED ME TO BETRAY MY SISTER ONCE. I WON'T DO IT AGAIN FOR YOU.
OH, THIS. GOOEY SENTIMENTALITY. I WAS PRETTY SURE YOU HADN'T RECOGNIZED HER. SHE'S NOT THE SAME PONY SHE ONCE WAS.
DAYBREAKER, COME ON, YOU'RE A WEAPON. YOU'RE MEANT TO DESTROY WEAK PONIES LIKE THIS. NOT TO GET ALL SAPPY.
ALL OF THAT IS DONE. I'M DONE WORKING FOR YOU. I'M MY OWN PONY FROM NOW ON.
A PRETTY SENTIMENT.
I WONDER HOW LONG I'LL NEED TO SHOCK YOU FOR YOU TO REALIZE HOW WRONG YOU ARE.
CLICK

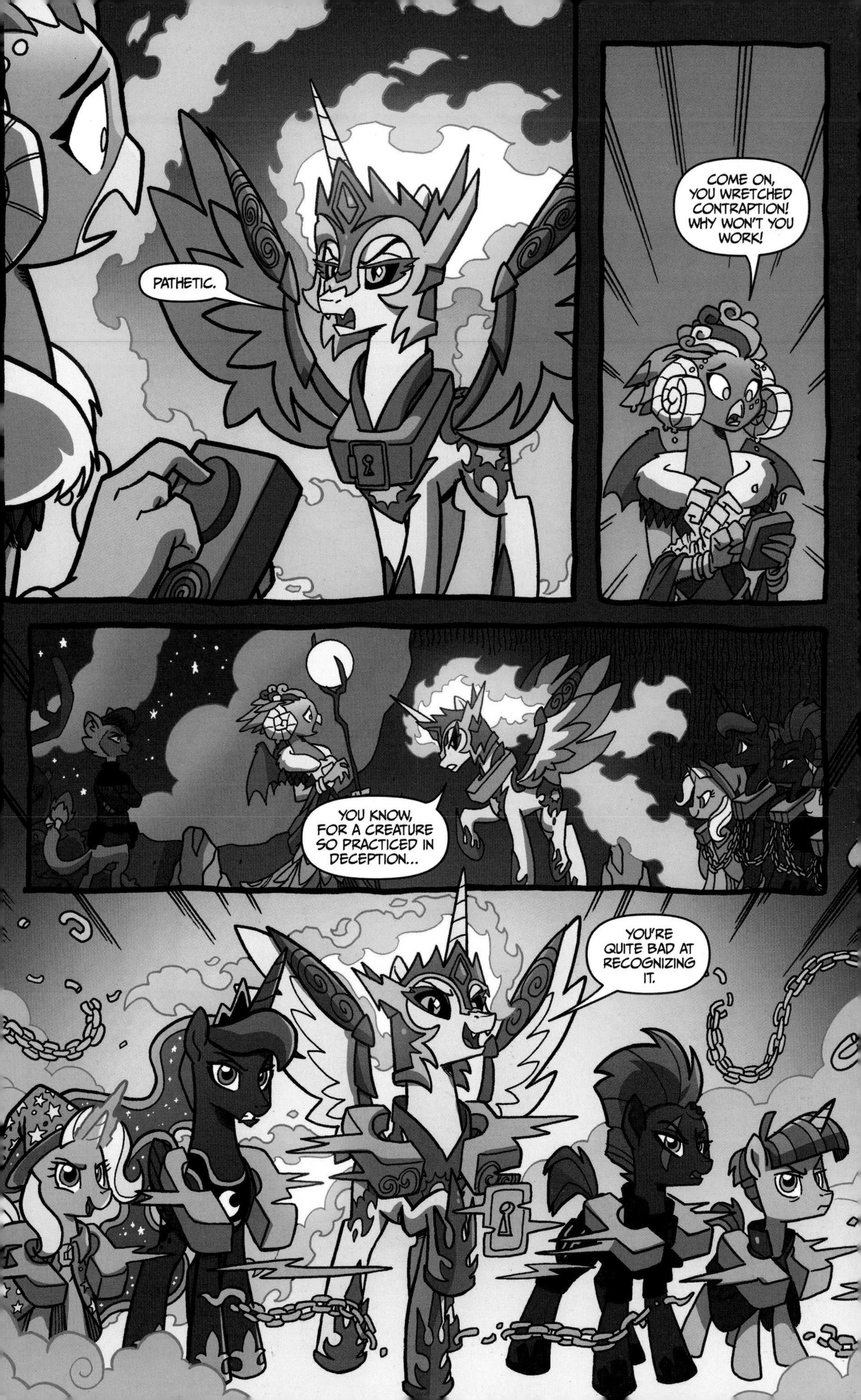
PATHETIC.
COME ON, YOU WRETCHED CONTRAPTION! WHY WON'T YOU WORK!
YOU KNOW, FOR A CREATURE SO PRACTICED IN DECEPTION...
YOU'RE QUITE BAD AT RECOGNIZING IT.

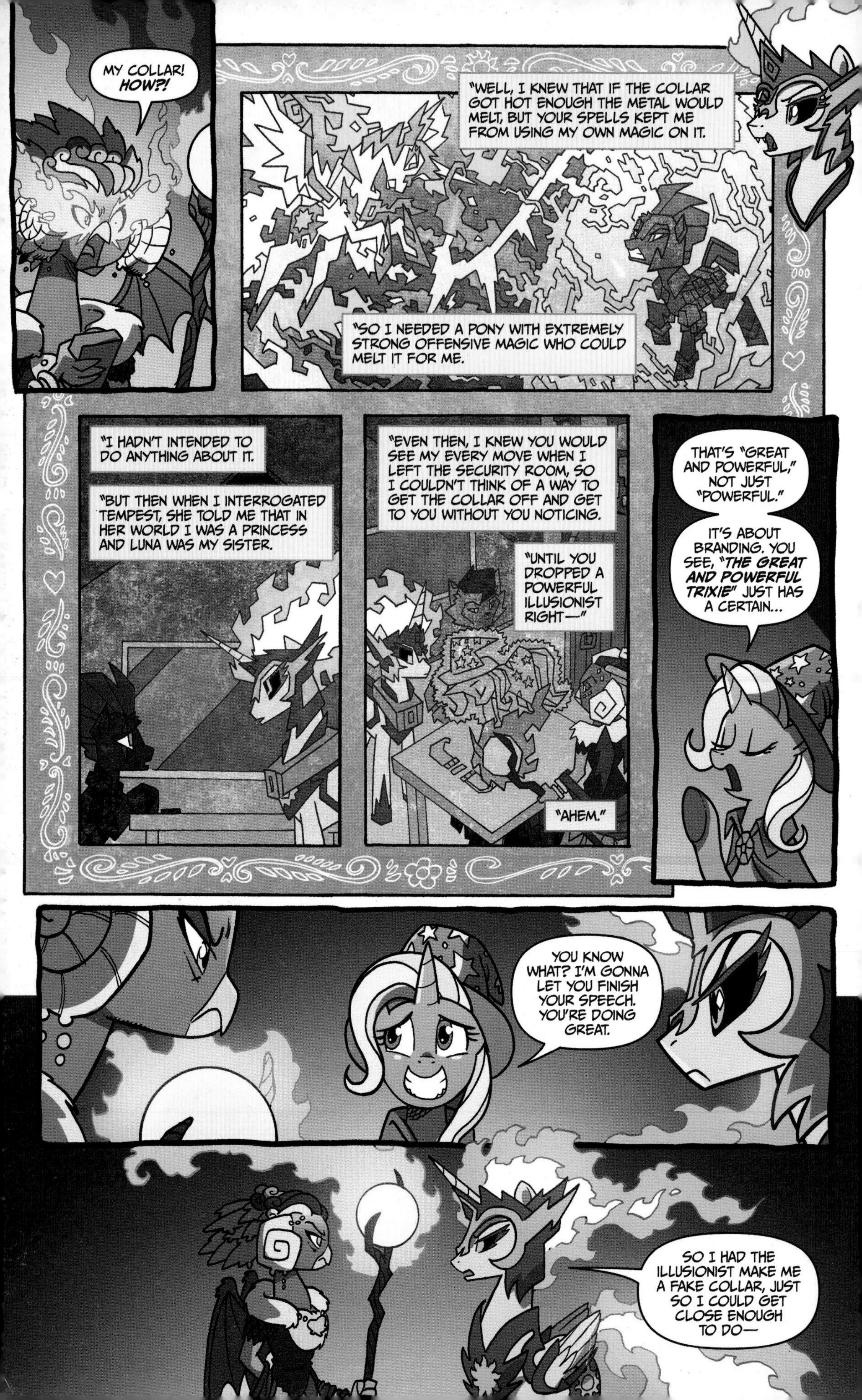
MY COLLAR! *HOW?!*
"WELL, I KNEW THAT IF THE COLLAR GOT HOT ENOUGH THE METAL WOULD MELT, BUT YOUR SPELLS KEPT ME FROM USING MY OWN MAGIC ON IT.
"SO I NEEDED A PONY WITH EXTREMELY STRONG OFFENSIVE MAGIC WHO COULD MELT IT FOR ME.
"I HADN'T INTENDED TO DO ANYTHING ABOUT IT.
"BUT THEN WHEN I INTERROGATED TEMPEST, SHE TOLD ME THAT IN HER WORLD I WAS A PRINCESS AND LUNA WAS MY SISTER.
"EVEN THEN, I KNEW YOU WOULD SEE MY EVERY MOVE WHEN I LEFT THE SECURITY ROOM, SO I COULDN'T THINK OF A WAY TO GET THE COLLAR OFF AND GET TO YOU WITHOUT YOU NOTICING.
"UNTIL YOU DROPPED A POWERFUL ILLUSIONIST RIGHT—"
"AHEM."
THAT'S "GREAT AND POWERFUL," NOT JUST "POWERFUL."
IT'S ABOUT BRANDING. YOU SEE, "*THE GREAT AND POWERFUL TRIXIE*" JUST HAS A CERTAIN...
YOU KNOW WHAT? I'M GONNA LET YOU FINISH YOUR SPEECH. YOU'RE DOING GREAT.
SO I HAD THE ILLUSIONIST MAKE ME A FAKE COLLAR, JUST SO I COULD GET CLOSE ENOUGH TO DO—

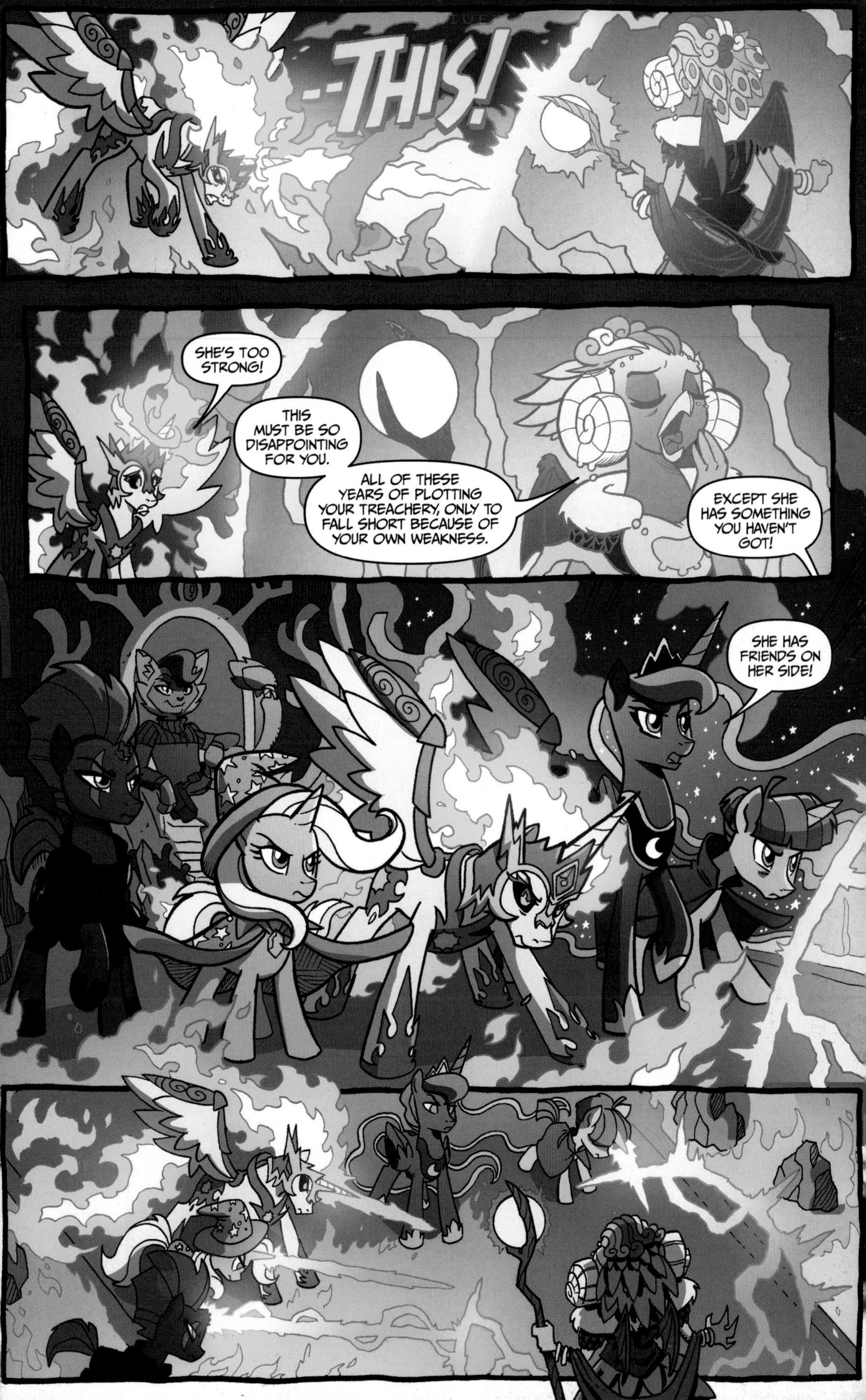
--THIS!
SHE'S TOO STRONG!
THIS MUST BE SO DISAPPOINTING FOR YOU.
ALL OF THESE YEARS OF PLOTTING YOUR TREACHERY, ONLY TO FALL SHORT BECAUSE OF YOUR OWN WEAKNESS.
EXCEPT SHE HAS SOMETHING YOU HAVEN'T GOT!
SHE HAS FRIENDS ON HER SIDE!

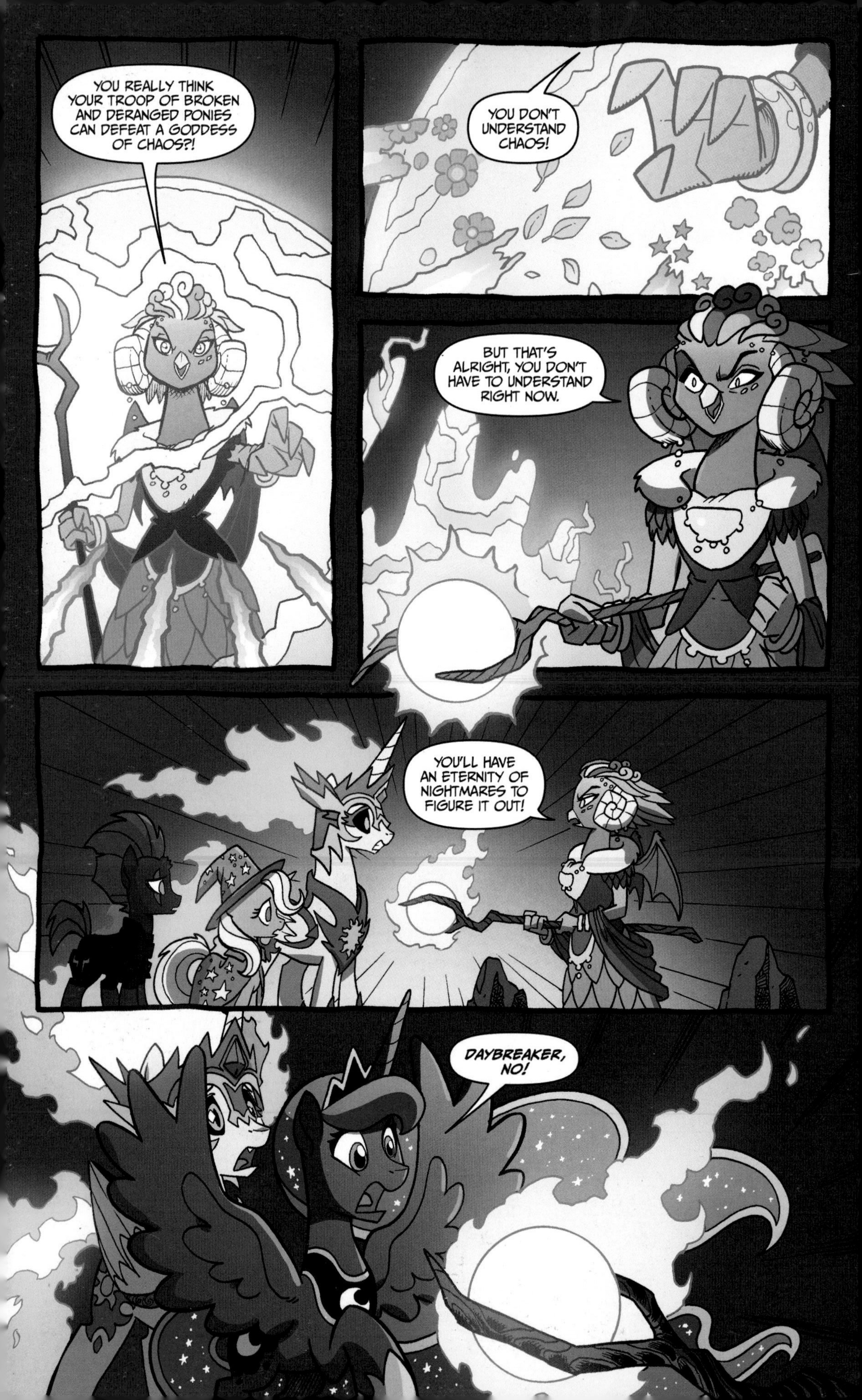
YOU REALLY THINK YOUR TROOP OF BROKEN AND DERANGED PONIES CAN DEFEAT A GODDESS OF CHAOS?!
YOU DON'T UNDERSTAND CHAOS!
BUT THAT'S ALRIGHT, YOU DON'T HAVE TO UNDERSTAND RIGHT NOW.
YOU'LL HAVE AN ETERNITY OF NIGHTMARES TO FIGURE IT OUT!
DAYBREAKER, NO!

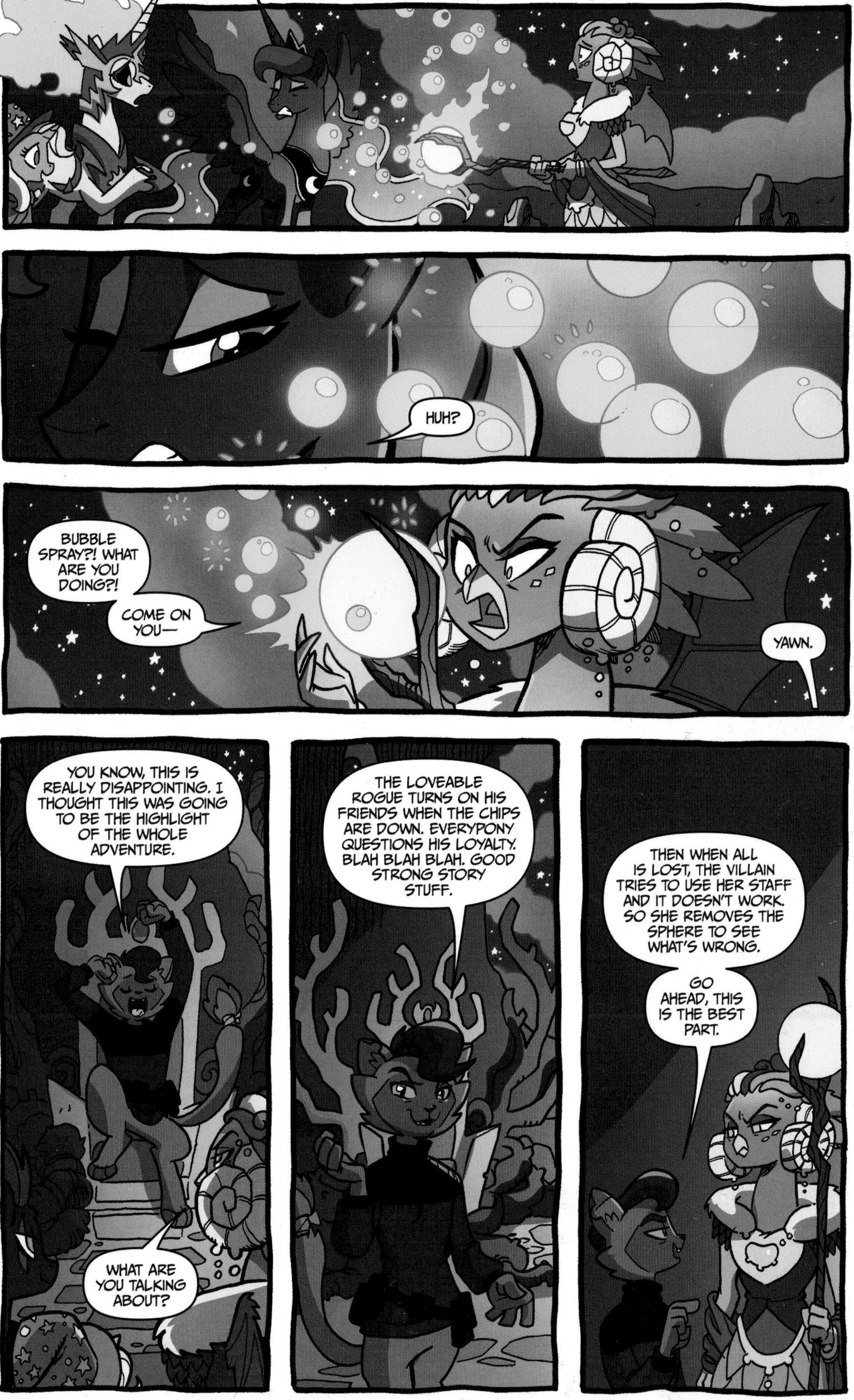
HUH?
BUBBLE SPRAY?! WHAT ARE YOU DOING?!
COME ON YOU—
YAWN.
YOU KNOW, THIS IS REALLY DISAPPOINTING. I THOUGHT THIS WAS GOING TO BE THE HIGHLIGHT OF THE WHOLE ADVENTURE.
WHAT ARE YOU TALKING ABOUT?
THE LOVEABLE ROGUE TURNS ON HIS FRIENDS WHEN THE CHIPS ARE DOWN. EVERYPONY QUESTIONS HIS LOYALTY. BLAH BLAH BLAH. GOOD STRONG STORY STUFF.
THEN WHEN ALL IS LOST, THE VILLAIN TRIES TO USE HER STAFF AND IT DOESN'T WORK. SO SHE REMOVES THE SPHERE TO SEE WHAT'S WRONG.
GO AHEAD, THIS IS THE BEST PART.

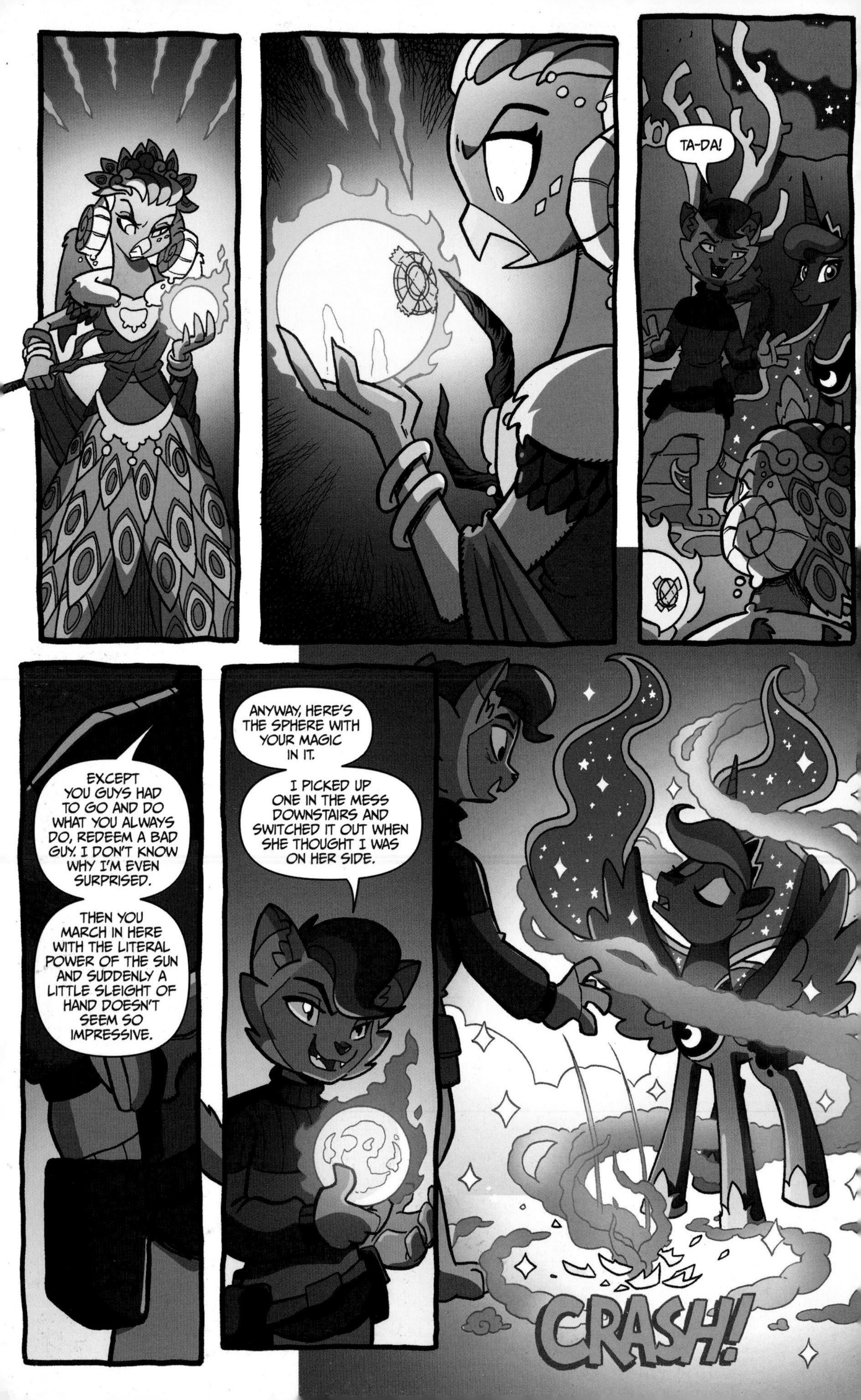
TA-DA!
EXCEPT YOU GUYS HAD TO GO AND DO WHAT YOU ALWAYS DO, REDEEM A BAD GUY. I DON'T KNOW WHY I'M EVEN SURPRISED.
THEN YOU MARCH IN HERE WITH THE LITERAL POWER OF THE SUN AND SUDDENLY A LITTLE SLEIGHT OF HAND DOESN'T SEEM SO IMPRESSIVE.
ANYWAY, HERE'S THE SPHERE WITH YOUR MAGIC IN IT.
I PICKED UP ONE IN THE MESS DOWNSTAIRS AND SWITCHED IT OUT WHEN SHE THOUGHT I WAS ON HER SIDE.
CRASH!

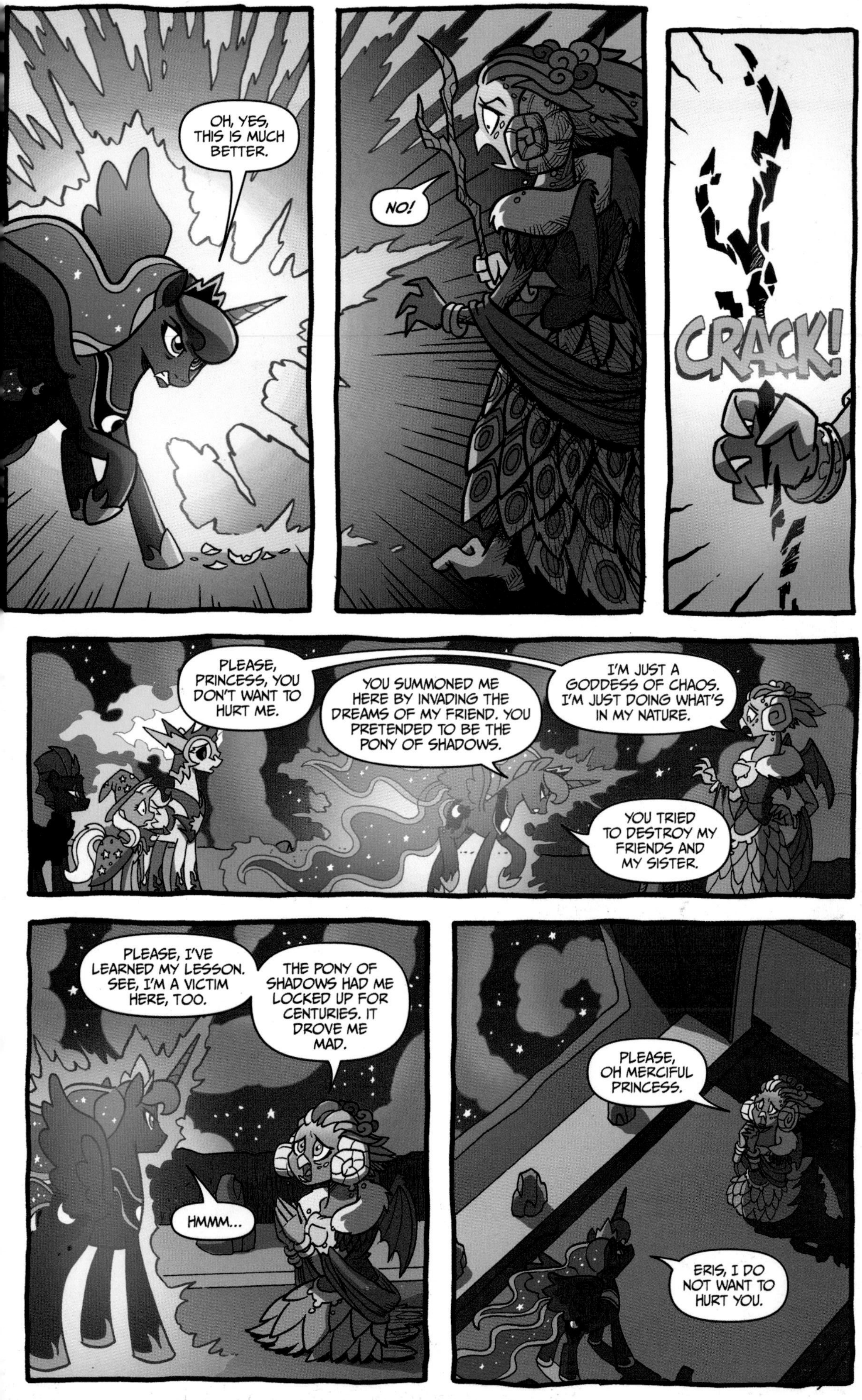
OH, YES, THIS IS MUCH BETTER.
NO!
CRACK!
PLEASE, PRINCESS, YOU DON'T WANT TO HURT ME.
I'M JUST A GODDESS OF CHAOS. I'M JUST DOING WHAT'S IN MY NATURE.
YOU SUMMONED ME HERE BY INVADING THE DREAMS OF MY FRIEND. YOU PRETENDED TO BE THE PONY OF SHADOWS.
YOU TRIED TO DESTROY MY FRIENDS AND MY SISTER.
PLEASE, I'VE LEARNED MY LESSON. SEE, I'M A VICTIM HERE, TOO.
THE PONY OF SHADOWS HAD ME LOCKED UP FOR CENTURIES. IT DROVE ME MAD.
HMMM...
PLEASE, OH MERCIFUL PRINCESS.
ERIS, I DO NOT WANT TO HURT YOU.

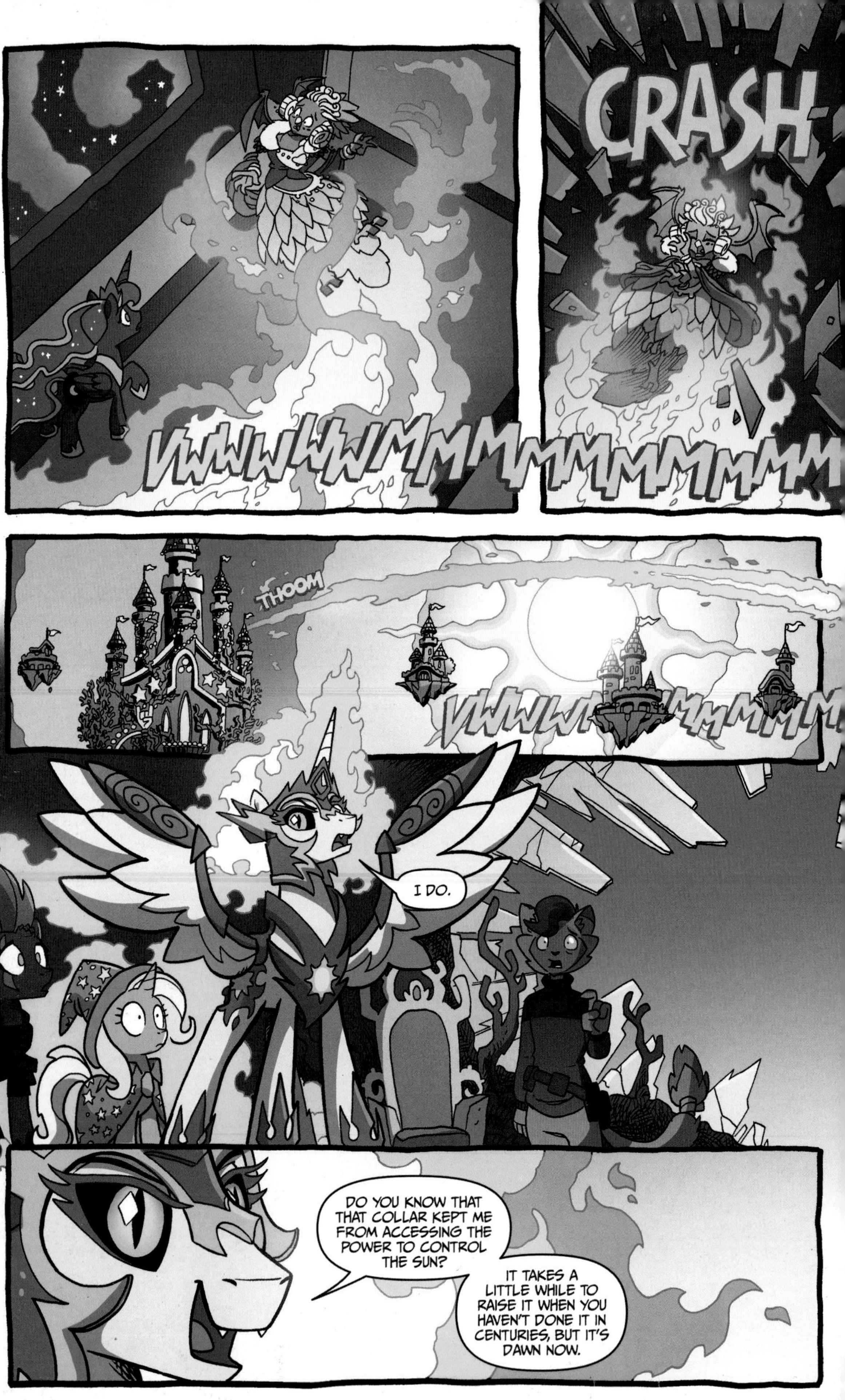
CRASH
VWWWWWMMMMMMMMMMM
THOOM
VWWWMMMMMM
I DO.
DO YOU KNOW THAT THAT COLLAR KEPT ME FROM ACCESSING THE POWER TO CONTROL THE SUN?
IT TAKES A LITTLE WHILE TO RAISE IT WHEN YOU HAVEN'T DONE IT IN CENTURIES, BUT IT'S DAWN NOW.

art by Jay Fosgitt

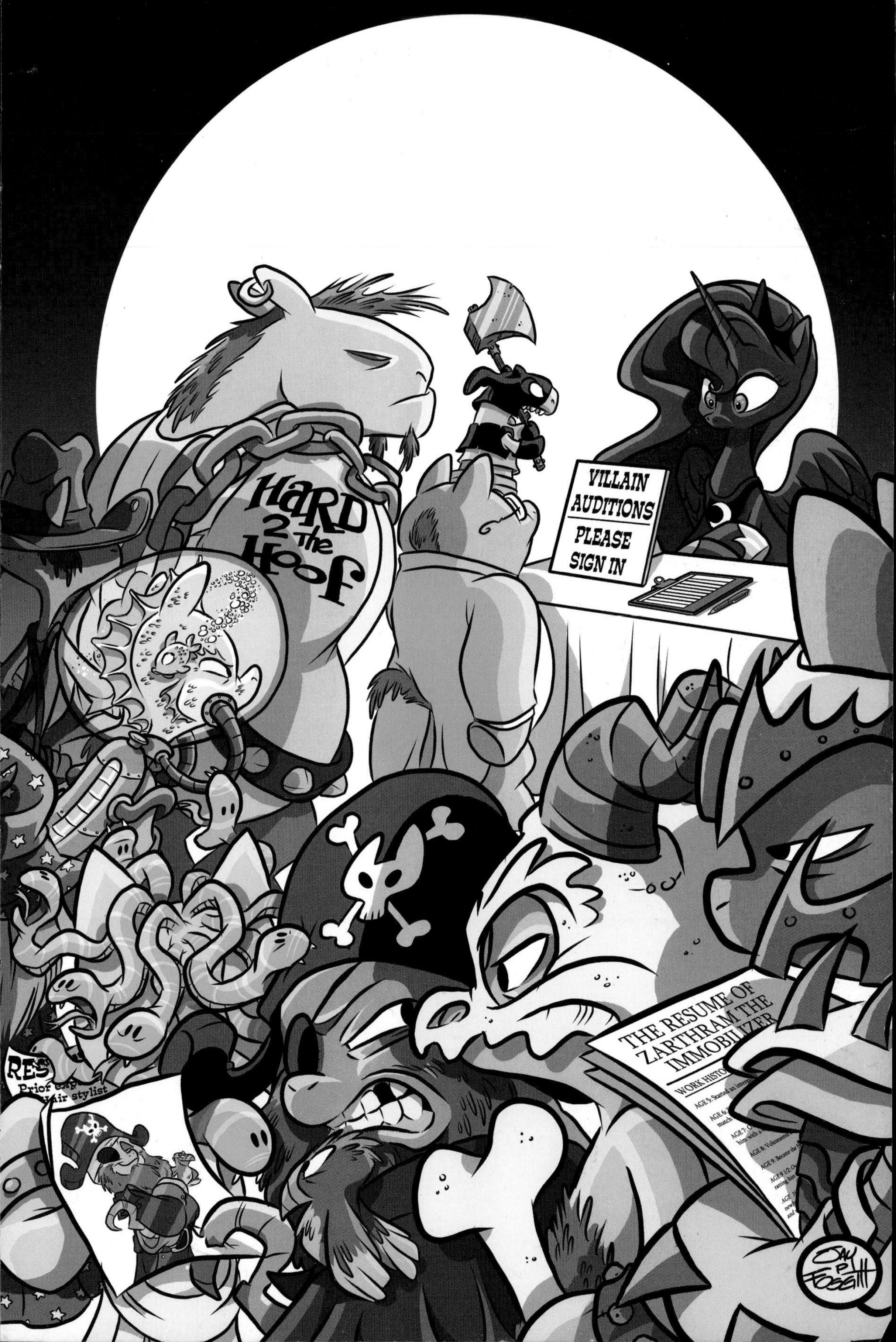

HARD 2 the Hoof
VILLAIN AUDITIONS
PLEASE SIGN IN
THE RESUME OF ZARTHRAM THE IMMOBILIZER
WORK HISTO
RES
Prior exp
hair stylist

art by Jennifer L. Meyer

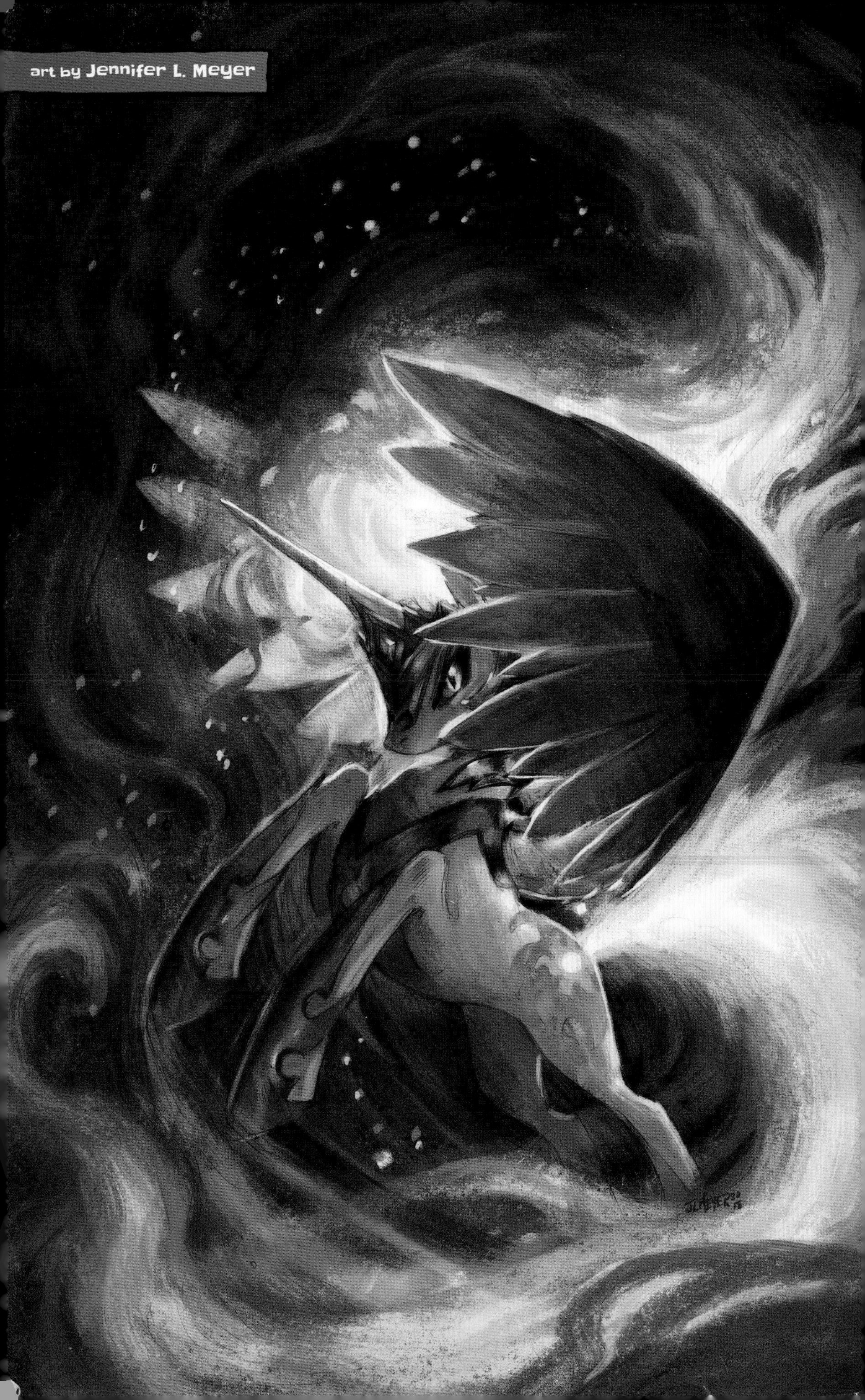

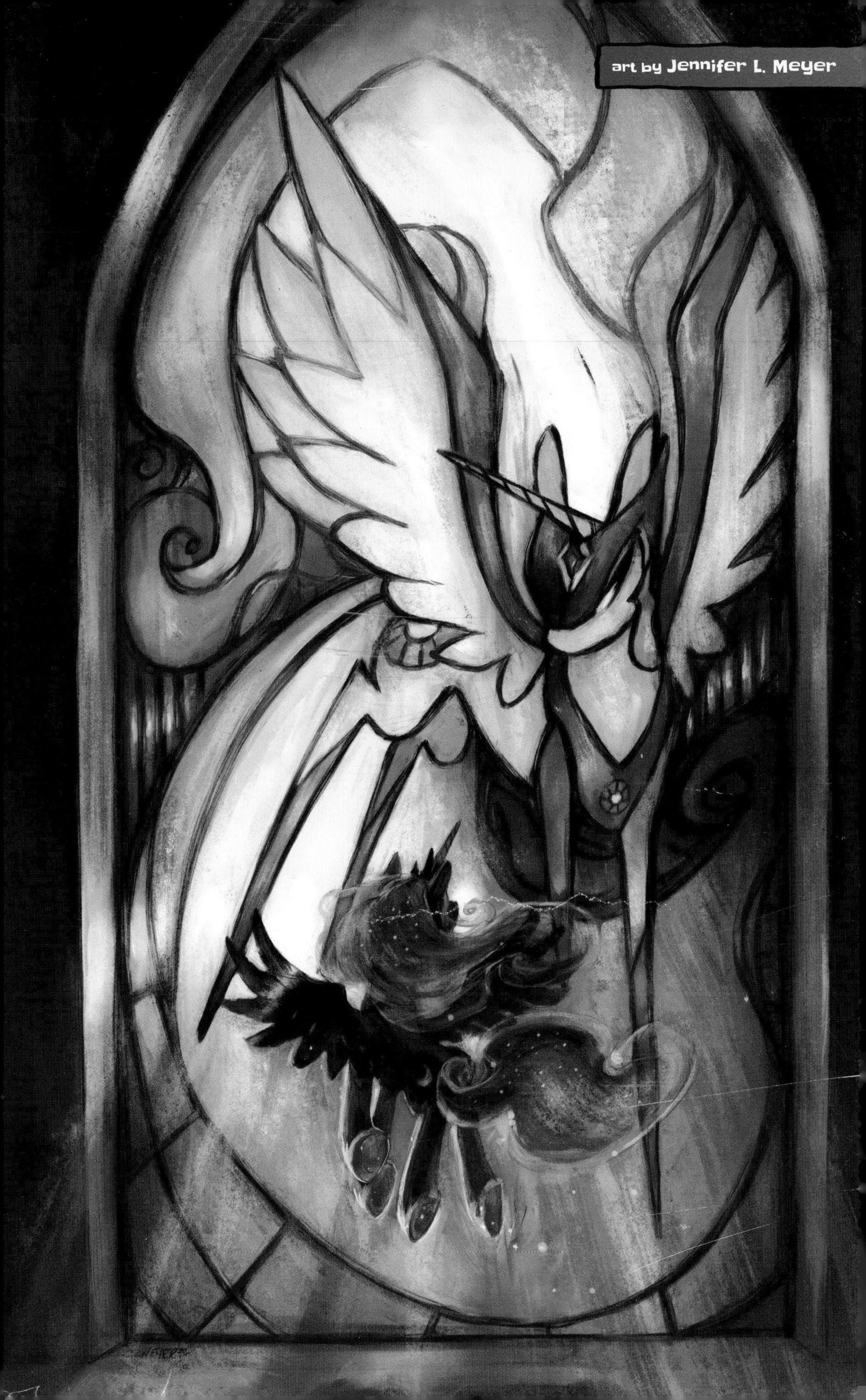

art by Jennifer L. Meyer

art by Jennifer L. Meyer

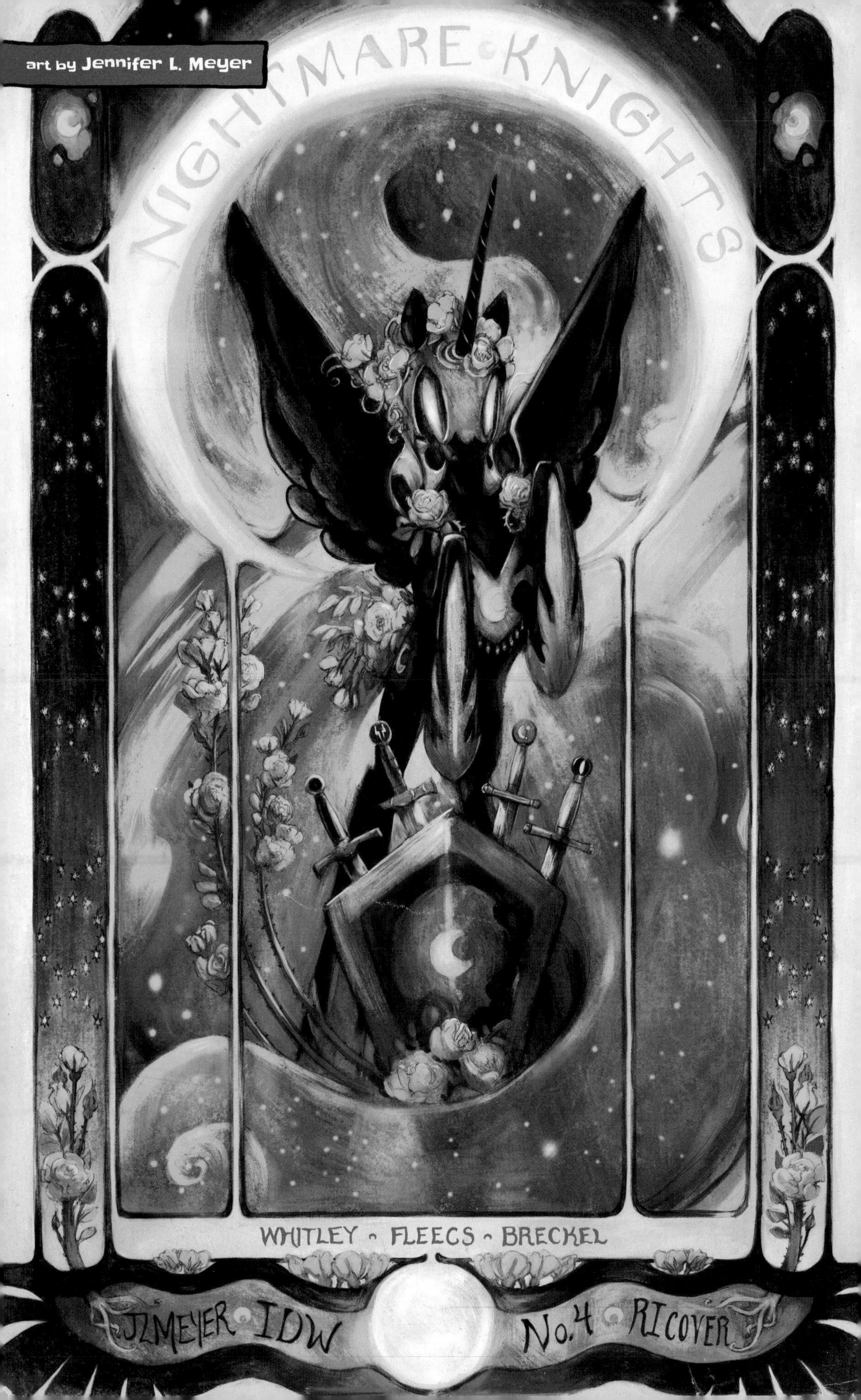
NIGHTMARE KNIGHTS
WHITLEY · FLEECS · BRECKEL
JLMEYER IDW
No.4 RI COVER

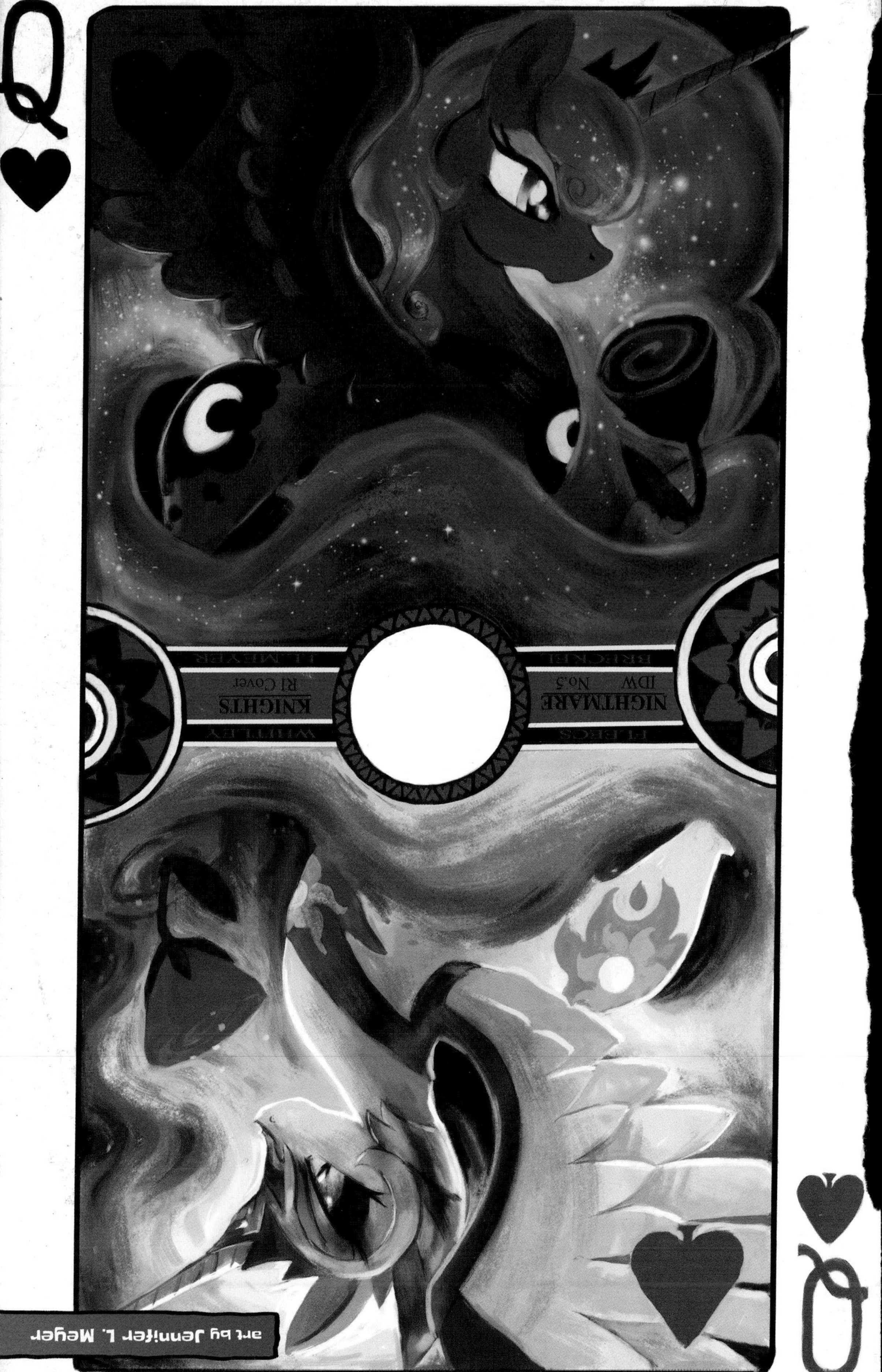

Q
Q
FLEECS
WHITLEY
NIGHTMARE
KNIGHTS
IDW No.5
RI Cover
BRECKEL
J.L.MEYER
art by Jennifer L. Meyer

my LITTLE PONY
Nightmare Knights

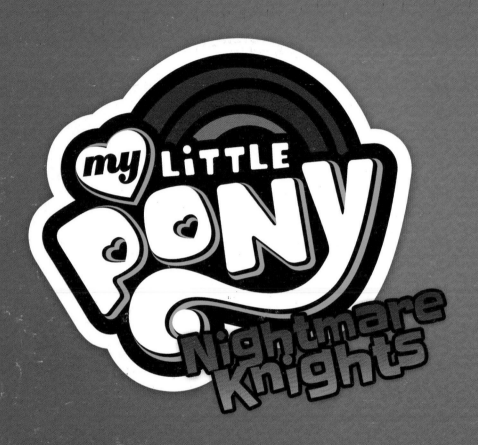